Jon Cleary, an Australian whose books are read throughout the world, is the author of many novels, including such famous bestsellers as *The Sundowners* and *The High Commissioner*.

Born in 1917, Jon Cleary left school at fifteen to become a commercial artist and film cartoonist – even a laundryman and bushworker. Then his first novel won second prize in Australia's biggest literary contest and launched him on his successful career.

Seven of his books have been filmed, and his novel, *Peter's Pence*, was awarded the American Edgar Allan Poe Prize as the best crime novel of 1974. He has also been awarded the 1995 Inaugural Ned Kelly Award for his lifetime contribution to crime fiction in Australia.

Jon Cleary's most recent novels have been *The City of Fading Light*, *Dragons at the Party*, *Now and Then*, *Amen*, *Babylon South*, *Murder Song*, *Pride's Harvest*, *Dark Summer* and *Autumn Maze*.

Acclaim for *Autumn Maze*:

'Cleary has produced another   d, absorbing novel br   g people and in   . *ian Review*

Dark Summer

'A well-crafted   written page turner with lots of social observation, colour and strong characterisation' *Sun Herald*

JON CLEARY

Winter Chill

This edition published by Diamond Books, 1999

Diamond Books is an Imprint of HarperCollins*Publishers*
77-85 Fulham Palace Road,
Hammersmith, London W6 8JB

First published in Great Britain by
HarperCollins*Publishers* 1995

Copyright © John Cleary 1995

The Author asserts the moral right to
be identified as the author of this work

ISBN 0-261-67088-3

Set in Sabon at
The Spartan Press Ltd,
Lymington, Hants

Printed and bound in Great Britain by
Caledonian International Book Manufacturing Ltd, Glasgow

For Cate

Chapter One

1

The four carriages of the Harbourlink monorail softly whirred their way above the three-o'clock-in-the-morning city streets. An occasional car or taxi sped down the glistening wet cross streets; in two of the main north–south thoroughfares garbage trucks banged and rattled at the quiet. The monorail, with its metallic whisper, drifted by dark upper-storey windows of department stores and offices, moved down the slope of Market Street, over Pyrmont Bridge and into the sharp curve that led above the Darling Harbour exhibition complex. It did not stop at the station there but continued on, a ghost train of the future, and swung back to head up into the city again, looking even more ghostly in a sudden squall of rain, going round and round on its endless circuit.

There was no driver and there was only one passenger. To those who knew the painting he was the spitting image (though he had never been known to spit) of the farmer in Grant Wood's *American Gothic*. Tall, gaunt, face weathered (not from farming but from sailing), the first impression of those who had met him was that he was humourless and forbidding. Yet the gaunt face could break into the most charming smile and his friendliness, though not legendary, was sincere and surprising. He had enough perceived contradictions to make him a good lawyer, which he was – or had been. Witnesses and judges and juries had never been quite sure whom and what they were dealing with till he had delivered his final argument. His name was Orville Brame, he was one of two senior partners in one of New York's most prestigious law firms and he was the incumbent president of the American Bar Association. Or he would have been incumbent if he had not died in the past hour.

He sat in the compartment immediately behind the driver's cabin, held upright with his thin arm pushed into the handrail beside him. His dark eyes were open and had any other passengers boarded the carriage at that out-of-schedule hour they might have mistaken him for a man who had drunk himself into a glassy-eyed stupor at some professionals' dinner. Except for the dark red stain on the front of his white shirt and the twist of agony that had turned down one corner of his thin-lipped mouth.

The monorail slipped along its track, over the street-lights, past the black mirrors of the windows, down and across the oily finger of harbour, along the front of the exhibition centre. The sightless eyes of Orville Brame stared out at the city he had left thirty years ago and to which he had never returned until now. And now he was past memories and regret, past the anger and trepidation he had brought home with him.

2

It had stopped raining when Scobie Malone got up at six o'clock for his regular morning walk. He went into the bathroom for the ritual start-to-the-day leak, splashed some water in his face, ran his hand through his dark hair, which always curled during the night. He went back to the bedroom, pulled on his track-suit and trainers, went out to the front door and opened it. Despite the rain the weather had got colder; a cold wind sprang up out of nowhere and blew through his bones. He went back into the bedroom and pulled on a sweater.

'Come back to bed,' Lisa murmured sleepily.

'Go back to sleep,' he said, resisting temptation.

Leaving the house he turned, like a trained dog, to the usual route, which took him down through several side streets to Randwick racecourse. The wind had blown the clouds away and the stars looked like frozen fireworks in the still-dark sky. He shivered as the cold bit at him. Of course *cold* was comparative; the Norwegians at February's Winter Olympics would consider this morning the brisk beginning of a summer's day. But he was not a Norwegian nor a Siberian nor an Inuit; he was an Aussie who knew when it was bloody cold and no argument. Comparing climate was like comparing one woman with another. An opinion he would not have quoted to Lisa.

Once out of bed and on his way Malone was always glad to be walking. His mind, like the cold engine of the nine-year-old Holden Commodore back in the garage, always took a little time to get started; the five-kilometre walk each morning eased him into the day. The racecourse provided a convenient circuit.

He walked briskly round the outer rail of the outside track, while the horses began appearing out of the lightening darkness, waiting for enough light for them to begin their training gallops. There was an occasional shout or obscenity from the jockeys and strappers as a horse played up, but the morning was too cold for any sustained burst of temper. On the far side of the course, away from the grandstands, Malone was alone. He began to run over in his mind the day that lay ahead of him at Homicide, the five murders that he hoped would be wiped from the computer by the end of the week. There had been a spate of murders in Sydney in the past month, some of them without obvious motive but all of them with suspects reasonably certain of committal. The eighteen detectives under Malone, as their inspector in charge, were usually not so fortunate in the cases that occupied them. With a bit of luck Malone might have a clean computer, nothing on the running sheets, when he went on leave in two weeks' time. At the thought of the holiday coming up, two weeks in the Queensland sunshine, he almost broke into a jog, but reason slowed his legs before they got out of hand. Jogging, he believed, was the invention of orthopaedic surgeons and urologists looking for future trade.

An hour after leaving the front door he was back at the Federation-style house that was home. As he opened the door again he heard the phone ringing on the small table in the hall. Claire, his seventeen-year-old, came out of her bedroom, picked up the phone and handed it to him as he came down the hallway.

'How do you know it's not for you?'

'Dad, civilized people don't ring at seven o'clock in the morning. It has to be someone from Homicide.'

She went on into the bathroom she shared with Maureen, the fifteen-year-old, and Tom, going on twelve. He looked after her, marvelling again at how much she resembled her mother in looks and temperament. There was no Irish in her, only Dutch.

'Scobie?' Russ Clements, sergeant and second in command, was on the other end of the line.

'Where are you, this hour of the morning?'

'Still at home. Peta Smith called me, she's just come back from Darling Harbour. She's got one she thinks you and I should handle.'

In his mind's eye the computer screen all at once began to mock him: the running sheets were off and running again. 'Why me? I have eighteen of you supposed to be working for me –'

'This guy was found in the monorail at three-thirty this morning, a single bullet wound in his heart.'

'In the *monorail*? At three-thirty?' Lisa, up and dressed, passed him in the hallway, raised her eyebrows and he nodded, equally puzzled.

4

'Peta said she'll explain it all when we see her. The point is, she thinks you and I should handle it. The dead man is – *was* the president of the American Bar Association. They're in town for an international law convention, you've read about it. I've put the morning conference off till ten-thirty. The monorail car, the scene of the crime, has been moved on to a siding.' He gave Malone instructions how to get there. 'I'll see you at eight-thirty.'

Malone put down the phone, turned to find Lisa standing immediately behind him. He looked at her. 'Why all dressed up?'

'I'm going to the dentist.'

'You didn't tell me.'

'You weren't listening, as usual. Well, anyway –' She headed back towards the kitchen. 'Have your shower.'

She seemed quiet, not inclined to talk, and he wondered how much trouble her teeth were giving her; she had excellent teeth and her visits to the dentist were usually no more than routine. He went in to shower and to get dressed, his mind slipping off in another direction. Murder was always a distraction, even though it was, for him, routine.

When he came out into the kitchen fifteen minutes later the three children, dressed for school, were at the breakfast table. 'You've got another murder,' said Maureen. 'It was on the radio.'

'I thought you only listened to Rod Stewart and other screamers?'

'Sometimes they interrupt with some news, if it's juicy enough.' He suspected that she would grow up to be that bane of all cops, a reporter. Till then he would love her.

'Who's dead? A politician?' Tom had just begun social studies and looked like following in his father's and grandfather's footsteps, politician-haters both.

'No, they said he was a lawyer,' Maureen told him. 'An American lawyer. Do many lawyers get murdered, Dad?'

5

'That's enough,' said Lisa. 'I won't have murder as a topic at breakfast.'

She had spoken in her formal voice, her Dutch voice as Malone and the children called it. He looked along the table at her. 'Your teeth hurting?'

'What? Yes, a little. Let's skip talk about murder and trips to the dentist, shall we?'

'My, we are touchy this morning,' said Maureen.

'Easy,' Malone warned her. He glanced again at Lisa, but she had bent her blond head and seemed engrossed in ensuring that she put the right amount of butter on her toast. He caught Claire's eye and she shook her head as if giving *him* a warning. He wondered if Claire, now on the verge of womanhood, was privy to confidences that Lisa was not giving him.

When he was leaving the house Lisa came to the front door to give him her usual farewell kiss. 'What's the matter, darl?' he said.

'Nothing. I'm going to the dentist at the wrong time of the month.' She kissed him. 'Drive carefully. Will you be home this evening at the usual time?'

'I'll call you.' He patted her behind. 'I love you.'

'Not just for *that*, I hope.'

He noticed she didn't smile when she said it.

He drove into the city under a polished sky. He always liked the light of Sydney; it seemed to add another dimension to whatever one looked at, but, of course, that was an illusion. He passed a Social Security office where a line of people had already gathered; no amount of bright light altered their plight, they stood there becalmed in the doldrums. The economy had begun its climb out of the past few years' recession, but it was accepted now that there would always be some who would never again get a foothold on the slope. It didn't make him comfortable to know that too many of them were men and women of his own age.

6

He found his way to Darling Harbour through the maze of one-way streets that always seemed to lead in the wrong direction. He parked the car in a No Parking zone and got out, shivering a little in the wind that sprang at him. Clements was waiting at the foot of a flight of steps. The big man, married for a year now, was a well-dressed shadow of the untidy bachelor he had been for so many years; well, almost well-dressed. To have made him sartorially smooth would have been like landscaping a landslide.

'Do your collar up,' said Malone. 'You're not one of those Pommy detectives in *The Bill*.'

Clements did up his collar, arranged his silk tie. 'There, how's that? Are we supposed to be impressing the Americans this morning?'

'I dunno. They haven't impressed *us*, killing their top lawyer.'

'We dunno *they* did it.' They climbed the steps and came out on to a narrow pavement that ran round a siding where a single monorail car was parked. Blue-and-white crime scene tapes had been strung round it, cracking in the wind like carnival stockwhips. Members of the Physical Evidence team were working inside and outside the car. They had once been known as Crime Scene members; but it was Malone's convinced belief that the New South Wales Police Service, once known as the Police Force and before that as the Police Department, had a secret body called the Police Name-Changing Team whose sole purpose was to confuse everyone, including the police.

Peta Smith stepped out of the car and came towards them. 'Morning, sir.' She was always meticulously correct when it came to protocol in front of strangers; besides the PE team there were four men in overalls standing close by. 'The body's been taken to the morgue. I've got all the particulars.'

'Anyone else here?'

'Phil Truach is inside with the PE team. And there are some uniformed guys.'

'What have you come up with?'

'Nothing so far.'

She had blond hair, cut short, and a pale complexion that freckled in the summer; outdoors she almost always wore a broad-brimmed hat; it upset some crims to be interrogated by a woman who looked to be on her way to one of the more conservative churches. Today she wore a navy-blue trenchcoat against the south wind and a matching rain-hat. She was better computer-educated than any of her male colleagues and had taken over most of the research duties, but she was as efficient and painstaking as any of the men when out on an actual job. She had a good figure, the result of diet and exercise, but she would always have to watch her weight. She was attractive and coolly friendly in a dominantly male environment and, as far as Malone could judge, not overly ambitious. He had remarked all these points about her, but it had taken time. He was not averse to working with women, but he was reluctant to be responsible for them. In them he saw his own daughters and the weight of responsibility there.

'Anything on the body?'

'Just some loose change and his convention name-tag. No wallet, no keys, nothing.'

One of the men in overalls approached them and Peta Smith introduced him. 'This is Mr Korda, the technical manager. He took the phone call from the security guard who found the dead man. Then he called Police Central.'

Korda was young, ginger-haired, with a frank open face that suggested he took the world at its own valuation. At the moment he looked bemused and resentful, as if murders shouldn't happen on anything with which he was connected. 'I just couldn't believe it when Murray, our security guy, that's him back there on his own –' He jerked his head over his thin shoulder at a thickset man in uniform who stood about ten metres from them. 'When he rang me. Who expects to get a call like that, three a.m. in the morning?'

'It happens all the time,' said Malone. 'To us.'

Korda ducked his head apologetically. 'Oh sure, I guess so. Sorry. Only . . . Well, when Murray called me, I got down here right away, I been here ever since. The cars were still going around with him, the dead guy I mean, sitting up there like a tourist. It passed me just's I got here, we hadda stand and wait till it come around again. It's not something I'm used to, standing there three o'clock in the morning freezing my butt off, waiting for a dead guy to arrive. I cut off the main power, got aboard and ran it in here to the siding after Murray had switched the power back on again.'

'There was nobody else on board?'

Korda shook his head. 'Murray was back there on the Convention station, that one in fronta the Novotel. We were on our mobiles to each other. While he was waiting for me, it went around five or six times. He said there was no one in it but the dead guy.'

Malone looked at Peta Smith. 'You talked to the security man?'

She nodded. 'His name's Murray Rockman. He bears out what Mr Korda has just told us.'

Malone beckoned to the security guard, who came towards them, nodding affably to both Malone and Clements. He was almost as tall as Malone at six feet but looked shorter because of the thickness of his body; the thickness was muscle, not fat. He had a broad-cheeked face, very fair hair and almost white eyelashes; he carried his peaked cap under his arm, like a serviceman or a police officer. Malone guessed that he was the sort of security guard who took his job seriously, with a lot of his spare time spent keeping fit.

'What time did you come on duty, Mr Rockman?'

'Eleven last night, sir. I was on the shift that knocks off at six.' He had a deep voice, every word almost perfectly articulated. He had no accent, but Malone was certain he

9

had not been born in Australia. He was one of those immigrants who had learned to speak English with more respect than the local voters showed. 'My beat is this side of the water.'

'Who employs you?'

'I'm with ABS Security, we do contract work for TNT.'

The alphabet was taking over the commercial world, Malone thought: TNT was the transport corporation that ran the monorail. 'When did you first notice the monorail was still running?'

'Three-oh-eight, sir.' Security men were usually not this polite; many were ex-cops glad to be free of what they looked upon as serfdom. Rockman, on the other hand, sounded like a man who would be in service all his life and would never resent it. 'I noted it in my book. I was down below –' he nodded at the pavement beneath their feet '– when I heard it go over the first time. Then I came up here and waited for it to come round again. That was when I saw the dead man in it.' He blinked, the white eyelashes catching the sunlight. 'I didn't know he was dead, of course. I thought maybe he was a drunk who'd been put in there by some of his friends. There was a lot of merriment last night over at the hotel, the lawyers settling in.'

'You saw nothing suspicious?'

'You mean did I see anyone else? No, sir.'

'Do you know how to drive the monorail?' asked Clements.

'Mr Korda has given us some brief instruction, just in case of emergency.'

'You didn't think this was an emergency?'

'Blame me for that,' Korda interjected. 'The instructions are they aren't to touch the cars without permission. When Murray called I told him to leave it alone till I got here. I live over in Birchgrove, that time of the morning it took me less than ten minutes to get here.'

'Righto, thank you, Mr Rockman. We have your work and home address?' He looked at Peta Smith, who nodded. Then as the security guard turned away, he said, 'What service were you in, Mr Rockman?'

The white eyelashes blinked again. 'You're observant, sir. The United States Marine Corps.'

'You're American?'

'Yes, sir, but I've been out here twelve years. I've become Australianized – I hope.' He smiled for the first time, showing strong white teeth. American teeth, Malone thought.

'You're still too polite.' Malone smiled in return. 'But there's time.'

Rockman smiled again, nodded and went off, not marching but walking briskly. Malone in his mind heard the cadence song of the Marines and it matched Rockman's step. He looked at the others. 'He didn't *sound* American.'

'He's a good man,' said Korda. 'One of the best.'

'You said you cut off the power. How come the train – is that what you call it? – how come it kept moving if there was no one at the controls?'

'Doesn't it have a dead man's handle?' Clements was a grab-bag of trivia that often produced an essential key. 'They used to have it on electric trains. Probably still do.'

'We have something that works on the same principle, a power button that cuts out after a certain number of seconds if the driver hasn't activated it. In this case someone – the murderer?' He said the word as if it were alien to his tongue, with a note of disbelief that he could actually be talking about a *murderer*. 'Well, someone had taped the button down and then must of jumped off. These trains only do about fifteen ks an hour. The door to the driver's section was still open when I pulled it up.'

'So you would suggest that whoever committed the murder, he knew how to run one of these trains?'

'Well, I'm no detective –' Then he ducked his ginger head again, gave an apologetic grin while the three detectives gave him smiles that told him he was right, he was no detective. 'Sorry. Yeah, I'd say that. You don't have to be a mechanical genius to drive one of these, but it'd help if you knew about the dead man's handle principle. Dead man's handle – that's pretty funny . . . Well, not *funny*, exactly. You know what I mean, the dead guy . . .' His voice trailed off.

'Let's have a look at the scene of the crime,' suggested Malone. 'Thanks, Mr Korda. Detective Smith will be in touch with you again.' Then, as he and Clements walked along to the parked carriage: 'First time I think we've had a mobile scene of the crime, isn't it?'

'It narrows the field a bit. We start looking for someone who knows how to operate a train like this. Would you know how?'

'It takes me all my time to start our lawnmower.'

'Who is your lawnmower – Lisa?'

They grinned at each other, two old married men; then they grinned at Phil Truach, another old married man, who stood in the carriage doorway. He was their age, but he would not make sergeant or higher until he transferred to another section of the Police Service; he had been in Homicide twelve years and had twice refused promotion or transfer. Murder, he said, was a crossword puzzle, and he was addicted to puzzles, he also said, though neither Malone nor Clements had ever seen him indulging his addiction. He was tall and bony with a lean, gullied face; he smoked forty cigarettes a day and he had a smoker's cough like the bark of a gun. Somehow he had so far avoided lung cancer or emphysema and the Homicide joke was that the Tobacco Institute paid him a monthly stipend for staying alive and on his feet.

He was one of the best detectives on Malone's roster.

'Not a skerrick, Scobie.' He never worried about protocol, no matter who was around. 'No prints, nothing – everything's been wiped clean.'

'No shoeprints? It rained last night.'

'There's a welter of muddy prints on the floor, you could never sort 'em out. The monorail was packed all day yesterday, I gather – all the Yank lawyers and their wives. The cleaners don't start work on the car till five a.m. By then we'd taken over this one.'

'How many bullets?'

'Just the one. It's still in the body.' Truach stamped out the cigarette he had been smoking; he knew how much the habit annoyed Malone, a lifelong non-smoker. 'This bloke Brame, he's top of the ladder, they tell me.'

'Where's the media, then?' said Clements, though he looked relieved that none was in sight.

'They've been and gone from here. Now they're all along at the Novotel interviewing the thousand Yank lawyers.'

'*How* many?'

Truach looked at Peta Smith, who had come up behind Malone and Clements. 'There's a thousand of them,' she said. 'Spread around every hotel in Sydney. This is the first international convention that's been in Australia and it seems everyone wanted to come. Plus their wives and girlfriends. And boyfriends, too, I guess,' she added, and Malone wondered if there was a note of prejudice in her voice.

'Who's home minding the store?'

'There are eight hundred thousand lawyers in the United States,' said Clements, grabbing in his mental bag again. 'I was reading the Law Society's Journal one day. One lawyer for every three and a half thousand of the population. There'll be enough left home to mind the store and chase ambulances.'

'Eight hundred thousand!' Malone shook his head.

'We don't have that many crims registered out here.'

The four detectives were silent a moment, aghast at the thought of the legal poison ivy spreading across the US. Malone had few prejudices, but one of them, as with most cops, was an aversion to lawyers.

He stepped past Truach into the carriage and looked around. There were three blue-upholstered seats facing three similar seats in the small compartment. There was none of the disorder one so often found at a murder scene; the compartment was neat and tidy, with none of the vandalism that occurred on the city's urban trains.

'When can we have the car?' said Korda, behind him. 'I wanna get it cleaned. We'll need it today, all the traffic.'

'Not today,' said Clements. 'Maybe tomorrow.'

The technical manager's face closed up, but if he was annoyed he kept it to himself. 'Well, okay, if you say so . . . But you know what a head office is like – at the end of the day all they're interested in is the bottom line.'

'You should work for the government,' said Clements. 'It's even worse. They can't *find* the bottom line.'

'Let's go along and talk to the thousand lawyers,' said Malone. 'If we can get one of them to confess, you can have the carriage back today.'

He and Clements went down to his car. On the opposite side of the road, atop a low cliff, was a row of warehouses, some of them now converted into apartment complexes; these had been the wool stores when wool had been the wealth of the country, but those days were gone, probably for ever.

The two detectives drove along to the hotel. It was French-owned and was one of the many-roomed hotels that had been built in the city in the past five or six years, completed just as the recession had begun and hotel rooms became as much a glut as wool and wheat. Malone gave the Commodore over to a parking valet who, though Australian, had a Frenchman's hauteur, especially when it came to cars that should have been traded in years ago.

'Leave it up here on the ramp,' said Malone, showing his badge. 'It'll give the place some tone.'

The two men walked, or were blown, in through glass doors to the concierge's desk; the architects, whoever they were, had not allowed for winter's south-west winds. The concierge referred them to Reception on the first level. They travelled up on an escalator and stepped off into the big lobby, which was crowded and echoed to the clamour of voices, all of them American. They squeezed their way through the throng, asked for the manager and were directed to his office.

He was a small neat man, French and polite; the owners back in France had realized that it would be pointless sending French arrogance to handle the native barbarians. With him were two Americans, both grey-haired, both grey with concern.

'I am Charles Champlain. This is Mr Zoehrer, vice-president of the American Bar Association, and this is Mr Novack, the American Consul-General.'

'A terrible tragedy, terrible!' Zoehrer was a big man with a big voice and big gestures; he flung his hands about, addressed Malone and Clements as if he were addressing a jury. 'His wife's due in today – God, what a way to greet her! *Orville's been murdered!*'

'She's on her way in from the airport now.' Novack, a short bulky man, had the calm air of a man who had, innumerable times, had to convey bad news. In a way, Malone guessed, a consul's job was not unlike a policeman's: you were everybody's target. 'Do you want me to handle it, Karl, or will you?'

'We'd better do it together,' said Zoehrer. 'I've only met her once before, at Clinton's inaugural. She's not a lawyer's wife, you know what I mean? Not one for conventions, stuff like that.' Then he seemed to remember that he was talking in front of strangers, non-Americans. He looked at

Malone. 'You getting anywhere with your investigations, sir? Inspector, is that right?'

Malone nodded. 'Sergeant Clements and I've just come on the case. Our Crime Scene team tell us they've come up with nothing. The only thing we can say is that it doesn't look like a mugging, something unpremeditated. He was lured on to the monorail, or forced on, by someone who knew what they were about. Or maybe he was shot beforehand and carried on to the monorail. At this stage we don't know. I have to ask this – would you know if Mr Brame had any enemies, someone who might've followed him from the United States? Was he working on some big case? I'm asking the obvious – the Mafia?'

The big hands were spread wide. 'Not as far as I know. Orville wasn't a criminal lawyer, at least he hadn't been in years. We lived and worked on opposite sides of the country. He was New York, I'm San Francisco and LA. Los Angeles. I guess all lawyers – civil as well as criminal – I guess we all collect enemies as we go along.'

There was a knock on the office door and a young woman put her head in. 'Mr Champlain, Mrs Brame has arrived. We've taken her up to her suite.'

'How is she?' asked the manager.

'It was hard to tell. Upset, I suppose, but she seemed to be holding herself together. Someone met her at the airport and told her on the way in.'

'Well, we better go up,' said Novack. 'Will you excuse us, Inspector?'

'Mr Novack, this is a murder case, on our turf.'

'Of course, how stupid of me. Let's go. I just hope she can handle it, four strange men coming in on her like this.'

When the four men stepped out of the manager's office into the lobby, a sudden silence fell on the crowd still there. The throng opened up and they went through and stepped into a waiting lift. As the doors closed they heard the clamour start up again and Malone glimpsed photographers and reporters trying to break through.

'I hope they didn't shut up like that when Mrs Brame came in,' said Zoehrer.

'They did, sir,' said the girl who was escorting them to the upper floor. 'It was eerie.'

'When you go back downstairs,' said Malone, 'see that none of the media get up to this floor.'

'Can I tell them you'll be making a statement later?' This girl had dealt with reporters before; hospitality management had taught her they were a necessary evil.

Malone sighed. 'They'll expect it. We never tell 'em anything, but they always write it down anyway.'

'The media,' said Zoehrer. 'Bless 'em, they think we can't do without them.'

He sounded sincere, as a good lawyer should, but Malone had the distinct impression that the big man would wring everything he could out of the media.

The four men entered the Brame suite, doing their best not to look like a threatening phalanx. Vases, large and small, of flowers decorated the big main room, an intended welcome for the wife of the president of the ABA; no one had remembered to remove them and they now supplied the wrong note, like a laugh at a funeral. Even the bright airiness of the room itself seemed out of place.

Joanna Brame was sitting in a chair, staring out of the big picture window at the city skyline on the opposite side of the narrow strip of Darling Harbour. As she sat there the monorail train came into view and slid round the curve beneath her like a pale metal caterpillar. She turned her head as the four men came in, but did not immediately rise. When she did at last stand up she did so with slow grace; there was none of the stiff angularity that Malone knew shock could bring. She was dressed in a beige knitted suit that showed no untoward bulges in her figure; a brown vicuna coat had been dropped on a nearby couch. She was tall with short grey-blond hair, the patrician look that came of a special mix of flesh and bone, and large grey eyes that had a touch of hauteur to them; Malone had the quick thought that Mrs Brame would not suffer fools gladly, if at all. She was also someone who could hide her grief and shock like an accomplished actor.

'Mrs Brame!' Zoehrer strode across the room, hands outstretched. 'I'm Karl Zoehrer, we met at the White House –'

She gave him her hand, held a little high, almost as if she waited for it to be kissed. 'Of course, Mr Zoehrer.' Then she looked at the other three men, waiting for them to introduce themselves.

Novack did so. 'There are no words to express our feelings over what's happened –'

'No,' she said and looked at Malone and Clements. 'Is it too soon to ask who killed my husband?'

'I'm afraid so, Mrs Brame. May we ask you some questions?'

'Can't the questions wait –?' Zoehrer all at once had become a heavyweight guardian angel.

'It's all right.' Joanna Brame held up a hand; Malone had seen judges call for quiet with the same gesture. She might not be a lawyer's wife, you know what I mean, but she would hold a jurist's view of things, she would ask questions as well as answer them. She had a low deep voice with some edge to it that, Malone guessed, usually got her what she asked for. 'Where is my husband? His – *body*?'

'At the city morgue.' Malone saw an excuse to get her away from the interruptions and interference he felt sure would be coming from Zoehrer. 'We'll need you to identify him. It has to be done by a relative.'

'Has his brother been informed?'

'His *brother*?' said Zoehrer. 'He has a brother here at the convention?'

'No, he's Australian, not American. He is a partner in a

18

law firm here in Sydney. Rodney Channing. You may know him, Inspector?'

Malone looked at Clements and left the answer to him. 'We've heard of him, Mrs Brame. But he's not in our line of work, he's not a criminal lawyer. It's a different name – are they stepbrothers?'

'No, brothers.' She reached for her coat; Novack helped her on with it. 'Shall we go?'

'I'll come, too,' said Novack. 'Your husband is an American citizen, I take it?'

'Naturalized. He was born here in Australia. Do you have a car? Thank you, Mr Zoehrer, I'll be more hospitable when I've done this – this duty.'

'Sure, sure.' Zoehrer looked as if it was the first time in years he had been dismissed. 'I'll be taking over the convention – I'll see there is someone to take care of you, Mrs Brame –'

She turned back in the doorway of the suite; Malone, immediately behind her, had to pull up sharply. 'I'll be perfectly all right, Mr Zoehrer. Thank you, though, for your concern.'

When Malone led the way out of the lift down in the lobby the crowd there had thinned out. There were still clusters of people around the lobby; they all turned their faces towards the lift as the doors opened. Even those with mobile phones grafted to their ears, the new street performers, the new clowns and mimes, said *Hold it* and stopped speaking to stare at the new widow. Cameramen and reporters swept in a wave towards Malone and the others, but he moved quickly towards them before they could get too close to Joanna Brame.

'Not now. There'll be a full statement later, but at the moment we have nothing definite.'

'How's Mrs Brame taking the murder?' That was from a fresh-faced television reporter, not one of Malone's favourite breeds.

'C'mon, how would you take it if your girlfriend was murdered?' It was not the sort of reply that the police manual recommended, but it stopped the questions long enough for Malone to make his escape.

Down on the lower level the doors opened and a gale blew in. Joanna Brame produced a brown beret from her coat pocket and jammed it on her head. A grey Cadillac with DC plates and a chauffeur was waiting for Novack. 'Will you ride with us, Inspector?'

'That's my car over there, sir. You know where the morgue is?' Novack shook his head. 'Sorry, why should you? You'd better follow us.'

It was a ten-minute drive out to the morgue near Sydney University. When the attendant on the front desk phoned through to Romy's office, she came out to greet them. 'This is Dr Keller,' said Clements and added with the pride that Malone had noticed since their marriage, 'my wife.'

Joanna Brame and Novack hid any surprise they may have felt and made no comment. Which surprised Malone, whose experience of Americans was that they commented on everything.

'I'll have your husband brought out. If you would go into that room there?'

Malone ushered Joanna Brame into the side room where the body could be viewed through a window. As he touched her elbow he could feel the trembling in her arm and, involuntarily, he pressed the elbow sympathetically. She looked sideways at him. 'I have done this before, Inspector. My first husband –'

Romy came into the small room as, on the other side of the window, a white-coated attendant wheeled in a trolley on which lay a green-shrouded body. A zip was pulled and Orville Brame's face was exposed, the mouth open, the eyes shut. It would be Malone's only glimpse of the murdered man and, as always, he wondered what events would pile on the death of this man about whom he knew nothing and would certainly never learn everything.

Joanna Brame drew a deep shuddering breath, took off her beret. 'Yes, that's my husband.'

'Orville William Brame?' said Romy.

'Yes.' She watched while the shroud was zipped up again and the trolley wheeled away; then she turned her back on the window and looked at Romy. 'Will there be an autopsy or anything?'

'It's a homicide, so yes, there has to be. We have to take out the bullet that killed him.' Romy's voice was soft, sympathetic; there was no hint of officialdom about her, though she was the deputy-director of the Institute of Forensic Medicine. In her white coat and with her dark hair pulled back she looked severe, but for the compassion in her dark blue eyes. 'We have to wait on HIV tests –'

'HIV? AIDS tests? For my husband?'

'It's standard practice these days, Mrs Brame, for every autopsy. It's no reflection on your husband.'

'He would be amused. He always tried to be beyond reproach.' But she said it with affection.

Malone thanked Romy and left Clements with her while he escorted Joanna Brame out into the street, where Novack joined them. They stood in the weak winter sunlight and the wind, coming up the street, tore at their hair so that they looked, to a passer-by, like mourners who had gone wild in their grief. Joanna Brame pulled on her beret again and Malone settled his pork-pie hat on his head. Novack evidently used a strong hair-spray, for his hair was set like concrete.

'You said you wanted to ask me questions, Inspector. Could it wait till this afternoon, say five o'clock? I'm really not in any fit condition –'

Malone hated any sort of delay in an investigation, but there would be others he would have to question. 'Five o'clock then, Mrs Brame.'

'Thank you, Inspector.' Novack took her arm and led

her across to the Cadillac. He opened the rear door for her, but she paused and looked back at Malone. The wind whipped away her words, but he thought she said, 'I may be able to help you.'

3

Driving back to the Hat Factory, which had indeed once been a hat factory turning out trilbies, fedoras, even bowlers once upon a time, and now housed Homicide, Clements said, 'Have you got the feeling there's a thousand lawyers sitting on your back?'

'I hope they're not all like that cove Zoehrer. I've just placed him. He's one of those big damages lawyers from California – Melvin Belli's another one. They invented that palimony thing. The way you used to play around, it's a wonder you didn't cop a palimony suit.'

'You know none of the girls ever stayed long enough. But let's drop that, I'm a married man now. So how do we handle this Brame case?'

'We're spread thin. Keep Phil and Peta on it and maybe we can spare John Kagal. I'll load the rest of the calendar on to the other fellers. At least three of the cases should be wound up this week or Greg Random will want to know why.' Random was the Chief Superintendent, Regional Crime Squad, South Region. 'I suppose we'll have to officially let the New York PD and maybe the FBI, I dunno, we'll have to let them know what's happened. I'll check it out with the Consul-General. In the meantime . . .'

'Yes?'

'Put Peta on to questioning Zoehrer and any other of the lawyers who might give us some light on why Brame was done in.'

'She's a bit young – inexperienced, I mean –'

'She's all right, Russ. And she's better-looking than you

or me. All these lawyers haven't come all this way just to discuss the law. Junkets like this one, for lawyers or doctors or politicians, they're an excuse for a tax-deductible holiday. A young lawyer on holiday, who's he going to let his hair down for – a good-looking sort like Peta or you and me?'

'You're sexist.'

'Only in a good cause.'

Back at his office, in the glass-walled cubicle that passed for the Homicide commander's domain, he ran through the computer sheets that had been neatly laid on his desk. There had been last-minute hitches in two of the murder cases; the other three on the list would be wrapped up and sent to the Director of Public Prosecutions by the end of the week. The Brame homicide looked as if it would get the full-scale investigation that the Americans would expect. It was going to be a round-the-clock job.

He reached for the phone to tell Lisa he would not be home for dinner. The phone at Randwick had rung four times before he remembered she would be at the dentist's. He waited for the answering machine to take over, but when it came on all he got was Maureen's voice saying, 'This is –' Then her voice cut out and he knew the machine had gone on the blink again, as it had twice in the past month. It was supposed to have been fixed and he wondered why Lisa, usually so meticulous in running the household, had neglected to call a technician.

He flipped through his small personal notebook, found the number of their dentist. 'May I leave a message for Mrs Malone? This is her husband.'

'Mr Malone, your wife isn't here.'

'Oh, she's left already?'

'She hasn't been in at all. She had no appointment –'

He thanked the receptionist and hung up. He sat back in his chair, puzzled and a little angry: why had Lisa lied to him? Was she planning some surprise? Then a memory came back, like a spasm of pain, and he felt a hollow sense of dread. Years ago, before any of the children were born, he and she had been in New York on a round-the-world honeymoon financed by a lottery win; an extravagance, one of his last, that he had insisted upon. Lisa, suffering a lost filling, had left their hotel and gone looking for a dentist. She had been kidnapped along with the wife of the then Mayor of New York and held to ransom by terrorists. It was ridiculous that history could repeat itself, but the agony of that search for her came back like new pain.

Then reason, the hook on which hope hangs, sometimes weakly, took over. Lisa had not gone to the dentist. So where had she gone and why had she lied to him, something she had never done before? He trusted her so absolutely that the thought did not enter his mind that she might have gone to meet another man. But where was she?

Chapter Two

1

He got her at home at four o'clock in the afternoon. 'Where have you been? I've called half a dozen times – you said you were going to the dentist's, I tried there –' There was silence at the other end of the line. 'Darl, for Chrissake, what's going on?'

Something that sounded like a long sigh came down the line. 'I'll tell you when you come home –'

'Tell me now. I'll probably be late – not before seven or eight, anyway –'

'No, I'll tell you when you come home.' There was a pause, then she said, 'I love you,' and hung up.

He put the phone back in the cradle and looked up to see Clements standing in the doorway. 'You look as if you've been talking to one of the Yank lawyers. Mr Zoehrer?'

'No, Lisa.'

'Oh?' Clements waited for further comment, but when none came he went on, 'Ballistics just called. They haven't got the bullet that killed Brame yet. The morgue's snowed under, dead 'uns everywhere.'

'The natural place for them.' His mind was still on Lisa.

'You want me to come with you to see Mrs Brame?'

'Who else?'

'I thought you might prefer Peta. The good-looking one.'

They left half an hour later to go to the Novotel. As they were leaving the big main room Peta Smith, taking off her trenchcoat and her hat, came in. 'Nothing, Scobie, nothing worthwhile. Brame was at a reception at the Darling

Harbour convention centre last night, but no one noticed anything out of the ordinary about him, I mean how he behaved. Nobody remembers seeing him after eleven o'clock, when someone saw him in the hotel coffee lounge with a guy.'

'Who?'

She shrugged. 'Who knows? Like I told you, there are a thousand lawyers in town – most of 'em are strangers to each other. Except the guys at the top.'

'Are they being co-operative?'

She smiled. 'I've had four invitations to dinner, six to drinks and two to mind your own business.'

Malone looked at Clements. 'Could you have done as well? Thanks, Peta. Get Andy Graham to help you set up the flow charts. Don't work late.'

'I wasn't going to. I accepted one of the dinner dates. That okay?'

'Just so long as you feed it into the running sheets.' But he grinned. 'Not with Karl Zoehrer, I hope? I don't want him suing Homicide for palimony.'

When he and Clements drove into the Novotel at a few minutes to five, the lawyers were filtering back from their afternoon session at the convention. Malone saw Zoehrer holding court in the lobby, but the big man did not see the two detectives and they escaped into the lift and rode up to Mrs Brame's floor.

She was waiting for them in her suite, in a rose silk dress and looking much fresher than she had this morning. With her was a handsome young man with thinning blond hair and the awkward look of a courtier new to serving the queen. And Malone knew now that Joanna Brame was the queen of whichever circle she ruled back home in the States.

'Adam, would you get the gentlemen a drink? This is Adam Tallis, an associate in our firm.'

Malone and Clements shook hands with Tallis and gave

him their drink preferences. Then Malone sat down opposite Joanna Brame. '*Our* firm? You're a lawyer, too, Mrs Brame?'

She smiled at that, a pleasant smile, then sipped the cocktail she had been holding when the two detectives had entered the room. 'Only by osmosis. I said *our* firm out of habit. My great-grandfather founded it back in – when was it, Adam?'

'1888.' Malone was certain that Joanna Brame had known the date, but she had neatly drawn Tallis into the conversation. 'Mrs Brame is a Schuyler.'

'Of Schuyler, Dr Vries and Barrymore,' said Malone and smiled at the surprise of the two Americans. 'I looked it up, Mr Brame's firm, I mean. I just didn't know you were related to it, Mrs Brame.'

'My great-grandfather, my grandfather, my father. And my husband.' She looked at her drink as if she saw reflections in it. Malone wondered if her first husband had belonged to the firm, but now was not the time to ask her. 'Somehow, I've never been able to escape it, the law. Even my first husband was a lawyer . . .' Then she looked up, threw off the introspection that had veiled her for a moment. 'Well, how can I help? Sit down here beside me, Adam. You may be able to help, too.'

'First, we have to establish what Mr Brame was doing out so late last night.'

'He may have gone for a walk. He did that every night, to unwind, he said. Whether we were at our apartment in Manhattan or at our place in Connecticut. I used to worry, especially in New York, but he told me he always kept to the well-lit streets.'

'Darling Harbour is reasonably well-lit,' said Clements. 'There just aren't too many people around at two or three o'clock in the morning.'

Malone said gently, 'Did your husband have any enemies?'

'Here?' She put down her empty glass. 'He hadn't been home for thirty years.'

'Not necessarily here. In the United States.'

'None that I know of. He was highly respected.'

'Popular?' He knew that popularity could breed enmity. That skater Nancy Kerrigan had been popular and she had had enemies.

'Well, perhaps not *popular*. My husband never courted that sort of thing. He used to quote somebody, I forget who. The more one pleases everybody, the less one pleases profoundly.'

'Stendhal,' said Tallis.

Malone didn't know who Stendhal was, but guessed he was a lawyer: he sounded like one. 'Would you know if he had any enemies, Mr Tallis? People he'd had business dealings with? Ex-clients?'

Tallis was handsome now, but one could already see the plumpness, like clouds of flesh, gathering around the cheeks and jowls, that would dim his looks and turn him into a fat middle-aged man. His voice was soft but reedy, unassertive, but at least his gaze was direct and Malone had the feeling he could be trusted. 'I had only just begun to work with Mr Brame, to assist him personally, I mean. I've been with the firm four years, ever since I came out of law school, but I was in a section that Mr Brame had nothing to do with. Clients' tax problems.'

'How big is the firm?'

'All told, I think we have about four hundred and fifty people on staff, including the partners and senior men.'

'So what were you assisting Mr Brame on?'

'Mr Brame handled half a dozen or so of our top clients.'

'Such as?'

Tallis named three corporations that even Malone, no student of American business circles, knew. 'You'd know those, I'm sure, Inspector. There were others, not so public, but all of them highly capitalized. There were times – well,

28

I – I was out of my league, the first month or so. Perhaps, like me, Inspector, you don't realize how much hidden money – well, not *hidden* – *unpublicized* money there is in our country. Mr Brame, in a way, was – *connected* to a lot of wealth. Riches.'

'No names, Adam.' Joanna Brame smiled, but there was no mistaking the fact that she was warning Tallis.

'Are you suggesting money might be behind his murder?'

Tallis was abruptly cautious. 'Well, no . . . I think we should wait till Mr De Vries arrives. He's the other joint senior partner. I called him first thing this morning, when we – when we got the bad news. He was leaving immediately, as soon as he could get aboard a plane. Fortunately he was in Seattle on business, on the West Coast. I think I should leave him to answer all questions about the firm.'

'Mr Tallis, we're investigating a murder here. We don't want the trail to go cold while we pay our respects to company protocol.' Crumbs, he thought, I'm starting to sound like a lawyer, God forgive me.

Joanna Brame interrupted, politely: 'Inspector, I don't think Mr Tallis is trying to obstruct your investigations. Though he was my husband's assistant, he was not privy to everything that Orville would have been involved with. I know – *knew* my husband. He carried everything very close to his chest. I think it would be advisable to wait for Mr De Vries.'

'Did he ever confide in you?'

Her gaze, like Tallis's, was direct. 'No, nor did I encourage him to.'

Why do I have the feeling I'm facing hurdles here? Is it because lawyers, even lawyers' wives, can't help blowing smoke? Or was it just a cop's prejudice? 'You mentioned Mr Brame had a brother here in Sydney. Were they close?'

'No. Anything but.' *Well, that was a direct answer, no smoke there.*

'Have you ever met Mr – what was his name?'

'Channing,' said Clements. 'Of Channing and Lazarus.'

'Never,' said Joanna Brame. 'Their father, his name was Lester Brame, was in Sydney during World War Two. He was a sergeant in some company or something that spent all its time in Sydney. Having a good war, I think it was called. He met and married their mother. My husband was born in 1943, I think. His brother was born ten years later. In the years between, I gather, the marriage had been an on-and-off affair. Finally, my husband's father went back to the United States – he was never a success here nor back home. My husband grew up and went to law school at Sydney University, then left immediately he'd got his degree and went to join his father. Lester Brame died the day after my husband graduated from Yale Law School. The brothers took sides in the marriage – it often happens. My – my brother-in-law took his mother's name, Channing.' She stopped suddenly, as if she had run out of breath, but it was surprise at how much she had revealed. She was, Malone guessed, not one given to opening family closets, not to strangers. He wondered if, though she was a lawyer's wife, this was her first encounter with a police investigation. She reached for her glass, saw that it was empty but waved a dismissing hand when Tallis gestured that he would refill it for her. 'I don't think my brother-in-law would have a clue, as you call it, as to who might have killed my husband.'

'I hadn't suggested he might have, Mrs Brame.' There was just a hint of stiffening in her face, but that was all. But Malone saw Tallis straighten up and he turned to him: 'You thought of something, Mr Tallis?'

'Well, no, not really –'

'Try me. I'll tell you if it's something worthwhile.'

Tallis hesitated, glanced at Joanna Brame, then looked back at Malone. 'I saw two letters from Channing and Lazarus, both marked as strictly personal for Mr Brame. They came in in the last month. I gave them to him, but he never made any comment on them.'

'Did Mr Brame ever dictate any reply?'

'Not that I know of. He may have phoned his brother, but I wouldn't know about that. You'd have to check the office switch records.'

'Or he could have called from home?' said Clements, who had been taking notes.

'He could have,' said Joanna Brame. 'He often made business calls from home.'

'Has Mr Channing been in touch with you since you arrived?'

'No.'

'That's odd, don't you think? He'd know of the murder. Common courtesy should have made him call you.'

'He wouldn't know I'm here. He may have called Mr Zoehrer or someone else from the Bar Association.' She seemed unconcerned at her brother-in-law's lack of interest. 'When may I take my husband's body home?'

'That will be up to the coroner, Mrs Brame. The police can ask for a delay, but I don't think there'll be any need for that. Not if we get co-operation and we find the murderer soon.'

2

'You have only a faint resemblance to Orville.'

'I've got my mother's looks,' said Rodney Channing. 'Orville always looked like our father.'

He was as tall as Orville had been, but thicker-set. He was better-looking than Orville, but his looks were fleshy; he had thick wavy hair with streaks of grey along the temples; he wore a medium-thick moustache that was already grey. He had smooth, almost unlined skin, and she wondered if he used lotions on it, something Orville had never done. He had Orville's eyes: dark, giving nothing away, waiting for the other man (or woman) to tell secrets first.

He had phoned just after six, a few minutes after the two detectives had left. 'I've only just learned you are here. I'd have called earlier if I'd known.'

He had said *Mrs Brame?* when she had answered the phone, but he had given her no name at all after that, not even now, ten minutes after he had entered the suite. They were strangers, not even linked by a common surname.

'Did Orville mention we'd been in touch?' There was no hint of Orville's voice in his, but that could be because of the accent. She was looking for similarities, though she was not sure why.

'No.'

'It was just business.' *Did he sound relieved?* 'Very formal.'

'Did he plan to see you while he was in Sydney?'

He hesitated, sipped the whisky-and-water she had given him. 'We saw each other yesterday. He came to my office.'

'Yesterday?' She frowned, getting the day right in her mind; the international date line threw the calendar out of kilter. 'Sunday?'

'I'd rather you didn't mention it to anyone – may I call you Joanna?' She nodded, coolly, and he went on, 'My wife and I have an understanding, I never bring my work home –'

'Mr Channing?'

'Rod.'

She nodded, but didn't say his name. She had married beneath her when she had married Orville, which is not to say she could have done better; diamonds and gold are always found beneath one, and Orville had been pure gold. But, with the quick antennae of the born snob, she was beginning to suspect that Rodney Channing was pure dross. 'I'm not expecting you to bring your work *here*. If you and Orville were engaged in something – *secret*, I don't want to know. Though I'm curious –' it hurt her to confess it '– what brought you together after all these years of – what do I call it? Did you hate each other?'

'What did Orville tell you?' He had a habit of stroking one side of his moustache, like an old silent film villain.

'He never told me anything, just that he wanted this part of his life – the Australian part – put behind him.'

'He'd become thoroughly American, hadn't he?'

'What does that mean?'

He back-tracked: 'I don't mean it in a pejorative sense. But he'd become American Establishment, hadn't he? Ivy League, all that?'

He had indeed become Establishment, but only because she had led him by the hand into it. Even after ten years with Schuyler, De Vries and Barrymore there had been the rough edges of his father on him; at least, from what Orville had told her of his father, she had assumed the rough edges had been those of Lester Brame. Her first husband, Porter Greenway, had been dead two years when she had married Orville, taken him out of the small apartment on Central Park West and into the ten-room apartment on Park Avenue and the house on ten acres in Connecticut. And, more important than addresses, into that part of American East Coast society that, come Republicans, come Democrats, come Roosevelt, come Reagan, or even Clinton, would be as rock-solid as Grant's Tomb. Even though Grant himself would never have been admitted as a member to the circle.

'Orville *proved* himself, Mr Channing. There was no lawyer in the Bar Association held in higher regard. I'm sure they'll tell you that, if you care to ask anyone in this hotel. The place is full of lawyers,' she said testily, forgetting he was one.

He showed an unexpected solicitude. 'Why don't you move out, go to another hotel?'

'Mr Tallis, one of my husband's –' She could not

accustom herself to the thought that this man opposite her was *family*. 'One of Orville's associates, he tried to get me into another hotel, but no luck. Every hotel in town is booked out. Orville was booked in here to be close to the convention centre. I have to stay here amongst what I suppose the police would call the principal suspects.'

'I'm not sure what the police would call them. I'm not a criminal lawyer, I've never had anything to do with murder.' He spoke as if it were an unspeakable subject.

'Have you no suspicions, Mr Channing?'

He didn't correct her on the use of his name; he seemed to accept the fact that their relationship was going to be distant. She wondered why Orville had not told him yesterday that she was coming to Sydney and could only guess that Orville had wanted to distance her from his brother.

'Suspicions? Why should I have any?'

For the first time she seemed at a loss. 'I don't know. I don't know why I asked that. I still can't accept that Orville was – *murdered*.' The word hung in the air like an obscenity. She looked away from him, out the window at the windswept night. 'I can't accept that he's *dead*.'

There was an awkward silence. Channing half-rose from his chair, then sank back. She turned back to him, frowning, as if he had been on the verge of committing some familiarity that would have offended her. She was fending off grief as if it were physically attacking her; she felt physically exhausted, her muscles stiff under the strain. She said, 'You haven't commented at all on his murder.'

He stroked the side of his moustache; she recognized now that it was a nervous habit. 'I'm the sort of lawyer, Joanna, who doesn't venture an opinion till he knows all the facts. I know virtually nothing of what happened to Orville, other than that he was shot while riding on the monorail.' He stood up. 'I must be going. How long will you be staying?'

'Only until they release Orville's body for me to take home.'

'He was born here. Why not bury him here?'

She had stood up, very straight. 'It would seem that you are a rather insensitive man, Mr Channing. Not at all like your brother.'

3

'I have cancer,' said Lisa. 'Of the cervix.'

He had got home just before eight o'clock, after she and the children had had dinner. He had eaten alone, while she busied herself at the sink and the children had gone to their rooms to do their homework. Afterwards he and she had sat listlessly watching television, a sitcom where the situation was banal and the comedy even worse. The mood had been constrained, his by suspicion, hers with her secret. Now they were in bed, with the light out, lying side by side with a stiffness uncommon to them. Then she gave him her secret and, with a low moan, he reached for her.

'Jesus, why didn't you tell me before?'

'I didn't want to scare you, in case it proved to be nothing. I had a pap smear last week, then Dr Newton called me on Friday and asked me to come in today.'

'You kept it to yourself all weekend?' It had been a good weekend. Sunday, the children, for a change, had had no social engagements; in a rare fit of extravagance, his wallet turning blue at the prospect, he had taken the family to lunch at one of the better restaurants in The Rocks, where the prices were tourist prices and the waiters expected tourist tips, preferably American and not your lousy local 2 per cent. Lisa had been her usual self, drily cheerful, attentive to him and the children; or so it had seemed. 'How bad is it?'

'If a woman is going to have cancer, the cervix is as good

35

a place as any. There's a better than even chance that it is localized and can be contained. I think I'd rather it's there than in my breast.'

He was still holding her to him. 'Don't start making comparisons, that's not going to make me feel any better. Is Wally Newton going to operate? When?'

'Soon's he can get me into St Sebastian's. He won't do the surgery, he's got a top man, Dr Hubble.' She freed her hand from between them, stroked his chin. 'Don't worry too much, darling. I'll make it.'

He rolled over on his back, his arm still under her. He could feel the life in her, the sensuousness that bound them together where love and lust merged; he shut his eyes against the thought of what might be eating away at that body. The Celt in him took over: he squeezed his eyes even tighter against the thought that he had already lost her. He felt the winter chill of death: not his own but of a loved one, which is worse.

'Have you told anyone? Your mother? Claire?'

He felt her turn her head, heard the rebuke in her voice. 'Do you think I'd have told anyone before I told you? I actually caught a cab down to the Hat Factory after I came out of the doctor's. But I couldn't bring myself to go in – I was looking for comfort, but it wouldn't have been fair to give you the news there – cry on your shoulder in front of Russ and the others . . . Then I thought I'd take myself shopping, I don't know why, or what I was going to buy. I sat in David Jones for an hour listening to that pianist they have on the ground floor near the perfumery counters. I got very sentimental listening to him . . .' Then she put her face against his shoulder and began to weep.

He held her to him, silently cursing God, in whom he believed and who had been good to him, but who, like all gods, demanded repayment.

4

In the morning they told the children. Perhaps it was the wrong time of day. Bad news, unlike good news, does not improve with keeping. It burst out of him at breakfast; instantly he was sorry. He should have allowed the children to go off to school and then gathered them to him and Lisa in the evening and told them. But then he might not be home in time this evening: there were murders to be solved, to delay him. Bad news, he now realized, was endemic. The way the world was going showed him that.

Claire and Maureen got up from the table and went and put their arms round Lisa; Maureen, the one who jeered at the world, was the one who burst into tears. Tom sat looking from one parent to the other, frowning, an almost resentful expression on his face, as if both of them had hit him. Malone reached out and put a hand on his son's arm.

'Mum'll be all right, I promise you. But keep it to yourself at school, okay?'

'Geez, d'you think I'd broadcast something like that?'

It was the second time he had been rebuked. Then the phone rang. He got up from the table, squeezed Maureen's shoulder as he passed her, and went into the hallway. It was Clements.

'There's been another one, Scobie. The security guard who found Brame's body. He's just been fished out of Darling Harbour.'

Chapter Three

1

They were putting the body into an ambulance as Malone arrived. He parked his car and walked out on to the broad expanse of promenade which fronted Cockle Bay, the headwater of Darling Harbour, which itself was no more than a small arm of the main harbour. Cruiser ferries were anchored at the landing stages and across the water a sour screech of music came from the pleasure grounds as someone tested the sound system. It was raining again, but the radio this morning had said there was still no rain west of the Blue Mountains, eighty kilometres from Sydney. Out there on the plains drought was breaking the hearts of farmers; there were some areas that had had no rain for two and a half years. This was a tough country, where people on the land died by degrees, though the rate of murder and suicide had risen sharply in the past twelve months. Someone had once called Australia the Lucky Country: the irony of it was a bitter taste.

The rain, like bitterly cold glass darts, came from the south on squalls of wind; facing the wind one could see the squalls coming, like dark waves of swifts ahead of their usual seasonal migration. The wind made it pointless trying to put up an umbrella and Malone pulled his hat down hard, turned up his raincoat collar and showed his back to the squalls.

'What happened?'

'A bullet in the head, then he was dragged across there and dumped off the end of the jetty.' Clements nodded to the crime scene tapes writhing and crackling in the wind like blue-and-white streaks of lightning. 'It looks like close range, almost an execution job. There's been a break-in over at the Convention Centre there. They're still checking what's been taken, they're not sure if a computer's gone.'

'They'd kill him for that? A bullet in the head for a computer?'

'The shit that's around these days, they'd kill you for loose change.' Clements turned his face into a squall of rain, as if to wash away his look of anger and disgust. He could be a charitable man but he had no illusions left.

'A bit coincidental, isn't it, two murders here in twenty-four hours?'

'I think you're stretching it a bit to connect this one with the Brame murder.'

Malone nodded. 'I guess so. I'm not thinking too straight this morning.'

Clements looked at him through another gust of rain. 'Something wrong at home? The kids?' He loved them as if they were his own.

'I'll tell you later.' Malone turned as Korda, the technical manager of the monorail, wrapped against the elements in a hooded wind-jacket with the monorail logo on the pocket, came towards them. 'Morning, Mr Korda. We didn't expect to be back so soon.'

'Christ Almighty, what's going on? Someone trying to fuck up the tourist business, drive all these lawyers outa town?' He turned his face away as the rain hit it. 'No, I take that back, that's bloody tasteless. But shit . . .' He looked after the departing ambulance. 'The ABS security guys are over there in the Convention Centre, you wanna talk to 'em?'

'Anything to get out of this rain and wind,' said Malone: that, too, was a tasteless remark. But his mind really wasn't here. 'Let's talk to 'em.'

Inside the foyer of the huge convention hall three men in

suits and raincoats were in a tight group, sober faces close together in discussion. They opened up as Korda introduced Malone and Clements. Two of the men nodded and the third held out his hand.

'I'm Jack Favell, managing director of ABS. Dreadful business, this. We've lost two of our men in the past twelve months, but this one seems senseless. A bullet in a man's head for nothing.'

'Nothing?'

'There's been a break-in, but it was either for show, to put us off, or Murray, the guy that was shot, disturbed them. Looks like they just held the gun against his head and shot him.' He was a short plump man, almost egg-bald and with dark shrewd eyes behind gold-framed glasses. Malone doubted that he had ever patrolled a security beat. 'Murray Rockman was a good man, one of our best.'

'How long had he been with you?'

'Three years.'

'Any family? A wife?'

Favell looked at one of his colleagues, a lean man with a battered face; Malone recognized him as an ex-boxer who had once been in the Police Service. 'Was he married, Ted?'

'He had a de facto, I think.' Ted Gilligan nodded at Malone and Clements. 'G'day, Scobie. Russ. Looks like you're busy, this and Sunday night's job.'

'We're hoping there's no connection,' said Clements. 'Where did Rockman live?'

'We'd have to look it up. Somewhere out in Arncliffe. You wanna go out there?'

Clements looked at Malone, who said, 'Send Peta. Do you run the security details, Ted?' Gilligan nodded. 'Rockman would've been armed. Did the killer or killers take his gun?'

'No, it was still in his holster. Your guys have taken it, but said they'd give it back to us.'

'It was still in his holster? If he was investigating a

break-in, he didn't strike me as the sort who'd be as careless as that.'

'That's the way we're thinking. The flap of the holster was still buttoned. Looks like he never had a chance to draw it. They just come up behind him and shot him in the back of the head.'

'An execution job?'

'Call it what you like. But if you catch the bastards –'

'Leave 'em to us, Ted,' Malone said quietly. 'Don't have your fellers go looking for them, okay?'

Gilligan nodded and Favell said, 'We shan't step on your turf, Inspector. But you'll understand our men are going to be a bit toey for a week or two.'

'Sure, we understand that. In the meantime . . . We'll send a detective round to your office, Detective Smith. Give her everything you have on Mr Rockman.'

'Her?' Gilligan raised his eyebrows.

'Things have changed since your day, Ted. We have tea and cakes now, instead of a beer.'

Driving back to Homicide Malone gave Clements the news about Lisa. The big man seemed to crumple. 'Oh Jesus! You better take leave.'

'That's what I want to do, but Lisa won't have a bar of it. You know what she's like, you can't argue with her.'

'I'll have Romy have a word with her.'

'No, you won't. Let Romy talk to her, by all means, but tell her not to mention me and work. Lisa's point is that if I take leave and stay at home with her, it'll only upset the kids more, make them worry more than they are now. She wants things to stay as normal as possible, at least till she goes into hospital.'

'When's she going in?'

'At the weekend. When she does, *then* I'll take leave.'

Clements shook his head, stared through the rain-spattered windscreen. The world outside was fragmented; here in the car it was little better. 'Christ, who'd believe in

God? A woman like Lisa . . . And the shit He lets survive!'

'She'll survive.' He would never forgive God if she didn't.

Having unburdened himself to Clements didn't help, but somehow he got through the rest of the day. One of the five murders on the calendar was suddenly cleared up with a confession, releasing Andy Graham and John Kagal; he sent Graham to follow up with Phil Truach on the Brame case. Peta Smith was sent out to ABS Security and John Kagal went with her. Just before four o'clock all four detectives reported back to him. There was no room for all of them, plus Clements, in Malone's office, so they repaired to the big main room.

'We could do with some coffee,' he said. Nobody moved, then he remarked that the four men were looking at Peta Smith.

She remarked it, too. 'The tea-lady's gone home. You want me to run after her?'

For a moment Malone was irritated; after all, he hadn't nominated her. Then he nodded to Kagal. 'You're nearest the kettle, John, okay?'

Kagal had the grace to smile as he stood up. 'Are you ever going to make a cuppa, Peta?'

'Not while it's taken for granted that I will,' she said, unsmiling. 'No milk in mine, thanks.'

'Sugar?'

'Call me sweetheart, not sugar. One lump.' Then she looked around the other men, Malone included. 'You'll learn. It may take a year or two, but you'll learn. *Sir*,' she said, addressing Malone.

He grinned, the only way out other than being bloody-minded. 'If I start a roster for coffee-making, you mind if I put your name on it? . . . Righto, what've you got for me?'

She gave him a grin in return; she was not a shrew. 'John and I went out to ABS, got Murray Rockman's file.' She handed it to Malone. 'Then we went out to the block of units where he lived in Arncliffe. One of the neighbours, a stickybeak – I'd hate to live next door to her – she said Rockman had had a girl living with him, but she'd left him about three months ago. He's lived alone since then, except for the odd weekend girl. The old biddy next door didn't miss a trick. His keys were in his locker at ABS, we'd taken those, so we let ourselves in. We found nothing, nothing but his clothes.'

She stopped and Malone said, 'You're going to tell us something, right?'

Kagal came back with the office tin of biscuits. Peta Smith looked at him. 'You want to tell them?'

'I'm making the coffee,' he said, but grinned at her.

'Bastard . . . Like I said, there was nothing in the flat but his clothes. No papers, no address book, no passport, nothing that might identify him – zilch. Either he'd cleaned everything out himself or someone had got there before we did.'

'The stickybeak neighbour saw nothing?'

'She said she'd been out shopping this morning, wanted to give us a rundown on where she'd been.'

'Any sign of forced entry?'

'None,' said Kagal, coming back with the tray of coffee cups. 'All we have of Mr Rockman is what's in his file.'

Malone opened the file. Two pages: but then he wondered how many of the world's voters and non-voters merited any more than two pages. Some lives, he knew, could be written on the back of an envelope and a small one at that. He had no conceit that his own life would warrant any more than a few pages and half of those would concern the deaths of other people. 'Born Caswell, Ohio, August 22, 1960. High school education . . . Blah, blah, blah . . . US Marine Corps, 1980–1983 . . . He told me yesterday he'd been out here twelve years. He must've come here straight after leaving the Marines. The file doesn't tell us much. The second page is just a resumé of his references. They all look okay.' He closed the file. 'But what sort of life did he live when he wasn't working for ABS? You checked if he has any record?'

'I'll do that now,' said Peta Smith and rose and moved across to one of the computers.

Malone sipped his coffee. 'Nice coffee, John. Your first attempt?'

Kagal raised his cup. 'Okay, make out a roster. Equality above all.'

'Don't let Peta hear you say that.'

Kagal smiled, drank his coffee. He was a good-looking young man, the best dressed of all the detectives, some of whom, in Malone's old-fashioned opinion, were real dudes. Kagal would never have any difficulty getting women's attention and perhaps even their devotion. His only fault, again in Malone's opinion, was that he thought he deserved everything that was offered him.

Peta Smith came back, picked up her cup and tasted it. 'Nice cuppa, John . . . Mr Rockman has no record. He's spotless.'

'He's bloody near invisible,' said Malone. 'Andy, you're the man with the contacts in the FBI. Get on to 'em, ask if they'll trace him for us. See what they have on him, if anything. At least there'll be his Marines record.'

Andy Graham sprang to his feet, spilling his coffee but managing not to splash any of it on his clothes. He went through life at a gallop, never in front, always trying to catch up. He grabbed Rockman's file from the table and was gone. All the others smiled at each other but said nothing. Andy Graham was lovable in his absence.

Malone turned to Clements. 'Anything yet from Ballistics on Brame?'

'Just come in.' Clements dropped a plastic envelope on the table. 'Clarrie Binyan says it's an uncommon one, not the usual calibre. It's a nine-millimetre ultra.

Clarrie's trying to trace the sort of gun that would take it.'

'Righto, your turn, Phil. How'd you go?'

Truach sighed, coughed. 'You ever tried to interview a thousand lawyers? You get a thousand opinions. The gist of it all, however, was that nobody saw nothing. One or two, the vice-president for one, Zoehrer, they do remember seeing Brame talking to someone in the coffee lounge Sunday night. A waitress remembered they walked out together, Brame and the other guy. She says she didn't look at the other man, she was looking at Brame, she'd been told he was the boss cocky and she was observing what a top man looks like. Seems she wants to be a writer, she's taking some writing course.'

'So she doesn't look at the supporting character?' said Peta Smith. 'She must write poetry.'

All the men, poetry lovers if ever one saw a bunch of them, nodded. Malone wondered if, between the lot of them, they could recite the first half a dozen lines from *The Man from Snowy River*. 'Did you get to see Mrs Brame, Phil?'

Truach was bouncing an unlit cigarette up and down on his palm, a hint that he was dying for a smoke; Malone ignored it. 'She was out, they told me. Making arrangements to fly her husband's body back to the States as soon's it's released. Seems it's harder to book a ticket for a coffin than for a livin', breathin' person.'

Clements ferreted in his trivia bag: 'D'you know that if someone kicks the bucket on an aircraft, they just throw a sheet over him and leave him in his seat? There's nowhere to put a stiff. How'd you like that, sitting beside a corpse when they serve you lunch?'

Malone glanced at Peta Smith to see how she was taking the deadpan macho humour, but she seemed unperturbed by it. He turned back to Truach. 'There's a brother here. Did anyone mention him to you?'

'No.'

'Russ, you and I'd better have a talk with the brother, what's-his-name?'

'Channing. Their offices are down in Martin Place. I looked it up.'

'I thought you might have.' He rose, looked at his watch. He wanted to go home, to be with Lisa, but she had said, *Do your job*. He would do it, as conscientiously as ever, but only because she had insisted. He was beginning to realize that she had run his life far better than he could have alone. 'We're always hearing about how late lawyers have to work. Let's go and see. Thanks for the coffee, John.'

'Any time,' said Kagal, 'the roster says so.'

'You're learning,' said Peta Smith and winked at Malone. He felt almost affectionate towards her as he walked out of the office.

2

'Let's walk,' he said when he and Clements were outside the Hat Factory. The rain clouds had gone and the late-afternoon sky looked like blue ice. The wind still blew, ambushing them at corners, snatching like a mad joker at hats and umbrellas. Malone, looking for something to lighten his mood, was reminded of the old joke of the bald man whose hair was blowing in the wind and he was too embarrassed to run after it. Clements had said nothing when walking was suggested, but now he looked at Malone as the latter smiled.

'Something funny?' Malone told him the joke and Clements went on, 'Keep laughing, that'll be the trick. Well, not laughing, but keep your spirits up.'

'Don't play counsellor with me, Russ.' Then he heard the abruptness in his voice. 'Sorry. I'm touchy, I'm still getting used to what's happened to her.'

'I understand, mate. But like I say, be optimistic. Don't be so bloody Irish.'

The walk along Elizabeth Street took them just over ten minutes. Over on their right Hyde Park was dark and dank, wrecked by winter. They passed the huge Park Grand hotel, repossessed within a year of its opening but now, fortunately, chockablock with lawyers; they glanced in, saw the packed lobby and hurried past as if afraid of being bombed with torts. As they passed David Jones, a door of the big department store opened and they heard the music: the pianist threw a few bars at them, memories were made of this and that, then the door closed again. As they reached Martin Place the street-lights came on and the clock on the GPO tower struck a quarter to five. The Channing and Lazarus offices were in one of the older buildings on the north side of the long narrow plaza.

The offices had been newly furnished, suggesting Channing and Lazarus might have been celebrating a good financial year. There were new beige carpet and tub chairs and a couch in a muted deep purple tweed; on the cream walls there were large brass-framed prints of several of the more restrained modern Australian paintings, no invitatory genitals or phallic flagpoles. The girl behind the modern teak desk, getting herself ready to leave, was as smart as the paintings, though perhaps a little more invitatory. At least she was spraying a musky perfume behind her ears as the two detectives walked in.

'Mr Channing?' She looked at them in surprise. 'Did you have an appointment?' Clements showed his badge and she looked even more surprised. 'Oh. I'll see if he's free.'

Rodney Channing was free, though he did not appear too glad to see them. He stood up as Malone and Clements were shown into his office. This, too, had been newly refurbished, but it was all leather, though not club-like. There were two paintings on the cream walls, one a landscape by Lloyd Rees, all airy light, the other a portrait of Channing in a style that Malone thought had died years ago. Rodney Channing, at least in the portrait, looked mid-Victorian, stern and forbidding, and Malone wondered why he had chosen to be painted that way.

'My brother?' Channing said when Malone explained the reason for their visit. 'We've been strangers to each other for thirty years.'

'We understand he was seen talking to a stranger Sunday night in the coffee lounge of the Novotel hotel. Was it you?'

'Sunday night? No, no it wasn't.' There was a pause, then he seemed to relax; or at least accept that the detectives were here to stay. He sat down behind his desk, gestured to them. 'Sit down. I saw my brother Sunday morning. He came here to my office.'

'Here? Sunday morning?'

There was a pause again: Channing seemed to be laying his words out like playing cards. 'I told you, we were strangers. I – I suggested here because I wanted to be sure we'd get on together, after so long. I didn't want to invite him to my home and have an awkward situation in front of my wife and family. I have three children, all youngish.'

'And did you? Get on together?'

Another pause. 'Not exactly. The separation, I suppose, had been too long.' Then there was a knock at the door and a woman put her head inside the room. 'Oh June! Come on in. This is Mrs Johns, our office manager.'

June Johns had been born to manage; one look at her told you that. She was in her late thirties, attractive, a little plump, wearing a blonde helmet of hair; but it was her manner, her wouldn't-miss-a-detail eyes, that caught the attention. Her smile would have cowed a stampede of bulls.

She shook hands with the two detectives, a firm handshake that let them know she wasn't cowed by *them*. 'Are we being investigated or something?' Her smile suggested that they had better not be. 'Law firms seem to have been in a lot of trouble over the past year. *Other* firms.'

'These gentlemen are from Homicide,' said Channing. 'They are investigating my – my brother's murder.'

'Oh? Any luck?'

Clements, the punter, thought she might have been asking if he had backed a winner at Randwick. 'Not so far. But it's early days –'

She turned away from him, looked at Channing. Malone had no idea of the ranking in a law firm, but he guessed that an office manager would have much less status than a partner, particularly one of the two senior partners. Yet Mrs Johns gave the impression that her status did not matter, at least not to her. Though she did call him – 'Mr Channing. Is there anything we can do to help?'

'We?' Channing fumbled one of the cards; or anyway, a word. 'How?'

'I don't know.' She looked back at Malone and Clements; she appeared to have taken command. 'Perhaps you gentlemen can tell us?'

Malone didn't answer her, just turned back to Channing. 'You never represented your brother's firm out here?'

Channing shook his head. 'We do represent three or four American firms, but never Schuyler, De Vries and Barrymore. I'm afraid we're too small to have interested them.'

'How big are you?' asked Clements.

'Forty all told,' said Mrs Johns. 'Two senior partners, four junior partners, six legal staff. And then the usual office staff, including myself. Nothing compared to Schuyler and partners. They're a small army.'

Malone wondered why and how the manager of a medium-sized Sydney law firm would know how big a major New York firm was. But maybe law-firm office managers, like defence chiefs, kept tabs on other armies. 'Would you know if Schuyler et cetera had links with other law firms in Sydney?'

'Oh, they're sure to have had.' Channing had risen to his feet when Mrs Johns had come in, but Malone and Clements had resumed their seats after greeting her. Channing looked as if he didn't want the meeting prolonged, but Malone was going to take his own time. 'But it'd be one of the big firms –'

'One of the small armies.' Mrs Johns made what sounded like a soft hissing noise, but Malone thought he could have been mistaken. There was no doubt, however, that she did not have much time for battalions of lawyers. 'We can check for you –'

'We'll do that,' said Malone, who did not like being managed and felt that Mrs Johns was cracking her office whip. 'We're investigating another murder down at Darling Harbour. It may or may not be connected with your brother's murder, Mr Channing.'

'Another lawyer? Someone from his firm?' Channing, with both hands on his desk, leaned forward: like a prosecutor quizzing a witness was the image that struck Malone.

'You knew someone from Schuylers was with your brother?'

'Well, no. I don't know why I – I asked that.'

He was standing in front of the painting of himself; Malone, a modest man, wondered at the vanity of someone who would seat himself in front of his own portrait. But there was the stiff, formal Rodney Channing gazing over the shoulder of the suddenly ill-at-ease real Channing. Then Malone knew that the portrait was Channing's own impression, not the artist's, of himself. It was intended to impress clients that the real Rodney Channing was the calm, solid man in the painting.

'No, it wasn't anyone from Schuylers. He's still alive, a young man named Adam Tallis. No, it was a security guard who was murdered. The same one who found your brother's body.'

'Coincidence?' asked Mrs Johns.

Malone had been looking at Channing, who had leaned forward on the desk again, frowning this time but saying nothing. Then Clements said, 'We're looking into that, Mrs Johns. We're not great believers in coincidence in the Police Service.'

Speak for yourself, thought Malone. He believed that coincidence greased the wheels of the world, otherwise fate would go off the track. The Celt in him wasn't entirely negative.

'A security guard?' Channing had straightened up again. 'What would he have to do with my brother?'

'We're not even trying to guess at this stage,' said Malone. 'Except that the security guard, too, was an American.'

Then the door, which was half-open, was pushed wide and another woman stood there, dressed for an evening out and holding a man's white shirt on a hanger. 'Oh, I thought . . . I'll wait outside.'

'No, come on in, come on in!' Channing moved swiftly round the desk, advanced on the woman and hugged her as if she were a client on whom the future of Channing and Lazarus depended; she could not have been more welcome if she had been Alan Bond or Christopher Skase back in their heyday. He took the shirt from her, introduced her to Malone and Clements. 'My wife Ruth. These gentlemen are from the police, they're investigating my brother's murder, they're just leaving . . . My wife and I have to go to a reception for the Americans, the Bar Association. The Law Society is putting it on . . .' Words were tumbling out of him, he was like a card trickster whose fingers had turned into fists. 'I have to change . . .' He held up the shirt. 'If you'll excuse me?'

'You go and change, sweetheart.' Mrs Channing stepped aside and pushed her husband out the door. 'We're running late. June and I will show the gentlemen out. I'm one

51

of the official hostesses,' she explained to the two gentlemen. 'I can't afford to be late.'

Ruth Channing had escaped plainness with the aid of a hairdresser, an aerobics instructor and a couturier, the latterday fairy princes who, for a price, would kiss any plain jane, or joe for that matter. There was also a vivacity that lit up her small pale eyes, that gave mobility to her thin lips. Malone guessed she would be a willing volunteer hostess, anything to advance her husband's career, one hand in the middle of his back guiding him. It struck Malone that, between his wife and Mrs Johns, Channing's kidneys might be black and blue from being steered in the right direction.

'I don't know why, I'm expecting all these Americans to look like Perry Mason. I have this crazy sense of humour –' She was one of those people who, afraid that the rest of the world was too dumb to be perceptive, would always help them with a description of her imagined better qualities. It was Malone's experience that those who claimed a crazy sense of humour often had no such thing if the joke was against them. 'It'll be the social death of me one day –'

And a sickness for your friends: Malone wondered why he felt so unkindly towards Mrs Channing. Then realized he had let Channing and Mrs Johns start the irritation. 'We must be going,' he said.

'Murder won't wait, will it?' she said.

He stopped dead. 'Pardon?'

'Didn't Perry Mason say that? Or was it Shakespeare?'

Then he recognized the brightness in the pale eyes, the width of the smile: she was high on some drug. He had read her wrongly. She was not a volunteer hostess; the pushing hand was in *her* back. There were wives like her everywhere, driven or pulled by their husbands into situations where they would always be off-balance, where they would have to fall back on some support they could not find in themselves. The portrait on the wall must forever mock the Channings. Malone wondered what the other partner, Lazarus, was like.

'Oh, murder will wait, Mrs Channing. We're very patient in Homicide.'

Her eyes widened, as if she had realized that, for him, murder was no joke. Then Mrs Johns stepped forward, took her arm. 'I don't think we need any more of this sort of talk. Show yourselves out, will you, Inspector?'

'Of course. We're used to doing that.' She gave him a look as sour as the note in his voice. 'Channing and Lazarus. Is there a Mr Lazarus?'

Mrs Johns paused in the doorway. 'Yes, Mr Will Lazarus. He's overseas at the moment.'

'America?'

'No, Europe. Excuse us. Will you be coming again?'

Malone shrugged. 'Who knows?'

'Telephone first.' Then she was gone, her hand in Mrs Channing's back.

Out in Martin Place the wind was still blowing; the evening was turning bitterly cold. Banners on the flagpoles lining the plaza crackled in the wind; they writhed so much it was impossible to tell what occasion was being celebrated. Malone looked up and down the slight slope of the plaza. It had the potential to rival some of the plazas of Europe, but it was cluttered. Give an Aussie planner an open space, he thought, and it would soon be filled up. He was waiting for the planners to be let loose on the vast Nullabor Plain in the interior. He and Clements walked up the slope under the winter-shredded trees.

'What d'you reckon?'

'Something smells,' said Clements. 'There's a connection.'

'Between the murders?'

'I dunno about them. No, between Channing and Brame, the two brothers. Maybe we should've tried to get more out of Mrs Channing.'

'She was up to her eyeballs on something. What sort of drugs do nice housewives take, women who don't want to be anything but housewives?'

Above their heads a banner crackled like a burst of machine-gun fire. The wind threw a handful of grit against their faces and they had to shut their eyes; a few leaves scurried after them like blind mice. 'She's probably on one of the designer drugs. You look at her? Everything about her is "designer". So's he. Between 'em they'd be wearing more logos than Nigel Mansell. Whatever she's snorting, it's still shit.' Clements had a hatred of drugs and contempt for those who advocated their legalization. He would press his argument over any number of beers. 'Half an hour with her and if she knows anything, we'd have it out of her.'

Malone shook his head, grabbed at his hat as the wind tried to rob him of it. 'Mrs Johns would never let us near her, not for that long.'

Clements looked sideways at him, eyes slitted against another burst of grit. 'I'd like half an hour with that woman.'

'You'd have to put a gun at her head. That woman wouldn't be able to remember the last secret she gave away.'

3

Romy was just leaving the Malone house when Scobie arrived home. He took her out to her car, opened the door for her when she had unlocked it. 'How was Lisa with you?'

'Sensible. She's worried, but more for you and the children than for herself. Wives and mothers usually are, good ones.'

He nodded; he had seen it too many times, in other homes. 'What are the chances?'

'Of recovery? Good. They won't really know till surgery, but if they have caught it early, if it's localized . . .' She put her hand on his. The wind had dropped while he had been driving home and the cold now had the night to itself; the roof of the car was almost freezing his palm. 'There'll be chemotherapy . . .'

'That knocks you around, doesn't it?'

'Scobie, don't think about the worst. Be optimistic.'

'That's what Russ told me.' He kissed her cheek. The two men loved each other's wives: it was another bond between himself and Clements. 'Was it you who did the autopsy on the American, Brame?'

'Yes. A gunshot wound, right through the heart. A close shot, there were powder marks on the chest. Most people are not quite sure where the heart is, but this killer knew exactly. One bullet – Ballistics have it.'

'Are you doing the autopsy on the other bloke who came in this morning?'

'Scobie love –' She smiled. 'We had six other *blokes* this morning and five women. Not all homicides –'

'Not all of them with a bullet in the head.' Homicide made you parochial about death. Then he looked around him at the night.

'What's the matter?'

'Nothing.' He couldn't tell her he had been looking for a sign of death here in the silent street. *Don't be so bloody Irish . . .* But were Celts the only people afraid of shadows? He must ask Clarrie Binyan some time if the Aborigines, the Koories, kept looking over their shoulders. Probably: more so than the Irish. 'The security guard, Rockman – did you do him?'

'He hasn't been done yet. Tomorrow morning, first thing. If the bullet's still in him, I'll hand it to Ballistics right away.' She got into her car, holding the door open while she looked up at him. In the door-light he could see the strain in her lovely, square-jawed face; her dark hair had been blown into a tangle and evidently she hadn't bothered to comb it. She and Lisa must have been too concerned with other things . . . Again he was angry at his pessimism. 'I gave up going to church years ago, we were Lutheran. But I'll be praying for you. You Catholics like Hail Marys, don't you?'

'We'll take anything you care to say.'

He closed the car door, the light went out. He watched her drive away. Her mother had died of sunstroke two years after coming from Germany to start a new life in the sunshine of Australia; her father, a triple murderer, had suicided. She knew all about the shadows of death, and not just because she worked in a morgue.

He went into the house, sat down beside Lisa to watch the seven o'clock news. 'Not getting dinner?'

'The kids are getting it,' she said. 'They insisted.'

He held her hand. On the screen in front of them the world, as usual, was falling apart; only calamity was news. 'Any word when you go into hospital?'

'Sunday. They'll operate Monday morning.' She felt the tension in him and she looked at him, leaning forward. 'Don't *worry*.'

'Aren't you worried?'

'Of course I am. But I'm not going to sit around asking *Why me?* Self-pity is no medication. I'll be all right.'

He kissed her, his arm round her shoulders, holding her tight. Then past the curtain of her loose-hanging hair he saw Maureen standing in the doorway, smiling at them. 'They're at it again,' she said over her shoulder to her siblings in the kitchen. Then, still smiling at them, 'Dinner's ready.'

His heart ached, which did nothing for his appetite, even though Claire and Maureen had cooked his favourite, steak-and-kidney pie, and Tom had opened a bottle of Riddoch '86 shiraz for him and Lisa. Still, for all their sakes, he did his best.

Later, in bed, Lisa said, 'You'd better grab what you can between now and Monday. After that there's not going to be much sex for a while.'

'I'll join the Vice Squad, pick up a bit down in William Street.' He held her to him, treasuring every familiar curve and hollow of her. 'Romy says there may be some chemotherapy after it.'

'That's the bit that upsets me. It can make some people very sick.' Then she lay away from him in the darkness. 'You haven't said a word how work is going.'

'I don't think it's important, is it? To us?'

'It is!' With one arm still under her, he felt her stiffen. 'People dying, being *murdered*, is important! God, darling, don't lose your perspective!'

He recognized that her anger was really fear; it would be cruel to argue with her. 'Righto, it's important. But I've never brought the cases home, not unless you've asked me –'

'I'm asking you now.' It was an order. Fear took many forms: hers would never be a quaking surrender.

Flatly, listlessly, he told her of the Brame and Rockman cases, of the lack of leads. 'I've met two wives so far, the brothers' wives. One of 'em could whip the UN into shape, the other one couldn't run a school bazaar without a snort of some kind.'

'She's a drunk?'

'Drugs. I don't mean she's a junkie, she's just one of those women scared out of her pants by how far her husband's gone.'

'That's the American wife?'

'No, the Aussie one, Mrs Channing. Not that I think Channing himself has got as far as he'd hoped. In his own way he's as unsure of himself as she is.'

'They're often the ones who drive their wives the hardest.'

'When you're out of hospital and cured, you want to join

Homicide as a counsellor?' He kissed her, patted her mount but went no further. 'I'm just glad you never drove me.'

'You never needed it. You just had to be steered, that was all.'

She knew his every weakness, including his overwhelming love for her.

4

Chief Superintendent Greg Random had come across to the morning conference from Police Centre. 'President Clinton, him and everyone down as far as me, we're all looking for a quick solution to the Brame case. I just thought you'd like to know.'

He never pressured any of the men under him; he had his own quiet way of ensuring efficiency. He had total confidence in Malone; he had been Malone's boss in Homicide until he had been promoted to the desk job he hated. At the moment he was resisting a new directive that wanted all police to be shifted every three years from one division to another. The directive was aimed at stalling corruption, at breaking up any too-cosy relationship between police and their contacts, ignoring the fact that cops and crims were two sides of the same coin. Headquarters was evidently under the impression that informers stood on street corners, like hookers, waiting for cops with ready money. Ivory towers, Random had confided to Malone, were not confined just to academe.

'The Commissioner tells me the FBI has offered to help and he's expecting to hear from the CIA, the National Security Council, NASA and the Daughters of the American Revolution any minute now. Seven hundred and forty district attorneys have offered to prosecute and the US Supreme Court will take over if our judges find it's too much for them. In other words, the bullshit has hit the fan. Excuse me, Detective Smith,' he said, for the moment carried away by his sarcasm.

'Can I get you some coffee, sir?' Peta Smith half-rose from her chair.

'Are you getting it for everyone?' Random looked around the all-male-but-one conference.

'No, sir. Just for you.' With not a glance at any of the other men.

His lean, lined face eased itself into a slow paternal smile. 'Better leave it, Peta. Otherwise this mob will think it's favouritism . . . So what have you got, Scobie?'

'Clarrie Binyan, over at Ballistics, called me. The bullet taken out of the security guard, Murray Rockman – it's the same calibre as the one taken out of Orville Brame, a rare 'un, a nine-millimetre ultra. Clarrie says he's making a guess, but he thinks there wouldn't be too many guns in this country that take that sort of bullet. One of them is a Sig-Sauer, made for a Swiss company but manufactured in Germany. It will take a silencer, which Clarrie thinks would have been used, and it's a pretty expensive piece, not the sort your ordinary hoodlum would use.'

'He's guessing?'

'Of course. But that's all any of us are doing at the moment. The point is, they've made their first mistake – they've made a connection for us.'

'And what's the connection?'

Malone grinned: to an outsider it might have looked like embarrassment. 'That's it. The bullet. We start from there.'

'That's not much to tell President Clinton.'

Malone suddenly realized that, for all his relaxed air, Greg Random was under pressure. Perhaps not from President Clinton, but the local political pressure would be just as heavy. In his mind's eye he saw the weight, like heavy die-stamps, falling on Random's neck: the Premier, the Minister, the Commissioner.

'No, it's not much. But why would the one gun be used, on separate nights, to kill a top American lawyer, here in Australia for the first time in thirty years, and a local security guard who's got nothing but a clean record and, as far as we know, never met the lawyer? All we have to do is start at either end and work towards the middle.'

'I'll tell Bill Clinton that.' Random rose to his feet. 'Maybe it's the solution to his national debt. Let me know when you've come up with *your* solution. Yesterday will be soon enough.'

He went his unhurried way out of the big room, leaving Homicide looking at their boss. Malone spread his hands. 'Any suggestions?'

Two-thirds of those at the table rose from their chairs. 'It's all yours, Scobie. We've got the one out at Penshurst.' And at Cronulla and Bondi and elsewhere: simple homicides, of plain people with no political pull.

Then Andy Graham, who had not been present at the conference, came in. 'The Chief would like to see you outside, Scobie. He's waiting on the front steps.'

Puzzled, Malone went out to the entrance. Random was there, his familiar pipe, always unlit, stuck between his teeth. 'Walk up to the corner with me, Scobie.'

The sky was clear today, there was no wind and the sun, though not warm, was bright, throwing pale shadows. Up ahead, on the other side of the road, was the concrete fortress of Police Centre; Malone sometimes wondered if it had been built as the last bunker of a Police Service that appeared always to be defending itself. Random paused outside a deserted restaurant car park. It struck Malone that he had chosen a spot where whatever he had to say he would not be overheard.

'Russ told me about your wife. I'm sorry to hear it. Cancer's a real bugger. My wife had a breast removed six years ago.'

'I didn't know –'

'Well, you don't broadcast your worries . . . When's she being operated on?'

'Next Monday.'

'Okay, take leave from Saturday night. Russ can take over from you.' Then he took his pipe out of his mouth and looked at it as if wondering why he was holding it. 'Unless you want to take leave now?'

'No. Lisa insists I keep working. But I'll go off Saturday night. Thanks, Greg.' He sighed, feeling drained of energy. 'I don't like leaving this Brame case. Or the other one, the security guard. Are you getting pressure?'

'Am I? Have you ever had the chain of command wrapped around your neck? You'd think the Pope'd been done in, not just a bloody lawyer. But never mind, do what you can up till the weekend. Then stay home with your wife. Give her my best. A nice woman.'

He abruptly left Malone, not rudely but because that was his way. Malone stood a moment, then jumped as a car, wanting to turn into the car park, tooted its horn. He walked back to the Hat Factory, apprehensive that one day he might be sitting in Random's chair. The chain of command, when applied by political pressure, could be a garrotte.

Clements and Andy Graham were waiting for him in his office. 'Andy's heard from the FBI.'

'They're thorough,' said Graham. 'They've come up with nothing on our friend Murray Rockman.'

Malone dropped into his chair. 'Sort that one out for me, Andy. They're thorough and they've come up with nothing?'

Graham looked flustered, one of his usual expressions. 'Yeah, I see what you mean. No, they've done their homework. They've been through all the records in Caswell, Ohio. Birth registration, high school, everything. They've checked the Marines, their enlistments, their service records. No Murray Rockman, ever. In either place,

Caswell, Ohio, or the Marines. Nothing.' He handed Malone the fax he held. 'Our guy never existed before he came to Australia.'

Chapter Four

1

The De Vries family had been lawyers for over three hundred years, ever since their arrival in New Amsterdam from Utrecht. Dutch Catholics, they had little to do with the predominant Dutch Calvinists and looked elsewhere for clients amongst the growing polyglot citizens of that growing city. Hendrik De Vries, the original immigrant, built up a clientele amongst the Jews from Spain and Portugal, and he passed on the practice to his two sons. Over the succeeding years, as New Amsterdam became New York, the fortunes of the family firm both flourished and flopped; as in all families that manage to survive the generations, it suffered occasionally from drunks, fools and incompetents. Eventually the firm, to survive, had to merge with Schuyler and Barrymore, to become Schuyler, De Vries and Barrymore. There was no Schuyler now on the board of partners and the last Barrymore had disappeared at the end of World War Two. There was, however, still a De Vries: Richard De Vries the Third. He was no drunk, fool nor incompetent; but the margin for error, on all counts, was narrow. Still, he owned 30 per cent of the stock and stock ownership has its own competence, as the other partners, when pressed, heartily agreed. Dick De Vries was kept afloat by money, which is more buoyant than balloons on Wall Street.

'I came as soon as I could –' He was a small man with a round face, flushed from too much claret and Scotch, and reproachful brown eyes, as if he blamed others for his failings. He had silver hair, parted in the middle like that of a dandy from the Twenties, and tiny ears laid flat along his skull. Though he had just got off a fourteen-hour flight, he was dressed as if on his way to the offices in Broad Street, Manhattan. He wore a dark grey suit from Fioravanti, a custom-made shirt from Kabbaz, a Racquet-club tie and black wing-tips by Vogel. Not for him French shirts and English suits and shoes: he was All-American. Except for his clipped accent: as a young man he had always tried to imitate Ronald Colman and Robert Donat and now the voice came naturally to him.

He even dresses and speaks like a lie, thought Joanna Brame: inside there is an untidy, useless little man trying to get out. Orville had told her that several times.

'Have they released the – er – body yet?'

'Not yet. Australians, it seems, have a fetish for red tape. Did you have a good flight?' Why am I asking him that? she wondered. But she had always had difficulty trying to keep a conversation going with Dick De Vries.

'Not really. These days, with a lot of people, the only thing first class about them is their ticket.' She agreed with him, but she wouldn't tell him so. 'To cap it all, everything here in Sydney is booked out. I'm having to share a room, something I haven't done since I was in college.'

'Whom with?' She still had the precision in grammar that her mother, who had sat at the feet of Henry James, had taught her.

'Young Tallis. It could be worse, I suppose, though there is hardly room to swing a cat. I could be sharing with one of those palimony shysters. Or an ambulance chaser from Chicago.' He had his own snobbery.

She was not embarrassed that she was staying alone in a suite in which she could have swung a Bengal tiger. She changed the subject: 'I am still coming to terms with Orville's death. The way he – he died.' For just a moment her voice faltered. Last night, lying awake in the strange bed, a huge bed that could have accommodated four people and so had an increased emptiness, reaching out on one occasion for the Orville who wasn't there, who would never be there again, there had been a long moment when she had wondered at the worth of going on alone; it was uncharacteristic of her to think that way, and she had been both frightened by the thought and embarrassed by it. She went on: 'The police don't think it was a mugging, anything like that. Why should anyone want to kill him?'

'You can't expect me to answer that? I've only just arrived.' He sounded irritated; but then he often sounded like that. 'Are the local police any good?'

'I suppose so. How would I know?' It was her turn to sound irritated; she despised herself for the pettiness. 'All police departments are different, I suppose. Just as people are different.'

'May I?' He helped himself to his second Scotch from the mobile drinks tray. 'The first thing, Jo –' She hated the name Jo, but she didn't correct him this time. ' – The first thing is to get you and Orville on a plane for back home. I'll stay here and handle things with the police.'

'His brother came to see me.'

He looked at her (cautiously?) over the rim of his glass. 'What's he like?'

She shrugged. 'I didn't take to him. He didn't seem very – upset by Orville's death. Murder.'

'From what Orville told me, they were never close.'

She was surprised. 'He discussed his brother with you?'

Again there was what seemed to her some caution. 'Once. Maybe twice. I don't remember how his name came up – oh yes. It was when Sydney was nominated as the venue for this convention. Orville mentioned his brother then. Yes, it was then.'

She was alert to nuances; she would have made a good lawyer. 'You sound a little hazy about when it was. Never mind,' she said before he could protest, 'the brother is here and doesn't seem too put out by Orville's murder. I'd better get used to calling it that,' she added, more to herself than to him.

'Perhaps I should contact him?'

'To what purpose? But please yourself.'

'Will you have dinner with me this evening? I understand the food in Sydney is edible and the wines are excellent.'

'I wouldn't be good company, Dick.'

He drained his glass, then stood up. 'Oh, by the way, did Orville leave any papers here? He brought a stuffed brief-case with him, I believe. Young Tallis told me he was the one who had to carry it. Lug it, was the phrase he used.'

'It's in the other room.' She rose and went into the bedroom. While she was gone he looked at the drinks tray, looked at his glass, then reluctantly put down the glass. When she came back she stopped in the bedroom doorway. 'It's not there.'

'Perhaps Tallis has it?'

'Perhaps. But he wouldn't have taken it without telling me –'

'Have you been out of here since you arrived?' His voice was quick with concern.

'No. Yes, yes, of course. I had to go to the morgue on – Monday? Two days ago? God, have I been sitting here that long?'

'We better get Tallis up here. What's our room number? Oh, yes.' He picked up the phone, asked for the room: 'Adam? Could you come up to Mrs Brame's suite? Yes, *now*.' He sounded irritated again; or edgy. He hung up the phone. 'We have to find that briefcase.'

'Pour me a gin-and-tonic, please. Light on the gin,' she said, remembering his heavy hand. 'Why did Orville bring papers all the way from New York to here? Were they ABA papers?'

'Some of them, I guess. Yes, some of them would be. But there would have been others –'

There was a knock on the door; De Vries went to it and opened it. 'That was quick, Adam.'

'I came up the stairs, I didn't wait for the elevator. You said *now*.' The young man was not impolite, but Joanna recognized where his loyalties lay; and was pleased for Orville's sake. 'Something wrong?'

'Mr Brame's briefcase is missing.'

Tallis frowned, looked at Joanna. 'You sure? It was there – damn! Come to think of it, I haven't seen it since Sunday afternoon, when I gave it to Mr Brame. He gave it to me to take care of Sunday morning when he went out to see his brother.'

'He told you he was going to see his brother?' said De Vries.

'Yes. He seemed – perturbed? I mean, at meeting him. But he didn't say why. But what's happened to the briefcase?'

'That's what – perturbs us,' said De Vries. 'Did you know what was in it?'

Tallis shook his head. 'It was locked all the time I had it. Mr Brame never told me the combination. But I can't understand . . .'

'Someone must have taken it while I was out at the morgue on Monday morning. Or – once I went down to the coffee lounge when the maid came in.' Joanna put down her glass, picked up the phone. 'I think we should call the police.'

'No.' De Vries held up a hand. 'No, not yet. Let's make sure no one here in the hotel has it. If there are ABA papers in it, Orville could have given it to one of the other officers. Karl Zoehrer, perhaps. Don't let's panic –'

'I'm not panicking, Dick.' But Joanna put down the phone.

'Mr Zoehrer's over at the Convention Hall,' said Tallis. 'There's a session on international law. He's chairing it. Mr Brame was scheduled to do it. I'll go over there now, find out if he has the briefcase.'

As the door closed behind him, De Vries turned to Joanna. 'We have to retrieve that briefcase and those papers.'

'That's why I think we should call in the police. There has to be a connection between it and Orville's – murder.'

'I think I need another drink.' He moved towards the drinks tray.

'No, I think you should go and lie down, Dick. You look as if you're suddenly suffering from jet lag.'

Then the phone rang. Reception wanted to know if Inspector Malone could come up to see Mrs Brame.

2

Malone preferred not to interview people on his own, but his resources were spread thin this morning. 'We want someone here to mind the store,' he had told Clements. He had looked around the almost empty big room; there were only two detectives at their desks, each of them head bent above papers. 'You're it, Russ. You can enjoy yourself answering the phone from the Commissioner, the Minister. Even Bill Clinton. Where's Andy Graham?'

'I sent him over to ABS Security to check on Rockman's references from his other employers. Then he can follow that up by going to see those firms, find out what he can about Rockman.'

'Peta Smith and John Kagal?'

'They're out looking for Rockman's ex-girlfriend.' Clements settled back in Malone's chair. 'This chair's a bit tight on the bum. If I'm moving in here next Monday, I'll bring my own. Good luck with Mrs Brame.'

When Malone knocked on the door of the Brame suite it was opened by a silver-haired man who didn't seem particularly glad to see him. 'I'm Richard De Vries. Come in – Inspector, is it? Your ranks are different from ours, aren't they?'

In contrast to De Vries, Joanna Brame looked pleased to see him. 'Do come in, Inspector. Have you some good news? Well, no, not *good* news –' She gestured, but not vapidly. 'Why should I be asking for that? If you've caught the murderer, it still won't be good news, will it?'

'No, Mrs Brame. And we haven't caught him. I'm sorry to say we're not much further advanced. Except –'

'Except?' De Vries was standing by the drinks tray. 'Drink?'

'Mr De Vries is the other senior partner. He arrived from the States only this morning.'

Malone shook his head at the offer of a drink, but noticed that De Vries poured himself a stiff whisky. But before the older man tasted his drink he said, 'You said *except*. Except what?'

Malone then explained about the murder of Murray Rockman.

'He was murdered near *here*? Is this a dangerous area where the hotel is?'

'It hasn't been up till now.' Malone knew he sounded defensive, like a local city councillor.

'It's starting to sound that way now.'

Malone ignored him and looked at Joanna Brame. 'The bullet that killed the security guard was the same calibre as the one that killed your husband.'

'But that proves nothing, does it?' said De Vries, drink still untouched, manoeuvring himself into Malone's gaze again. 'How many calibres of bullets are there?'

'This one is an uncommon one. Our Ballistics unit are looking into it, they think they know the type of weapon that would fire such a bullet.'

'Are they any good?'

'Our Ballistics unit? They're considered as good as any in the world.'

De Vries then took a gulp of his drink and Joanna said,

'I'm sure Mr De Vries didn't mean to imply that they were not as good as –'

'The FBI?' Malone smiled, but with an effort. He hoped this was not going to develop into a battle of the flags. He was not particularly nationalistic, seeing nationalism only as an upmarket name for tribalism (and look at what *that* was doing in the rest of the world), but he did have pride in his own Service. 'We hold our own, Mrs Brame . . . We're now trying to find the connection between the two killings. We still don't know who was the man who spent half an hour with your husband on Sunday night.' He looked at De Vries, reluctantly. 'Would Mr Brame have discussed with you meeting anyone in particular while he was out here? A client, maybe?'

De Vries put down the glass, as if Joanna's reproachful stare had taken all flavour out of his drink. 'As far as I know, his only interest in coming here was as president of the Bar Association, that was all. I don't believe he knew anyone here in Sydney.'

'Except his brother.'

'Well, yes, his brother.'

'And he knew nobody else here? No local lawyers?'

'Well, yes, I suppose so. We have association with –' He named one of the biggest law firms in Sydney. 'He could have met one of their partners.'

'I'll check on that,' said Malone, but wondered why, if a partner from a top law firm had met with Brame on the night of his murder, he had not come forward. Lawyers might be obstructive in court, but they were usually not obstructive towards police work, especially murder.

'There is something, Inspector –' Joanna ignored De Vries's warning look. 'We think something has been stolen from here. My husband's briefcase. Mr Tallis, you met him the other day, is checking if someone else has it. Mr Zoehrer, for instance.'

'Do you know what was in it?'

'None of us know, not even Mr Tallis.'

She was sitting opposite Malone, the morning light striking across her face, almost sympathetically: it didn't betray any lines of age. In an instant of sensation Malone felt he could be looking at Lisa in ten or twelve years' time (he had no idea how old Joanna Brame was); or as he had always expected Lisa to look. He had never thought of Lisa's dying; or if he had, he had closed down the thought at once. Now, looking at this composed, good-looking woman opposite him, he saw her turn her head towards De Vries, the lift of the chin exactly as Lisa's lifted, and all at once he had to turn away. But she had caught the movement.

'Are you all right, Inspector?'

'What? Oh yes.' He stood up and walked to the window and looked out. The monorail train glided past, packed with passengers, all of them safe from bullets of any calibre. 'Were you going to tell us about the briefcase?'

'Of course,' she said; but he had turned round and saw the closed-up face of De Vries. 'But it's being missing can't have any significance, can it? I'm bewildered, Inspector.' But she didn't look it. 'Are you sure this isn't just random killing? My husband and the – the security guard?'

'We don't think so.' But he didn't elaborate. 'Was your firm, Mr De Vries, engaged in any big lawsuit before Mr Brame left to come here?'

'Yes. Yes, of course. A firm the size of ours, we always have lawsuits on our books. But none that would invite murder. Our clients are not – well, the Mafia, for instance. They come mostly from the *Fortune* Five Hundred. You've heard of them?'

'Vaguely.' Malone smiled, not wanting too much friction at this stage. Mr De Vries seemed to be making an effort to be abrasive. '*Fortune* is a magazine you don't find too often around police departments. Not even in New York, I should imagine.'

Joanna looked pleased at the rejoinder, but De Vries's look said Malone was an uppity cop. 'Well, then, you appreciate the sort of clients we have. Not the sort one finds in *LA Law*.'

'Never watch it,' Malone lied. 'So for the moment we're at a dead end. But we're often there in a homicide. People kill for the simplest reasons and for the most obscure ones. More so than in any other crime. We'll find a reason for these killings, maybe tomorrow, maybe not for months. But we'll find it.' He sounded more confident than he felt. 'When are you leaving for home, Mrs Brame?'

'Not before Monday, at the earliest. So I'm told.'

I'll be off the case by then: but he kept that to himself. 'I'll be seeing you again before then. Nice meeting you, Mr De Vries. You must be feeling the jet lag by now, you look pretty peaked. Take care.'

He left them, went down in the lift and as he stepped out of it into the upper lobby he bumped into Adam Tallis. 'Mr Tallis – just the man I wanted to see. Can I buy you a coffee?'

'Well, they're waiting for me upstairs –'

'But you're empty-handed, aren't you? The briefcase – Mrs Brame told me about it. Come and tell me a little more about it.' He had taken the young man's elbow and was guiding him towards the nearby open café. 'If Mrs Brame complains because you've been too long, blame me. We cops are used to taking the blame for most things.'

They sat down by a window, a waitress took their order and went away and they were alone, nobody seated near them. 'Righto, tell me about the briefcase.'

'Righto.' Tallis, now that he was seated, seemed to accept his hijacking. 'I thought only people in English comedies said that.'

'No, that's right-*io*. I've said *righto* since I was a kid. Some things stick on your tongue. I also say *crumbs*, which breaks my kids up. Are you married, Mr Tallis?'

'No, I live with a girl. It's two years now, so I guess you could say we're almost married.'

'A lawyer like you?'

'No, an actress. TV. She's in a soap, so every third week or so she's in desperate trouble.'

'So are we, Mr Tallis, and we don't have any script writers to help us out.' The waitress came back with two coffees and a pastry for Tallis. 'Righto, we've got to know each other. Now let's talk about the briefcase. I gather no one knows what was in it?'

'I certainly didn't.'

'Yet as I understand it, you were Mr Brame's personal assistant. Sort of.'

'Look, I got on well with Orville, I was his protégé, I guess. But he always played things close to his chest, that was his nature. He was all for Schuyler, De Vries and Barrymore, he'd never worked for any other law firm, but still – well, there was always something private about him. You were never sure what he was thinking.'

'Did you know what his address was going to be to the Bar Association? I suppose there would have been a president's speech?'

Tallis nodded, and said round a mouthful of pastry, 'There always is. But Orville didn't give me a hint what he was going to say. It would've been a good speech, though. He was famous for being to the point.'

Malone stirred his coffee. 'I wish we could find some point to his murder.'

Tallis cleared his mouth, was silent for a long moment; then: 'I thought of it this morning – about three months ago he said something. He said, "If anything happens, look to the past."'

'What did he mean?'

Tallis shrugged. 'Search me. I asked him what he meant and he just smiled. He had a way of smiling – enigmatically, I guess. Not putting you down as if you were dumb, but leaving it to you to find your own answer.'

'And did you?'

'No. I thought about it for a while, then I forgot it. Till this morning.'

Then Malone's pager beeped. Tallis looked at him in surprise. 'You don't carry a mobile phone?' He produced his own, like a badge of office.

Malone grinned, held up his wrist to show his watch. 'Not even a digital watch. Us fellers who say *righto* and *crumbs*, we're a little slow when it comes to technology. Our twelve-year-old son has to set our VCR for me.' Homicide had been issued with mobile phones, but so far he had resisted the temptation to carry one. A gun was enough hardware. 'I'd better go –'

'I don't know I've been much help –'

'Everything will fall into place sooner or later. I'll be seeing you again, I'm sure. Oh –' He paused. 'Mr De Vries was the other senior partner – how did he and Mr Brame get on?'

Tallis shifted uncomfortably. 'You can't expect me to answer that –'

Malone was standing over him. 'I do expect you to answer it.'

Tallis stood up. He was almost as tall as Malone, but thicker in build; he was so close to Malone that it looked as if he were challenging the detective. Then he stepped away. 'I'm sorry, I guess you have to . . . Let's say they were partners in name only. Between you and me, Dick De Vries is not the brightest lawyer on the board. On top of which, he has a drink problem.'

'Did they ever have open disagreement?'

'Not that I know of. Dick would run a mile to avoid a fight – Jesus, what am I saying?' Malone had paid the bill and they had come out into the lobby. 'Don't quote me, okay? I'm sounding damned disloyal to the firm. I shouldn't be telling you our office politics.

74

You're not suspecting Dick of anything, for God's sake?'

'Mr Tallis, I used to play cricket. It's a little like baseball, even down to abusing the umpire, which we didn't do in my day. One thing the games have in common, you learn everything you can about the other team's weaknesses. Mr Brame belonged to a team, Schuyler, De Vries and Barrymore. I'd like to know everything I can about them. Because I've got a feeling that if we don't solve Mr Brame's murder, Schuyler, De Vries and Barrymore are going to be making noises I don't want to hear. De Vries sounds to me as if he'd make the loudest noise. I want to be prepared. See you later. Take care.'

He went down to his car, which, under the reproachful eye of the commissionaire, he had parked in the driveway rather than have a valet take it away. He got into the car out of the wind, picked up the car phone and dialled Homicide. Russ Clements came on the line: 'Any luck?'

'Nothing concrete. What's happening?'

'Peta has called in, she's out at the Miranda shopping centre. She's found Rockman's ex-girlfriend. Her name's Dicey Kilmer.'

'Daisy? You sound like an Italian with an Aussie accent.'

'No, Dicey. D-I-C-E-Y. Short for Christ knows what.'

'Righto, tell Peta to bring her in. I'll be back in ten minutes –'

'No, that's why I called you. She won't come in, not here, not anywhere where there's cops. She'll only talk to you at Miranda, in some coffee lounge near where she works.'

'She's scared of something?'

'Shit-scared, though that wasn't how Peta described it.'

'I should hope not, we want some bloody decorum around Homicide.'

'Watch yourself, you're talking to the man in charge here. I'll tell Peta you're on your way. The Rodeo coffee lounge in Westfield Shopping Centre. Dicey Kilmer.'

3

'I loved Murray, his definition.'

Malone and Peta Smith looked blank. 'What definition was that?'

'His muscle definition. He had pectorals, my mouth used to water. We were both body-builders, that was how we met, the gym. We bumped into each other, the same mirror, you know? We used to strip, admire ourselves, each other. The gym, the bedroom, wherever. Vanity, I suppose you'd call it, but what's the harm in that? He was beautiful, Murray, with his clothes off. Good at the leg-over, too, though not all body-builders are, the steroids get to 'em.' Malone did not dare ask what the leg-over was, but she told him anyway: 'The sex bit, you know.'

Malone kept his eyebrow muscles under control, not wanting their definition to show. 'What can you tell us about him, Miss Kilmer? I mean besides the body-building?'

'Well –' Dicey Kilmer was just the wrong side of pretty: her blunt features did not quite match. But she was bursting with health: her blue eyes could not have been brighter, her blond hair shinier, her skin clearer. And the body in the tight blue dress had all the hard firmness of a mannequin, though it moved with more grace. 'Well, actually, I dunno that much, now I been adding it all up. You live with a guy a year, more, you'd think you'd know him, right? Then you sit down and add it all up and waddia get?' She shrugged. 'I dunno.'

'We don't know anything about him ourselves. Did he ever talk about what he did before he met you?'

Dicey Kilmer sipped her pineapple juice, while Malone and Peta Smith poisoned themselves with caffeine. They were seated in the coffee lounge on the third level of the almost-new shopping centre. The shops, with their well-designed fronts, had none of the worn look that Malone had seen in the older centres; this was suburban shopping at its best, American-influenced. The heart might be dying in the city itself, but out here on the outskirts retail was alive and well. Or appeared to be.

'Practically never. Oh, he was good company, but trying to get him to talk about himself – forget it. Once or twice I, you know, persisted, and he got sorta angry, told me to shut up. I didn't like that, so I hit him. That was a mistake . . .' She rubbed an invisible bruise on her arm.

'Did he have any friends?'

'Friends? No. Acquaintances, more like, he had a few. Guys he worked with, people like that. He did have one friend – acquaintance – call him what you like. He used to ring Murray every week, never come to the flat, just ring and ask for him. They'd talk sometimes for half an hour. I asked him once who the guy was, he said he was someone he'd known in Melbourne. Sometimes I'd answer the phone, I'd try to be polite, you know, *friendly*, but the guy never wanted to know me.'

'Did they talk business?'

'I dunno. Most of the time Murray spoke some foreign language, I dunno what it was. It could have been Hungarian or Russian or Bulgarian, I wouldn't have a clue. This is supposed to be a multicultural country, but we know bugger-all about other languages, right? I once asked him what it was and he said it was Esperanto, he'd met the guy at an Esperanto club in Melbourne. It sounded like bullshit to me, but I let it go. About three months ago he got a call from the guy and it seemed to change him.'

'What way?'

'I dunno, it made him – sorta secretive. God knows, he was never an open book, but now he was worse. Moody, too. That was just before I left him.'

'Why did you leave him?'

She crumpled the drinking straw into her glass. From a music store opposite there came the sound of Artie Shaw and *Begin the Beguine*; there were no young shoppers visible and this was the Golden Oldies Hour, aimed at reviving the itch in pensioners' arthritic feet.

'My music,' said Malone, though he preferred Benny Goodman to Shaw and was too young to have heard either of them in their heyday.

But Dicey Kilmer seemed not to have heard him or the music; she was looking around the coffee lounge. 'I'm always keeping an eye out, I was always expecting Murray to come looking for me. I dunno he'd of known where to find me, I didn't come from Sydney originally. I came from the country, Cawndilla, just the other side of Brewarrina. I like it here, this centre. No wogs, you notice? Nobody knows why, but all the ethnics, they go to Roselands or somewhere else. But here, you look around. All Anglo-Saxons, you notice? Just like in the bush.' She might not be muscle-bound, but she was stiff with prejudices. 'Why'd I leave him? One night he'd had too much to drink, he'd broken training, and he was sorta talking to himself, we were in bed. He said they'd kill us if we ever said too much. I asked him what he was talking about and he sorta seemed to wake up he'd said too much. He told me to shut up again and turned over and went to sleep. I lay awake for a long time that night and that was when I decided to leave. Things'd been cooling, you know, between us . . .' She looked at Peta Smith, not at Malone. 'You know when it's time to leave, right?'

'Yes.' Peta Smith also didn't look at Malone; he was the outsider, the male. 'But no one's ever threatened to kill me. He never said who *they* were?'

Dicey Kilmer shook her head. 'Nah . . . Do you think *they* killed him?'

'We don't know.' The two women were having a one-on-one conversation; Malone might just as well have not been there. 'If you felt threatened, why didn't you go back to, where was it, Cawndilla?'

'What's to do in the bush? There's no jobs, not in my line of work. I'm a beautician. I work in a place down on the lower level.' She caught Malone's enquiring eye. 'What's the matter?'

'You're not made up. All the beauticians I've seen, they wear more make-up than Dame Edna Everage.'

For the first time since they had sat down she smiled. 'They'd kill you if they heard you say that. You mean the false eyelashes, all that? I put 'em on when I start work. Today's my half-day, I don't start till one o'clock. I don't look like Claudia Schiffer, Linda Evangelista, them top models, but I try my best and it's what the customers – the *clients* – it's what they look for.'

'Well, Dicey –' Then Peta Smith smiled, too. 'Dicey. Is that your real name?'

Her smile widened; she seemed at ease now with the two detectives. 'Nah. I was christened Rosemary Edith, but my mum always called me Dicey. I had a pretty dicey birth, they didn't think I was gunna make it, so she always called me her dicey baby. It stuck and I got used to it. My whole life's been dicey, I guess.' She looked at Malone, the smile abruptly gone. 'You think they might try to kill me? I'm scared, tell you the truth. That was why I couldn't come anywhere near a police station, be seen talking to a cop. I dunno I'm safe here, but –' She looked around her, at the Anglo-Saxons, no wogs. Then she looked back at Peta Smith. 'How did *you* find me?'

'Detective work.' Peta Smith smiled, but gave no other explanation. 'We can arrange protection, if you like.'

She looked worried, but she shook her head. 'Nah, let it go. If someone turns up – well, I'll let you know. Poor Murray –' She doodled with her finger on the table-top. Then she looked at Peta, a faint shine of tears in her eyes. 'It's just struck me, he never once told me he loved me. Are all guys like that?'

'No,' said Malone. 'If you don't mind me butting in?'

She blinked, wiped her eyes with the back of her hand. 'No, I guess they're not. You married?'

'Yes.' To a woman I love very much, one whom I tell that to every day.

'Good luck to her. You?' To Peta Smith.

'No, not yet.'

Malone said, 'When Detective Smith searched your flat, where you lived with Murray, she found nothing, not even a piece of paper with his name on it.'

'That was him, all right, come to think of it. If he got a letter or anything, not that he got many, he'd burn 'em. I asked him about it, he'd just say there was too much paper in the world. He'd grin, but I think he meant it. Maybe he was right.'

'Did he have a bank account?'

'Yeah, he'd get a statement, but he'd even burn that. The Commonwealth Bank in Martin Place, the head office. He once told me I ought never bank at a local branch. That way the staff got to know you and all your business. There it was again, the secrecy bit.'

'Maybe I shouldn't say this, but he doesn't sound the best of company.'

'You mean why did I stay with him? Because he had a good side, he could be real nice when he wanted to be. F'rinstance, he loved flowers, especially carnations, said where he come from, everyone loved flowers.'

'I wonder where that was?'

'Ohio, America.'

Malone shook his head. 'We've checked there.'

'Well, wherever it was. He started a garden in the backyard of our block of flats. He'd bring me a bunch . . . No, he was nice when he wanted to be.'

Then all three stood up. Peta Smith reached into the small briefcase she always carried. 'Here's my card, Dicey. You think of anything, anything that'll tell us more about Murray, call me. In the meantime look after yourself. And I don't mean just the muscle definition.'

Dicey Kilmer gave them a final smile and walked away along the gallery towards an escalator. Going down the escalator she looked back at them and waved. 'She's still scared,' said Peta.

'How *did* you find her?'

She looked up at him, grinned. 'The stickybeak who lived next door to them gave me her name. Then I have a friend in Social Services . . .'

'That's against the rules. The Civil Rights mob would have you strung up if they knew.' He took her arm as they went down the escalator. 'Let's hope *they*, whoever they are, don't have a friend in Social Services.'

4

'Were you surprised when I phoned you?'

'Of course.' Joanna Brame was not rude, just direct; she had the assurance that can come with class, education and wealth. Which, she had noted, Milly Channing did not appear to have. 'But we *are* daughter-in-law and mother-in-law. So . . .'

'I asked you here because I thought you'd like to get away from all those lawyers. There are lawyers here, I suppose, but they're all retired. Or should be. Rod made me an associate member here, he loves his golf. He comes all the way over from Roseville to play here.'

'You play golf?'

'Oh no. I'm a bowler.'

'A *bowler*? You go to tenpin bowling alleys?' What sort of women did that, except factory workers' wives?

'Oh no! *Lawn* bowls. It's very popular with women in Australia. We dress all in white – white hat, white skirts, white shoes. Very old-fashioned, it's the last, what do they call it, the last bastion of the old-fashioned. I'm very old-fashioned now I'm old. I wasn't when I was young, but. That was how I met the boys' father. I threw myself at him, as they used to say. Many times I wished he'd ducked and I'd missed. He was a bastard, a sonofabitch, a failure, a woman-chaser – you name it, that was Lester. Thank you,' she said as the waitress brought them their oysters. She had spoken without heat of her ex-husband and her smile for the waitress suggested she might have just switched from telling an amusing story to her guest. When the waitress had gone she went on, 'But I loved him, bastard and all – why I kept taking him back. Till the day came when I could stand it no longer – or him. That was when he went back to America. Enjoy the oysters, we think they're the best in the world.'

Joanna, enjoying the taste of the first oyster, was at the same time taking stock of her hostess and their surroundings. She recognized the Royal Sydney Golf Club as being upper-class, the sort of club her father and her two husbands had belonged to back in Connecticut. The big dining room was not crowded, but the diners had the look of people who had money to spare: the cashmere and alpaca sweaters of the men, the well-cut suits of the women, most of them middle-aged or elderly. It was, obviously and to use Milly Channing's word, a bastion.

Milly herself looked slightly out of place; or rather, ill at ease. Joanna could not quite put her finger on what the other woman lacked; unless, of course, it was class. But, she knew from experience, in these days an expensive and exclusive golf club did not necessarily stamp class on its members. There were members of the club in Connecticut who would never be classed as *class*, not in her opinion, not even if God canonized them. Though, being Episcopalian and Republican, she did not believe in canonization.

Milly Channing was in her early seventies, but she had somehow held age at bay; she looked younger, except for her brown eyes, which, Joanna suddenly realized with a pang, were Orville's eyes. There, the years of pain and disappointment had made their mark. She seemed to smile easily, but the smile took just that much longer to reach her eyes. Her grey hair had been blonded, her make-up was restrained and she was dressed conservatively in a dark green suit with gold buttons. Yet somehow, Joanna felt, Milly Channing did not *belong* here.

'I'm Jewish,' Milly said abruptly; and Joanna felt guilty, as if her thoughts had been read. 'Or anyway, half-Jewish. Did you know that? My father was a money-lender.'

'Am I supposed to be shocked?' Whatever her faults, Joanna had never been anti-Semitic.

'No–o.' She had a way of drawing out her words, as if not sure that they were presentable. 'I understand there's still a lot of anti-Semitism in America. Did you see *Schindler's List*?'

'No.' She had sympathy for those who had been through the Holocaust, but she preferred not to dwell on the horrors of the past. The present, God knew, was barely endurable.

Milly looked around her. 'My father would be pleased I'm a member here. And that Rod is, too. Jews weren't allowed at one time to be members here. Then we had a Jew as our Governor-General, Sir Isaac Isaacs – you can't sound more Jewish than that, can you – back in the Nineteen-Thirties. That upset the apple-cart. They had to offer to make him a member, though I dunno whether he joined or not. My father tried to join, the same time, but they black-balled him because he was a money-lender. In the Depression he used to lend money to half the members of this club, but they couldn't stomach him playing golf with them. Not so long ago some of them were in debt to the banks for millions, but they still played golf with the bank's directors. Different people, different standards.'

'You sound bitter.' The club in Connecticut, too, had once banned Jews as members.

'Oh no, no, I'm not. What's the point of bitterness? I mean about something like that? I used up all my bitterness with Lester. Did you ever meet him? Lester?'

'He was dead long before I met Orville.'

Milly Channing nodded, a sharp little nod as if annoyed at her own obtuseness. 'Of course. Orville didn't write to me that often, just my birthday and Christmas. Anything happened between those dates, he never seemed to make anything of it.'

'You mean he didn't tell you your husband had died? Or that he and I had married?'

'Well, ye–es. But I – I suppose I tried to stop thinking about them, the two of them . . . But it never works, does it? I mean, you can't stop thinking about them. I remember everything about Orville, now he's dead. Everything about him when he was young.'

Joanna suddenly felt the tears start; not for the other woman but for herself. But she had never cried in public, certainly never in a strange eating place, and she was not going to start now. She lowered her head, blinked her eyes and kept the tears at bay. 'Why did Orville cut himself off from you and his brother?'

'He never told you? No, I don't suppose he would have, he was like that even when he was young. Kept things to himself.' She chewed on an oyster as if it were a lump of gristle. 'He idolized his father and he always blamed me that we didn't get on, that the marriage broke up.'

'Why? Your husband sounds, as you say, a real son-ofabitch.'

Milly smiled. 'You don't look to me like a woman who'd say a word like *sonofabitch*.'

'Every woman, at least once or twice in her life, meets a sonofabitch.' But she didn't elaborate.

'I don't know why Orville took Lester's side, but he did. Rod took my side. I – I walked out on Lester, went to live with another man and took the boys with me. That – that

84

was another of my bad choices. It lasted a year and I – I walked out on him, too.'

'Another sonofabitch?' She liked the sound of the word.

'No, not really. Just a bad choice. But by then the damage was done. Lester had gone back to America and Orville told me when he was, I dunno, ten or twelve, some day he was going to go and live with his father. And he did that. He walked out on me and Rod just the way I'd walked out on Lester.' She looked across the table at Joanna, suddenly direct. 'Was he a good husband to you? I'd never forgive him if he wasn't.'

'Yes,' said Joanna, the tears close again. 'The best. Much, much better than my first husband.'

'Oh, you'd been married before?'

'Yes. He died, he was an alcoholic. He was killed in his car while he was drunk.'

'Two of 'em.' Milly's face suddenly aged with sympathy; the pain in her eyes was shared. 'Oh, my dear! We're unlucky, aren't we?'

'Yes.' All at once Joanna felt a warmth for the other woman. She had never been one to make friendships with women; there were no sorority sisters from her Bryn Mawr college days, she belonged to no women's groups, no charity committees. But suddenly she felt a bond with this woman across the table from her, this stranger, this *bowler*. 'Yes, we are.'

'Who could have done it? To Orville, I mean.'

'I have no idea. Did he come to see you before –?'

'Yes. Early Sunday morning. He said he was going to see Rod, at Rod's office.'

'How was he?' The oyster plates had been taken away, been replaced by plates bearing small *filet mignon* and, thank God, no French fries. The TV commercials she had seen in her hotel suite had told her that the locals *loved* what they called chips. Sometimes she thought the world's taste buds were in the lower bowel. 'Was he – worried?'

'I don't think so. Unless he was worried about meeting me. I mean, a mother-and-son reunion after, what, thirty years? It wasn't easy, for either of us. But I'm glad he came to see me, that I saw him before . . . Did you have to identify him? I understand you have to do that, some relative.'

'How did your other son feel about Orville?'

'We–ell –' Milly cut her steak as if she were cutting a diamond. 'Well, not too loving. Actually, he often said he hated Orville. For leaving me, going with his father.' She looked up then. 'Actually, there was a lot of envy, I think. Orville was always the bright one, he got a much better pass at university than Rod did when he went there. And of course, Orville did much better in America. I mean, he was top of the tree, wasn't he? Big time, as they call it.'

Joanna did not want to ask the question, but had to: 'Did Rod hate Orville enough to want to see him dead?'

Milly put down her knife and fork with a clatter. 'That's a terrible thing to ask.'

'I know.' Joanna put down her own implements, pushed her plate away. 'Have the police been to see you yet? They will ask you the same question if you tell them what you've just told me.'

Milly looked at her own plate, then pushed it away. All at once she looked her age; the bloom, artificial though it may have been, had died. 'You think I should keep that to myself? No, they haven't been to see me, not yet. Perhaps they don't know I'm still alive. We're often forgotten, us oldies. Orville forgot me. Or did his best to.'

'Rod's firm sent two letters to Orville, both marked personal. I presume they would have been from Rod. Did he ever mention anything to you, about doing business with Orville?'

Milly signalled for the waitress to take away their plates. 'No, the steak was fine, dear. It's just that we – well, we haven't as much appetite as we thought.' Joanna listened impatiently to this; she couldn't understand people who had to make explanations to the help. The waitress took the plates and went away after the two women had declined dessert. Then Milly looked back at Joanna. 'I don't come here that much. I feel – uncomfortable. I don't think you'd feel uncomfortable anywhere, would you?'

I'd feel uncomfortable in a women's bowling club. 'I don't know, I don't test myself. I'm what other people call a snob.'

Milly smiled, a weak smile but genuine. 'Not many people would admit that . . . Rod is a snob, but he'd never admit it.'

'Is he ambitious?'

'Rod is forty-five years old – can you still be ambitious at that age? I've always supposed ambition was something you had when you were young. I wanted to be a singer, the Australian Connie Boswell, before your time, I'd say . . . Did you have ambition?'

'I didn't need it,' said Joanna.

Milly smiled again. 'No, I suppose you didn't. Lucky you,' she said without malice and, unexpectedly, made Joanna feel embarrassed and ashamed. 'Yes, I think Rod is ambitious. He'd love to be up there, top of the tree. I heard him telling Ruth, she's his wife, a couple of weeks ago, he said he was about to make the biggest deal of his career. I didn't ask him about it, I wasn't supposed to have heard, they were out in their kitchen. But he sounded excited, though angry too, they were sort of arguing about something, the way couples do. Then he mentioned Orville, but I didn't catch the rest. Yes, Rod is ambitious, still.'

A foursome of elderly golfers had come into the dining room, bringing their bar talk with them. Everyone turned to look at them, but the men seemed oblivious of the disturbance they were creating. Though she knew none of them, Joanna recognized them for what they were: top of the tree, Establishment. They were recognizable anywhere in the world, their accent made no difference. Orville had been one of them, though quieter; he would never have created a disturbance. Remembering Rodney now, she knew, even from the one meeting, that the younger brother would never be Establishment. Snobbery was a fault, but sometimes it gave one a deadly accurate eye.

'I think Orville and his brother had some deal going,' she said. 'Whatever it was, the deal killed my husband.'

'Cain and Abel – is that what you're saying?'

'No. But I'm going to ask the police to talk to your son again.' For a moment she had been coldly brutal. Then she saw the pain in the other woman's face and she put out a hand, though she didn't touch Milly Channing. 'I'm sorry, Milly. But I can't bury Orville and not know why he died.'

Chapter Five

1

That afternoon Malone went up to the Central Criminal Courts in Darlinghurst to hear the verdict on a murder case against a couple, both heroin addicts, who had killed their infant son. A deal had been struck and the charge reduced to involuntary manslaughter; the couple were sentenced to two years' imprisonment with a non-parole period of eighteen months. Malone walked out of the court seething with disgust. Phil Truach, who had worked on the case from the beginning, was waiting for him.

'Why do we bother, Phil?'

'Good question. Sometimes I think I'd do better in the Fraud Squad. At least there you can expect the villains just to get a slap on the wrist, get a light sentence, they don't even have to take a toilet kit to jail. The fucking judiciary, all they're interested in is the letter of the law. They never see what we see. But then, the Fraud Squad –' He lit a cigarette, puffed on it, keeping the smoke away from Malone. 'There's no mystery in fraud, is there? Villains commit fraud because of greed, nothing else. Or maybe to get out of financial trouble. But homicide . . .' Another drag on the cigarette. 'There's a hundred reasons for murder. That's the bit keeps me in Homicide.'

'That couple in there –' Malone nodded back at the old sandstone courthouse with its pillared front. 'They killed that kiddy. Injuries like he had, that wasn't manslaughter. They beat him to death.'

Truach stopped, looked towards four street kids, none

of them more than fourteen or fifteen, who stood looking in through the bars of the high railing fence. 'Maybe the kiddy's better off dead. With parents like that, where would he finish up? With those kids out there?' The kids seemed suddenly to recognize that the two men were cops. They shouted something obscene, gave the middle-finger salute and ran off down the street. The incongruous thought struck Malone: would Orville Brame ever have had to defend a street kid in New York? Or would his brother have, here in Sydney? The two lawyers belonged to another world.

'Anyhow, back there, it's over, Scobie.' Phil Truach had no children and, if he felt any anger about murdered infants, he hid it better than Malone. 'Let's go back to thinking about the Brame case. There's mystery there, all right. What've we come up with? Bugger-all. I think maybe we're looking in the wrong place. Maybe the answer's back in New York.'

They walked towards Malone's car. The sky was grey, like frozen sludge; the wind strained at anything in its path. The few trees in the courts' yard had the iron look that some trees get in winter; the bare branches bent in the wind like lengths of hawser. Malone had not brought his raincoat and he was cold. He ducked into his car, slamming the door after him, and Truach slid in on the other side, throwing his cigarette into the gutter.

'What do you mean? Back in New York?'

'Some deal, something dirty that Brame was mixed up in. You ever see that film *The Firm*? Read the book? The Mafia was mixed up in that, they *ran* the lawyers.'

Malone shook his head as he took the car out into Oxford Street and round the back of the law courts. The male prostitutes, whose beat was along the high stone wall that backed the court complex and what had been the old Darlinghurst jail, were not in evidence; it was either too early for them to pick up the businessmen looking for a stopover on their way home or the cold had frozen their salesgoods. 'Brame's firm is simon-pure in that regard. I had John Kagal query a couple of the top firms here. Schuyler, De Vries and Barrymore would have been fussy about taking on Jesus Christ.'

'There's always a first time. I think we should get permission to go through all Brame's papers.'

'Yeah, it might –' He was not averse to Truach's suggestion; he always had a ready ear for whatever came from his men. Maybe he should have thought of the idea himself; his mind had begun to slip gears. 'I'll talk to his assistant, the young bloke, Tallis. We'll come up against all the lawyer–client bullshit, but maybe . . . No, I'll talk to *Mrs* Brame. I think she has a lot of clout there. And after all, it's her husband's murder we're investigating.'

He dropped Truach off at Homicide and drove on over to the Novotel at Darling Harbour. The sky had lowered still further and when he got out of the car rain was slanting in from the south-west. He parked the car in the driveway and winked at the concierge as he was blown in through the main door.

'I know it's not a Rolls or a Porsche, but it's better-looking than Columbo's.'

The concierge just gave him a sour look; after all, he wasn't a guest, just a cop. Malone went up the escalator to the main lobby, and had just reached the reception desk when Richard De Vries touched him on the arm.

'Looking for Mrs Brame? She went out to lunch, she's probably gone shopping. Women do that, takes their minds off their problems. Or maybe she's gone to try to get rid of the red tape that seems to be binding up her husband. Perhaps that should be Orville's shroud, red tape. We lawyers are entrapped by it all the time. May I buy you afternoon tea?' He led Malone towards a side room off the lobby. 'I have tea every afternoon back home in the office. There are certain English customs one has to admire. Not many nowadays, but afternoon tea is one of them. Are you an Anglophile, Inspector?'

'The name's Malone. What do you think?'

'Of course. But not all the Irish have been Anglo*phobes*.' They sat down in deep chairs with a low table between them. A waiter approached and De Vries gave his order. 'Two teas, made in the pot, not with tea-bags. Earl Grey for me. Malone? Green tea, perhaps?'

'Earl Kerry for me.'

De Vries smiled at the waiter. 'Mr Malone is Irish. Earl Grey for two. And cakes, cream cakes.' The waiter disappeared and De Vries settled back in his chair. 'Well, how is the investigation going?'

Malone shrugged, dodged the question. 'You look a lot fresher than you did this morning.'

'I'll flake out this evening, no doubt. Yes, I had a nap, I feel a little better. Why did you want to see Mrs Brame? Don't you think she should be spared all this? Have you come up with something?'

Malone hesitated a moment. 'I was going to – well, maybe you're the one I should've seen first, anyway. We want permission to go through all Mr Brame's papers in his office.'

De Vries's elbows rested on the arms of his chair; his fingers were laced together. The affability of a few moments ago had abruptly disappeared from the round bland face. 'You're asking a lot! Don't you have lawyer–client confidentiality in this country?'

'Of course we do.' Malone kept his tone even. 'I'm not suggesting *we* go through the files. That would take too long, anyway. We'd have to get the New York PD to do it for us, there'd have to be warrants . . . You can fax your office this afternoon and have someone start the search.'

'Why?'

'Because we think New York should have been our starting point. The more we think about it, the more we

92

think Mr Brame was involved in some deal that got him murdered. Why was his briefcase stolen, all his papers in it?'

'Have you talked to any of our associate firms here? For instance –' He named the two top firms in Sydney. 'They'd know if there was any deal we were handling for them –'

'We've talked to them, they know nothing. The deal, if there is one, might not necessarily have anything to do with Australia.'

De Vries shook his head. 'It's a long, long shot. I would have known if Orville was involved in something like that. We shared information – we were the two senior partners, but I was the senior, you know.' For a moment he sounded like some small boy claiming a right. 'But I'll do it if you insist, fax the office.' He looked at the slim gold watch, almost a woman's watch, that he wore. 'It's one a.m. back there. I'll see the fax is waiting for them when they come in first thing in the morning. What do you want to know?'

'Anything that will link to his murder. Was he planning to see anyone out here, stuff like that.'

De Vries tilted his head. 'Inspector, you sound as if you suspect Orville of having been up to something.'

'Not at all. Maybe he was murdered because he refused to get up to something, whatever it was.'

De Vries stared at him, then turned abruptly as the waiter wheeled a tray up to them. 'Ah, here we are! Tea and cakes. Cream cakes, too! They look almost French, something from a real *pâtisserie*.'

'This is a French-owned hotel, sir. And I'm from Paris myself. Shall I pour?'

'No, leave it. Thank you.' De Vries shook his head as the waiter went away. 'The world grows smaller by the day. Fancy, French waiters *here*.'

'Yes,' said Malone. 'We don't have to use the Aborigines any more as servants.'

He smiled as he said it, but De Vries wasn't taken in. 'I

apologize, Mr Malone. This *is* a civilized country. Milk?'

'Black, with no sugar.' Malone bit into an éclair. 'Simple-minded civilized. We don't kill each other as frequently as other countries do.'

'You've made your point, Mr Malone,' said De Vries, voice sharp as the silver knife cutting his cake. 'Back to our subject. What about the other murdered man, the security guard who found Orville?'

Malone wondered who had briefed De Vries on the second murder. 'We're making a little progress there . . .'

He looked out at the lobby filling up with lawyers returning from their afternoon session. They had the look of students who had been freed from a boring lecture, as if they had been subjected to a topic that held nothing new for them. Three or four of them came into the side room, glanced around and went out, as if they had been looking for something more exciting than two men chatting over tea and cream cakes. Malone wondered if the murder of the Bar Association's president would be an agenda item for discussion before the convention ended.

'The security guard was an American,' he said. 'Or claimed to be.'

'Claimed to be?' De Vries paused with the piece of cake halfway to his mouth.

'We had his record checked by the FBI. It was fake.'

'You've already been in touch with the FBI? You move fast.' De Vries swallowed the cake, took a sip of his tea. 'Where do you think he came from then?'

'We don't know. Not from here, we're pretty sure of that. He wasn't Australian.' Malone wiped éclair cream from the corner of his mouth.

De Vries sipped his tea again, nodded appreciatively. 'A good cuppa, as the English say. There's no connection, is there, between Orville's murder and the security man's?'

There was no apparent real concern on De Vries's part that there might be a connection between the two murders.

This was a tea-and-cakes chat, with De Vries leaning forward to take a pastry, a napoleon, and murder with no more weight than gossip.

'We think there might be a connection.' He had never been very good at playing the enigmatic, but today's effort was not bad.

It made De Vries pause and look at him; cream oozed out of the napoleon as he pressed down on it. 'In what way?'

'I'll let you know when we're more certain.' He was not sure why he was lying like this, playing De Vries with a line that had no bait on it. Then through the room's open doors he saw Tallis crossing the lobby. At once he was on his feet and caught the young American before he got to the lifts.

'Mr Tallis –' Then he saw the briefcase in the young man's hand. 'Yours?'

'No.' Tallis held up the briefcase. 'It's Mr Brame's – empty. They just handed it to me at the desk, said it had been found down in the basement.'

Malone took the briefcase and led Tallis back into the side room, where De Vries still sat in his chair, the napoleon half-eaten. 'Tea, Adam? I'll get them to bring another cup, another pot.'

'No, thanks.' Tallis sat down, looked up at Malone, who had remained standing. 'There's nothing in the briefcase, not a single paper. The lock had been forced. Whoever took it, cleared it out.'

'That's Orville's? Of course, I recognize it now.' Again De Vries's interest seemed only perfunctory. He took a final mouthful of the pastry, chewed it, swallowed, wiped cream from his lips, then said, 'I gave it to him, actually. When he joined me as senior partner. We went to Mark Cross and he chose it himself. He liked it immensely –' Then it seemed to occur to him that he was talking too much but saying nothing. He wiped his mouth again. 'But that's all irrelevant, isn't it?'

'Yes,' said Malone quietly but bluntly. 'Where did you say it was found, Mr Tallis?'

'They said down in the basement, it had just been brought up.' He held out a hand. 'Shall I give it to Mrs Brame?'

'I'll keep it, we'll need to look at it for fingerprints. I'll be in touch, tell Mrs Brame.' He nodded to De Vries. 'Thanks for the tea. Don't forget that fax.'

De Vries's brow clouded a moment, then cleared. 'Oh yes. Of course. I'll send it off immediately.'

Malone left them and went out to the desk. A pretty young girl, non-French, recognized him. 'You're one of the police officers, right?'

'You're keeping an eye on us?'

'We keep an eye on everyone, sir.' But her smile told him he might be one of the favoured ones. 'The briefcase? One of our maintenance men brought it up. Mario Valetta.'

Malone asked directions to the basement, went down in the lift and was told by a maid sorting laundry where he could find Mario Valetta. He headed down a long corridor, came to a door, opened it and found himself in a large room humming with the motors of a huge air-conditioning plant. Mario Valetta was a young Italian shaking and bobbing his head to the music coming out of the Walkman earphones he wore against the constant hum of the air-conditioning. Malone had to tap him on the shoulder to get him to turn round. He pulled aside one of the earphones.

'Yeah?'

Malone held up the briefcase, jerked his head towards the door behind him, then walked out into the corridor. Valetta followed him, slipping the earphones down round his neck. 'Michael Jackson, I listen to him all day.'

'I thought you'd have gone for Pavarotti.' Malone showed his badge.

Valetta smiled, showed a broken tooth in the left side of his mouth. He was tall and thin, with a nose like a knife-blade and bright cheeky eyes. 'Nah. I left all that opera stuff when I come out here with my parents when I was a kid. You think *La Traviata* means anything today?'

'The way he's going, maybe Jackson won't mean much in a year or two.' He held up the briefcase again.

'They told you upstairs I found it? Yeah, stuffed down the back of one of the air-conditioners. This morning.'

'Any idea how long it'd been there?'

Valetta shrugged his thin shoulders. 'Who knows? I don't think it was there day before yesterday, not Monday morning, anyway. I cleaned the place up Monday morning, it's my house-keeping day, like.' The gap-toothed smile was friendly rather than cheeky. 'But it could of been dumped there Monday afternoon.'

'Who comes down to the plant room besides you?'

'There are four of us, we work around the clock, six hours a day, six days a week. We got an enterprise agreement with the Frogs run the hotel. Six days a week but a four-day break every month.'

Malone wasn't interested in enterprise bargaining, the new cure-all for industrial trouble; he doubted that the police would ever be offered such a bargain. 'You were on all day Monday?'

'Yeah, like I told you. Look, you're not thinking any of the other guys stole that?' He nodded at the briefcase. 'No way, mate. If they had, they wouldn't of been dumb enough to leave it down here, would they?'

'Who else has access to the plant room?' The two of them had to stand against the wall as an overalled man went past pushing a huge wheeled basket full of laundry.

'Anybody, I guess. The door ain't locked. But nobody comes in, why would they wanna?'

'You know all the staff?'

'Everybody works down here, yeah.'

'You see any strangers down here Monday afternoon or yesterday?'

97

Valetta screwed up his thin face; his sharp nose actually moved sideways. 'Nah, can't remember anybody. Not *strangers*. One of the security guys, Murray, that's all I know him as, I saw him out here in the corridor. He said he was looking for one of the maids. He gimme a wink, you know, like he had something going with her. The poor bugger, he's dead, they fished him outa the harbour yesterday. But you'd know all about that.'

'Yes. Murray Rockman. Did he name the maid?'

'Well, no, come to think of it, no. He just said he was waiting for one of the girls.'

'He didn't work for the hotel as a security guard.'

'No, he was with, I dunno, TNT, I think. But working this side of the water, with the monorail and that, I'd see him around. Poor bugger,' he said again. 'Who did him in?'

'I wish we knew. Thanks, Mario. We'll probably be in touch again.'

'You think he had something to do with that?' He nodded at the briefcase again.

'You never know. Enjoy Michael Jackson while you can. You ever notice that opera singers last longer than pop singers?'

'You mean you're an opera fan?' He sounded incredulous, as if Malone, a cop, had just expressed a regard for Jack the Ripper.

'No, I just like people who last. It's the conservative in me.'

'You sound just like my dad.'

Malone left him and walked along to the lifts. When he looked back the young Italian was walking back towards the plant room door. The phones were clamped over his ears again, his head was bobbing and shaking to whatever message the fallen idol Michael Jackson was giving him.

2

'Dad, will Mum die?'

Malone was angry at the question; but then he recognized where his anger sprang from. His own fear was as large as his son's. 'Tom, people all die eventually. Even you will.'

'Gee, thanks.' Tom, though still wet behind the ears, was already approaching the dryness of his father and grandfather. 'That wasn't what I asked you, but.'

'Tom,' said Con Malone from where he sat in the chair across from his son and grandson, 'I'm old enough to be your grandpa –'

'You *are* my grandpa.'

'That's what I said. Don't interrupt. Kids today are always interrupting. What I'm telling you, when I was your age, a little older, I got something wrong with me. The doctors told me it would never be cured –'

'Was it cancer?'

'Well, no –'

'What was it?'

'It was a broken elbow. They told me it'd never be straight again. But look –' He held out a sweatered arm.

'Ah, come *on*, Grandpa! A broken elbow isn't the same as cancer!'

'What we're trying to tell you,' said Malone, 'is that we all die in God's own good time. The only people who die in their own time are people who suicide. Mum has no intention of dying. Ninety-nine per cent of the women who have what Mum's got, they recover and live for ever.' He wasn't at all sure of the percentage of recovery from cancer of the cervix, but percentages were like statistics, the next figure along from lies and damned lies. He had to believe that, even if Tom didn't. 'Mum will live to have grandkids, the same as Pa and Ma have. Your kids.'

Brigid Malone came in from the kitchen, sat down

beside Tom and ran her hand lovingly over his thick dark hair. Malone could not remember her ever doing that to him; the talent for showing affection had come late in life, but not too late, for Brigid Malone. But even now she never kissed Malone himself or showed her cheek for him to kiss.

He looked at his parents, relics of another age. Con, built like a tree-stump though splintering now at the edges, had worked most of his life on construction sites or on the wharves; he still had all the old-time militancy of the unions that had controlled those jobs. The termites in the stump of him were racism, bigotry and an antagonism towards authority, including bosses and police. Brigid was stiffer in her morals than her husband and riddled with the bigotry of xenophobia and religious bias. She had once been a pretty woman, but that was long ago and she had never had the vanity to keep her looks from fading.

'What are we talking about?' she said.

'Mum's cancer,' said Tom.

Her hand froze on top of his head. 'That's not something to talk about!' She looked accusingly at her husband and her son, the idiot men. 'What's got into you two?'

'I brought it up, Gran –' Tom ducked his head out from under her hand, 'I was just asking.'

'Well, don't let's talk about it any more. Let's talk about something else.'

'How's your murders going?' said Con, going in the wrong door, as he often did in conversation.

'Con!'

'Simmer down, love. Tom knows what his father does, don't you, son? If he has to have a copper as a father, he's entitled to know what he does. I used to tell Scobie about working in the wharves.'

'The fights and the strikes,' said Brigid. 'It's a wonder he grew up to be normal.'

'Are you normal, Dad?' said Tom, hiding his grin.

Malone rarely brought his work home with him; and

never to discuss it with the children. But to rebuff his father now would only arouse the old man's resentment. For all Con's remarks about 'mug coppers', Malone knew that his father took pride, though he would never confess it, in Malone's rise in police ranks. If ever he rose to be Commissioner, which in his own mind was highly unlikely, his father would be hernia-stricken with a twist of pride and shame.

'We're not getting very far,' he said. 'But it's early days yet.'

'Are you going to keep working while Lisa is in hospital?' said Brigid.

'No, I'm coming off duty at the weekend, I'll take a week's leave. More, if I have to.' Then instantly regretted the last remark when he saw Tom's quick sideways glance at him.

'Good,' said Brigid and looked at Con as if that should settle any further discussion about murders.

But Con was not to be put off: 'Are the Yanks interfering? All them lawyers out here.' He was anti-American, anti-British, anti- any sort of imperialism; he was anti-lawyers, whom he saw as an empire in themselves. 'I'd stand up to 'em, I were you.'

'They're not interfering, not yet. He was an Australian, you know, the lawyer who was murdered.'

'I know that.' Unlike most of the voters, Con still read newspapers; his idea of news was not illustrated headlines on television. 'So someone who knew him back then, they might of done him in?'

'My mother used to tell me,' said Brigid, 'that anything a man did wrong, you looked for it in his past life.'

Malone had never met his maternal grandmother; she had never followed her daughter to Australia. But Brigid was always quoting her and he could picture the stout old lady in the farmhouse in Galway laying down her maxims like tarot cards. Aileen McGoldrick, though no more than a figure in a faded sepia photograph, was a real presence in his mind. An only child of parents who had no siblings of their own, he clung to any image that suggested family. It was why he did his best to give his own children a sense of continuity.

Then his ear, a little late, registered what his mother had said. 'What did your mother tell you?'

Brigid looked at him, puzzled. 'Why? She said that anything a man did wrong, you looked for it in his past life. We had a murder once in Ballyreagh –' Tom turned his head to look sharply at her, but she just patted his hand. 'Well, never mind. It shouldn't be talked about.'

'Ah, come on, Gran. Talk about it. We watch murders every night on TV.'

'Just shows what the world's come to –'

'Mum,' said Malone, 'don't leave us up in the air. There was a murder in Ballyreagh and your mother said something about it. What happened?'

'Come on, love,' said Con. 'You're a bugger for leaving things up in the air.'

'Watch your language –'

'In front of the kid,' said Tom. 'Come on, Gran, what happened in Ballyreagh?'

'A man murdered his brother. And that's all I'm going to tell you.'

Then Lisa and the two girls, the pots and pans washed and put away, the dishwasher sloshing quietly, came in from the kitchen. The two girls and Tom went on into their bedrooms to do their homework and Lisa took Tom's place beside Brigid.

'What are we talking about?'

'Nothing,' said Brigid, closing her own door on a conversation that obviously had no appeal for her.

Con opened another door: 'Are you in private health insurance?'

'Yes.' Lisa was calm about what lay ahead of her; or appeared to be. 'We're covered fully.'

'Bloody doctors,' said Con, adding another item to his hate list. 'They charge the bloody earth, think everyone's a bloody millionaire like themselves. There should be a law against 'em.'

'If there was, you'd still find something else to complain about,' said Brigid.

'Bloody oath, I would.'

'I'll come out and cook for Scobie and the children,' Brigid told Lisa. She put a hand on her daughter-in-law's; long years of pent-up affection were seeping out of her, like water out of a gourd worn thin by age. 'I'll see they eat properly.'

Thick stews and corned beef and cabbage and sausages and mashed potatoes, thought Malone: his mother paid no heed to dietary fads; multiculturalism had introduced nothing new into her menus. Nor would Con have let her. Though Malone noticed that every time his parents came to the house for dinner, they cleaned their plates of everything that Lisa, an experimenter, put in front of them.

'They'll appreciate some good plain food,' said Lisa, knowing that tomorrow her own mother would suggest that *she* come over to cook, bringing her European menus with her. The rivalry between mothers-in-law could equal that between mistresses. But she would not worry about it, would leave it to Claire to sort out. Claire might have bigger problems to solve in the near future, she thought; and instantly was amazed at the cruelty of the thought. She would have to teach herself, *now*, that self-pity was no medication.

At nine-thirty Malone drove his parents home to the narrow terrace house in Erskineville where he had been born. Erskineville was a tiny inner-city enclave that had staved off gentrification longer than most inner suburbs; but lately elaborate brass door-knockers, brightly painted balcony ironwork and strains of Mozart and Vivaldi had become discernible. As soon as Malone pulled up the

Commodore, Con was out of the car and through the front door, chasing his bladder to the bathroom.

'He shouldn't drink wine,' said Brigid. 'It works on him worse than beer.'

Malone helped her out of the back seat, where she always rode, sitting up straight with regal dignity. 'Mum, why did one brother kill the other? In Ballyreagh?'

'Jealousy.'

'Jealousy? Over what?'

'Over a girl.' She was at the front gate, only a yard from the front door, which had a black iron knocker, none of your fancy brass stuff.

'Who was the girl?'

'Never mind,' she said and, showing none of the affection that she had allowed to leak out of herself earlier in the evening, she went in and closed the door in his face.

He stood there in the cold dark night, realizing once again how little he knew and understood his mother. He got back into the car, unutterably sad, and drove back to Randwick. By then a sabre moon had come up, slicing the clouds into tatters as they slid across its face. As he walked towards his front door a camellia fell from its bush, hitting his foot with a soft thud. He started and, unintelligently, was abruptly afraid; then, just as suddenly, was angry with himself. Seeing an omen, for Chrissake, in a falling flower! He would have to start hiding his pessimism from Lisa.

She was in bed, reading another book by another Chinese woman.

'Aren't there any Chinese *men* writers?' he said as he got in beside her.

'Probably. Your feet are cold, keep them to yourself. Women always write the truth better than men.'

'You could've fooled me.' Remembering some of the female depositions he had had to read. He picked up his own book, a biography of Al Capone, read two pages and took in not a word, and put the book down. 'I think a man killed his brother over my mother.'

'*What?*' She dropped her own book.

He told her of his cryptic conversation with his mother. 'In all her life, she has never told me why she came to Australia. I'd ask her and she'd just say, Adventure. You know what she's like, she's not adventurous at all. She's never been out of the State, hardly even out of Sydney. She got off the boat fifty years ago, nearly, she went to stay with some Irish family in Erskineville and she's never moved out of the district. It's hard to believe –' He shook his head. 'Some feller killing his brother over her.'

'You don't know what she was like when she was young.' Lisa closed her book, China forgotten, trying to imagine rural Ireland and the girl, hidden somewhere in Brigid, who had inflamed enough passion to cause a murder.

He put out his own bedside light, lay in the darkness holding her to him. Then he said, 'I wonder if Rod Channing killed his brother? Jealous over something?'

3

Commissioner John Leeds had a passion for neatness. In his appearance, the lay-out of his desk, the curriculum he laid down for the Police Service: he was notorious for his insistence that nothing constructive had ever come from a mess. No one who had the knowledge dared tell him of Beethoven and others who had made something constructive out of the mess on their desks.

Now he was presiding over a mess of epic proportions; or so he was being told by the large, gesticulating man in front of him. Karl Zoehrer was saying, 'It's not my place to criticize, Commissioner, but there appears to be a lack of *effort*. If Mr Brame's murder had taken place back in the

States, there would instantly have been a major hunt, a task force –'

Malone caught Novack's eye: the Consul-General looked embarrassed by Zoehrer's approach. Two of the other men at the conference, Assistant Commissioner, Crime, Fred Falkender, and Superintendent Greg Random, merely looked stone-faced; they were accustomed to criticism, though usually from the natives, not from foreigners. Zoehrer was still talking: 'How many police are assigned to the case?'

'Sufficient,' said Leeds without reference to either Falkender or Random. 'This is not a hunt for a serial killer, Mr Zoehrer. Our resources are limited. I appreciate the American way is for saturation –'

'I remember reading about the murders of some backpackers out here last year. You used, what, five or six hundred men on that?'

'Three hundred,' said Fred Falkender, who had been in charge overall. He was a squarely built, muscular man who had a normally jovial face; today there wasn't a hint of humour in it, it had only the flush of rising bad temper. 'But there we were looking for more graves, for possibly more bodies, we were searching for clues months old –'

'Did you catch the killer?'

'Yes, we have a man in custody.'

Zoehrer nodded; it was difficult to tell if it was a nod of congratulation. 'Well, I'd like to see a more concentrated effort on this case –'

'May I say something?' said Novack, stepping in with the thin-ice step of a diplomat who spent half his time unravelling contending flags. 'Has the investigation come up with a motive for the murder?'

Leeds looked at Malone, who had been silent up till now. Despite the difference in rank, there was no remoteness in the relationship between the two men. They had once been involved in a case where Malone had had to protect the Commissioner's reputation; in the years since the case had never been referred to again, but a bond had been established. Leeds had never offered any favouritism for the debt, that would have been against his nature, and Malone had never looked for any. But there was an understanding between them that was not common between men of such different ranks.

'Inspector?'

Malone knew the onus was on him. It was all very well to say that the buck stopped at the top, but that was never really the case: it was no more than political rhetoric. Between the top and himself there were other supposed buffers: a Deputy Commissioner, Assistant Commissioners, Regional Commanders. In the end, however, it was the officer in charge of the day-to-day investigation who had to supply the answers.

'None so far, sir. We think there's some connection between the Brame murder and that of the security guard Rockman and we're working on that.'

'What connection?' Zoehrer might have been interrogating a witness, one whom he considered hostile.

'They were killed by the same gun.'

'The security guard's own gun? Are you suggesting the guard shot Mr Brame and then shot himself?'

'Not at all. The guard was shot in the back of the head. It would be a bit of a contortionist's act, to do that.'

Random's lips twitched, but that was the only reaction, except from Zoehrer, who glared. 'How many men have you on the case?'

'Enough,' said Leeds, taking the question away from Malone. He had seen the latter bristle and he knew that Malone's tongue could make this meeting even messier. 'May I ask why you are here, Mr Zoehrer, representing the Brame interests and not – is it Mr De Vries?'

'Dick De Vries has no experience of criminal trials. His firm specialize in deals, litigation, matters like that.' His tone seemed to imply that Schuyler, De Vries and Barrymore knew none of the excitement of being a lawyer. 'Dick asked me to look into it. I'm here representing the Bar Association, too. Orville Brame was our president, a highly regarded one. There are a thousand of our members here in Sydney, all wanting to know why Mr Brame was murdered.'

'I'm sure there are three and a half *million* Sydneysiders who'd also like to know why. Every one of them is on our back. That's why Inspector Malone and his team are doing their best to give you all an answer as soon as possible.' Leeds rose from behind his desk. One of his talents was that he knew how to close a meeting. 'You will be kept informed, Mr Zoehrer. You too, Mr Novack.'

Zoehrer and Novack stood up and Malone waited for some stiff remark from Zoehrer at being so curtly dismissed. But Karl Zoehrer, for all his bluster and grandstanding, knew the rules of any game of law. A lawyer's domain was in court, not here in the police chief's room.

'I'm sure your men will do their best, Commissioner.' He turned to Malone. 'I hope I didn't sound too much of a Doubting Thomas, Inspector?'

'Not at all, sir,' said Malone, practising being oily but still unable to resist throwing a little grit into the oil: 'The Bible doesn't say so, but Doubting Thomas went on to be a cop. He's our patron saint.'

'Is that so? No wonder I've found life difficult with our own guys back home.'

The two Americans were ushered out by Fred Falkender and the door closed. Leeds gestured for Random and Malone to sit down. 'I didn't know that about St Thomas.'

'Neither did I, sir. I just had a sudden vision.'

'Here in College Street? I've never seen this as the road to Damascus . . . Am I right in thinking you're getting nowhere on these cases?'

'This isn't an open-and-shut case,' said Random defensively. 'We –'

'Greg, you're not talking to Mr Zoehrer. I know it's not an open-and-shut case – I've read the summaries. But I have to tell the Minister *something*. And the Premier. What have you come up with, Scobie, that I can make sound as if you're making progress? Will it help if we put extra men on it? Say another three hundred?' The Commissioner allowed himself some bitterness.

'We don't need any more at the moment, sir. We're not chasing bodies on this one . . . I'm going back to talk to Channing, Brame's brother.'

'You think he knows something?'

'I don't know, sir. But I'm convinced Brame wasn't killed by some stranger, someone who had no connection with him. Whether he was done in by the security guard and then someone did *him* in, I don't know. But the only person in Sydney who knew Brame was his brother.'

'And his mother,' said Random, who had read today's summaries in his usual non-summarily way.

'Peta Smith and John Kagal are out seeing her now. We slipped up there – we thought she was dead. Nobody mentioned her, not even Channing. Or Mrs Brame.'

'There are some other people you've forgotten,' said Leeds. 'The thousand American lawyers here in town. Why wouldn't one of them have killed him?'

'Don't depress me, sir.'

Leeds smiled. 'Okay, keep at it. Don't hold any press conferences, Greg. We'll handle all that from here. Bullshit from headquarters always sounds more authoritative. Don't quote me.'

As Malone and Random rode down in the lift from the twentieth floor of the Avery building, police headquarters, Random said, 'How's your wife?'

'Fine, she says. I'm the one with flutterguts.' They got out of the lift, crossed the lobby and went out into College

Street. Across the road in Hyde Park the wintry sun shone on the pale bulk of the Anzac Memorial, the monument to other dead. *Other* dead? What the hell was he thinking of? He threw off the mood as if it were a filthy cloak. 'Greg, I don't think we are going to wrap this one before Sunday.'

'Do you want to take leave now?'

They walked up College Street. Four youths in dirty jeans, ragged sweaters and baseball caps were just ahead of them; coming from the opposite direction were four senior boys from Sydney Grammar, the exclusive private school a hundred yards down the street. The four youths stopped, forming a barricade across the pavement; the schoolboys slowed, then stepped off the pavement into the gutter and walked past the sneering street kids. As the schoolboys passed Random, he said, 'Sensible tactics, fellers.'

The boys nodded and passed on. Random looked at Malone. 'Do your kids go to private schools?'

Malone nodded, but made no reply as he and Random caught up with the four youths, who still blocked the pavement as they jeered back at the disappearing schoolboys. 'You're blocking the footpath, sport,' he said to the biggest of the youths.

'So? It's a public footpath, ain't it? Are you a fucking pig?' With a glance down the street towards headquarters.

'Pull your head in, son.' Malone sounded more patient than he felt; he looked at another of the youths. 'Take your mate away, he's only making a nuisance of himself.'

'What else's he got to do? Eh?'

Malone had no answer to that. Random walked past him and he followed him. Random said, 'You can't win, Scobie. Social problems are not our problems, thank Christ. Let's stick to what we've got. So do you want to take leave now?'

They caught the traffic lights and went down Wentworth Avenue. This had once been the mecca for motorcyclists. There had been icon names on the shop-fronts:

Rudge-Whitworth, Ariel, BSA, Indian, Harley-Davidson; Con had told Malone of the great dirt-track riders of the past, Tommy Benstead, Lionel Van Praag. It was a world Malone had been too young to know, but, like the Hollywood of the silent film era, it had held glamour for him. There had been no bikies in those days, Con had told him, no beards, no helmets, no studded leathers. Now there were only one or two shops left; the motorbikes were out in the suburbs. The past was disappearing from the heart of the city.

'I'm tempted. But I hate leaving anything half-done.'

'Okay, stay with it. I'll take over, with Russ Clements doing the donkey work. But don't leave me out on a limb, pointing the finger at someone and leaving me to prove it. You mentioned the brother?'

Malone grinned, held up a finger. 'Intuition, I can feel it on the wind.' It was a joke between them: Random's father had been a farmer who tested the weather with a finger to the wind. 'I don't think he would've pulled the trigger, but he might know who did. Both Russ and I got the feeling he wasn't telling us all he knew.'

Back at the Hat Factory he ran through the running sheets on the computer, looked at the flow charts on the wall of the incident room; the only consoling figures were that there had been no new murders in South Region since the weekend. Other areas had had their homicides, four of them, but they were no concern of his. For once he was glad of the regional system.

He was about to leave with Clements for a visit to Channing and Lazarus when Peta Smith and John Kagal came back to the office. 'Did you see Mrs Channing? The mother?'

'A nice woman,' said Kagal, who never referred to any female as a lady, not even the tea-woman. 'All smiles and no information. A true mother.'

'Would she know what her son does? Either of them?'

'She knows they are lawyers – or were, in Brame's case. But I'm sure that's all she knows. We'd be wasting our time with her, Scobie.'

Malone looked at Peta Smith. 'You agree?'

She nodded, then opened her briefcase. 'I think you should look at this.' She handed him her notebook. 'I got all that from ABS Security's records.'

Malone scanned the notes written in her neat hand. 'You checked the records with someone at ABS?'

'With Ted Gilligan. He's a real old-timer, isn't he? He actually took his hat off when he was speaking to me. Murray Rockman was on the scene of two previous homicides. He wasn't the one who discovered the bodies, but he was on security detail at the time of the murders. One was out at Carlingford, the other out at Homebush – neither of them would've been in our region.'

Malone looked at Clements, then back at Peta Smith. 'Are you suggesting Rockman did the hit in each case?'

'I don't know. But he was *there*, Johnny-on-the-spot on all occasions. Three murders in two and a half years.'

'Four,' said Clements, 'counting his own.'

'Who were the victims at Carlingford and Homebush?' asked Malone.

Peta Smith took the notebook back from Malone, looked at her notes. 'Both small businessmen, owned their own businesses. A Yugoslav named Pijade, out at Carlingford, and a Chinese, Samuel Lee, at Homebush. Pijade owned a plastics firm and Lee an import firm, stuff from Asia. Both very profitable, I gather.'

'Was anyone ever charged with the murders?'

'Nobody.'

'What happened to the firms?'

'They were sold up, I understand. They're still going, but under new owners. But ABS no longer have the security contract.'

'Check the new owners. You do that, John.'

'Sure. Coffee, Peta?'

She smiled at Kagal. 'That'd be nice, sugar. Or do you want me to call you sweetie?'

'If I can interrupt –' said Malone. 'What about Rockman's bank account at the Commonwealth?'

'My next stop,' said Peta. 'I've already got the warrant.'

'Take John with you.'

'No, I'll be all right, it's only routine.'

He didn't argue with her: to do so would be sexist, would say that he didn't think she could be as independent as the rest of the team. 'Righto, come back with something that'll clear everything up for us.'

4

At lunchtime, all his paperwork done, Malone rang Lisa at home. 'How're you feeling?'

'I've just finished ironing four of your shirts and four of Tom's. How do you think I feel?' Then her tone softened, a sigh came down the line like a feather against his ear. 'Darling, I'm *okay*, okay? What I have doesn't knock you down suddenly like a stroke or a heart attack. And it's not like the 'flu, it doesn't make you miserable.'

'It should, the thought of it. It makes me bloody miserable.'

'Just keep your mind on your work.'

'I'd like to knock off now and come home.'

There was silence for a moment, then she said, 'No, don't. I'm determined I'll come out of this all right. But if we sit around holding hands, thinking these might be our last days together –' She broke off, but he had heard no sob in her voice. Then she came back on the line: 'Darling, let's stick to routine.'

'Stuff routine!' Then he realized at once that he was making it no easier for her; he was concerned only for himself. He, too, sighed, said quietly, 'Sorry. You're right. The time to start holding hands is after your op.'

'Isn't it nice that we love each other so much?' she said and hung up.

He put his phone back in its cradle; she had always had a talent for the last word. He was smiling when he looked up to see John Kagal in the doorway of his office. 'I just got some good news,' he said, but didn't elaborate. 'Have you got some?'

'I don't know whether it's good or just intriguing. I checked on the new owners of those two firms out at Carlingford and Homebush. They were bought by two different companies –' He looked at his notes: 'Bern Investments, B-E-R-N, they bought the plastics firm. And Alps Securities, who bought the import outfit, the one owned by the Chinese.'

'What's the intriguing bit?' He knew that Kagal was a bugger for stretching things out; he would have turned the Sermon on the Mount into a filibuster. 'Fill me in. Intrigue me.'

'Both companies could have a Swiss connection. Bern, the Swiss capital, and the Alps.'

'You're stretching it, but yes, let's say you're right. Maybe there's a lot of Swiss money invested here – God knows, they'd have enough, what their pharmaceutical companies make. From what I read, overseas money has been pouring in here this past year.'

'There's more –'

I knew there would be.

'The lawyers who handled the takeovers, both of them, were Channing and Lazarus!' Kagal sat back, closing his notebook with a snap; somehow he managed not to look insufferably smug. 'Oh, what a tangled web we weave, et cetera et cetera.'

'Don't start quoting Bob Dylan at me.'

Kagal smiled. He and Malone had been at odds when he

first joined Homicide, when, almost unconsciously, he had tended to air his superior education. Now there was mutual respect. 'Do you want me to find out who's behind Bern Investments and Alps Securities?'

Then Peta Smith came in carrying a plastic shopping bag. She laid it on Malone's desk and took out a large manilla envelope. 'The bank took a little convincing that Mr Rockman wouldn't be calling to collect this. The warrant was sworn out in the name of Murray Rockman, all we knew. Seems his full name was Alexei Murray Rockman.'

'Alexei?'

She nodded. 'Banks can be as pedantic as lawyers, it seems. But someone else had been in, trying to get the box opened. They produced a letter, supposedly signed by our friend Murray. The bank wouldn't accept that. They wanted a letter from a solicitor, saying Murray, or Alexei, was dead and the solicitors had the authority to open the safe deposit box. The guy, whoever he was, went away and said he'd be back. I've told the bank if he comes back, to ring us immediately and someone will be down there to invite him up here. Right?'

'We'll look forward to talking to him. *If* he comes back . . . Let's see what you've got.'

'An East German passport. The GDR – the passport would be obsolete now, wouldn't it? It was issued in Dresden in 1987. Didn't Murray say he'd been out here twelve years?'

'I'm beginning to think Murray was something of a liar.'

'The passport's in the name of Alexander Repin, with Murray's photo, born Wriezam May 20, 1957. The passport pages are pristine –'

'Pristine?'

'It's a word I picked up from John.' She and Kagal gave each other a smile; the small war between them seemed to be over. 'Not an immigration, entry or exit, stamp on it.

Looks like it was another of Murray's lies, to be used in an emergency.'

'He should've kept it up to date. What else?'

'There's this.' Peta emptied the last of the items from the envelope; among them was a gun. 'A Tokarev, a Russian make.'

'Does it fire nine-millimetre ultras?'

'We'd have to check with Ballistics. But it doesn't look as if it's been fired recently. And then there are these.'

She dropped a bundle of papers on the desk and Malone picked it up. 'Share certificates? BHP?' The Big One, as it was called in its own advertisements: the largest company in Australia. He riffled through the certificates. 'Ten thousand shares. Where's Russ?'

'Here,' said Clements, who had just come in and stood in the doorway.

'You're the stock exchange expert. What would ten thousand BHP shares be worth?'

'I don't own any myself, they're outa my bracket. But right now they're worth about eighteen dollars a share, give or take a few cents.'

Malone dropped the certificates back on his desk. 'One hundred and eighty thousand dollars' worth. Not a bad investment for a security guard on, what, five, six hundred bucks a week?'

'But they're not in his name.' Peta had picked up the bundle. 'They belong to Bern Investments.'

'We're getting into foreign territory here.' Clements was still leaning against the door jamb. 'We don't want to have to go asking the Securities Commission for help. They'll then suggest we get the Crime Authority into it . . .' The four detectives contemplated all the bureaucracies out there, waiting like a giant swamp to engulf them. 'There's gotta be a better way.'

'Put the share certificates back in the envelope,' Malone told Peta Smith. 'Take it back to the bank, tell 'em to put it back where it belongs. If someone comes back to collect it, get 'em to stall him and get on the blower to us.'

'Wouldn't it be better if we staked it out?' said Clements.

'Of course it would,' he said irritably; his mind had slipped out of gear again. 'You take the first shift, Peta, then I'll have Andy Graham relieve you. The safe deposit vault closes when? Four o'clock, five? I assume it's not open round the clock?'

'I don't think so. What do I do if someone comes back while I'm there?'

'Get on the blower and we'll have someone down there within five minutes. You stand by here, John. You can come with Russ and me, Peta.'

'Where are we going?' asked Clements.

'Down to talk to Channing and Lazarus about Bern Investments and Alps Securities.'

He saw the look of mild chagrin on Kagal's face at being excluded. *But that's the way it is, son. Your turn will come, you'll have the rank some day.* From what he remembered of the Bible, even the angels pulled rank.

5

Weekdays the city council put on free entertainment for the lunchtime crowd. The shallow amphitheatre in Martin Place was given over to brass bands, singers, rock bands and gymnasts: today a rock band was testing the cracking level of the surrounding granite walls. Malone and Clements left Peta Smith to go into the Commonwealth Bank. Not so many years ago almost every school child in the country had known of this stately building; their money-boxes had been tin miniatures of the bank. Nowadays children didn't have money-boxes; they had bank accounts or, if they were lucky and so were their parents or grandparents, they had trust accounts. Malone privately thought the industrialized world was raising a crop of creepy little Croesuses.

They continued on down towards the building that housed the offices of Channing and Lazarus. The rock band's singer's voice followed them, telling them he'd got the world on a string.

'He's welcome to it,' said Malone.

'I remember Sinatra singing that. Great.'

'It was a different song, then,' said Malone, dating them both.

The Channing and Lazarus offices were on the middle floor of the building; it was perhaps a sign of their standing, the rents in Martin Place were not cheap; Malone wondered how long they had been here. The receptionist told them Mr Channing was in court this morning, but perhaps Mr Lazarus could see them?

'I thought Mr Lazarus was overseas?' said Malone.

'He got back last night. Unexpectedly,' said the receptionist, then looked as if she should have bitten her tongue on the last word.

Then Mrs Johns, the office manager, appeared, almost materializing out of the walls, or so it seemed to Malone. 'Mr Lazarus? Oh no, he's too busy at the moment. Maybe you could come back, Inspector?'

'I'm afraid not, Mrs Johns. I know it's bad manners, but we police never think people are too busy to see us. It's a conceit we have.' The woman irritated him, but he was in an irritable mood; and then she was trying to manage him and Clements and that wasn't on. 'Tell Mr Lazarus we're here and getting a little impatient.'

She did not like being ticked off in front of a junior; she glared at the receptionist before she turned the glare on Malone. 'Bad manners is right. I'll see what Mr Lazarus has to say.'

She disappeared, this time through an inner door, and Malone grinned at the receptionist. She was in her late twenties, he guessed, not unattractive, the sort of girl who would make a career of sitting at a reception desk and enjoying it. She smiled at him and said softly, 'Take no notice of her. She would've liked to run a concentration camp.' She had learned about concentration camps from seeing *Schindler's List*: history and education now came on the Big Screen. 'Smoodge to her, she likes men who do that.'

Malone looked at Clements. 'You're nominated.'

The camp commandant reappeared. 'Mr Lazarus will see you.' She stood aside to allow the two detectives to pass her, then she followed them into an inner office. 'Mr Lazarus has asked me to stay, to fill him in on anything that has happened while he's been away.'

For the first time Malone noticed that she had a slight trace of accent, though he could not place it and he would not dare to query her. Though she was not old enough to have known concentration camps, maybe she had come from a country where they had been part of recent history. In the past thirty or forty years Australia had become a babel of accents, though now most of them had been overlaid by the flat local one.

Will Lazarus was waiting for them. Except for the Armani suit, hanging on him as if he had lost weight since he had bought it, and the eye-shattering tie, he would not have been out of place in a pillage of seventeenth-century pirates. He had black hair, worn rather long, a neatly trimmed black beard and moustache and a black eye-patch. The whiteness of his wide smile was almost dazzling against its black surrounds. His handshake was ex-cruciatingly firm, his vigorous voice told them he was delighted to see them, he was always willing to help the police. Malone thought he could still be a pirate; he was a complete contrast to his partner Channing.

'A dreadful business, the Brame murder. Rod, my part-ner, rang me about it, I was in Zurich. Have the police, I mean have you made any progress?'

'A little. May we sit down?' He and Clements sat down, neither of them glancing at Mrs Johns, who obviously thought they were making themselves too much at home.

'Of course. Sorry, I'm not quite with it this morning. I'm still getting over the jet lag.'

Lazarus's office reinforced the pirate image. There were prints of sailing ships on the walls; a cabinet in one corner held a collection of antique pistols; crossed swords, like a stripped-down coat-of-arms, hung on the wall between the two tall windows that looked out on to Martin Place. Lazarus had stopped short of flying the skull-and-cross-bones. Malone wondered if clients were supposed to take the decorations seriously.

Lazarus saw him eyeing the crossed swords and smiled and touched his eye-patch. 'That's how I lost my eye. I used to fence.'

'I thought you wore masks?'

'We do. Mine slipped.'

'A nice collection of guns,' said Clements. 'Are you an expert on antique weapons? Guns of any sort?'

One eye, it seems, is less revealing than two; the white smile still remained there amid the black beard, but the dark eye showed nothing. 'No, I'm just a collector, not an expert. Now how can we help you?'

Mrs Johns had pulled up a chair and seated herself beside Lazarus's desk. There had been no invitation from Lazarus to do so; evidently she had her own autonomy in the office. 'I think you would do better to wait till Mr Channing comes back from court.'

The thumping of the rock band had been coming through the closed windows; the singer was ghost-busting, to finish up the gig. Then abruptly it stopped and in the sudden silence those in the room heard the shrill ringing of an alarm-bell.

'Do you respond to those alarms?' said Lazarus and offered another wide smile.

'They're never for us, not in Homicide . . . We'll talk to Mr Channing later. In the meantime . . . Mr Lazarus, what do you know about two firms, Bern Investments and Alps Securities?'

It was a bean-ball, right at the batsman's head; Malone had often bowled it when he had been playing cricket. Of course you apologized profusely, saying the ball had slipped, but neither the batsman nor the umpire believed you: it was part of the game. In this case not one head but two heads ducked; or so it seemed. At least both of them reared back in their chairs as if to let the bean-ball whizz by. Lazarus was the first to recover: 'What should we know, Inspector?'

'They are clients of yours, right?'

Lazarus frowned, as if they were unfamiliar clients. 'Yes, we've done business for them.'

'Very little,' said Mrs Johns, letting them know she was the one who kept the files. And she would keep them efficiently, Malone guessed.

'Are they Australian owned?'

'They are registered here, I believe.'

'That wasn't what I asked.'

'They are proprietary companies, privately owned –'

'Don't fartarse around, Mrs Johns –' Then he stopped. This woman really did get under his skin; yet he knew she was only doing her job. 'There we go again, with our bad manners. But we're not playing games, we're investigating a murder. Two murders. Now, are they Australian owned?'

'*Two* murders?' said Lazarus.

'A security guard, worked for TNT on the monorail – where we found Mr Brame's body. The guard, we think, was killed with the same gun.'

'Jesus, what's going on?' But Lazarus had leaned back, asked the question of the air above him and didn't look for an answer.

'Are the companies Australian owned?' Malone repeated.

'What makes you think they may not be?' Lazarus tilted his head forward again.

'Their names,' said Clements, taking over the bowling. 'Bern and Alps. That suggests they might be Swiss-owned.'

Lazarus and Mrs Johns did not look at each other; but Malone had the distinct impression that something had passed between them. Maybe the dead eye behind the patch had winked at her. Then Lazarus said quietly, all the vigour gone from his voice, 'They are subsidiaries of a holding company, ZPH.'

There were the initials again. Where had all the old names gone: Broken Hill Proprietary, Colonial Sugar Refineries, Australia and New Zealand Bank? 'ZPH – what does that stand for?'

'Zurich Private Holdings.'

'Based in Zurich?' asked Clements, and Lazarus nodded. 'They're registered in Zurich, in a German-speaking canton, and they don't have a German-language name?'

'Zurich Private Holdings is registered here in Sydney but not listed on the Exchange.'

'Where are the directors? Here or in Zurich?'

'Zurich.'

'And you've just come back from Zurich? From seeing them?'

'Yes.' Answers were coming now like drawn teeth. Then Malone's pager beeped.

6

'Even we don't know how much wealth there is in here,' said Mr Axt.

Peta Smith had ambition but no envy. She slid the safe

deposit box back into its slot and looked along the banks of boxes. 'How many boxes are there?'

'Thirteen thousand and not enough.' Mr Axt, the safe deposit manager, was a tall heavily built man who dressed like a floor-walker; though Peta was too young to have witnessed those perambulating paragons from the old department stores. He had clients in this underground chamber who had more wealth than any shoppers back in the days of Farmers and other stores that had employed floor-walkers; he treated them with deference and went home each night wondering how much they really were worth. 'People are more safety-conscious these days. Foreigners, mostly,' he said and one eyelid flickered, though she was not sure that it was a wink.

She had seen those who had come into the vault while she was waiting for Mr Axt. 'Asians?'

'At least fifty per cent of our clients. Hong Kong, mostly. Lots of those of the Jewish faith, too.' He had dropped his voice. 'They've been robbed in the past, I suppose, in other countries. So they're careful and who can blame them? Australians, generally, are not careful, except those who have something to hide.'

'Do you have many of those?'

He smiled, the eyelid flickered again. 'How would we know? You think Mr Rockman had something to hide?'

'We think so. We're just not sure what.' They passed through the round doorway, like a temple entrance. She nodded at the door itself. 'What does that weigh?'

'Thirty tonnes. It's the second biggest in the world, the biggest is in Milan.' Again the smile and the tic of the eyelid. 'For the benefit of the Mafia, one supposes. Or those corrupt Italian politicians. We have none of our politicians amongst our clients,' he said and sounded almost patriotic.

'Was the door made here?'

'No, by Chubbs in England. When they landed it in

Sydney in 1927 there were no trucks that could handle it. So it was hauled up from the wharves on a wagon drawn by twenty, *twenty*, draught horses, Clydesdales.'

'Well, call me at once if the gentleman comes back who wants the Rockman box. I'll sit over there, out of the way.'

'There won't be anything – well, dangerous?'

'Nothing like that, Mr Axt. It'll just be routine.'

She took a seat not far from the enquiry counter, from where Mr Axt or one of his staff could easily signal her. Sitting there in her neat trenchcoat, her rain-hat on her lap, her small briefcase beneath the hat, she looked serene and not at all out of place: a secretary waiting for her boss to arrive to collect papers, a career woman with her own box there inside the vault. She was watching an elderly Chinese couple helping each other up the steps into the vault when Mr Axt, leaning over the counter, signalled her.

She got up and crossed to greet the well-dressed slim man who had turned towards her when Axt had pointed her out to him. 'This is Mr Ballinger, Detective Smith.'

Peta showed her badge, not officiously but merely as identification. 'I wonder if you would mind coming down to our office for some questions, Mr Ballinger? I can have a car here in five minutes for us.'

'May I ask why?' He was middle-aged, short and slim, neat as a store dummy in his well-cut covert topcoat, a white shirt with a conservative blue tie showing in the V of the coat. He had a thin, square-jawed, flat-cheeked face, a wide mouth and he wore thick-rimmed glasses, the sort she thought had gone out of fashion when Buddy Holly died. Yet, though she had taken all this in, the odd thought struck her that he was anonymous-looking, that he would not be noticed in a crowded room.

'You know Mr Rockman was murdered? We know nothing about him and we are hoping you may be able to tell us something.'

For a moment Ballinger looked as if he were about to

refuse, then abruptly he smiled. 'Of course. Shall we wait upstairs?'

Peta Smith called Homicide, asked for back-up, then she and Ballinger went up the marble stairs to the main banking floor. The number of people coming down to the vault seemed to have increased: Peta wondered if they were coming down to lunch on their deposits.

'Did you know Mr Rockman?'

'He was my cousin. That's why I'm here.' He held up a folded letter, but didn't offer it to her. 'He left a will. I gather there is something in his safe deposit box he wanted me to have.' His English was precise but she could detect a faint accent in it. 'I have no idea what he had in mind. Do you know what is in the box?'

'No,' she said.

They were now walking through the main banking chamber, towards the doors out on to Martin Place and the cacophony of the rock band. Mr Axt, escorting her out earlier, had told her about the bank, how its banking chamber was one of the largest in the world, how the glistening green scagliola on the thirty-seven ('count them') columns that supported the high decorated ceiling had been applied by imported Italian tradesmen who had worked behind screens so that the then-secret process would not be disclosed, how marble and bronze and mosaics had been used throughout in the building in a style that not even the crazy spending of the Eighties could have afforded. She liked such grandeur and she resolved that she would transfer her account from her suburban branch to here, just so that she could come and walk among the splendour of the past. She had a yearning for the past and regretted missing it.

'The car won't be long,' she said. 'We'll wait for it in Elizabeth Street. You don't mind coming?'

'Not at all,' he said. 'Anything I can do to help –'

He stood back to allow her to go out through the doors

into Martin Place; then he followed her out into the storm of music. It hit them like a physical blow; Peta shook her head as if the aural thugs had assaulted her. Then she felt the two jolts in her back and the excruciating pain as one of the bullets shattered her spine. She went down in a heap, saw Ballinger step past her and disappear, then her vision blurred and she felt something warm coming out of her mouth as she coughed. The music storm suddenly stopped and somewhere an alarm-bell began ringing. Her vision cleared for a moment and she looked up into the horrified face of Mr Axt.

'I'm dy –' she whispered in surprise, then abruptly there was only silence and blackness.

Chapter Six

1

'We should never have left her on her own!'

'Scobie, dammit, stop blaming yourself! For Chrissake, how were we to know he'd actually shoot her in the street! The fucking crowd saw nothing – everyone was looking at the fucking band –' Clements's anger had no direction; he looked as if he wanted to beat at walls. 'If we'd been with her, he'd have shot all three of us. The guy's a *killer* –'

Clements looked around them. He had taken Malone aside when he saw how upset the other man was by Peta Smith's murder. Over the years there had been other police officers killed, men they had known sometimes for years; this was the first time a woman officer had been killed and Malone was taking it hard. Too hard, in Clements's opinion. He himself was angry and upset, but he did not think they should take the blame for what had happened.

They were in the main banking chamber, away from the stares of the crowd outside in Martin Place. Peta's body had been taken away and the Physical Evidence team had arrived and were at work; this section of the main hall had been roped off with the usual blue-and-white ribbons. Customers and bank staff had been herded to the far side of the big square of counters; the counter on this side, the foreign currency desk, was deserted. Half a dozen senior bank officials stood in a nearby group, looking as if lost in their own domain.

'Come on, mate, snap out of it!'

Malone had the odd feeling of stepping back into himself,

as if for a few moments he had been let loose in another character. Normally he was in control of his emotions; sometimes it had been difficult, but the effort had always been successful. He was as surprised as Clements at his reaction to Peta Smith's death. 'I'm all right, Russ. Let's talk to Mr Axt.'

Axt was still visibly shaken by what he had witnessed. 'I was coming after her – she'd left her hat on the counter when she phoned –' He looked around for the hat, but it was nowhere in sight. His large round face was pale and he kept working his mouth, as if afraid he might not be able to control whatever he had to say. 'Sorry. I have a daughter about her age . . .' He was in his shirtsleeves, one cuff bloodstained. He had cradled Peta Smith in his arms, holding her to him while he yelled for help; someone had since taken away his bloodstained jacket. 'It all happened so quickly.'

'Would you know the man again if you saw him?'

'Yes, yes, of course –' Then he stopped and his thick eyebrows came down to touch the top of his gold-framed spectacles. 'I *think* I would, I mean if you put him in, what do you call it, a line-up? But I'm not sure. He was small and thin, he wore thick-rimmed glasses . . . You wouldn't believe it, would you? He came here twice, and yet . . .'

'We'd believe it,' said Malone. 'Sometimes we've had six people give six different descriptions of someone we've wanted to interview. How was he dressed?'

'Very smart, I remember *that*.' Clothes made the man in his eye: Malone knew how numerous his sort of observer was. 'He looked – *English*. You *know* – he wore an English-type overcoat, covert-cloth, I think they call it. He carried his hat in his hand, but it was an English hat, too. You know, a soft brown hat, a trilby. He was thin – but I've said that. Come to think of it, he was – *anonymous*. I guess that's the word. Anonymous.'

Malone didn't want to tell him that thin people generally

were more anonymous-looking than stout people: that would be a rude comment on Mr Axt's own build. 'Did he ever get down into the actual vault?'

Axt was gathering himself together, a large task. He was not so innocent as to be totally shocked by what had happened: hold-ups and the occasional killing occurred regularly in banks, or so it seemed these days. But they usually occurred in bank branches, not here in head office. He *was* shocked that he had held a dying girl in his arms, a stranger who had looked at him in the last seconds of her life with her eyes full of a terrible fear. It was a sort of confession and it unsettled him that she had laid it on him. It made him wonder to whom he would confess his own fear of dying.

'What? No, we never gave him a pass to go into the vault. But he did come downstairs –'

'Did he appear upset when you refused to let him look at Mr Rockman's box?'

'You mean yesterday? No–o.' He seemed to be having trouble putting the days together in his mind. 'No, he just accepted it. He was very polite, said he understood the reason. Then he got up and left, he wasn't in my office more than a couple of minutes. Come to think of it, I suppose he didn't want me to remember him, right?'

As a detective Malone didn't like other people playing detective; but occasionally the amateurs were on the right track.

'Mr Axt, I want you to talk with one of our officers, so we can build a picture of Mr Ballinger.'

'Of course, of course.' Axt was eager to help, as if he was embarrassed at his poor memory of Mr Ballinger.

Malone left him, had a few words with the senior bank officials, then he and Clements went out through the roped-off entrance where Peta Smith had died. Both men stepped round the white outline where her body had lain, not even glancing at it; she was not to be remembered as a rough sketch. Once outside they stood a moment looking up and down Martin Place, almost as if hoping the murderer would obligingly come back to the scene of his crime. The rock band had packed up and gone to wherever bands disappeared to when the music stopped; a group of young people stood some distance away staring at the fluttering crime scene tapes as if expecting something festive to happen.

'Let's go back and continue with Mr Lazarus,' Malone said.

When his pager had beeped, his first thought was that Peta was calling him from the bank up the street to tell him that the man they were looking for was at hand. Then, as he asked for permission to use Lazarus's phone, he realized that if Peta indeed wanted him she would not have paged him but would have called him direct at the Channing and Lazarus office. He dialled Homicide and was put through at once to John Kagal. The younger man had been distressed, but his message was clear. Malone had put down the phone, stood up and was at the door before he stopped and looked back at Clements. *Peta's been shot.*

'You're all right?' said Clements now. 'You think we both are?'

'I'm not going back to the office to sit staring at the bloody wall. Come on.'

Two minutes later he was glad he had not gone back to his own office. He and Clements got two birds with the one visit: Channing was back from his court appearance and he and Lazarus were having a sandwich lunch in Channing's office. Both men got to their feet as the two detectives were ushered in by the receptionist. Mrs Johns was apparently still out at lunch, a long one, Malone hoped.

'We heard the brief report on the radio,' said Lazarus. 'She's dead?'

Malone nodded, fired a wild one: 'Shot, we believe, by someone connected with our other two murders.'

'They shot a *police officer*?' Channing's voice finished on a high, almost squeaky note.

'I don't think they're too careful about who they shoot. The president of the American Bar, a security guard, a woman detective –' The sarcasm was rougher than usual, but it was sarcasm born of anger. Not at Channing but at the whole circumstance that had brought about Peta Smith's death. 'I think you have to start giving us a few more facts, Mr Channing. You too, Mr Lazarus.'

'Facts? What sort of facts?' Channing looked at his partner. 'You told them all we know, didn't you? You and June?'

'Not quite,' said Malone, getting in first. 'We were talking about a client of yours in Zurich when Sergeant Clements and I were called away. Z-something-or-other.'

'ZPH,' said Clements, notebook open in his hand. 'Can we sit down? This may take some time.'

He sat down and Malone did the same. The two partners stood a moment, looked at each other, then they sank almost gingerly back on to their chairs. An outsider witnessing the moment would have assumed that Malone and Clements were the hosts and the two lawyers the guests. Except that the latter were at the big wide desk, Channing behind it and Lazarus to one side. As if their appetites had simultaneously disappeared, both men folded the paper that had wrapped their sandwiches and put the small packages to one side.

'Zurich Private Holdings,' said Clements. 'Is it Swiss-owned?'

'It is Swiss-based, but the company is registered here.'

'Mr Channing –' Clements was showing a lot of patience. Malone let him hold the floor: the big man was doing all right. And he was the expert of the two of them on business affairs. 'Don't let's start playing games again, like we did yesterday. Is ZPH Swiss-*owned*?'

The partners exchanged glances and Channing said,

'You know them better than I do, Will.'

'Thanks,' said Lazarus and sounded as if he had been left out on the end of a slim limb. 'Sergeant, we have no idea who owns ZPH. They deal with us through a Swiss bank and I'm sure they've satisfied the bank they are legitimate, whoever they are. The old Swiss blind eye doesn't apply any more.' He touched his eye-patch and smiled, like the quick flashing of a piano keyboard. 'They have been perfectly above board in their dealings with us, prompt in paying their bills. We have handled several takeovers for them.'

'How many?' said Malone.

'Seven or eight. Eight.'

'We'd like a list of them,' said Clements. 'ZPH has an office here in Australia?'

Lazarus shook his head. 'No.'

'They're registered here and they don't have an office?'

'Not as such. They're just a name on a door.'

'Whose door?'

There was a slight hesitation, a rubbing of the eye-patch as if the socket behind it had begun to itch. 'Ours.'

'You said they paid their bills promptly.' Clements was not letting up. 'On what account are the cheques drawn and where?'

'I'm afraid I'm going to have to draw the line there – that's confidential between us as lawyers and our clients.' Lazarus's voice had a rasp to it now.

Malone took over again, changing the tack a little: 'What about Bern Investments and Alps Securities?'

Again the slight hesitation, the pause of someone stepping off a kerb: 'Yes, they have an office here.'

'You know, Mr Lazarus,' said Malone, 'I'd hate to play poker with you. You take forever to put your cards on the table.'

'I guess it's because I'm a lawyer.' Lazarus gave him a cold eye.

'Probably. What's the address of Bern and Alps or are they on your door, too?'

'They are just up the road, in Castlereagh Street.' Channing came in, as if afraid of an unnecessarily rough reply from his partner. Channing was a smoother, Malone guessed, a man forever pouring oil, even on untroubled waters. The forceful portrait behind him mocked him. 'In the building with the trees in front of it. They have the one office. It's only small, just a manager and a typist, Mrs Johns tells me. No more than a mail-drop, I'd say.'

'But you deal through them rather than direct with ZPH?' said Clements. 'Most of the time, that is?'

'Yes.'

'How many times have you been to see the directors of ZPH in Zurich, Mr Lazarus?' said Malone. He and Clements were now working the old switch-the-bowling technique. It was an old ploy, ancient under other names. 'Play a quick card on this one. We can always check.'

'Half a dozen times.' Then Lazarus added, as if Malone were already checking: 'Four times in the past three months.'

'What are the names of the directors?'

The cards were played slowly again: 'There are only two, as far as I know. Or have met. Mr Federal and Mr Dietrich.'

'No Mr Ballinger?'

'Who?' Both partners frowned.

Malone held back on that, said instead, 'Do the directors of ZPH ever come to Sydney?'

'Occasionally,' said Channing. He and Lazarus were now trying the switch-the-bowling technique; but they were purely defensive.

'We take it they are Swiss?'

Malone had looked at Lazarus because the bearded man, given his temperament and the fact that he now appeared tired, suffering from jet lag, seemed the more likely to make the give-away reply. But it was Channing who answered, 'As far as we know, yes. Swiss-German. We've never asked to look at their passports,' he added, but managed a smile with it.

'Well, we can ask the manager up at Bern Investments. He should know.' Malone stood up. 'Unless they're somehow involved in our murders, we're not really interested in what ZPH do here in Australia, so don't get your balls in a knot on that account. We don't interfere in the affairs of the Securities Commission.'

Both lawyers glared at him: Lazarus's one eye was the more baleful.

'All we're interested in is finding who murdered three people. Your brother, Mr Channing. The security guard. And especially our colleague Detective-Constable Smith. Especially her.'

With that he turned and left the room, so quickly that he had to wait for Clements out in the reception lobby. The latter caught up with him: 'Next time you're gunna leave me sitting there like a shag on the rock, let me know.'

'I had to get out of there before I did my block.' Malone stopped beside the main office door. On it, in small gold letters, was a table of at least twenty names. 'There, in the middle. ZPH Proprietary Limited. I wonder how many other companies are just names on that door, nothing more?'

'Don't complicate things, mate. Simmer down. You're boiling.'

They waited for the lift doors to open. When they did, out stepped another irritant: 'Hello, Mrs Johns.'

She looked startled; or disturbed, as if afraid she had missed something by not being here. 'Oh! I didn't think you'd be back. Not when I heard what had happened –' She gestured, handbag in one hand, a plastic shopping bag in the other; she looked awkward, something one wouldn't have expected of her. 'They said a policewoman had been shot –'

Malone nodded. 'One of our colleagues, someone both of us worked with. We think there's a connection between her murder and here –' He jerked his head, taking in the reception lobby and the offices that lay behind it. 'G'day, Mrs Johns. We'll be back, I'm sure. Keep an eye on the files.'

Clements had been holding open the doors of the lift. Both men stepped in and the doors closed. 'Jesus,' said Clements, 'you were a bit strong then, weren't you?'

'You think they'll sue us? No worries, chum. I may be way off beam, but it's not going to hurt to make them worry. They know much more than they're telling us, so they're not going to throw shit at the fan by issuing us with a writ.' The anger at Peta Smith's murder was building up in him again. 'Let's go and talk to Bern Investments. If *their* bloke starts giving us the runaround, I think I'll knock his bloody teeth in!'

Clements was silent till they reached the ground floor. Then as the doors opened he said quietly, 'Don't take this mood home to Lisa, okay? She's got enough to worry about.'

Malone knew then where his fear and anger came from. He felt the pain of death, not his own but the death that brings the sense of loss that overwhelms. When he had lifted the green plastic shroud and looked down at Peta Smith he had been looking at Lisa.

2

The Bern Investments office was in a high-rise block that appeared to grow out of a rain forest. It had been the architect's whim to plant trees that grew thick and tall in the forecourt; the bones of failed entrepreneurs of the Eighties were said to lie among the under-growth. Today the forest just looked drab and forlorn in the winter drizzle that had started in the last half-hour.

Malone and Clements rode up to the floor where Bern Investments and Alp Securities had their office. The names of both firms were lettered in gold on the thick oak door; there was no welcoming lettering, no Knock and Enter. But the door of the office was locked; there was no reply to their knock. They rode down again to the lobby. The man behind the reception desk there was pale and dismal, as if looking out on the rain forest day after day had depressed him beyond hope. Malone, mood lightening, wondered if he were anti-conservation.

'Bern Investments? Yeah, Mr Dourane went out no more than five minutes ago, just before you got here. His secretary was with him.'

'Dourane – how do you spell that?'

'D-O-U-R-A-N-E. You want to leave a message?'

'No, thanks, I think they got a message.' Malone and Clements walked out into Castlereagh Street, stood against a wall to shelter from the drizzle. 'Lazarus or Channing called them as soon as we left their office. We'll check on Mr Dourane, find out where he lives. You'd better warn Immigration, too, just in case. He may be a true-blue Aussie, for all we know, but true-blue Aussies flee the country just like other buggers.'

'You're starting to label everybody connected with this as shonky.'

'Wouldn't you?'

He looked up and down the long narrow street. A courier on a bicycle, head down against the drizzle, pushed into the wind coming from the south, looking like a crippled bird under his plastic cape. They were ubiquitous, these couriers, descendants of the military despatch riders, risking life and limb as they wove in and out amongst the shellfire of abuse from motorists and pedestrians. They were a bloody nuisance.

Malone sighed: he had his own couriering to do: 'I'm

going out to see Peta's dad. He'll be at work, unless he's already got the bad news. He's out at Newtown, he works in a liquor warehouse.'

'You want me to come with you?'

'No, you trace Mr Dourane. Find out where he lives, use all your dirty illegal contacts in Social Services or Telecom or whatever. I'll be back in an hour and we'll go and see him.'

'How will you get out to Newtown?'

'I'll be rash and take a taxi.' He hated even spending the office petty cash. Given time and the opportunity, he could have reduced the National Debt. 'I'll drop you off on the way.'

The taxi driver was young and talkative, with a long lugubrious face that hid a cheerful nature. 'Bloody awful weather, isn't it, but we shouldn't complain. We're still breathing, right? You're cops? You been on that shooting down in Martin Place? A woman cop. Well, her troubles are over, right? No disrespect, but I'm right, right? You drive a cab and you gotta be philosophical or what's the point? I'm a computer analyst, I been looking for a job two years now, I've written I dunno how many letters, always the same reply, up yours, yours sincerely. But I'm still breathing, right?'

Clements got out at the Hat Factory and Malone continued on with the driver. 'You going home?'

'No,' said Malone from the back seat. 'I'm going out to tell a man his daughter's dead.'

'Oh,' said the driver and was silent for the rest of the journey. When Malone got out of the taxi the driver shook his head as the fare was held out. 'It's on me, mate. I wouldn't be in your shoes for quids.'

Malone stood in the thin rain and watched him drive away, all his irritation at the driver's talkativeness suddenly gone. There was still charity to be found without one's having to dig for it. Feeling better but still apprehensive he turned to go into Horlicks Liquor Centre.

Here in Newtown he was less than a mile from his parents' house, where he had been born and reared; these streets had once been his streets, but he had always managed to avoid the street gangs. This particular street was a narrow one-way thoroughfare of mostly one-storeyed terrace houses, their doors and windows shut against the cold and the rain and the intruders who had not been a menace in his day. On the opposite corner of a side street was a small mum-and-dad store, a survivor against the supermarkets, a tiny fort that, despite the defiance on its windows – We'll Meet Anyone's Prices! – was fighting a losing battle. Malone turned and went into the Liquor Centre, a two-storeyed warehouse that had a faintly familiar air, though for the moment he couldn't place it.

Peta Smith's father was just leaving for home. He was a well-built, red-headed man who, in normal circumstances, might have been as cheerful as the taxi driver. His gingerlashed eyes were dim now, but there were laugh-lines around them and his wide mouth, even now, could smile a weak welcome to Malone, whom he had met once at a police function. 'You didn't need to come, Mr Malone. I know how hard it must be for you.'

'Better me than a stranger – Lou, isn't it? How did you know about it? You know how it happened?'

'Not the details. One of my mates heard it on the radio. I want to get home before the wife hears about it.'

'She's probably being told right now. They'd have someone from the local station go to see her. Where d'you live?'

'Marrickville. I better be going, my car's out the back –'

He led the way through the low banks of stacked wine cases, of beer and whisky and gin; there was enough liquor here to drown a world of sorrows. Several men stood aside to let Smith and Malone pass, murmuring condolences, standing there with the awkwardness of men unaccustomed to handling sympathy. Malone detected a sweetly sickly smell, as if a case of sweet sherry had been dropped: he had tasted the same smell on cheap drunks. Unconsciously he wrinkled his nose and Lou Smith nodded and made a face.

'Marsala,' he said. 'I dropped a case of it when they gave me the news.' They paused at the rear door of the warehouse. 'Can I give you a lift?'

'No, I'll be okay. Lou –' He put a hand on the other man's arm. 'We'll get whoever did it. We have some clues –'

Smith nodded absently. 'Sure. But it doesn't really matter now, does it?'

'It does to us. Peta would've expected it of us.'

Smith pondered that a moment, staring out at the rain. 'Yeah, I guess so. It just doesn't help – not now, anyway.'

'There'll be a counsellor call on you and Mrs Smith –'

'No, thanks.' He shook his head stubbornly. 'The wife and I weren't brought up that way. You can't handle grief on your own, there's something wrong with you. The world is full of bloody psychiatrists and analysts and social workers and priests and the world gets worse by the day. You wonder who's to blame.' Then he suddenly leaned against the door jamb and began to weep.

Malone kept his hand on the other man's arm; to withdraw it would be almost a withdrawal of sympathy. Back in the warehouse the other men stood unmoving amongst the thousands of bottles. The rain stopped, dripped from the lintel of the doorway like heavy tears. Lou Smith shuddered with a deep sob, dried his eyes with a red handkerchief, a splash of colour in the greyness.

'Sorry. I'll be okay by the time I get home – better to get rid of that now. Have you ever lost anyone?'

'No.' Not yet.

'We lost Peta's brother. AIDS. He got it through a transfusion.' There was no mistaking the defensiveness in his voice. 'Two years ago. And now this –'

'Peta never mentioned it.' But then why should she have?

Two years ago she had not been with Homicide, he hadn't known she existed. Unable to think of anything else to say, he said, 'We'll find him, Lou. Trust us.'

Lou Smith nodded. 'Yeah, you said that. Good luck. But really, right now I don't give a damn. Thanks for coming.'

He left abruptly, running across the shining asphalt of the parking lot to a pale green Toyota. He drove away without looking back at Malone, going too fast and having to jerk to a stop as he was about to turn into the side street and a truck, horn blaring, came past. Malone hoped he would reach home safely.

He went back into the warehouse, asked to use the phone in the manager's office and called for a taxi. Then he went out and stood in the front doorway to wait for it. As he stood there he suddenly remembered why the place was familiar. He had been six years old, on his way home from primary school, and he had stopped when he had seen the crowd outside what had then been a bakery. A man had shot his girlfriend, who worked in the bakery, then come out and shot himself outside the entrance. His body had been lying on the hot pavement, it had been the middle of summer, and a baker's apron had been thrown over the man's head and upper chest. A pool of dark blood lay on one side of the body, flour sprinkling it like a baker's decoration. It had been his first sight of death.

3

Clements was waiting for him back at Homicide. The atmosphere in the office was heavy; for all their chauvinism, the men had liked and respected Peta Smith. To add to their mood was the police culture: killing a cop was the unforgivable sin. There were half a dozen detectives in the big outer office and they all looked at Malone when he came in. 'How'd it go?' said John Kagal.

'I only saw her father, he was pretty cut up, like you'd expect. I told him we'd get the bastard. Understood?'

All the men nodded. The triple murder case had all at once become personal.

Malone went into his office, slumped down opposite Clements. 'Well?'

Clements looked at his notebook. He had a prodigious memory, but he never neglected taking notes. Police officers with faulty memories were sitting ducks in a court. 'Mr John Dourane lives out at Arncliffe, would you believe, two streets away from our dead friend Murray Rockman. I don't know the secretary's name, so I couldn't check on her.' He looked at his watch. 'You wanna go out and talk to Mr Dourane now?'

Malone was weary, washed out: all he wanted was to go home. But he heaved himself out of his chair, took his hat and raincoat off the hook behind his door. The raincoat was a Burberry, a present last Christmas from Lisa's parents, another of the expensive presents he resented their giving him. It irritated him that his resentment was ungracious and unnecessary; Jan and Elizabeth Pretorius could well afford the gift, but all his life it had been as if presents were some form of charity. Once again, as an hour earlier, he had a memory of childhood, of his father going out on a long strike down on the wharves, and him and his mother going to the local St Vincent de Paul depot for him to be outfitted in clothes to wear to school. Each time he put on the raincoat he felt he was still being outfitted by someone else. His stupid outlook annoyed him, but he could do nothing about it.

They rode out to Arncliffe in an unmarked police car. The rain had gone, the sky had cleared, the wind had dropped; but the cold remained like iron against the skin. They crossed a polluted stream where detergent floated like dirty snow, turned under a railway line and found the street where Mr Dourane should be living. As they got out of the car Malone was glad of the Burberry.

Arncliffe lies about five or six kilometres south of the heart of Sydney. Originally its rich black soil had been covered by thick timber, an ideal hide-out for convicts escaping from the colony, a haunt for footpads preying on the occasional traveller heading south, and a camping ground for roving Aborigines who killed the convicts and the footpads as fair game. The forest was thinned out as bark collectors, sawyers and charcoal burners moved in, the rich soil was exposed and the wealthy landowners set up their small pretentious mansions. Time passed and so did the fortunes of the landowners as the chills and influenza of capitalism, recession and depression, came and went. Properties were cut up, streets were laid out. Gone were the convicts and the footpads and the Aborigines and the charcoal burners and the wealthy farmers. In came the railway and suburbia. A municipality was formed, graft arrived and civilization was complete.

A 747 roared low overhead, planing down to the airport two kilometres away. Malone looked up and only then saw the mosque on the hill, its white minaret looking like a lighthouse that had lost its sea. Then on the other side of the road two women in black *chadors* went by, eyes averted, dark ghosts who disappeared into a house where a man stood on its porch staring at the two strangers who had just got out of their car.

Then Clements, who wore his prejudices casually, like the tie of a not particularly distinguished school, said, 'We're in Arabia, mate. Wogland.'

Then Malone remembered the tensions of three or four years ago, when Lebanese youths from the district and veterans from the local Returned Soldiers League had clashed. Graffiti, the new banners of war, had splattered walls; a war memorial had been defaced. Reason on both sides had eventually prevailed, but even now the peace was uneasy; racism, on both sides, simmered like hot mud beneath the veneer of community relations. Worst of all the police had the reputation of not understanding Arab culture and there had been one or two ugly incidents since the Arncliffe clash. Malone all at once wished Mr Dourane lived somewhere else. Say on the North Shore, where the veneer was thicker, though still only a crust.

'Dourane? Is that a Muslim name?'

'I dunno. I thought it might of been French. Maybe he's French-Algerian, French-Moroccan, one of those North African wogs.'

The houses in the street were modest, on fifteen-metre lots. The Dourane house was larger than the others, on a double block. A walled verandah ran across the front of the house and the entrance was at the side. A driveway led up one side of the house to the entrance; a late-model Saab was parked there, its boot-lid raised. As the two detectives walked up the driveway a man came out of the entrance carrying two suitcases. He pulled up when he saw Malone and Clements, stood stockstill with the two big suitcases almost pulling his arms out of their sockets. Then he let them drop and raised his arms as in a gesture of surrender.

'Mr Dourane?' Malone introduced himself and Clements, showing his badge. 'May we have a word?'

Dourane was tall and broad-shouldered, with a dark mane of hair, a lean handsome face and an air of panic. Malone raised himself on his toes, waiting for the man to turn and bolt; Clements had eased his way up the far side of the car, ready to come at Dourane from the rear. Then Dourane dropped his arms and flipped his hands outwards as if to say, *What's the use?*

'You want to come in the house?' He had a deep pleasant voice, thickened at the moment by unease. 'The neighbours –'

'What about your bags?' said Clements.

'I'll put them in the boot –'

'No, I'll help you carry 'em back inside. I don't think

143

you'll be going anywhere for a while, Mr Dourane.'

For a moment Dourane again looked as if he might try to escape, then he shrugged and picked up both suitcases and led the way up some steps into the house. As they came into the hallway a young woman came through from the back of the house.

'Linda, these two gentlemen are from the police.'

Her mouth opened and she blinked. She was tall and slim, with auburn hair that might or might not have been tinted, light blue eyes and lips that reminded Malone of the pout of the current crop of teenage models. She was dressed in a dark blue suit, had her handbag under one arm and carried a dark blue topcoat and a blue-and-white silk scarf. She was going away; or had been: 'You've come for *us*?'

There was no mistaking the emphasis on the word; Malone picked it up: 'There's someone else?'

'No,' said Dourane, putting down the bags. 'There's no one else. Let's go into the living room.'

He led the way into a room that had a mix of furniture, of East and West. There were two brass side-tables, one of them holding a polished copper coffee pot, the other a *hookah*; a comfortable suite of a couch and two deep chairs; a Persian rug on the plain beige Axminster; a television set under a lurid portrait of Saddam Hussein. The dictator balefully eyed the two Western scumbags.

'Where were you going, Mr Dourane?' said Malone.

'Surfers Paradise, the Gold Coast. Just a holiday break, to get away from the cold.' Malone couldn't argue with that; he and Lisa and the children had been looking forward to the same escape with their now-cancelled holiday. 'What is this about? We are not used to visits from the police.'

'May we sit down?' It seemed that nobody today was offering the police a seat.

'Of course. Please sit.' At times Dourane's accent thickened, there was an awkward formality to his phrases. He was beginning to look uncomfortable. 'Do you wish to talk to my wife, also?'

'I think she should stay. Does your wife work with you at Bern Investments?'

Dourane glanced at his wife, then nodded. 'Yes, she acts as my secretary.'

'Then I think she should stay. She would know what's in the files.' Then he bowled the first beamer: 'Do you know a man named Murray Rockman?'

Out of the corner of his eye he was watching Mrs Dourane. She lifted her head at the name, but it was Dourane who said, 'No, I have never heard of him.'

'He lived just two streets away. He was murdered Monday night. He worked for a security company that provides security for a company owned by Bern Investments. I thought you might've read about the murder.'

'No.'

'It was also on TV.'

'No.'

'Mrs Dourane?'

She was sitting on the arm of the couch, still carrying her handbag and topcoat, still eager to be off to the Gold Coast. 'No, I'm sorry, I've never heard of him.'

'You're not interested in reading about murders in the newspapers?' said Clements. 'When the victim could be called a near-neighbour?'

'I never read the newspapers.'

Malone had never actually heard anyone make that claim before, but a recent survey had reported that 65 per cent of the adult population now got all their news from television. The written word was no longer held in respect, the voters wanted pictures.

Mrs Dourane was remarkably composed, ready, it seemed, for any questions. Malone began to wonder if she had previous experience of police questioning. She said, 'There's too much violence, who wants to read about it all the time? Or watch it on TV? That's when I get up and do something else.'

'Sensible,' said Malone. 'What d'you know about ZPH, Mr Dourane? Zurich Private Holdings.'

Dourane took his time, gathering his thoughts as he might gather papers on his desk. 'They own the companies I work for. Several of them, including Bern Investments.'

'Do you know the directors of ZPH?'

'I've met only one of them.'

Here we go, drawing teeth again. 'He has a name?'

Dourane bit his bottom lip, then nodded. 'Mr Federal.'

'Federal? As in Federal government?'

Dourane smiled, as if the idea was ridiculously amusing; his smile was mirrored by his wife's. 'Yes, I suppose so. Mr Martin Federal.'

'And he's what? Swiss?' There was always a point to repeating questions: sometimes you got conflicting answers.

'I believe so.'

'How often does he come to Sydney to see how ZPH is going?'

There was just the faintest hesitation. 'He comes and goes.'

'We all do that, Mr Dourane, come and go. Do you have an address for him?'

'No. He stays in hotels. The Ritz-Carlton, the Regent. Expensive ones.'

'Is he in town now?'

'No.'

He's lying, thought Malone: he had seen the true answer in Mrs Dourane's face. 'Dourane? Are you French? Or French-Swiss?'

'No, I am Afghan.' The chin lifted a little.

'Are you descended from the Afghan camel drivers who came out here last century?' Even as he said it, Malone knew it was an insult, one he hadn't intended.

Dourane was insulted, there was no mistaking that. 'My people were the Douranees, most of us Pathans. The British never conquered us, not even in their great days. My ancestors were never camel drivers.'

'You've put your foot in the camel dung, Inspector,' said Mrs Dourane, looking pleased.

'I apologize. You're not Afghan, are you?'

'No, I'm fifth-generation Australian. There might even be some Abo blood in me, but I don't think so. Certainly no camel driver's blood.'

Clements stepped in before the questioning could be side-tracked. 'Do you know a Mr Ballinger?'

Dourane's frown of puzzlement looked genuine. 'Ballinger? No. Who is he?'

'He's the man who just shot and killed a colleague of ours. It'll be on TV tonight, if you care to look.' He glanced at Mrs Dourane. 'But I thought Mr Channing or Mr Lazarus would have told you about it when they called to say we were coming up to your office.'

The Douranes' faces went stiff. Then the front doorbell rang. Mrs Dourane half-rose, but her husband gestured for her to sit. 'It's nobody, a hawker or someone. Leave them.'

The bell rang again, a finger staying on the button. Clements rose. 'I'll go.'

He went out into the hallway, opened the door and Malone heard him say, 'Well, hel–*lo*, Mrs Johns! Come right in.'

The two of them came into the living room. Mrs Johns wore a tan trenchcoat with a fur collar, a scarf over her head, carried a large handbag and two travel agents' envelopes. She looked very uncomfortable, had completely lost her air of management.

'Are those Mr and Mrs Dourane's tickets for the Gold Coast?' said Clements.

'What? Yes.' She held them out towards Mrs Dourane,

who was closest to her, but Clements intercepted them. 'You have no right –'

Clements ignored her, took the airline tickets from the envelopes, looked at them, then looked at Dourane. 'Thai Airlines, two first-class tickets to Zurich via Bangkok. A roundabout way to the Gold Coast, Mr Dourane. Or does Zurich have a Gold Coast, with all those banks there?'

There was silence in the room. From somewhere, perhaps the house next door, there came a wailing; someone sounded as if he was practising a prayer, perhaps an apprentice muezzin from the mosque on the hill. It was an eerie sound to Malone's and Clements's ears; Mrs Johns also looked startled. Dourane just looked annoyed, like an unbeliever who knew the futility of prayer.

Then Malone said, 'Righto, Mrs Johns, you want to tell us what's going on?'

She drew herself together, physically. 'No, I don't think I do. Has Mr Dourane told you anything?'

'Nothing.'

'Then that's the way it stays, Inspector. You know, lawyer–client confidentiality.'

'You're not his lawyer, Mrs Johns.'

'Don't split hairs, Inspector. I'm employed by Mr Dourane's solicitors.'

The prayer next door suddenly stopped in mid-note, as if the praying one had been choked off or, worse, given up hope. Malone stood up. 'You had better come back to Homicide with us, Mr and Mrs Dourane. You can get on the phone to your office, Mrs Johns, and tell either Mr Channing or Mr Lazarus they'd better come up to Homicide and look after their clients.'

'There's no necessity for all this –'

'Oh, I think there is, Mrs Johns. When we have three murders on our hands, especially one of a policewoman, there's always a necessity. It's what you lawyers call due diligence.'

It has been said before: the North Shore of Sydney is a social state of mind, not a geographical location. The nearest body of water is some kilometres away, its shoreline never visited by the majority of the North Shore elements. Monogamy is still the preferred way for the married; living in sin is no longer frowned upon but neither is it blessed. Homosexuality occasionally raises its airy-fairy head but, like voting Labor, it is not considered socially acceptable. McDonald's and Pizza Hut have invaded the region, but they are looked upon as unavoidable social necessities, like regimental brothels in other invasions elsewhere. In the upper reaches of the North Shore money doesn't drip from the eaves of the mansions like silver wistaria, but Mercedes and BMWs are left lying around like expendable toys.

Rod and Ruth Channing lived at Roseville, the southern verge; anywhere south of there was submerged territory, socially speaking. In recent years there had been newspaper references, prompted by real estate agents, to some area called the Lower North Shore, but the use of the adjective showed where it figured on the social scale.

Joanna Brame knew none of this; nor would she have cared to know. She was the better class of snob, one who protected only her own class structure; she was uninterested in classifications in other societies. She had come to dinner here at Ruth Channing's unexpected invitation and as an excuse to avoid having dinner with Karl Zoehrer. She was glad that, back home, a continent would separate her from him.

The Channing house was in a quiet tree-lined street – 'This is one of our better areas, madam,' the hire-car driver had told her. He was garrulous, but it had already occurred to her that any Australian behind a wheel was that way; they seemed to assume that any passenger in the back seat was dying for a dialogue. 'Very solid. But I guess they all have problems like the rest of us, eh?'

'I'm sure,' said Joanna, hoping he wouldn't go on to tell her about *his* problems.

When Ruth Channing opened the front door, Joanna immediately smelled the liquor on her breath. 'Mrs Brame! How nice to meet you after all these years –'

What years were those? 'Mrs Channing.'

'Oh no, no! Ruth. *Ruth!*'

The poor woman, thought Joanna, she thinks I'm the Queen; she hoped Ruth, *Ruth*, wouldn't curtsey. Then, behind her hostess, standing in the doorway of a room, she saw Milly Channing, who smiled and came forward like an old friend with hands outstretched. 'Come in, Joanna. I had no idea you were coming till Ruth told me. These are my grandchildren. Do you have any?'

'No.'

'Oh, I'm sorry. What a rude, dumb question! Say hello to Mrs Brame, kids, and then buzz off.'

The three children, a boy and two girls, grinned at their grandmother, who was obviously a favourite of theirs, smiled and said hello to Joanna and then buzzed off. Milly said, 'They're not brats, any of them. Ruth has done a wonderful job with them.'

Ruth had been standing with the front door still open, as if frozen either by the cold night air or Joanna's arrival. Then abruptly she came alive again, closing the door a little too sharply, and coming forward to take Joanna's coat.

She saw the label inside the coat. 'Bonwit Teller! I used to dream of shopping there.'

'I've had it for ages,' said Joanna and instantly felt it was somehow the wrong thing to say.

'Take Mrs Brame into the living room, Milly, get her a drink. What would you like?'

'A martini?'

That seemed to push Ruth into the closet where she was

about to hang the vicuna coat. Milly came to the rescue: 'I don't think they've made a martini in this country since the 1920s. Would you like a gin-and-tonic? Ruth does.' She was heading for a mobile drinks tray, something that Joanna thought *had* gone out in the 1920s; her back was to Joanna as she offered the comment on Ruth's preference. The look on Ruth's face told Joanna a barb had hit the target.

'Gin-and-tonic would be fine. It used to be Orville's favourite drink. That and Australian beer. He always kept the refrigerator stocked with some beer called Fosseys.'

'Fosters,' said Milly and turned round with a gin-and-tonic and a small glass of beer. 'I drink it myself, just a glass or two.'

Women drinking beer? It didn't happen in Joanna's circle. She and Milly sat down and Ruth came into the middle of the room and stood awkwardly. 'I have to see to something in the kitchen. Will you excuse me?'

She was gone as if from a flying start; Milly smiled after her. 'You've got her scared. She thinks you must be at least the President's mother.'

'The president of the Bar Association? I'm his wife. Was.'

'No, President Clinton.' Milly sipped her beer, lowered her voice. 'Just as background – Ruth has absolutely no confidence in herself, she hates everything she has to do as Rod's wife. But basically, as all the young people say these days, she's a very nice person. I'd like you to remember that, please?'

'Of course,' said Joanna and thought what a very nice person Milly was.

She was taking in her surroundings with that practised eye that does not need to move in its socket; *House and Garden* editors, mothers-in-law and proper snobs have it. This, she guessed, was what she always called a safe house; not in the espionage sense but in the choice of furnishings.

No outlandish decorator had been allowed to roam in these rooms; it had been decorated from suggestions in those middlebrow home and garden magazines, to which she herself would never think of subscribing, for middle-brow housewives. There did not appear to be a single item in the room that hinted that Ruth Channing had any taste of her own; except, perhaps, the mobile drinks tray. Or was that the husband's choice? Orville had had idiosyn-crasies, such as collecting beer coasters, of which she had had to cure him.

'What?' Milly had said something.

'I said the police had been to see me. Yesterday. A very nice young woman detective and a very nice young man.'

'What did they ask you?' Joanna sipped the gin-and-tonic; it was weak by her standards.

'This and that. Nothing, really. What could I tell them about Orville? They did ask me what the relations were between him and Rod, but I told them nothing on that. It's not a mother's place to tell Cain-and-Abel stories. I'll bet Eve didn't.'

Joanna smiled; she enjoyed this woman's company. 'Were there detectives in those days? The Garden of Eden PD.'

Then there was a key in the front door and a moment later Rod Channing called out, 'I'm home!' Out in the hall there was the commotion of the children greeting him, Ruth called from the kitchen and then Channing came into the living room, hair blown by the wind, his nose red as he wiped it with a handkerchief. 'I'm getting a cold . . . Hullo, Mum.' He kissed her on the cheek with what looked to Joanna like genuine affection, then he turned to her. 'Mrs Brame –'

'Joanna,' she said, hoping she didn't sound like Ruth, *Ruth*. It was time to start making concessions, if only for Milly Channing's sake.

'Joanna. I'm sorry I'm late. I've just come from a meeting

with the police. I had to put in an appearance for a couple of clients, get them released. The police have made a mistake, but I could have been there for ever, trying to argue the matter with them. Drink? Oh, I see you have one. I'll get one, myself. A whisky is what I need with this cold coming on.'

Here's another one I've scared, thought Joanna. What was the matter with the Channings, husband and wife? 'Is it anything to do with Orville's murder?'

He turned to look back at her, the Scotch whisky bottle held over his glass. 'What made you ask that?'

'I don't know –' She didn't know. 'I suppose that's all I can think of when the police are mentioned.'

He poured the whisky, a double measure, no ice, took a gulp of it. 'Yes, actually, it does have something to do with Orville. Or so the police think. But they're wrong. There's an inspector named Malone –'

'I've met him,' said Joanna.

Channing looked at her, took another gulp of his drink, then said, 'I'll wash up. Won't be a sec.'

He went out of the room almost on the run and Milly said, 'He's always like that, always in a rush. I ask him where he's heading, what he's going to do with all the minutes he saves, but he never answers. We took our time when I was young.' Then she shook her head. 'No, I never took my time with Lester. I should have.'

Then Ruth came back into the room, looking more composed, as if she had been pulled together by another gin-and-tonic. 'Dinner is ready. Would you take care of the wine, Milly? Rod'll be out in a minute.'

The table was too elaborately dressed for a family dinner; Joanna wished Ruth would not try so hard to impress her. Yet she realized at the same time that it was the other woman's nervousness that had resulted in this table for which all the best glass and silver and linen had been brought out. All that spoiled the effect was the sight of Milly, a *woman*, pouring the wine. Joanna's mother, the dowager of Southport, would have thought that was taking equal rights too far.

The children had evidently already been fed, a fact that gave Joanna some relief. She had never been comfortable with children since her years at the Spence School almost forty years ago. Anyone under the age of twenty-five always left her wondering about the future of the world, *her* world.

Channing came back and took his place at the head of the table. He had a few graces, Joanna noted: he thanked his mother for pouring the wine. He had changed his shirt and tie, had sleeked down his hair and the redness had gone from the end of his nose. He caught Joanna's glance at his vivid tie and he flipped a finger under it. 'My Olympic tie. I'm on one of the organizing committees.'

The Olympics? She had a vague recollection of reading something about Sydney's holding the Olympic Games in – when was it to be? She was not a sportsperson, though she had attended tennis matches with Orville. If Rod had worn his tie to impress her, he had failed: she thought it looked like a badly suppurating piece of heart surgery. 'Eye-catching,' she said. 'Are you on one of the committees, Ruth?'

'Oh no, thank God!' Seated now, Ruth looked more at ease; or the half a glass of wine she had already drunk had fortified the gin-and-tonic. 'Rod isn't going to get me into *that*. I couldn't care less about sport.' She looked along the table at her husband and gave him a smile as spurious as a waiter's. 'Darling.'

The pumpkin soup was excellent; so were the roast beef, the vegetables and the wine. Joanna never toyed with a meal; she enjoyed her food. When the crème brûlée turned out to be as good as what had gone before, she had to hide her surprise. The crème only began to turn sour when Milly said, 'Rod, the police came to see me yesterday.'

154

He put down his spoon; it clattered against the side of his plate. He stroked his moustache, pulling at it as if to make sure it was still there. 'You? Why, for God's sake?'

'I *was* your brother's mother,' Milly said tartly.

He picked up his spoon. 'No, I meant why trouble you? They're poking their nose in everywhere.'

'We have an interest in what happened to Orville.' Milly nodded at Joanna, including her in the *we*. 'I didn't mind them coming to see me.'

'Who was it? Inspector Malone? He's a real pain in the –' Then Channing stopped, glancing at Joanna.

'A real pain in the ass. It was the worst that Orville could say about anyone.' She had expected Ruth to be shocked by her apparent fall from grace, but was surprised to see she wore a silly expression of befuddled amusement. The wine glass in front of her was now empty.

'No, it wasn't him,' said Milly. 'It was a nice young detective named Kaggle or something like that. And a very nice young woman named Smith.'

Channing put down his spoon again, carefully this time. 'She was shot this afternoon, just after lunch. In the Commonwealth Bank in Martin Place, just up from our offices.'

Milly frowned as if she could not take in the news. 'I missed it, I didn't watch the news this evening . . . Shot? You mean *killed*? Who by?'

'They don't know.'

Joanna said carefully, 'Why are Inspector Malone and the police so interested in your clients? Are Orville's murder and now this young woman's murder connected?'

Channing pushed his plate away and Ruth, having refilled her glass and taken a sip, said, 'It's not spoiled, is it? The crème brûlée? It's so easy to spoil,' she explained to Joanna and Milly.

'Of course not,' he snapped, for a moment sounding as if he had forgotten that the other two women were at the table. Then he looked directly at Joanna, his manner still brusque: 'I told you, the police have got it all wrong about my clients.'

She did not like his attitude at all, but this was not the place to attack him, at his own table. Good breeding is a handicap at times, a fact she had realized long ago but which she had never attempted to conquer. 'Yes, of course.' She went back to finishing the crème brûlée, turning her head away from Channing to smile at Ruth: 'It is beautiful. There is a knack in making it, my cook tells me, and obviously you have the knack.'

'You have staff?' said Ruth over the rim of her glass and made it sound as if Joanna ran a battalion.

'Doesn't everyone?' said Milly and laughed, somehow making the remark inoffensive. Joanna, too, laughed and after a moment, his face slowly crumbling as if he were in pain, Channing also broke into a laugh.

Ruth put down her glass and for a moment Joanna thought she was going to break into tears. But then from somewhere in the ruins inside her she dredged up a laugh. She pushed the glass further away from her and once again gathered herself together. Poor woman, thought Joanna, she looks as if she spends all her time picking up the pieces of her life.

'You must get to know us better,' Ruth said. 'All three of us. I, for one, would like to know more about Orville. It's not usual, not where I come from, to have a brother-in-law who was a total stranger.'

'She came from a small country town,' said Channing, not sounding at all helpful.

Joanna said, 'I didn't know him at all – well, hardly – when he first came to work for my father. I was still married to my first husband. By the time we were – *acquainted*, he was highly regarded. And highly respected, which is another thing altogether, don't you agree, Rod?' Her tone was light, but it still sounded like a challenge.

He didn't reply at once and it was Milly who said, 'Very different. Some of our entrepreneurs were highly regarded, but nobody respected them.'

'You're old-fashioned, Mum,' said Channing.

'No, I think Joanna and Milly are right.' Ruth sounded very sober now. 'You have clients you don't respect.'

'You're giving away business secrets. Let's have coffee, shall we?'

He has no respect for his wife, thought Joanna; and was glad the discussion of Orville had been chopped off. She really didn't want Rod and Ruth Channing to learn anything about him; he was hers and she did not want to share him with these two people. With Milly, yes, but not with Orville's brother and sister-in-law.

The rest of the evening was small chat like sour after-dinner mints. Channing and Ruth, at odds with each other, appeared suddenly uninterested in Joanna. She suffered the atmosphere with good manners, then at ten o'clock looked at her watch, stood up and said, 'My driver will be waiting. It's been a lovely evening . . .'

'Could you give me a lift back to town?' said Milly. 'Rod usually drives me home or puts me in a taxi –'

Channing didn't seem disposed to do either tonight; he looked at Joanna too eagerly. 'If you wouldn't mind? Mum can catch a cab from the city . . .'

'I'll have the driver take her right home.' Her tone suggested he had left his mother in the middle of a frozen tundra. She did not like Rod Channing and was glad that an ocean *and* a continent, in a few days, would separate him from her.

As she and Milly, wrapped up against the night cold, went out the front door, Ruth said, 'When will you be going home? To America, I mean?'

'They tell me Orville's body may be released by the coroner Saturday. I'm booked on Sunday's plane. We are,' she added, as if they might think she was going to abandon Orville.

Ruth put a hand on Joanna's gloved one. 'I'm sorry we had to meet this way.' Was Joanna's ear too sharp or was there a double meaning to the remark? 'It'll be a sad journey but a safe one, I hope.'

'Thank you, Ruth,' said Joanna and turned her hand over to press that of this sad, suppressed woman.

Going home in the hire car nothing much was said between the two older women; Milly seemed unnaturally quiet. As if sensing something was wrong, even the driver was silent. When the car drew up outside the Novotel, Milly said, 'Would you mind if I came in for a moment? There's something I want to talk to you about.'

Telling the driver to wait, Joanna took Milly up to her suite. When they walked in Milly looked around in approval, but made no comment. Joanna, taking off her own coat, gestured for Milly to do the same. But she shook her head.

'No, I'm not staying. I don't want to sound like I'm playing Miss Marple –'

'Who?'

'Miss Marple. Agatha Christie.'

'Oh.' She never read detective mysteries. She read Henry James and Edith Wharton, her mother's favourites, and Louis Auchincloss, whom she knew, and John O'Hara, the outsider but the one with the sharpest ear if not eye of them all, all authors who had written about the world she knew. None of them, as far as she could recall, had ever written about a detective. 'Have you been – *investigating*?'

'Just keeping my eyes and ears open. I was talking to Ruth before you came tonight. She'd had a coupla stiff gin-and-tonics – she was scared of meeting you, you know. But then she'd be scared of meeting the Virgin Mary.'

'A lot of us might be,' smiled Joanna.

'Well, yes, she was a Jewish mother. Anyway. She repeated what Rod had told her a week or two ago, that he was about to put together something that would make them millions in fees. He told her he'd just been waiting for Orville to arrive. And then . . .' Abruptly she stopped and shut her eyes.

Joanna took both her hands; in just a few hours, two meetings, she had come to feel close to this plain-spoken woman. 'Milly –'

Milly blinked away the tears. 'I'll be all right. Strange – I'm missing Orville more now than when he was alive, though I hadn't seen him in thirty years . . . You told me he was a good man, decent –'

'He was. He was the most honourable man I've ever met.'

Milly shook her head. 'That's what I can't understand. He and Rod were linked in something that Rod told Ruth they couldn't talk about. Something that, when it got out, would make them a fortune. Something so big and dirty it got Orville killed!'

'No!' But even as she made the denial she felt the cancer of doubt. Perhaps, after twelve years of living with him, she had never really known the secret Orville. As much as with the way of his death, she was struck with the horror that perhaps there had been another man behind the man she had loved. She remembered something Adam Tallis had told her, something that Orville had said: *If something happens, look to the past.*

What if there had been something in those eighteen years between Orville's arriving in the United States and his marrying her, some debt that had been called in with his death?

5

'It was like trying to stick labels on a barrelful of eels,' said Malone. 'Channing says he's not a criminal lawyer, but today he did a criminal job on us.'

'We couldn't hold the Afghan and his missus,' said Clements. 'Not even confiscate their air tickets. All we could do was get Channing to promise they wouldn't leave Sydney till we talked to 'em again. I wouldn't put money on them staying around, but we've got someone tailing them, just in case.'

When Malone had come home and told Lisa of Peta Smith's murder, she had insisted that they go through with tonight's invitation to have dinner with Russ and Romy Clements.

'I know how you feel about Peta Smith, I knew how you'd feel when I heard it on the radio. My first thought was, thank God it wasn't you.' He pressed her arm at that. 'I'm upset about her, though I didn't know her. But I *need* to get out. Ever since Monday when I gave you the bad news, we've sat home here holding hands – I've felt your worry, it runs out of you like – like blood. I don't want to watch TV – every time we turn it on, there's something about hospitals or disease or surgery. I don't know what TV programmers would do without the medical profession. I'm not being selfish or callous about Peta Smith, darling. But we're going out tonight. We're not going to sit at home and think about death!'

She was not given to dramatics or hyperbole; at times she could be as laconic as himself. This evening, however, she had spoken with passionate denial; she would not allow them to think of death or the possibility of it. She was determined to escape, if only into the humdrum of looking at another woman's new home.

Romy, from her arrival in Australia twelve years ago, had lived with her parents in a flat in Glebe, one of the city's inner suburbs. Her mother had died and she had stayed on with her father; till two years ago, when, after committing three murders, he had taken his own life. On her marriage to Russ she had insisted that they had to start a new life in a new house. It had taken them longer than they had anticipated to find what they wanted and it had been only a month ago that they had moved into this old Victorian house in Drummoyne overlooking the waters of Iron Cove. They had a substantial combined income, but it had been Russ's racecourse winnings that had enabled them to meet the price of the house without having the roof cave in under the weight of a mortgage. The ponies had, as he had told Malone, at last provided him with something solid. His only worry was what Internal Affairs would think of a detective-sergeant who could afford a waterfront home.

The four of them were at dinner now, at the dessert and coffee stage. Romy said, 'Do you think these people had anything to do with Peta's murder?'

Malone glanced at Lisa, but it was as if she were carefully avoiding his eye. He recognized the look, the one she adopted when she knew shop talk was unavoidable. 'There's a connection, but maybe it's one they don't want. We don't know that the cove who shot her was the one who shot Brame and Rockman.'

'We haven't done the autopsy yet, so the bullets are still in her.' Then Romy abruptly reached across and put a hand on Lisa's. 'Sorry. That won't make the pear tart taste any better.'

Lisa smiled wanly; Malone had noticed over the past week that amusement no longer came easily to her. 'I've been through it before.'

'No, I've never lost a detective before.' At once Malone cursed the loose cannon of his tongue.

'No,' said Lisa. 'It is different this time. Sorry.'

It was Clements, the bumblefoot in relations, who saved the moment. He raised his wine glass; there was just enough in it for a toast. 'Forget it. Here's to you, Lisa. A complete recovery and no pain.'

Later, while Clements and Malone made an attempt at cleaning up in the kitchen, Romy and Lisa stood by the wide bay window in the living room looking out across the flat sheen of Iron Cove. The night was chillingly cold, the stars polished by it. The darkness seemed to have an edge to it; over the city to the east the sharp-edged moon looked ready to chop buildings in half. On the opposite ridge, across the water, the tower of the old mental asylum could just be distinguished, looking for all the world like an Italian campanile, though the only bells that had ever rung there had been alarm bells.

'You're happy here?' Lisa said.

'Yes. I'm glad I stayed, in Sydney, I mean. Going to Adelaide would not have been an escape. Marrying Russ has been my true escape.'

Her father had committed none of his murders in their old home, but it would have resonated with his presence. Nothing had been brought from the flat in Glebe, none of the heavy Bavarian furniture that had been to her parents' taste, none of the steel engravings of nineteenth-century pastoral scenes: the past had been discarded. Lisa hoped that Romy's escape would be permanent.

'How do you feel?' Romy said.

'Worried. But don't tell Scobie. He worries even more than I do.'

Romy put her arm round her; they stood close together like sisters bound by a common fear. Still, Romy said, 'Twice I've thought the end of the world had come. First, when my mother died, two years after we landed here in Australia. I thought I'd die from grief, but I got over it. Then when my father –' She paused: she still had not come to terms with the fact that he had been a cold-blooded murderer, the worst kind. When he did what he did, I wanted to curl up and die. Before I learned the truth, I was doing the autopsies on the people he had –'

She stopped again and Lisa murmured sympathetically, unable to find words.

'But Russ stood by me –' Romy gestured ' – and here I

am. We are. Alive and happy. You will be, too, Lisa.'

Lisa thanked her by squeezing her waist. 'How does Russ feel about the shooting of Peta Smith?'

'Very bad, just as badly as Scobie, though he tries not to show it. He argues pragmatism, that police are always going to be shot, it's the nature of their job, but it's still hurting him.' Then she smiled. 'Let's go in and see how the New Age men are doing.'

The New Age men were not doing well at all. The dishwasher had been stacked and started, but the pots and pans were still in the sink. 'We've been talking,' said Clements lamely.

'Leave them.' Romy kissed Malone on the cheek. 'Take Lisa home. You have had a bad day.'

He was grateful for her consideration; Romy knew not only how to take a man apart, she knew how to keep him together. He kissed her, looked over her shoulder at Clements. 'How'd you manage it?'

'I dunno. I ask myself the same thing about you, when I look at Lisa.'

'These foreign dames, they have no taste.'

It was end-of-the-night prattle, that comes with bone-weary tiredness, but it sent the Malones home on a light note. But going home in the car, Lisa, leaning away from him and looking at him sideways, said, 'Don't take leave.'

'Don't what?' He pulled up at a red light.

'Stay on the case. Especially find out who killed Peta Smith.'

'No, I can't do that.' The light, as so often happens at a late hour, seemed stuck on red. A car, engine revving, had pulled up beside them; in it were two youths and two girls, loose with drink. Suddenly, the driver unable to contain his impatience, the car jumped the light and sped, with a scream of tyres, across the intersection. Another car, coming from the right, blared its horn in a loud nervous shriek, propped, skidded to one side, then drove on while the offending driver and his vehicle disappeared into the night. 'Stupid bastard!'

'Let him go, let him kill himself and his friends.' Lisa sounded casually callous; but she wasn't interested in the stupid driver and his friends: 'I said, find out who killed Peta. Stay on the case.'

He shook his head. 'No.'

'Yes.' She did her best to sound adamant, sensible; in her heart she wanted him by her throughout every minute of the surgery. 'Be there during the op, but come and see me after it just twice a day. Stay on the case.'

'Why?' The light was still red. A car went across the intersection at speed as the light turned green. 'Another stupid bastard! That's how accidents happen . . . You want me to?'

No, I don't. 'Yes. I know this one is eating at you. Stay with it till you've solved it.'

He leaned across and kissed her. 'Watch it,' she said. 'That's how accidents happen.'

Chapter Seven

1

At ten the next morning Romy rang Malone. 'I came in early. I've done the autopsy. Ballistics have the bullets.'

An hour later Clarrie Binyan came across from Ballistics at Police Centre. His dark Aboriginal face had a blue tinge from the cold morning air; he wore a heavy overcoat, a scarf and a tweed cap. 'I'd ask for a transfer up north if I could trust the Queenslanders. My mumma came from up there, on a mission reserve. They treated her like dirt.'

'I'll bet your mumma wouldn't recognize you now.' There was no racial edge between himself and Binyan, but he was always cautious about asking what the Aborigine's life had been like before he had joined the Police Service. He felt a sense of guilt, but he didn't question himself too much on that, either. 'You look like a rah-rah footy fan on your way to a rugby game. You got leather patches on your elbows?'

Binyan held up his elbows. 'Clean.' He laid a plastic envelope containing two bullets on Malone's desk. 'Standard Thirty-eights. Not the same gun that killed Brame and Rockman.'

'Bugger!' said Clements, who had followed Binyan into the office.

'Relax,' said Binyan, who never looked otherwise but relaxed. 'The news isn't all bad. We've identified the gun that killed the other two. Police divers came up with it this morning, over in Darling Harbour – they've been down there since Tuesday morning. It's the make I suspected. A

Sig-Sauer P Two-thirty, a Swiss piece but it's made in Germany. It fires nine-millimetre ultras, the sort we found in both bodies. It's also a very expensive piece, your ordinary run-of-the-mill hitman wouldn't be using one.'

'Any prints on it?'

'Fingerprints have seen it. Nothing. It was coated in mud.'

Malone looked at the two bullets in the envelope. 'I hope Peta didn't feel those,' he said quietly, almost to himself.

The other two men glanced at each other, then Binyan wound his scarf more tightly round his neck. 'When's she being buried?'

'Some time next week, soon's the coroner okays it.' He had remained staring at the bullets; now he looked up. 'Thanks, Clarrie. I hope that's the last we have to send you.'

'Are you kidding?' said Binyan and left.

Malone had meant, *the last bullets that would kill a police officer*; but Binyan had gone before he could explain.

Greg Random had assumed overall command of the investigation and seven detectives were now working on the three murders. Andy Graham had taken over the flow charts and the consolidation of the running sheets. Evidence was being accumulated, but it was like trying to knead flour that wouldn't bind. Malone had begun to worry that his concern for Lisa was preventing his getting a grasp on what they had gathered.

'We're not doing so well,' said Clements. 'We're shorthanded. We've got the tail on the Douranes and the one on Channing. I've had to ask for the loan of some uniformed guys, put them in civvies. We're stretched, mate.'

'What about Mr Federal?'

'John Kagal's been around the top hotels, checking if Mr Federal has been staying in any of them, like Dourane said.'

'What about the Douranes?'

'We got a warrant and had their house searched. Nothing. No weapons, no paperwork, nix. It was as if they had been expecting us before we got to them yesterday.'

'Righto, get John in here.'

Clements stood up and tapped on the glass that looked out on to the main room. Kagal, who had been working in front of a computer, stood up and came into the office. He was as impeccably dressed as ever, but somehow he seemed to have shrunk inside his clothes. His dark handsome face had aged, all the near-cockiness was gone. He sat down in the spare chair and shook his head.

'It's like a morgue out there.' He didn't appear to notice the inaptness of his remark. 'Only now she's gone do we realize how much she fitted in. I should've been with her yesterday, you know.'

'Then we might of been missing the two of you,' said Clements, his voice a little too sharp. 'What did you get out of the hotels?'

'I've just been putting it into the computer.' Kagal sat up straighter, squared his shoulders in the Serafino suit. 'He was at the InterContinental. Martin Federal, Swiss passport. He came in last Friday and checked out yesterday. Half an hour after Peta was shot.'

'Are we to take it Mr Federal and Mr Ballinger are the same man?' said Malone.

'Could be.'

'Did you get a description of him?'

'Vague. Thin, average. He hadn't stayed there before, so they couldn't tell me much about him, the way they could with a regular. He moved around, it seems. He's been in Sydney four times in the past three months, stayed at a different hotel each time. The Ritz-Carlton in Macquarie Street, the Regent, the Hilton. Looks like he didn't want to leave an impression on anyone. He never ordered a car through any of the hotels, never had a meal in any of their dining rooms, not even breakfast.'

'Must be a new breed of businessman. I thought they all tried to make an impression,' said Clements.

The three of them pondered for a moment the accepted immodesty of businessmen as distinct from their own low profiles, then Malone said, 'How did he pay his bills?'

'Cash, every time.'

'I didn't think hotels took cash any more.'

'They do when the guests have been guaranteed by a respectable firm, the one making the booking.'

'Who made all the bookings?'

Kagal's face came alive; he suddenly seemed to fill his suit again. 'Channing and Lazarus.'

2

The girl on the reception desk gave Malone a dazzling smile; she was the only one at Channing and Lazarus who was prepared to welcome him. 'Both Mr Channing and Mr Lazarus are in court this morning. All day.'

He pulled up one of the purple-tweeded club chairs close to her desk. 'Maybe I don't need to see them. Do you do all the hotel bookings for the firm? For the clients, as well?'

She raised an eyebrow, as if to say, *What's this about?* A call came in on the small board and she answered it, connecting it to somewhere else in the offices. Then she gave Malone her attention again, but warily. 'I don't know I should be answering questions. I work here, y'know.'

Don't pull the client confidentiality act on me, please. 'I appreciate that, Miss –?'

'Piric. Pam Piric. That was how I used to answer the phone when I first started here. Pamela speaking. I used to work for Avis, you know. Then Mrs Johns heard me one day and blew her top. Said this was a law office, not a car rental agency.'

'How long has she been here? Long?'

'Oh no, two years I think. She was here when I came eighteen months ago. She's efficient – God, is she!'

He let Pamela keep on talking; the tongue has collapsed more walls than pickaxes ever have. He should know: once upon a time his own tongue had undermined him more times than he cared to count. 'Where is Mrs Johns now?'

'In her office. She doesn't sit out front here, I'm all on my own. It gets pretty boring at times.'

'But you're kept busy?'

'Oh yes.' She answered another call, made another connection. She was more relaxed now, less suspicious of him. 'We've got very busy over the last six months, since we expanded.'

'That goes against the trend. Most of the law offices I read about, they've been reducing staff, not expanding. I'm glad to hear it, for your sake.' He gave her one of his own dazzling smiles, a rare sight; he was not dour, but a dry grin, barely showing his teeth, was his usual expression of flattery. 'Did you book Mr Federal into the Hotel Inter-Continental last Friday?'

'Mr Federal?'

'Yes, a director of ZPH. He came in from Zurich, I believe.'

'What's going on?' Mrs Johns stood in a doorway, all brassy indignation. 'How dare you come in and start interrogating our staff without seeing me!'

Malone stood up, put the club chair back in its place against the wall, gave the dry grin this time to the receptionist.

'Thanks, Pamela . . . You're wrong, Mrs Johns. I wasn't interrogating your staff, we were just passing the time of day.' He wasn't going to stand the girl up against a wall to be shot by the office manager. 'May I see you in your office?'

'I'm busy.'

'Who isn't, now the recession's turned around? Miss Piric was telling me how much the firm has expanded in the past six months.'

That was a mistake, the tongue rolling on too long. 'I thought you said you were just passing the time of day?' said Mrs Johns.

'Oh, we were. This and that.' He abruptly lost his patience: 'Come on, Mrs Johns! Let's go into your office, whether you're busy or not.'

But as he followed the office manager out of the reception lobby he winked at Pamela Piric and she gave him a surreptitious smile, which Mrs Johns did not see. He might need Miss Piric again; receptionists were a filter in which scraps of information stuck like paper in a storm-water grille.

Mrs Johns's office was a small cubicle off the main room, where a dozen women sat in front of word processors. She paused by her office, then, as if it would belittle her to entertain him in such a small space, she led him on into a medium-sized boardroom. Malone was aware of eyes staring into his back as fingers paused and words stopped being processed.

In the half-hour wrangle at Homicide yesterday afternoon over the detention of the Douranes, June Johns had been ready to explode. To Malone's surprise it had been Channing, showing unexpected firmness, who had kept her in check. Dourane and his wife had been very quiet, letting Channing argue for them. Mrs Johns had in the end turned sullen, saying nothing for the rest of the meeting, not even when she was leaving.

She seated herself at the head of the large teak table and looked across at Malone as if she were a lawyer and he was a client whose chances of being acquitted she thought were pretty poor. 'So what is this all about?'

'I thought that would've been pretty obvious. It's about

the three murders we're investigating.' Then he bowled his favourite weapon, the bean-ball: 'Do you know Mr Martin Federal of ZPH, the Swiss firm Mr Channing and Mr Lazarus represent?'

She ducked that one without effort. 'No.'

'Righto, let's try again. Did you instruct Miss Piric to book him into the Hotel InterContinental last Friday? And before that, over the past three months, into the Regent, the Ritz-Carlton and the Hilton?'

There was a moment's hesitation. 'Yes.'

'And you've never met him?'

'No.'

'So you booked him in on the instructions of Mr Channing?'

'I suppose I must have.'

He grinned, without humour. 'You're a beaut, Mrs Johns . . . What about a Mr Ballinger?'

'Who?' There was no hesitation, not the slightest gathering together of any defences.

'Mr Ballinger. He shot and killed Detective Smith yesterday afternoon.' His voice suddenly grated; he stopped, to soften it. 'I asked you about him yesterday at Homicide.'

'No, you never mentioned him to me.'

She had him there: maybe he had not asked her about the mysterious Mr Ballinger. He and Clements had concentrated on Dourane and his wife and, once Rod Channing had arrived, had got nowhere.

'Why are you so obstructive?'

'A good office manager protects her employers. From what I read, the police protect each other.'

'What did you do before you came here, Mrs Johns?'

'This and that.' A tiny sarcastic smile.

He went back on another tack: 'On whose authority did you guarantee Mr Federal's charges at those hotels?'

Again there was the slight hesitation. She was wearing a mustard-coloured wool skirt and a brown blouse with buttoned cuffs; she paused, one hand at her wrist as if she had just found a loose button. There are a hundred ways of covering hesitation: Mrs Johns, it seemed, was a past mistress at the ways. She fiddled with the button: 'Damn! I'm going to lose that . . . I've forgotten whether it was Mr Channing or Mr Lazarus.'

'Come on – June, isn't it?'

'No, it's Mrs Johns.'

So much for the familiar approach, as the unofficial manual advised; he accepted the rebuff with a grin. 'I was just trying to put you at ease. You seem a little uptight.'

'I don't think so. You're the one who's uptight. Or off-course. Whatever. You're trying to make perfectly legal connections into something criminal.'

'Killing one of my colleagues is criminal, Mrs Johns. Not to mention Mr Brame and a security guard named Rockman. If I'm uptight, it's about those murders!' His mood changed abruptly; it was time to go. He stood up, but paused, standing close to and above her. 'Don't get yourself too involved with what's going on at Channing and Lazarus, Mrs Johns. You might be too loyal to your bosses!'

It was a reckless statement, but his mention of Peta Smith had brought the dead girl back into his conscious-ness; guilt stirred him up like a poison. He went out of the boardroom without a backward glance, strode past the stares of the word processors (words were now processed, for Chrissakes, like food and waste!), and was outside the lifts, not smiling at Miss Piric as he swept by her, before his feelings cleared. The two other people in the lift, a girl and a middle-aged courier, glanced cautiously at the tall man who got in, moving his face as if checking whether he had broken his own jaw.

'You okay, sport?' said the courier.

Malone looked at him, struggled for a grin. 'It's okay. I've just bitten my tongue.'

Joanna Brame had taken a trip across into the city proper. She had had breakfast in her suite and watched the CNN news segments that the hotel ran for the benefit of its American guests. But why, she had wondered, would anyone want to look at the news that assaulted one from the television screen? President Clinton was still besieged, still falling in the polls; she had not voted for him, but his failure gave her no satisfaction. From Rwanda, misery stared at her with huge accusing eyes; she was always charitable when disasters struck, but at the moment she had her own misery. The Middle East appeared at long last to be creeping towards peace but, though she hated the phrase and the sentiment, she could not have cared less. Her world had abruptly narrowed and she felt no shame that she did not want to look outside it.

She had not called for a cab or a hire car, but had chosen to ride over into the central business district on the monorail. Without knowing it, and certainly not wanting to know it, she had ridden in the very car in which her husband had been murdered. She had not made the trip as a tourist, but as an escapee from the suffocation of her hotel suite and the possible attentions of Richard De Vries and Karl Zoehrer. The return to New York could not come quickly enough, even though it would mean the saddest journey of her life. No one, not even the dead, should have to endure a 10,000-mile funeral.

She never strolled the streets of Manhattan, not even the reaches between 57th and 65th and between Fifth and Lexington; the homeless, a councilman had told her at a charity dinner, were kept lower down the island, like debris swept into unvisited corners. She had never been mugged or accosted, but she had friends who had been. She rode in limousines past the waste of the city, both human and otherwise, and, though she admired other cities,

American and European, would not want to live anywhere else but in New York and, of course, the country estate in Connecticut.

Today she strolled through Sydney, listening to the flat accents and syncopation that made English sound like another language. She had decided that one should not be attacked by grief while in a foreign land. Despite the superficial American look of Sydney, she felt alien here; she would have been less alien in France or Italy, which she knew better. She kept her grief at bay by shutting her mind to all but externals.

She marvelled at the cleanliness of the streets, at the shine on the girls' hair, at the bright sunshine on a cold winter's day, at the absence of panhandlers and derelicts. She window-shopped through a huge cupola-topped building called the Queen Victoria Building: restored to its Victorian splendour, she was told by a shopkeeper, by an Asian company. She found another pleasure, another restored gallery of shops called the Strand Arcade, and when she finally hailed a cab to be taken back to her hotel she was filled with regret and grief that she had never had the chance to share the excitement of his home city with Orville. And wondered how much, if at all, he had missed it.

She had no sooner entered her suite than Dick De Vries and Adam Tallis knocked on the door. With a sigh of annoyance that she managed to conceal she invited them in.

'How is the convention going?' She really had no interest in the convention. She respected lawyers and their work, appreciating, if only with wifely good humour, Orville's belief that the law, and not love, made the world go round. A thousand lawyers in one spot, however, stopped the world dead. Here in front of her was one lawyer who, again in Orville's belief, could do the deed on his own. 'Have you been attending the sessions, Dick?'

'No. Adam is doing that for us.'

'And what have you all come up with, Adam? A thousand conflicting opinions?'

He smiled. 'So far, all we've been doing is reviewing the past. It's a legal trick of the trade.'

De Vries looked disapproving, but changed the subject. 'Anything new from the police on Orville? Dammit, you'd think they would have come up with something by now. They haven't been near us in two days.'

'I think they're probably preoccupied with the shooting of that woman detective,' said Tallis. 'She was the one working on Mr Brame's case and that of the security guard.'

Joanna frowned. 'Rodney Channing mentioned her last night –'

De Vries interrupted her: 'Last night? You saw Channing last night?'

'I had dinner at his home. With him and his wife and mother. You seem surprised, Dick?'

'Eh? No, no. After all –'

'After all?' She wasn't going to let him get off the hook, not after his attempt at policing her movements.

'After all, he is your brother-in-law. Did he have anything to say? I mean, about Orville's – about Orville's case?'

'Nothing at all. But I gather the plot, as they say, is thickening.' She shook her head. 'I never thought I'd hear myself say that. Someone warned me that we mustn't start playing Miss Marple.'

'Playing who?'

She was saved by the phone; she had once remarked to Orville that it had been invented by a dramatist and not by Alexander Graham Bell. This time it was Reception telling her that Inspector Malone was on his way up. She hung up and said to De Vries, 'Inspector Malone must have heard you complaining, Dick. He's coming up.'

'With some news, I hope,' said De Vries, voice more clipped than usual.

Joanna was grateful for the interruption of Malone's arrival, but disappointed when he told her he had no further news.

'I heard about the killing of your young woman detective,' she said. 'It must have been a dreadful shock to you.'

Malone nodded. 'It was totally unnecessary. She just wanted to question the man, not arrest him.'

'Do you know who the killer was?' said De Vries.

'No. A man named Ballinger, but we don't know if that's his real name. We think he's connected with the killing of Mr Brame and the security guard Rockman.'

'Christ, this is getting out of hand!' The English accent for the moment was gone; the voice was nasal Yankee.

Malone looked at him curiously, but said only, 'That's what we think, Mr De Vries. Have you been in touch with your New York office about what might be in Mr Brame's files?'

'Yes.' The voice was under control again. 'Nothing. I'm going back with Mrs Brame on Sunday, I'll check myself if there is anything in the files.'

Joanna was surprised she was going to have company on the flight; the prospect didn't please her. 'You didn't tell me, Dick –'

'There'll be formalities in Los Angeles when we take the, er, body in. I'll handle all that for you, I don't think you should be subjected to it.'

'Thank you.' She was not ungracious. 'Inspector, why do you think there is some connection between all these killings? My husband, who's never been under threat in his life, leaves New York and in a matter of days . . . It's all too bizarre.'

'Mrs Brame, when you've been involved in crime as long as I have, you find there's no such word as bizarre . . . Did

Mr Brame make any trips to Europe in the past three months? To Zurich in particular?'

Joanna frowned. 'No. The only overseas trip Orville made this year was to Japan. I went with him, in April.'

De Vries had looked at his watch, then moved to the drinks cabinet. 'Do you mind, Joanna? The sun is over the yardarm, or wherever it's supposed to be. My partner was a very keen yachtsman, I'm not,' he explained to Malone. 'Drink?'

'No, thanks.'

'Joanna? Adam?'

Nobody, it seemed, wanted a drink right now; he sighed and turned away from the cabinet empty-handed. 'Well, I'll wait. Sorry, Inspector. I interrupted you –'

'Mr De Vries, did you make any trips to Europe this year?'

'Did I?' He looked at Tallis, but before the younger man could answer he said, 'Yes, I did. I went to Zurich. One of our clients is Credit Suisse, one of the top Swiss banks.'

'When was that?'

'Last month. It was a quick trip, I was there just two days. No more, really, than a courtesy call.'

'Credit Suisse wouldn't have referred you to a Zurich firm called ZPH? Zurich Private Holdings?'

'No–o. What do – ZPH? – what do they do?'

'I gather they're an investment company. Channing and Lazarus represent them out here. One of their directors, Mr Federal, is here in Sydney right now, but he seems pretty elusive. That was why I asked if Mr Brame had been to Zurich – I thought he might have been planning to meet Mr Federal while he was there.'

Joanna, watching both men closely, wondered at De Vries's studied nonchalance and the casual, almost naïve approach of the detective. Her father had been a criminal lawyer and as a college student she had gone to watch him in the cut-and-thrust of court proceedings; she had a dim memory that the bludgeon had been rarely used, that cross-examination had been mostly a matter of stroking and counter-stroking; or at least that was how her father had operated. Then the flood-money Eighties had come along and Schuyler, De Vries and Barrymore turned away from crime, or anyway the more violent sort, and gave its attention to mergers, litigation and the defence of clients who had never bothered to read the law when it came to the difference between the right and wrong ways of making money. Orville had been a master at mergers, suffered the pursuit of litigation and had a profound dislike of clients who thought greed was an excuse for breaking the law.

She watched Malone and De Vries: stroke and counter-stroke were being applied here. But did the detective suspect Dick De Vries of something? Orville's partner was stupid at times, incompetent at all times, but he wasn't a criminal. Yet . . .

'I wouldn't know about that,' said De Vries and looked at his watch again; the gesture was studied, as if time were of absolute importance to him. 'You'll have to excuse me, Inspector. I have a lunch appointment. With Karl Zoehrer,' he told Joanna. 'Would you like to join us?'

She would like nothing less. 'What a pity! I've already told Adam I'll have lunch with him.'

Tallis caught on, looked at his watch. 'I've booked us for one o'clock.'

'Oh well, some other time.' De Vries did not sound disappointed that his invitation had been declined. 'Goodbye, Inspector. Let us know as soon as you've come up with something?'

'Of course, Mr De Vries. Why should we keep it to ourselves?' His tongue was on the loose this morning, but De Vries had begun to irritate him with his evasion and superior air.

De Vries gave him a hard look, then left, closing the door sharply behind him. Joanna said, 'I don't think you and Mr De Vries hit it off, am I right, Inspector?'

'We don't hit it off with 50 per cent of the people we meet, Mrs Brame. It comes with the job. Yes, Mr Tallis?'

The young man hesitated, then gestured awkwardly. 'No, it doesn't matter.'

'No, Adam,' said Joanna. 'Everything matters. If you were going to tell Inspector Malone something, out with it!'

There was no mistaking the sharpness in her voice; she was his boss's, or late boss's wife. 'I feel I'm being disloyal, Mrs Brame –'

'Who to? My husband?'

'No. Oh no, not him.'

'Who, then? Mr De Vries?' Tallis nodded. 'Well, that's up to you, Adam. But you worked for my husband, not Mr De Vries. I don't apologize for being so blunt – but I think you owe your loyalty to my husband. Tell us what's on your mind!'

Tallis looked at each of them in turn, taking his time, as if afraid of the jump that lay ahead of him. Jobs for young lawyers in prestigious New York firms were plums reached for each year by a thousand graduates; if it became known that he had spoken against the remaining senior partner, he would be out on Broad Street with the other panhandlers. At last he said, 'Mr De Vries said he'd called New York to check if there was anything in the files. I talked to Connie Letoni this morning –'

'Miss Letoni is – was my husband's secretary,' Joanna explained to Malone.

'Connie said she hadn't heard from him since he left New York.'

'What about his own secretary?' said Malone. 'Does he have one?'

'She's away, on her honeymoon. Connie is handling both offices, with both senior partners away.'

'What about a fax?'

Tallis shook his head. 'She'd have mentioned that if one had come in. She's very efficient.'

'I can vouch for that,' said Joanna. 'But why did Dick say he'd talked to the office when he hadn't? Unless he's forgotten. He's always been slipshod, Orville was always complaining to me about him. Forget you heard me say that, Adam.' He nodded and smiled weakly; then Joanna looked back at Malone. 'I had dinner at my brother-in-law's last night. His mother, my mother-in-law –' she said it almost as a query, as if she had not come to terms with having such a relative, a common disease in human relations. 'She told me that her son Rod was working on something that would bring in the biggest fees his firm had ever earned. Some deal that he couldn't even tell his wife about.'

'But he didn't mention your husband's name in connection with it?'

'Well, no–o . . . I'm sorry, Inspector. Perhaps I shouldn't have –' She was suddenly helpless; she felt useless. 'I'm chasing wild geese. But anything that will tell me why Orville was killed . . .'

Malone's pager beeped. 'May I use your phone?'

She gestured at the phone on a side-table; he moved to it, picked it up and dialled Homicide. Clements came on the line: 'We've just had a call from Dicey Kilmer. She's having a fit, she says *they* have found her.'

'Where is she?'

'Out at Miranda, in the Fit-to-Measure gym. I'll meet you there. In the meantime I've asked Miranda to send two uniformed guys down to the gym, just in case.'

Malone hung up. 'I've got to go. Mrs Brame – and you too, Mr Tallis – what you've just told me, keep to yourself. I'll talk to Mr De Vries, don't either of you have a word with him. I can't give you orders, but take it as one, okay?'

Then he was gone and Joanna looked at Tallis. 'I think we'll have lunch up here, Adam. I don't think I can face a restaurant full of lawyers, not today. My father, who was a very cynical man, once told me that the law was built on the interpretation of lies. I think I'm being caught up in a mesh of lies, Adam.'

She dared not confess to him that one of the liars might have been Orville.

4

'What are you doing *here*?'

'Where else was I gunna go, I'd feel safe? When I got back to the flat this morning, I'd been shopping, when I saw that someone had been through all my things – Jesus! They took nothing, far's I could see, but all the drawers were open and the cupboards, like they were searching for something, I dunno what . . .' Dicey Kilmer paused, gulped in a deep breath. 'I was coming to gym anyway, I was all dressed for it, so I come here and rung you from here. I know all the people *here*. Look at the guys – you think someone is gunna come in here and do me over, all that muscle standing around waiting to be used? And the girls – they'd tear anyone to pieces, someone tried any rough stuff with me. You should see what some of 'em carry in their bags – Mace, steel bodkins, one girl's got knuckledusters.'

'Dicey, these guys are using guns,' said Clements. 'They don't beat people up, they kill them. All the muscle in this gym isn't gunna stop a bullet.'

She nodded morosely. 'Yeah, I know. Still, where else was I gunna go till you turned up? Thanks anyway. I mean for those two guys in uniform. They were here five minutes after I called you. They were all over me like a rash, being protective.'

'You shouldn't wear such a tight outfit,' Malone grinned.

The Fit-to-Measure gymnasium was obviously popular.

At one end a dozen men worked on weights; muscles and sweat-drops stood out as if heralding an explosion of flesh. At the other end music started up, loud and rocking; no swans floated through a dance here. In front of a mirror-wall a moustachioed, bald-headed Narcissus, erotically in love with his own reflection, led two or three dozen women and half a dozen men in an aerobics class. In some cases fat bounced like jelly in an earthquake; some of the women and one or two of the men looked as if they were giving birth. The huge room reverberated to the thump-thump of the music, the mirrors told the aerobists that they were one in a million; or, they hoped, soon would be. Malone and Clements, in suits and hats and ties, not a muscle in sight, looked like drop-ins from another planet.

Malone yelled above the music, 'Is there somewhere else we can go?'

'There's a fruit-juice bar down the hall.'

Dicey Kilmer led them out of the gym and down a narrow hall to an area of plastic-topped tables and spindly chairs designed for narrow bums and anorexic aerobists. She bought three juices and she and the two detectives sat down at a table, Clements's ample behind straddling his chair as if it were a saddle. The beat of the music could still be heard, but here it wasn't so deafening.

'Do all you fitness fans finish up with impaired hearing?' Malone was trying to settle Dicey's nerves; she was still on edge. 'It makes a nice picture. All those sleek healthy bods leaning forward with their hands to their ears saying, Eh, what'd you say?'

Dicey smiled. 'You're trying to cheer me up, right? Well, I feel better now you're here. When I got back to my place this morning, saw what they'd done, I was scared sh – well, I was scared. I got the shakes, truly.' She held up a hand, looked satisfied that it was no longer shaking.

'We'll have the Fingerprints fellers go there, see what they can dig up. But to be honest, I wouldn't expect much.

There were no prints when they cleaned out Murray's flat.'

'They'd been through there, too? I didn't know that. Jesus, what are they after?' She sucked noisily on the straw in her juice. Malone and Clements, not pineapple lovers, had hardly touched theirs. 'I took nothing with me that belonged to Murray . . . I saw the news last night. About what happened to Peta Smith. That made me sick, I got the shakes then, too.'

'I think we're going to have to put you in protective custody, Dicey. For a week or so, anyway.'

She shook her head. 'No, no way. What does that mean? Staying locked up in my flat all the time, guys crowding me – I've seen it in the movies. Gimme Richard Gere, then okay –' She tried for some humour, but it was too heavy, she couldn't raise even a weak grin. 'No, thanks. You wouldn't let me go to work, would you?'

'I can't see two guys sitting under hair-dryers keeping an eye on you,' said Clements. 'Richard Gere, maybe, he's got enough hair for a perm, but not our guys. We could ask for women officers, but I dunno any station that has enough women to fill a twenty-four-hour roster, two at a time. The area commander would tell us to get lost.'

'I could go home,' she said without enthusiasm.

'To, where was it, Cawndilla?'

'Yeah. I've got two weeks' holidays coming up. If I explained – or maybe you could – to Antoinette –'

'Who?'

'Antoinette, she's my boss. Her real name's Aggie, Agatha, but who'd go to Aggie's for a shampoo and facial? Only the old bags from the Bargain Bag Store. That's a joke.' She smiled, humour creeping back into her like blood that had stopped flowing.

'Will Aggie – Antoinette understand if we explain?'

'She's a real nice person, she'll understand. But Cawndilla?' She made a face. 'I thought I'd got away from that place.'

'I think you'll be safe there,' said Malone quietly. 'We'll ask the Cawndilla cops – is there a station there?'

'Four cops, there used to be. Booking drivers, running in Abos for being drunk, nothing exciting.'

'Well, we'll ask 'em to keep an eye on you, but not to crowd you. Someone turns up to worry you, get in touch with me or Russ immediately, okay? I'm sorry it has to be this way, Dicey, but you made a bad choice when you picked Murray.'

'The story of my life.' She stood up, as fit as she could possibly be on the outside, a quicksand of feeling on the inside. 'When's it gunna end? I mean, how soon are you gunna catch them?'

'Soon,' said Malone and did his best to sound confident and reassuring. 'Let's go and explain the position to Antoinette.'

5

Karl Zoehrer and Richard De Vries and twenty other American lawyers sat in the public gallery of the New South Wales Legislative Assembly and watched another demonstration of the old saw that the first rule of democracy is the survival of the politicians who profess belief in it. The Assembly was called the Bear Pit by the local voters and though it did not stage fist-fights and other entertainments such as one saw in the Japanese Diet or the roundabout parliaments of Italy, there were abuse and jeers and rude signs that reminded the older visitors of Earl Long and other exuberant democrats.

The Leader of the Opposition, Hans Vanderberg, an elderly vulture in an ill-fitting suit, was on his feet criticizing the Police Minister. 'Why is not more being done to expedition the solving of the present spattle of murders? How many police officers are being employed on the cases? A stitch in time doesn't save any thread –'

'He's called The Dutchman,' Rod Channing, the party's guide, told Zoehrer and De Vries. 'He came out from Holland nearly fifty years ago and he's been mangling the language ever since. He does it on purpose – I'd bet he could recite *Paradise Lost* if it would get him votes. He was Premier for three terms and he hates the idea of being in Opposition.'

'Just like home,' said De Vries.

'Is he interested in impressing us?' asked Zoehrer. 'Or the local voters?'

'With all due respect, Karl, he couldn't give a fig for you visitors. If you're not a voter here in New South Wales, you don't count – and that includes the rest of Australia. He's just latched on to this topic because it's opportune.'

'Just like home,' said De Vries again.

The Police Minister, bald and handsome, rose to his feet. He knew all about murder: his own son had been a victim and he had applied all his ministerial pressure during that investigation. 'The Honourable Member, who was once himself Police Minister, knows very well that, like that of miners and speleologists, most police work is done beneath the surface.'

'He'll have got him with speleologists,' Channing whispered.

'I am assured by the Commissioner that progress is being made –' Tom Sweden looked up at the gallery. 'Today we have as guests a party of distinguished American lawyers. I should like to assure them that my Service is doing everything in its power to solve the murder of the Bar Association's president and we are hopeful of a solution any day now. But as lawyers, I am sure they understand the need for prudent delay –'

'Just like home,' De Vries said yet again.

Down in the body of the chamber, on a bench reserved for officials, Greg Random sat with Commissioner John

Leeds. They looked at each other and Leeds muttered from the side of his mouth, 'You heard that?'

'Like an earache, sir,' said Random.

The Dutchman was on his feet again, arms akimbo increasing the image of an aged bird unable to fly but still ready to pick at any carcase. 'The Minister, in his usual form, is beating about the mulberry bush. He talks about prudent delay, but like some Greek fishmonger once said –'

'There goes the Greek vote,' said Random.

' – like he once said, prudent delay is just another name for specious cowardice –'

'Thucydides,' said Zoehrer. 'This guy's smarter than he lets on.'

Channing nodded. 'But he'll never let the public know. Australians have always been suspicious of orators, they think they're bullshit artists. Your man, William Jennings Bryan, or even Roosevelt or Churchill wouldn't ever have got a vote out here.'

Down in the chamber Random was staring up at the gallery. 'What's the matter?' asked the Commissioner.

'Channing, the solicitor, he's up there with the Americans. Malone has him on our list as the principal suspect.'

Leeds frowned, dropped his whisper even lower. 'For Chrissake! You mean he thinks Channing committed the murders? And he's up there with Brame's successor?'

'He doesn't know whether Channing used the guns, but Channing knows who did.'

The Commissioner looked up at the gallery. Channing looked down and the two men's eyes met. There was no nod of recognition from either; they had never met. The voice of the Police Minister cut across the gaze: 'I reiterate, the police are hopeful of a solution any day . . .'

Chapter Eight

1

When Malone and Clements got back from arranging a police escort to take Dicey Kilmer home to Cawndilla, there was a message from Phil Truach on Malone's desk to call him on Truach's mobile phone. Malone did so.

'Where are you?'

'I'm standing here in the freezing bloody rain, my balls frozen off –'

'I didn't ask you how you were. I asked where you were.' He looked out the window at the rain which had started half an hour ago, thick and slanting on the wind.

'I'm in Martin Place, opposite the Channing and Lazarus office. Channing has just come back and gone in with two guys, one of them's Zoehrer or whatever his name is – the guy who's taken charge of the lawyers' convention. I dunno who the other guy is. Pink-faced feller with, I think, grey hair. He's wearing a raincoat and one of those tweed hats the rah-rah boys wear to footy matches.' Truach followed soccer, had only contempt for the fans of rugby union. The new opium of the masses came in various weeds. 'They've just come back from Parliament House, Channing's been a guide or something to a group of Yanks finding out how our system works. As if anyone could tell 'em,' he murmured, and Malone guessed he had mumbled the words around a freshly lit cigarette.

Truach was one of those rostered to keep surveillance on Channing. Surveillance had been decided upon yesterday after the interrogation of Dourane and his wife. Malone knew that Joanna Brame and Milly Channing had visited Channing's home last night; he knew, too, that Channing had spent some time in court this morning. Now he knew something else, something Mrs Johns hadn't told him, that Channing had been spending time with Karl Zoehrer and someone who might be Richard De Vries. The time with Zoehrer was understandable: Channing had said he was on the Law Society's welcoming committee. But why with De Vries who, as far as he knew, had no connection with the convention? He was falling into that trap that was always at a policeman's feet, the bog of suspicion.

'Righto, Phil, I'll be down.' He had been hoping to leave the office early to spend an extra hour or two with Lisa. He hung up and went out to Clements in the outer office. 'I'm going down to have another word with Channing – I think De Vries might be with him. I'll have a word with him, too. Anything on Dourane and his missus?'

'I just checked with Rockdale, they have two guys in plainclothes watching them. They've been at home all day.'

'Not coming into their office? Get a warrant to search the office. Have the Rockdale fellers bring them in to Castlereagh Street, I'll meet you there in an hour. It's more than likely I'll have Channing or Lazarus or both of 'em with me.'

'What'll I tell the judge about the warrant?'

'Dream up something. If we're wrong, they can always sue us – which I don't think they'll ever do.'

'You're getting reckless.'

'You've punted on long shots, haven't you?'

'All the time. But I always take each-way bets. Place or show, as the Yanks call it.'

Because of the difficulty of parking around Martin Place, Malone took a cab downtown. He rode in the back seat, an elitist attitude by local standards, and the driver, a huge Fijian, recognizing a cop when he saw one, made no effort at conversation. Which Malone, who would have bitten his head off, appreciated.

He walked down Martin Place, hat pulled down, raincoat collar turned up against the wind and the rain, the ropes of the flagpoles above him cracking like stockwhips. Phil Truach, putting out a cigarette as soon as he saw him, was waiting in the foyer of the Channing and Lazarus building.

'They're still upstairs. I haven't spotted the other partner, Lazarus, so he could be up there, too. You want me to come up with you?'

'Better not, Phil. They don't know you, let it stay like that. You could be tailing Channing for the next week.'

Truach looked out at the weather. 'Thanks. Yell if you want any help, though. You're going up to face three or four lawyers.'

'I'm an honest man.'

'When did that matter?'

Malone rode up to the Channing and Lazarus floor, and was greeted with a big smile by Miss Piric. 'Nice to see you again, Inspector. Who do you want to see this time?'

'Will it get you into trouble if you get through direct to Mr Channing without going through Mrs Johns?'

'I'll say you held a gun at my head.'

'Don't joke, Pam.'

Instantly she was sober. 'Oh God, that was stupid . . . I'll get Mr Channing.'

But on that instant Mrs Johns came through the door that led to the main office. She pulled up, her face abruptly stiffening. 'Unannounced again, Inspector?'

He was tired and on edge, really in a bad mood. 'Don't let's muck around, Mrs Johns. I want to see Mr Channing – *now*!'

'He has a client with him –'

'Not a client. Mr Zoehrer, from the American Bar Association, and another man named De Vries.' He was gambling, not a usual habit, but tiredness does not breed caution. 'Are you going to take me in or am I going to barge in? I'm still investigating three murders, Mrs Johns, I'm not here about a parking ticket.'

There had been grit between them from their first meeting; now there was gravel. She appeared unsettled by his aggression, almost as if she believed she had had him tamed. She looked at Miss Piric, but the receptionist was searching for the Retreat Mode button on her computer. Mrs Johns looked at Malone again, turned sullen, spun on her heel, almost a military drill manoeuvre, and disappeared.

'Thank you,' said Miss Piric, 'you've ruined my day.'

Malone made a gesture of apology, waited a minute, looked at his watch, then strode towards the door through which the office manager had disappeared. Almost as if she had been waiting for him to move, she opened the door in his face. 'Impatient again, Inspector?'

'Always, Mrs Johns. Time, tide and Homicide wait for no man. Or woman.' It was cheap, bargain-basement wit, but the gravel between them had worn him raw.

Channing and Lazarus were waiting for him in Channing's office, the bearded man on his feet by a window, Channing behind his desk. Neither man looked welcoming; indeed, they just stared at him, waiting for him to speak first. He did so, gesturing towards a door that, he guessed, might lead to the boardroom where he had talked with Mrs Johns this morning. 'If Mr Zoehrer and Mr De Vries are in there, you might ask them back in. They're both interested in our investigation.'

The partners looked at each other, then Lazarus moved to the connecting door and opened it. 'Karl. Dick. Inspector Malone thinks you might like to join us. Okay?'

The two Americans came in, Zoehrer striding as if into a courtroom, De Vries looking a little uncertain, as if he were unsure that this was the *right* courtroom. Immediately the four men were confronting him, Malone knew he had become reckless, had come too far. He was in a pit with four lawyers, no place for a cop ever to be.

Retreat was out of the question; there was nothing to do but take over. He sat down in one of the clients' chairs opposite Channing behind the desk; he gestured to Zoehrer and De Vries to sit on the couch against one wall. Lazarus hesitated, then with a half-smile dropped into the second clients' chair.

'Go ahead, Inspector,' he said and adjusted his eyepatch, like a marksman settling himself in front of the target.

Malone turned to Zoehrer, who was lolling on the couch as if he had been in this office all his working life; only the fingers drumming slowly on his ample belly suggested he might not be as comfortable as he looked. 'Mr Zoehrer, I understand you're a criminal lawyer?'

'Yes. I do other briefs, of course.'

'In Homicide, my only brief is criminal work. You are as keen as I am to find out who murdered your colleague Mr Brame. We at Homicide have a problem. We have *three* murders, all of them connected, we think, and the connection in each case leading us to this office –'

'Now hold it!' Channing half-rose from his chair, but was waved back down by his partner. He sat down, took out a handkerchief and blew his nose.

Lazarus said equably, 'Do we need to discuss this in front of Mr Zoehrer and Mr De Vries? Your question should be put to us, not Mr Zoehrer.'

'I haven't put a question to him yet, Mr Lazarus. I'm just after him for advice – unpaid, of course, Mr Zoehrer. I understand your fees are quite high, but maybe you'll work *pro bono publico*, I think you Americans call it?'

Zoehrer had looked slightly amused, but now he frowned. The big man was flamboyant, but Malone guessed the flamboyance could be all part of the act that was Karl Zoehrer, lawyer. Malone had seen the technique in local courts, lawyers aping actors playing lawyers: the studied pause, the planned spontaneity, the quip with one eye on the jury and the other on the judge, an ocular acrobatic that, Malone was sure, was taught in first year Law. But Zoehrer was putting on no act now; indeed, he suddenly looked more than a little uncomfortable. He sat up, drawing in his belly. 'Inspector Malone, I think you had better leave me out of this –'

'Me, too,' said De Vries and fingered the knot of his tie as if it were too tight.

Malone went on as if neither man had spoken: 'Three people have been murdered. The first was the brother of Mr Channing. The second was a security man who was on the scene at two previous murders at firms which have now been taken over by a client of Channing and Lazarus . . . You didn't know that?' The two partners had sat up, both looking startled.

Lazarus was the first to recover. 'We had no idea . . . Why didn't you tell us before?'

'I'm telling you now . . . The third victim, Mr Zoehrer, was one of my detectives, killed by a man we believe had a letter of reference from Channing and Lazarus. If you were the prosecuting attorney in this case, would you ask for a warrant to search all the files of this office?'

He was alone here, out on the longest limb he had ever ventured upon. He was punting on a long-shot, that if Channing and Lazarus had something to hide, as he suspected they had, there would be no lawsuit, not even a complaint to the Commissioner.

The four lawyers were silent for a long moment. Channing looked angry, Lazarus had become suddenly imperturbable, his good eye as dark and blank as his eye-patch. Both De Vries and Zoehrer looked plain uncomfortable, like executors who had turned up at the wrong family for the reading of a will.

Then Zoehrer said, 'The laws are looser in that regard in the United States, Inspector – our system runs differently –'

'I appreciate that, Mr Zoehrer,' said Malone, though he was sure that the big man was dissembling; and in his heart he couldn't blame him. 'But I know you're as impatient as I am to solve Mr Brame's murder. Under your system would you apply to have the files of Channing and Lazarus searched?'

Lazarus broke his silence, but made no movement to rise. 'I think this has gone far enough. You are making inferences, Inspector, that could be taken as slander.'

'If that's the case,' said Zoehrer, rising heavily from the couch, looking abruptly relieved, 'I think it best if Dick and I leave. This is a domestic matter.'

'I've never thought that boundaries were drawn in the matter of murder,' said Malone, still seated.

His tongue had slipped up again: Channing picked it up at once, his voice thick with his cold: 'You are wrong there, as you well know. You can't investigate a murder outside this State, the boundaries stop you.' He stood up, walked to the door with Zoehrer and De Vries. 'We'll straighten this out, Karl. Dick. I'm sorry you've been subjected to it –'

Malone had remained in his chair. He was feeling much less relaxed than he looked, but, though policemen are less theatrical than lawyers, at least in non-violent situations, they are sometimes better actors. They have to be: criminals are more often than not a very discerning audience. 'I think you'd better stay, Mr De Vries. I have a few questions about your New York office. Goodbye, Mr Zoehrer. I'll be in touch.'

Zoehrer nodded, looked at the other three lawyers, then departed abruptly. De Vries stood in the open doorway as if undecided whether to run or stay; then he closed the door and came back and sat once more on the couch. Lazarus's patched eye was towards Malone; he was looking at Channing, who had returned to his seat behind the desk. Then the bearded man turned his good eye on Malone, but not before the latter had recognized that some message had passed between the partners.

'We'll be putting in an official complaint to the Minister,' said Lazarus. 'We'll be asking for your removal from the Brame case because of extreme prejudice.'

'That's your prerogative, though I wouldn't fancy your chances, not on those grounds. More than half our time we operate with prejudice to some degree or another. We leave justice and impartiality to the jury and the judge. That's the law, isn't it?' Then he turned away and looked at De Vries. 'Mr De Vries, you told me this morning you had been in touch with New York and there was nothing of any consequence in Mr Brame's files.'

'Correct.' De Vries was sitting so awkwardly on the couch that he gave the impression of being all bones.

Malone shook his head. 'Not correct at all, Mr De Vries. One of my men –' He would not point the finger at Tallis, Schuyler, De Vries and Barrymore's own man – 'One of my men was in touch. You haven't spoken to or faxed your office since I talked to you the other day. Why, Mr De Vries? Have you remembered something you'd rather we didn't know?'

'Jesus Christ!' Channing banged the arms of his chair.

'Relax, Mr Channing. I'm just trying to find out why everyone connected with these cases is so evasive.'

'Are you always as roughshod as this?' said Lazarus, who had remained much calmer than Malone had expected.

'No, I don't think so. I was going along in my usual way on the first two cases. But when Detective-Constable Smith was shot . . .' But, of course, his nerves had been ragged before that murder. The public, however, is careless of the fact that a policeman has a private life. None of these men would bother to ask him what life was like at home, if he had a wife, if he had personal problems: it was out of the context of what they were involved in.

'That was unfortunate.'

'It was unnecessary, Mr Lazarus. And that's why I'm being so roughshod . . .' He managed to keep his voice under control. 'So why didn't you contact your office, Mr De Vries?'

The interruption by Lazarus had given De Vries enough time to compose himself. He leaned forward on the couch, elbows on his knees, hung his head as if in embarrassment. 'I clean forgot, Inspector, but I just couldn't bring myself to admit it earlier. I made a note – my memory isn't what it used to be. Then I forgot even the note – I can't remember where I put it. On my bedside table, I think –'

Crumbs, another bloody actor! Or was he? Joanna Brame had said that her husband had criticized De Vries as incompetent and slipshod. Wearily Malone said, 'What sort of lawyer are you, for Chrissake?'

'That's a fucking insult!'

'Of course it is, Mr De Vries. It was meant to be.' He was certain he was in no danger from De Vries; the American would report him to no one. He turned to Channing. 'Why did your brother come to see you last Sunday morning?'

Both Channing and Lazarus had watched the clash between Malone and De Vries with no show of emotion, but there was no doubting their careful attention, like men who had a stake in what the American divulged.

'I told you,' Channing said. He now sat with his hands together, his fingers steepled: another actor, thought Malone, 'it was a – a reunion – to patch things up –'

'I don't think so, Mr Channing. It was to talk to you about something that led to his death that night.'

'Oh, this is fucking preposterous!' For the first time Lazarus showed angry reaction; he leaned forward as if he might throw a punch at Malone. 'I'd advise you to get out now, Malone, before I get on the phone to the Minister.'

'You know the number? It's 380-0500.'

It was brazen, but it had the effect: Lazarus sat back,

breathing heavily. He adjusted his eye-patch, as if the dead eyeball behind it, if there was one, had popped out against the patch. There was silence in the room, then De Vries abruptly stood up. 'I'm going. I'll send that fax off to New York this evening, Inspector.'

'Do that. I'll look forward to hearing from you.' He did not rise from his chair, he felt he owed none of these men any courtesy.

De Vries nodded to Channing and Lazarus and was gone out the door before either man could escort him out. He left the door open and Lazarus, moving like a man whose muscles had set, stood up and went to close it. He didn't return to his chair but went across to a window and looked out at the rain, which had increased.

'What do you think we have to hide, Inspector?'

'I don't know. But my guess is it's something to do with the Swiss firms you represent. Another guess is that Mr Brame also had some connection with them.'

'He didn't mention it to me,' said Channing after a long moment.

You're a liar, thought Malone. He looked up at the portrait above Channing. There was no resemblance between the man and his painted image. Man, Malone had once read in a judge's summing-up, is made up of the values in which he believes; Channing's values, it seemed, had no relation to those the artist had put into the painting. There was no suggestion of deceit in the portrait; there was in the face behind the desk. There was a hint of leadership and vision in the painted eyes; none at all in those staring at Malone across the desk. The artist had found no uncertainty in his sitter; or, finding his own values in his fee, had not looked for it. Portraits such as this one hung in offices and boardrooms and palaces all round the world: honesty had never been a requisite for a commissioned portrait painter. Malone looked closer at the man and thought he saw something else the artist had missed. Fear?

He took a stab: 'What are you and Mr Lazarus afraid of?'

Channing swung round in his chair, the steepled fingers collapsing, looked at his partner by the window. Lazarus turned slowly, once again adjusted his eye-patch; Malone, thick with suspicion, wondered if the patch was no more than affectation, a complement to the heavy black beard.

'We're afraid of nothing more, Inspector, than violating a client's confidence.'

I'm being stone-walled here. He had faced batsmen like this, those who knew they couldn't win but were determined not to lose.

He bowled a long-hop, the sort of careless ball that sometimes trapped even the most careful batsman. 'You're an expert on guns, Mr Lazarus. Have you ever seen a Sig-Sauer P Two-thirty?'

But Lazarus was not a careless batsman. 'I told you the other day, Inspector, I'm not an expert, just a collector. No, I've never seen a, what did you call it, a Sig-Sauer. Why?'

Malone ignored his question; the ploy had failed. He stood up.

'I'm going up to one of your clients now. We're getting a warrant to go through Bern Investments' files. One or both of you can come if you wish.'

The effect on both men was as if he had hit them under the heart with a rising ball, every fast bowler's treasured shaft of malice. Lazarus actually leaned back against the window, put a hand to the eye-patch; Malone thought for a moment that he was going to tear it off, that the charade was over. Channing flopped back in his chair, beat one hand up and down on its arm. Neither said anything, waiting for the other to speak. Malone felt a spiteful delight that lifted some of the weariness from him.

'Why, for Chrissakes?' Lazarus said at last.

'I'll tell you that when we've seen the files. Coming?'

The two partners looked at each other again, then Lazarus said, 'I'll get my coat,' and disappeared through a doorway into his own office.

Channing, left alone with Malone, stared morosely at the detective. 'You're doing your best to ruin us.'

Malone shook his head. 'It's not my job to ruin anyone. If you think you're being ruined, you're doing it yourself. I'm shitty towards you and Mr Lazarus because you're protecting the bastard who killed my woman colleague. You gave a letter of reference to Ballinger –'

'Who? You said that before.' Channing stood up, came round the desk. 'About giving a letter of reference. I've never heard of anyone named Ballinger – have you, Will?'

Lazarus, pulling on a black raincoat, came back into the room. 'Ballinger?' He shook his head. 'Who's he?'

'Try his other name – Federal.'

Both men were suddenly wary. Lazarus said, 'Go on.'

'You gave him a letter of reference so that he could have access to a safe deposit box belonging to Murray Rockman, the security guard who was murdered.'

'We'd never heard of Rockman till you told us about him. Did you see the letter?'

All at once he saw that he had trapped himself: he was not even sure that Axt, the bank vault manager, had ever seen any letter. 'Well, no–o –'

'I think you've just shit in your shoes, Inspector.' Lazarus wound a black-and-white scarf round his neck; it complemented the beard and the eye-patch. He looked even more piratical, almost sinister. 'It's not a legal term, but I think you get my drift.'

2

Malone and Lazarus walked up Martin Place without speaking, as remote from each other as two men walking on opposite sides of a street. The wind and the rain frisked at them, as if urging them to walk closer together. A drain had been blocked in the shallow amphitheatre where the lunchtime concerts were held and water lay there like a small wind-ruffled lake. A street musician stood in a doorway out of the rain, playing an Irish jig, trying to warm himself as well as the passers-by. Malone noticed that Lazarus wore thick leather gloves, black of course, and wished that he had worn the pair that Lisa was always trying to press on him.

Clements, the Douranes and two young plainclothesmen were waiting for them at the entrance to the Castlereagh Street building. They stood in the lobby out of the rain, while outside the deep glass walls the rain forest suggested nothing but deep-green misery. The party crowded into the lift and went up to the offices of Bern Investments and Alps Securities. No one spoke, they could have been a group of strangers. Malone, standing close to Mrs Dourane, could feel the heat of her body and smell her heightened perfume. Yet she looked at ease, almost bored.

Only when they got out of the lift did Clements say, 'You've got a key, Mr Dourane?'

The Afghan nodded, but first he had looked at Lazarus, who just gave him the blank stare of the eye-patch. Dourane opened the heavy oak door and the group moved in. There were two rooms to the offices, both larger than Malone had expected, as if walls or partitions had been knocked down. The door to the inner room was open; in the far wall two windows looked out on to the street. Both rooms were expensively furnished, as if to impress: but to impress whom, Malone wondered. The carpet was luxuriously thick, the big desk in the inner room was not last week's antique, the leather chairs and couches had been made by craftsmen proud of their work, the antique prints on the walls looked expensive. But what clients did the two companies have to impress? Or was all this for the comfort and convenience of an executive who came in from Switzerland for only a few weeks each year, someone accustomed only to the best?

'Would you open the filing cabinets for us, Mrs Dourane?' There were two in the outer room, another two in the inner, metal disguised as oak. 'Sergeant Clements has shown you the warrant, I take it?'

'A piece of paper,' she said, the pouting lips curling at one corner.

'That's all we need, Mrs Dourane. Pieces of paper have hung people, finished wars, got cheating husbands into trouble with their wives – and vice versa. We know all about paper. Open the cabinets, please.'

She produced keys, opened the cabinets, slid open the drawers. They were empty. Her back was to Malone and Clements and she remained like that a moment; when she turned the pout had become a smirk. 'We've been burgled, Inspector. What now? Got a piece of paper that covers that?'

'Do you know anything about this, Mr Dourane?'

But Dourane's shock was genuine. 'No, no. I don't understand how –'

Lazarus had been standing back, like a passer-by who had stopped to see what was going on. Malone glanced at him, half-expecting a smirk such as Mrs Dourane had given him, but the lawyer remained impassive.

Malone turned back to Mrs Dourane. 'Let's look in the other office.'

She walked ahead of him, her hips in a lazy swing. She might once have been a model, one who had never made it on to a cover, who had spent her working life in the back of the book. But she exuded confidence; or contempt. She opened the cabinets in the inner office: they, too, were empty. She gave Malone the smirking smile. 'Do you think we came back here last night and cleaned out the files?'

'No, we know you didn't do that. We've had you under

surveillance since yesterday afternoon.' He gestured at the two young plainclothesmen. 'You haven't any report on Mr and Mrs Dourane sneaking out during the night, have you? These are Constables Dash and Yalwyn,' he said to Lazarus. 'For the record.'

'There was nothing in the log, sir.' Dash did not look as if he might live up to his name; he was solid and stolid, a brick wall of reliability. He was fair-headed, freckled and destined for sun cancers. 'Last night's shift reported that Mr and Mrs Dourane went to a restaurant in Rockdale, but that was all.'

'You bastards,' said Mrs Dourane, but addressed herself to Malone and Clements.

'Righto, let's have a look at the computer,' said Malone, but even in his own ears he didn't sound hopeful.

They went back to the outer office and Clements sat down in front of the computer. 'You work this?' he said to Mrs Dourane.

'Yes.'

Malone, standing beside her, felt the heat in her again. She was apprehensive; abruptly he felt hopeful again. 'Test its memory, Russ.'

But the computer produced nothing; its memory was as blank as that of a bankrupt entrepreneur who couldn't remember where he had mislaid an odd million or two. 'Nothing,' said Clements. 'It's been wiped clean.'

Mrs Dourane visibly relaxed; she produced a packet of cigarettes from her handbag and lit one. She blew smoke, a little theatrically. 'You could have saved that warrant for another occasion, Inspector.'

'Who else has keys to this office and these cabinets?' Malone asked Dourane.

The Afghan had been nervous from the moment they had entered the offices. His forehead was glistening, but it was difficult to tell whether it was sweat or water from his rain-drenched hair. He was wearing a tan raincoat and

Malone could see his hands moving inside its pockets like rats looking for a way out of a blind hole. His voice was a mumble: 'No one, as far as I know.'

'Who gave *you* the keys?'

Dourane glanced at Lazarus. 'Can I answer that?'

Lazarus said to Malone, 'We assume it was the leasing agency for the building –'

'That would be for the office,' said Malone. 'Not for the filing cabinets. Come on, Mr Dourane, don't hold us up. You don't want to spend another couple of hours down at Homicide.' He looked at his watch. 'It's time we all went home.'

Dourane chewed on his lip; there was no arrogant lift to the chin now. Perhaps he wished he *were* a camel driver, lost somewhere in the remote Outback. At last, giving up, he said, 'Mr Federal, my boss, gave me the keys. When I first started here two years ago.'

'Did he say he would keep a spare set of keys?'

'No.'

'But he could have?' Dourane nodded. 'How much autonomy did you have?'

Dourane glanced at his wife, who gave him no encouragement at all; then he looked back at Malone. 'None. I did only what he told me. While he was here and even from Zurich – he phoned every day.'

'Well,' Malone gestured at the cabinets and the computer, 'it looks as if your boss cleaned you out. You might be out of a job, Mr and Mrs Dourane – I hope you arranged for redundancy pay. Righto, you can go. Constables Dash and Yalwyn will drive you home.'

'Are they still to be under surveillance?' said Lazarus.

'Until we find Mr Federal, yes. I think it's safer, don't you? We wouldn't want them killed, too, would we? Feeling okay, Mrs Dourane?' It was cheap stuff, but he was exhausted now. He hadn't been able to resist the crack when he had seen her lean back sharply against the open cabinet, pushing in the top drawer. 'It's a possibility, you know.'

'You really are a shit,' she said, and Malone saw her husband wince.

'Not in front of the young men, please. Take them home, fellers.'

Malone and Clements were left alone with Lazarus. Clements looked around the room. He and Malone had visited offices such as these back in the Greed Decade, when entrepreneurs and other assorted bigheads had surrounded themselves with the extravagance of mad kings. He had once described such offices to Romy and she had drawn the comparison with the royals, calling them Down Under Ludwigs and Farouks. Most, if not all of them, had gone down the tubes, leaving no monuments except debt. These two rooms, however, suggested they had been furnished for the long run.

'Who else worked here besides the Douranes?' he asked Lazarus.

The lawyer shrugged. 'No one, as far as I know. I've only been in here twice before.'

'To see Mr Federal?'

Just the merest hesitation: 'No.'

'All this, a lay-out like this, just for Dourane and his missus to work in? Come *on*. If Federal has been coming to Sydney regularly these last twelve months or so, you've seen him.'

'Okay.' Lazarus sat back on the desk behind him. 'I've met him. Once here and once in Zurich.'

'What's he like? Describe him to us.'

Lazarus unwound the scarf from round his neck. He was beginning to look hot, though the central heating in the office had apparently been turned off. He peeled off his thick gloves and looked at his sweating palms.

'He's, I dunno, about fifty, maybe a bit more. Average-looking, you'd hardly notice him in a crowded room. He is thin, he wears horn-rimmed glasses, you know, the sort that went out years ago –' He was fashion-conscious; his own glasses, if he wore any, would have the rims of the moment. But Malone guessed that that one good eye would have 20/20 vision, would pick up every detail between here and the horizon. 'He speaks excellent English, but then so many of the Swiss do.'

Malone looked at Clements. 'He's our Mr Ballinger, all right.'

'What's he *like*?' said Clements. 'Aside from his looks?'

Lazarus thought a moment. 'It's hard to say. Precise – I mean he knew exactly what he wanted to tell you, his instructions. But he wasn't – overbearing? I mean he didn't try to ride you, not like some clients who think money is some sort of whip. He was polite, but stand-offish. He'd take advice, but you always knew who was in control. He was *Swiss*, I guess.'

Malone knew no Swiss and he wondered why other nationalities always seemed to have reservations about them. 'Mr Lazarus, I think you'd better watch your shoes, if you get my drift. He's our killer, at least he killed Detective Smith, and he may try to kill you too, if you know too much. You want to tell us all you know? *All* of it?'

Lazarus took his time, began pulling on his gloves. 'No, I don't think so,' he said, but he sounded like a man who wished he had an alternative.

3

That night Malone, despite his weariness, which he would never have confessed to her, took Lisa to dinner.

'I'm glad you're taking Mum out on her own,' Claire told him as he stood in front of the hallway mirror fixing his tie. 'Go out and be young lovers. Again.'

'Thanks, Dorothy Dix.'

'Who's Dorothy Dix?'

The signposts of different generations: a few months ago he had had to ask her who Kurt Cobain was. 'She used to give me advice when I *was* a young lover. And Grandpa, too, probably.'

'*Grandpa?*'

'Yes, I think he was young once.' Lisa was in the main bedroom, but he lowered his voice anyway: 'How has Mum been with you and Maureen and Tom?'

'Fine. Sometimes I've caught her staring out the window, you know, but who wouldn't? She's certain, though, she's going to be okay. She will be, won't she?' Anxiety clouded her young face.

'Romy and Mum's own doctor, they both say the chances are better than fifty–fifty. You know Mum, she'll make the chances better than that . . . How's school?'

Claire would sit for her Higher School Certificate this year; next year she would be at university. 'It's okay . . . Dad, what would you say if I joined the police after I've finished uni?'

'No.' He was flatly adamant.

'Why?'

'Do you need to ask?' He looked in the mirror and saw that, with his usual approach to dressing, he had put on his police tie. He began to untie it.

'You mean Peta Smith? I wasn't thinking of Homicide or anything like that. I'd like to be on the forensic side. Mother Brendan says I've got an analytical mind.'

'So has your mother. We don't want two of you in the family.'

'Come on, Dad. Stop treating me like a child. Here, give me that!'

She almost grabbed the tie from round his neck, went along the hallway into the main bedroom, was back in less than half a minute with another tie. In the meantime he stood in front of the mirror analysing his looks. Shopworn, he thought, too long on the job; it was beginning to show, like skin left too long in the sun. But he had survived, which was more than Peta Smith had done. He took the tie Claire had brought.

'That's the one Grandma Pretorius gave me last Christmas.' Another gift he hadn't wanted.

'Gucci. Just be grateful she didn't give you an Olympic tie – you'd have strangled her with it . . . Think about me joining the police. I'm really keen on it, Dad.'

He knotted the tie, looked at her in the mirror. 'Somehow I never expected you to be the one. Maureen, maybe. Or Tom. But not you. Why?'

'What would you like me to be? A lawyer?'

He wrinkled his nose. 'There are too many of them. I don't know, really, what I want you to be. I've been waiting for you to tell me.'

'So I just have. Think about it, there's plenty of time before I graduate.'

He put his hand behind her head, kissed her on the forehead. 'We'll talk about it then, okay?'

Lisa came into the hallway in a pale green wool-knit suit, a classic-cut camel-hair topcoat over her arm, her hair drawn back in a chignon, discreet gold ear-rings dangling. Malone smiled at her, all his tiredness abruptly evaporating.

'Not a bad-looking couple,' said Maureen from the living-room doorway. 'I think we can let 'em out of the house.'

'You look terrific, Mum,' said Tom.

'What about me?' said his father.

'Are guys supposed to look terrific?'

Claire made a face, looked at her father. 'A typical ocker. Maybe you think he's what a police recruit should be?'

'The spitting image of me when I first joined.'

He took Lisa to Level 41, a restaurant they had not

previously visited, on the top floor of a high-rise commercial building in the heart of the city. He felt the pain in his hip as he looked at the prices; the money in his wallet gave a new meaning to the term hard currency as it calcified with shock. But he managed to hide his dismay, told himself this was a night not to be celebrated at the Black Stump steakhouse or Pizza Hut.

But Lisa saw the hidden pain, smiled at him. 'You're not thinking of this as the Last Supper, are you?'

'Don't say that!' He reached for her hand.

'It was a joke, darling. Relax, I'm not going to spend the evening being miserable. What sort of a day did you have?'

'Miserable.'

He looked out of the glass walls of the restaurant, at this city that always quietly thrilled him with its beauty. The rain had stopped, the wind had polished the night air to a startling clarity. The city lay below them, stretched away to the stars that might have been the lights of another metropolis. To the north and seemingly just below them, ferries crawled like fire-flies across the splintered mirror of the harbour. To their left the Harbour Bridge looped in a comet of light and beyond it the commercial district of North Sydney flashed its bright signs like electric business cards. On the outer edges of the city were still the scars of last summer's dreadful bushfires, but they were hidden now in the darkness.

'It's a beautiful city. It's a pity it needs law and order.'

'When they settled in the first caves, the first community, they needed law and order,' she said. 'Even cricket needs an umpire. None of you cricketers ever trust each other to be fair and play the game.'

'That's heresy.'

'Of course it is. We women are good at that. Just imagine what religion would have been like if we'd been allowed to run it, instead of a lot of blinkered men.' Then she cocked her head to one side.

'What's the matter?'

'Am I hearing things or is the place full of American voices?'

Then he, too, became aware of the voices. 'It's the lawyers. I guess there was nothing official on for them tonight.'

He looked around, but saw none of the lawyers he had met; there was no sign of Zoehrer or De Vries or Tallis. Then he saw Joanna Brame sitting at a table not too far from them; she looked up and caught his eye and smiled, ducking her head in a small bow. He smiled back, wondering if she was with De Vries and he had disappeared for the moment. If he had, he hoped he would not come back, even if it meant deserting Mrs Brame. He had had enough of the New York lawyer for the day.

'Whom are you smiling at?'

'Mrs Brame. She's on her own, back there behind you.'

Lisa glanced over her shoulder. 'She's eating alone, there's no other place set. Do you want to ask her to join us?'

'No.'

'I shan't mind, so long as you don't talk shop. I'd like to meet her. From what you've told me, she's interesting. She sounds like someone out of that movie we saw last year, *The Age of Innocence*.'

'Not quite. I can tell you, Mrs Brame is far from innocent. If she joins us, we don't tell her why we're having a night out.'

'Of course we don't.' Her tone was a little sharp and he realized how insensitive he had been. He remembered something he had overheard an American say: Never ask an Aussie how he is, because he'll tell you in great detail. 'We'll tell her we come here once a month as a regular thing.'

'On a cop's pay?'

He didn't want Joanna Brame to join them, but he knew

Lisa's curiosity about people. Before their marriage she had lived the diplomatic life in London as private secretary to the Australian High Commissioner; he had met her there while on his first big case. She had been a witness, silent admittedly, to the lives of prime ministers and presidents and ambassadors. She had given up all that to come back to Australia to be a policeman's wife, to be a mother, to live in a shrunken world about which she never complained. But she had never lost her interest in the wider world, she read more than just newspapers and magazines, she looked at people and, with her analytical mind, saw more than vacuous faces and heard more than vapid voices. If she wanted to meet Joanna Brame, he owed it to her.

He got up and went along to the other table. 'I see you're eating alone, Mrs Brame. My wife and I would like you to join us. Would you?'

'Are we to talk shop, Inspector?'

'My wife has just laid down the law on that one. It's purely social. I'd like you to meet my wife.' He hadn't intended to say that, but it was true.

Joanna Brame gathered up her handbag. 'I've ordered, I'll just have them serve me at your table.' As they moved towards Lisa, she said, 'She is a beautiful woman, Mr Malone. You are very fortunate.'

'Thank you.' Malone was aware that heads had turned as he and Joanna Brame moved from one table to the other. By now they all knew who Joanna Brame was; he hoped none would remember who he was. It wouldn't do for the lawyers to think that he was on the same sort of expense account as themselves. That was his father coming out in him again, Con's attitude of *us* and *them*.

The two women met with no constraint between them, but with no gushing. A waiter brought an extra chair and Joanna sat down. 'I'm grateful to you for this invitation. I shouldn't have come here tonight, but I'd been told about this view. I haven't had a chance to admire it, people have been coming up ever since I arrived, giving me their condolences. It's very kind of them, but I find it hard to play the grieving widow in a public place.'

'You should've worn dark glasses,' said Malone. 'That usually warns people off.'

'I only wear dark glasses when I'm with so-called celebrities. Their glare hurts my eyes.'

Lisa laughed and Malone was suddenly glad he had invited the older woman to their table. 'Be our guest and admire the view.'

'Do you come here often?'

'Once a month,' said Lisa, lying with a diplomat's skill.

Joanna, who had no idea what a detective-inspector, indeed any police officer, earned and anyhow thought the menu prices, by New York standards, ridiculously low, said, 'For some reason I've always dined at ground level. I must go up in the world.' Dismissing Le Cirque and La Grenouille as if they were basement fast food outlets. 'Would you let me order champagne to toast the view?' A waiter appeared and she looked at Malone. 'What should I order, Mr Malone? Domestic or French?'

'No, you're our guest,' said Lisa. 'You order, Scobie. A bottle of Roederer will do nicely. It's a woman's champagne.'

Crumbs, he thought, she thinks she's back on the diplomatic circuit. But this evening he could deny her nothing and he ordered the champagne even as his money and credit card fused like rock in his wallet.

The longer the meal went on the more Malone accepted Joanna Brame's place at the table. Slowly he realized that Lisa had been right in wanting the American woman to join them. Left alone, he and she would inevitably have begun resurrecting memories, trying to avoid talking about the present and the immediate future; the dinner would have, after all, been a Last Supper of sorts. Joanna did not talk about her own tragedy; she hid her grief without putting on any embarrassing mask of gaiety. As he watched he saw something of the Lisa of long ago emerging. She and Joanna Brame found a mutual interest in art, even similar tastes; both were traditionalists, though not stuffy. Their taste in music and opera ran along similar lines; both of them remembered seasons at Glyndebourne. But it was more than culture that loosely bound them; it struck him with something akin to jealousy that Lisa could step into Joanna Brame's world and *belong*. He was the outsider, the milkman at the artist's door, the gatekeeper at Glyndebourne.

Then Joanna said, 'Oh, I'm sorry, Mr Malone. I've taken over your night out. Like . . . No.' She stopped.

'No? No what?'

She looked across the table at Lisa. 'I've been determined not to mention my husband –'

'I've noticed. No, go ahead . . .'

'Well –' She stroked her temple with a hand that bore only one ring, a platinum circle studded with a large emerald. All at once the strain of the last few days showed, the grey eyes had no animation in them, the cheeks were slack. 'This afternoon I remembered something. About two months ago, when Orville was preparing to come out here for this convention, he was tidying up his papers before an LBO –' She smiled wanly at Lisa's puzzlement. 'Leveraged buy-out. Even wives learn the jargon after a while.'

'Not when you're a Homicide detective's wife. Scobie protects me from those.'

There was an awkward silence for a moment, as if Lisa had prodded a corpse with her toe. Then Joanna went on, 'Orville had handled this takeover and it had taken months of his time. He said he was tired of the negotiating and he'd like a rest from it. But first, there was one he had to look at in Australia. He didn't say any more. We were interrupted by someone –' She frowned, trying to put her memory to work. 'We were at our place in Connecticut – yes, guests arrived . . . It may mean nothing at all, Mr Malone. LBOs have been a way of life for lawyers these past ten years. American lawyers, anyway. I don't think my father would have handled more than half a dozen in his whole life. Though they were not called leveraged buy-outs in his day. They were politer.'

'Everyone was politer in the past,' said Lisa, smiling. 'Or anyway, it's nice to think so.'

The bill, including the champagne, came to three hundred and eighty dollars. Curiously, Malone felt it had been worth it. They took Joanna down to her hire car, shook hands with her, recognizing that she was not one for the social peck on the cheek, not on a first occasion. 'You are a very lucky pair,' she said, got into the car and was driven off.

Going home Lisa said, 'I'll give you the money for the champagne out of house-keeping.'

He took his hand off the wheel, squeezed her thigh, then her mount, behind which the cancer lay. 'No, it made you look happier than you have for the past week.'

'Have I looked unhappy?' She was unhappy at the thought.

'Occasionally. Claire said she had seen you staring out the window a couple of times. But I do that, too, at work.' Then he said, 'I'm going into the office tomorrow morning, okay?'

'I told you, don't stop work on my account. I meant it.'

'I'm glad I married you.' Then he confessed: 'Tonight, for a while, I wondered if I'd made a mistake. No, if *you'd* made a mistake. Marrying me.'

She could read him like a book, every page cut and in large type. 'When Joanna and I were talking? Darling, that was another life. If I were still there, would I have you and the kids?' She lifted his hand from her crotch, kissed it. 'You can have memories without having to have regrets. If

He went back into his office, rang the Stock Exchange, found a girl on duty who gave him the home number of the secretary of the Exchange. He rang Mr Langer at his home in Pymble, was invited to come out at once.

He drove through the Harbour tunnel, moving at a sedate seventy ks an hour while the weekend traffic hurtled by him as if it had got word that the tunnel was about to collapse. Some months ago a group of kids had been clocked taking their cars through the tunnel at up to two hundred ks an hour; in some age groups there was no line drawn between heroics and stupidity. He hammered his horn as another idiot, a grey-haired one this time, cut across in front of him.

He continued on up the freeway on to Pacific Highway and then north into the *real* North Shore. Pymble was where the professional classes, so-called, lived: if any blue-collar workers lived here, the blue collars were by Lacoste or Ralph Lauren. John Langer lived on the west side of the railway line, which put him one notch down on the social scale.

He came down his driveway to meet Malone as the latter pulled up. He was a small man with thick, prematurely grey hair, lively eyes and a flat husky voice as if he had been choked by smoke. Which might have been: the reserve on to which his house backed was a reminder of last January's bushfires.

'We're rebuilding the back of the house,' he explained as they walked up the driveway. 'We were lucky the whole lot wasn't burned to the ground.' He gestured at the two houses, or their ruins, on the west side of his own house. 'You can see what the fires did there. Wiped out, entirely. The owners just don't want to come back here, they've said they don't care if they never see another bush or tree . . . What can I do for you, Inspector? At the Stock Exchange we don't get too many enquiries from Homicide. We have suicides, but they don't concern you, do they?'

For the moment Malone did not want to talk murder. 'Takeovers, Mr Langer. Have there been any big attempted takeovers in the past few months that caused any talk on the Exchange?'

'Sure, several of them.' He named three. 'Once the economy started to pick up just before Christmas, when the market started to climb, buyers came out of the woodwork. Not that I'm suggesting they were all shonky,' he added, though not hastily.

'That's when takeovers start happening, when the market starts rising?'

'Not necessarily. A takeover or a merger can happen at any time. But back in the Eighties it was a real dog-fight. The entrepreneurs – no names, so don't ask me – they were buying up everything they could lay their hands on and the governments, Federal and State, were turning a blind eye to it. They thought it was a garage sale. Now the buyers are more cautious. More honest,' he added, again not hastily. He gestured at his house, a two-storeyed white brick, still disfigured by the bushfire graffiti of scorch-marks. The brand-new ochre bricks of the half-completed back section, so far unpainted, looked like a huge scabrous sore against the main part of the house. 'Not all of them, of course. We've had buyers down here wanting to buy us out, buy up the ruins of those two places next door. Offering insulting money, but as brazen as those jokers back in the Eighties.'

Malone looked at the empty swimming pool, the lawn with the blackened soil still showing through in patches, at the dark skeletons of some of the trees in the bushland reserve at the back. Some of the trees had sprouted green promise in the autumn, but the winter had killed it off; it would be another spring before the bush came truly alive again and even then the black scars would still show as reminders of what had been and what would surely come again.

'Are the firms that are taken over, are they usually burnt-out companies? I mean burnt-out as far as management goes?'

'Often, but not always. What are we leading up to, Inspector?'

Malone then told him of the murders of Brame, Rockman and Peta Smith. 'None of them knew each other, but there's a connection. No names, but all the arrows on what we call our flow chart lead back to a particular firm of lawyers. We don't suspect them of the murders, but we believe they know something of why the murders happened. I think it may have something to do with a takeover. A big one that so far hasn't got into the papers.'

Langer picked at the wool of the thick sweater he wore. 'You're asking me to open a can of worms.'

'I guess so. But whatever you tell me, the public or the press will never know, not till you tell them.'

'You want to come inside, have some coffee?'

Malone hesitated, then shook his head. 'No, if I come inside it puts it on a more personal level. I'm asking you as the secretary of the Stock Exchange.'

Langer looked around him. 'I'd been in that office only two days when the market collapsed in 1987. Black Tuesday. We'd just taken out the mortgage on this place . . . Okay, I see your point. Yes, we've been looking into some share buying that worries us. Us and the Securities Commission. So far we've kept it to ourselves, though we think one or two of the financial columnists have sniffed it out.'

'Who's being bought and by who?'

'BHP and Ampolex. The buyers, we guess, are interested in the oil search by both those companies. The buying is spread over half a dozen companies – seven, if I remember rightly. None of them well-known or, as far as we can gather, even remotely connected to the oil business.'

'Any of them publicly listed?'

'No. BHP got in touch with us only last week, and then,

a day later, Ampolex. Twelve per cent of BHP has been bought up and 18 per cent of Ampolex.'

'Are they still buying?'

'No, not as far as I know.'

'Twelve per cent of BHP and 18 per cent of Ampolex – what would that add up to?'

'In dollars? A helluva lot. I couldn't tell you off the top of my head, but the total would run into several billion.'

'And nobody noticed that much money being spent?'

'Inspector, we're not dumb or blind on the Stock Exchange. We may have been back in the Eighties, but not now. Neither would BHP be blind. They have a team who do a daily graph on shares bought and sold – all big companies do. Of course we were aware of the buying up of the shares, we watched the price rising, though it didn't jump alarmingly, probably because the buying was spread. But there was no open bid as there was back in 1990 when Holmes A'Court tried to buy the controlling interest in BHP. He had Buckley's chance, incidentally, but over in the West in those days pie-in-the-sky was the main meal of the day. Don't quote me,' he said and grinned, looking suddenly younger, a grey-haired schoolboy. 'The prices went up, but it was only a couple of weeks ago that we woke up there were seven main buyers. Last week we found out the buying was spread amongst twelve stock-brokers. Some here in Sydney, some in Melbourne, Adelaide, Brisbane and Perth. We're all part of the Australian Stock Exchange. There's no Sydney Stock Exchange, or Melbourne, as such.'

'You know the names of all the buyers? Which stock-brokers they bought through?'

'I'd have to run through the computer. I can do that for you first thing Monday –'

'Mr Langer, I can't wait till then. I'm trying to hang on to half a dozen strings at once and some of them might slip out of my hand at any moment. Plus the fact that the widow of the American, Mrs Brame, is still here in Sydney waiting for the release of her husband's body. It'd please me if I could tell her who murdered her husband before she takes him back home.'

Langer looked dubious. 'Will it please her?'

'Yes, it would. The relatives of murder victims want just as much as the police to see the murderer caught. It's not just revenge – though more often than not, that's the main reason. But it, well, it's a putting an end to it in their own minds. As much as you can put an end to something like that. Can we go back to town *now*?'

Langer made no attempt to hide his reluctance; he looked at the house. 'The builder is due here at noon . . . Okay, I'll have my wife ask him to wait. Do you know where the Exchange is? Follow me in my car.'

He went into the house and Malone walked back down the driveway to the unmarked Commodore. Two boys were skate-boarding in the roadway, the screech of the wheels like fingernails against a blackboard. A couple stood arguing in their front garden under the drooping bare branches of a large Japanese maple, as under the ribs of a giant umbrella that had lost its silk. Malone saw nor heard none of it, taken up by the feeling of anticipation that had begun to creep through him; not excitement, he was too experienced for that, but the anticipation of an unexpected door opening. One that might lead nowhere, but experience had also told him that doors always led somewhere. Only in imagination or dreams did they open on blank walls.

Langer came out of the house; a woman followed him, standing on the front porch and looking curiously down at Malone. Langer came down the driveway, snapped at the skate-boarders, as they came too close to him, waved to the quarrelling couple across the street, got into a blue Mercedes that was parked at the kerb, started up and led Malone back to the city. He drove fast, as if under instructions from his wife to hurry back, and Malone had trouble keeping up with him.

The Saturday streets downtown in the financial district were almost deserted, as they are in most cities; as if money, like blood, was cut off for the weekend. The Stock Exchange was in Bond Street, not much more than a lane buried at the feet of high-rise commercial buildings. The big main room was deserted, but in a side room operators at computers were keeping an eye on overseas exchanges.

'It's still Friday on Wall Street,' said Langer. 'We watch to see if they sneeze, then we'll catch cold. We're financial hypochondriacs,' he said and gave the boyish grin again. 'Don't quote me, but this past week the markets world-wide have gone haywire.'

He led Malone into a room where there was a bank of six computers. A plump young woman followed them. 'Can I help you, Mr Langer?'

'Oh, Julie. This is Inspector Malone. Can you dredge up for us the share buying in BHP and Ampolex over the past two months?'

The girl sat down at one of the computers and began to tap at the keys. Green figures and letters came up on the screen and Malone watched with his usual incomprehension of the marvels of modern technology. He was a technological idiot; in another age he knew he would have had trouble understanding the mechanics of the chastity belt; Tom, a genius like all twelve-year-olds, had told him his relations with a computer 'mouse' were like those between Tom and Jerry. But he was not a modern Luddite and he admired what the computer and its operator could do. Julie, who in modern office protocol seemed to have no other name, was adept at her trade; information, it seemed, flowed out of her fingertips. She turned away from the screen.

'That's all the buying up to yesterday. The price on both stocks has gone the way of the market since Monday.'

Langer perused the figures on the screen. 'Okay, take out these buyers –' He handed her a slip of paper on which he had scribbled seven company names. 'Give us their total purchases in BHP and Ampolex.'

More keys were punched. 'Overall, since May 7 when the buying started, the seven companies have bought two hundred and twenty million shares in BHP, that's roughly 14 per cent of the total share-holding. Ampolex, they've bought 12 per cent.'

'How much did the BHP shares cost them?'

More keys, more figures. 'The price varied, but I'd say they paid out around four billion dollars.'

'And Ampolex?'

The fingers worked again. 'Roughly two hundred million.'

'None of that would be enough to give them control?' asked Malone.

'No,' Langer said, 'but it might give them a seat or two on the board if they demanded it. Though it might be difficult with BHP, there you're dealing with the Establishment, it'd be like trying to chip your way into Ayers Rock.'

'When did the buying stop?'

'From those seven companies?' Julie worked the screen again. 'Yesterday week. They've bought nothing this week.'

Nothing since the murders. 'Were Bern Investments and Alps Securities the biggest buyers?'

More keys: 'No, the buying looks pretty evenly spread.'

'Who did the buying?'

The screen had the information: 'It was spread around. Six stockbrokers –' Julie read out the names. 'In Sydney, that is. Another two in Perth, two in Melbourne, one each in Brisbane and Adelaide.'

'All middle-sized or small firms,' said Langer. 'That all you want, Inspector?'

Malone thanked Julie, then followed Langer out of the

room and down to his own office. 'Well, does what we've told you help you at all?'

Malone looked at his notebook. 'The first thing that stands out from my point of view is that the buying stopped this week, after the first two murders . . . What about the other five firms besides Bern and Alps?'

'The Securities Commission checked on them. They're all proprietary companies registered here. We checked the directors, most of them seem to be Australian, at least they've got Anglo-Australian names. Don't quote me to the Ethnics Board or whatever.' Again he grinned. 'But who the directors are doesn't mean much. Back in the bottom-of-the-harbour days –' in the Greed Decade when companies had risen and sunk like the Loch Ness monster – 'the wiseguys used to almost pick passers-by off the streets, borrow their names, pay them a coupla thousand bucks and send 'em on their way. We traced the director of one company, he was a wino, lived in the Matthew Talbot hostel, couldn't keep his own balance, let alone a balance sheet. We haven't interviewed any of the directors of these companies yet.'

'What about lawyers? Do companies have to nominate their lawyers when they register?'

'Not necessarily. Usually lawyers do the registration for a company but their name doesn't have to be on the certificate of registration. It would be on the prospectus, of course.' He looked shrewdly at Malone. 'You said everything pointed back to a particular firm of lawyers. I think you owe me their names, just so's we can keep an eye on them if this investigation blows up in our faces.'

Malone took a moment, then said, 'Channing and Lazarus. But do me a favour, don't approach them till I give you the word. And don't mention them to the Law Society. Like I told you, we don't suspect them of the actual murders or even having anything to do with them. But we're hoping they can lead us to the killer. Or killers.'

'You think someone connected with the seven companies are the killers?' He shook his head in disbelief. 'Even back in the Boom, the wiseguys didn't go around killing people.'

'How do you know?' said Malone and Langer looked at him wide-eyed. 'Even in Homicide we don't get to hear of all the murders committed. Now can I have the names of all the senior partners in those stockbroking firms and their home phone numbers if you have them.'

'You're going to contact them all *today*?'

'I can't wait, Mr Langer.' He could not tell him the real reason why he could not let the weekend pass and him do nothing. He would be going off the case tomorrow night: it was *his* case up till then and, as ever, he could not stomach the thought of leaving it unfinished. 'Incidentally, how big a buy would those shares in BHP and Ampolex add up to?'

'We talked about that with the Securities people. Combined, it would be the biggest buy-up in our history in cash terms. It's going to be very interesting when we find out where the money is coming from.'

'I think I can tell you that,' said Malone. 'From Switzerland, a company called Zurich Private Holdings. But where it *really* comes from . . . Your guess is as good as mine.'

2

It was not easy to find the partners in the six Sydney stockbroking firms. Malone drafted John Kagal and Phil Truach, both on weekend duty, to help him. At one number all they got was an answering machine that told them to call back Monday – 'a trade unionist stockbroker?' said Truach. The other five yielded up either the men themselves or directions from a family member as to where they could be found. 'Okay,' said Kagal, 'let's take the four top names or we'll be running around like blue-arsed flies all weekend.'

Malone should have made that suggestion, but his energy, if not his determination, was running out. He took two of the names and gave one each to Kagal and Truach, with a list of questions to be asked. Then he went out, got into the unmarked car and drove over to Birchgrove.

Birchgrove is a tiny area jutting out into the harbour from the south side. Once it had been a mix of workers' cottages and middle-class merchants' houses; narrow streets ran down from its ridge like paved gullies. Over the past twenty years it had become a refuge for the more successful writers and artists, some of whom would have died of shame if they had had to look at the harbour from its north shore, 'over there' among the silvertails. At the end of the point was a cricket oval where Malone had played in the lower grades in his teens and where, once only, he had scored fifty runs, even if most of the runs came from sliced shots that would have embarrassed a blind golfer.

Colin Salmon, of Salmon, Bryce, lived in a refurbished two-storeyed Victorian house with a narrow garden running down to a jetty where a small yacht was moored. A teenage boy and girl were at work on the boat and a woman in slacks and sweater had just reached the jetty with a picnic basket. Salmon, in jeans and sweater and boat shoes, and Malone stood on the narrow terrace between the house and the slope of the garden.

'You were lucky to catch me. Saturdays are our day on the boat.' Salmon was Jewish, tall and slim, with grey wavy hair and a deep voice that had a touch of South African accent. There was a steeliness to him that suggested he knew more about life than its mere commercial side, that it was more than just buy and sell. In his eyes there was pain not quite hidden. 'What can I do for you?'

Malone explained as briefly as he could, keeping the details to a minimum. He would have preferred to have told Salmon nothing, just asked his questions, but then the stockbroker would have been within his rights to walk away and answer nothing. 'We're trying to tie together a lot of things –'

Salmon nodded. 'I understand, Inspector. As far as I know, nothing we did for Bern Investments and Alps Securities – they were the only two we bought for – as far as we know there was nothing underhand about the deal. We were surprised at the size of the orders, but their money was always forthcoming, almost cash on delivery. We were asked not to publicize the buying, but we never do that, anyway.'

'When were you first contacted and when did you get instructions to stop buying?'

'They first got in touch with us about two months ago – I can't remember the exact date but I can have it looked up. We started buying immediately.'

'And when did they tell you to stop?'

'Last Monday.'

'The money, was it paid on local cheques?'

'No, they explained that to us before they instructed us to start buying. The money came by telegraphed bank draft from Switzerland. The Trade Bank of Zurich. I usually don't remember where a client's cheques came from, but this time we were dealing in big money.'

'Did you have instructions who to buy from?'

'We were told to buy from any source, but to go lightly on institutions like the insurance companies. I thought at the time that they didn't want to make waves, but I didn't make a point of asking them why. We did have to go to the institutions eventually, they hold so much of the stock, but we did it as discreetly as we could. Actually, it was rather exciting in a quiet way, raiding.'

Like a Zulu? Malone almost asked, but caught his tongue in time. 'Who gave you instructions to buy? Was it a Mr Federal?'

'No, it was a Mr Dourane. He wasn't Australian, but I haven't a clue where he came from. He could have been an Arab –'

'He's Afghan. Top drawer, I believe, so he told me.'

Salmon twisted his lips. 'That's a new one. We really are multicultural, aren't we?'

Malone grinned. 'When the South Africans were out here in the summer, who did you barrack for in the cricket?'

Salmon smiled. 'South Africa, of course. You can take multiculturalism too far, don't you think?'

Malone didn't ask the obvious question: *Are you going to go home to the new South Africa?* People's big decisions were not the business of strangers.

'Do you want me to keep quiet about your visit?'

'Yes. Except if Mr Dourane gets in touch again. He might like to know we're getting closer and closer to what this is all about.'

'Are you?' said Salmon shrewdly.

But that was not an answer you gave to a stranger.

He drove back across town and out to Rose Bay where Clive Kelty, of Kelty and Kelty, gave much the same information on the BHP and Ampolex buying. He was a rotund bald man who came off his tennis court, red-faced and seemingly glad to be distracted, to listen worriedly when Malone told him of the murders.

'Are we likely to be, you –'

'I don't think so, Mr Kelty. They're not serial killers, not of stockbrokers.' Kelty smiled sickly, as if he had been hit in his round belly by a smashed volley. 'So you were never contacted by anyone but Mr Dourane?'

Kelty shook his bald head. Behind him a mixed doubles game had started; a woman let out a squeal of fright and Kelty shook his head again. 'I hate playing with women, if they're not shrieking, they're giggling . . . No, we met only Dourane. Sometimes we'd get a query from a woman asking if the purchases were going through, said she was *Mrs* Dourane. She came once to pick up some share certificates. Good-looking woman,' he said appreciatively.

'I've met her,' said Malone. 'Don't think she'd play tennis.'

'No, probably not. There was never anyone else we met or spoke to.'

'You didn't think that out of the ordinary, an instruction to buy millions of dollars' worth of shares in two of the biggest companies in Australia and you know nothing about the companies doing the buying?'

Kelty wiped the sweat from his face with a towel; Malone wondered if he played tennis during the summer. 'Inspector, stockbroking is like bookmaking, it's a cut-throat business. We steal each other's experts, seduce each other's clients. Oh, we're all very gentlemanly, but it's a tough game and you make a dollar where and when you can. Yes, we checked on the companies we were buying for, they're all registered and above board, we did that when we added up the size of the buying order. When the first bank draft came in, as promised, we – well, we did what every other firm in the business, even the Establishment ones, would have done. We went ahead with the buying. Stockbrokers aren't a regulatory body, we leave that to those who have the authority. This country is over-run with interfering bodies.' Malone waited for him to say the country was a socialist state, but Kelty suddenly seemed to realize he was talking to someone who belonged to a regulatory body. 'Will that be all?'

'For the time being, Mr Kelty. We'll be in touch again, I'm sure.' Then, unable to resist it, he added, 'If a stockbroker is murdered, I'll let you know.'

He smiled as he said it, but Kelty, despite his trade, was not a man who appreciated the sardonic. Or perhaps he was not looking forward to going back on court, where the squeals had increased. Malone, who had cancelled his own game of tennis this afternoon, knew the chauvinism that prevailed on a court.

He drove back to town through a cold cloudless day in which the air at times seemed scattered with falling diamonds. Back at Homicide Kagal and Truach returned with repeats of what Malone had learned. 'Everything's above board,' said Phil Truach.

'Except the murders.'

'Sorry. Except the murders.'

'Could the Arabs be behind all this, trying to add to their corner on the oil market?' Kagal had done Economics at university, then, for no reason he had ever explained, joined the Police Service on graduation. Malone believed the economists were a bigger blight than lawyers and he sometimes wanted to ask Kagal what he thought of his old discipline. 'I got on to one of my old uni mates who's on the *Financial Review*. He dug out a copy of BHP's last annual report. They're into oil search all over the globe. They are in Algeria, they're in partnership with the Russians in the Pechora Sea, wherever that is. They're in partnerships in Argentina, the Gulf of Mexico, they're offshore Vietnam – that's just some of their overseas oil search. That's all besides what they're doing in Australia, places like the North-West Shelf. I don't know anything about Ampolex, but you can bet your boots you won't find 'em just drilling in some backyard. It *could* be the Arabs.'

'Which Arabs?'

'Well, I dunno. I'm putting the theory, not making a case.'

An economist's answer, thought Malone: Kagal still had the virus in his blood. He grinned at the younger man, then looked at Truach. 'You know the definition of an economist, Phil? A bloke who knows thirty-five ways of making love but doesn't know any girls.'

Truach just nodded, looked as if he were dying for a cigarette; Kagal smiled and waved an acknowledging hand. 'Okay, we're good on theory. But who else is there to point the finger at? Maybe the Yanks, but I don't think so.'

Malone said, 'Let's stick to those we know and what we know, forget the Big Picture. What about Mr and Mrs Dourane? We still got surveillance on them?'

'Yes,' said Truach. 'Just to make sure, we've put a phone tap on them.'

'Who authorized that?'

'Russ. He said you had enough on your mind. He sent me down to Judge Bristow for the warrant.' Malone knew Bristow, knew that the police always tried to get to him if possible. He believed law and order was the eleventh commandment and, Malone was sure, would have issued a warrant against Jesus Christ, then gone to church on Sunday.

Malone had been prepared to bristle at Clements's going over his head, but just in time he recognized that Russ had acted with the best of intentions. He himself should have suggested the phone tap, but the idea had not even crossed his mind. He felt a sudden temptation to take himself off the cases, to go home and spend the weekend with Lisa and the children. But he knew that would not work: his worry and concern for Lisa would throw a blanket of misery over all of them. Better to stay on the job, as Lisa had suggested.

'Anything from the taps?'

'Nothing worth following up. Just calls from friends. And Mrs Dourane's sister, who evidently doesn't like Muslims.'

'I wonder why Mr Federal hasn't been in touch? He'd know by now what's happened. There's been nothing from Immigration, has there? He hasn't tried to catch an overseas flight?'

'Not as far as we know. We'll get him, Scobie,' said Truach and sounded much too reassuring, like the doctor who had assured Lisa everything would be all right. 'Coffee? I'll get it.'

He rose and went out of Malone's office and Kagal said, 'I don't think I'll be able to drink coffee again without thinking of Peta.'

Then Phil Truach was back in the doorway, an unlit cigarette between his fingers. 'There are two ladies here, Inspector. Mrs Brame and Mrs Channing.'

3

Early that Saturday morning Joanna Brame had been on the phone to New York. She had called Orville's secretary, the second call she had made in the last eight hours. The first call to Connie Letoni had been to the latter's apartment on East 84th Street; she had caught the secretary just before she had been leaving to go downtown to the law offices. The second call was to the offices themselves, where Connie had stayed behind when most of the staff had gone home.

'I thought it best if we weren't interrupted, Mrs Brame.' Connie Letoni was a thirty-five-year-old divorcee whom a lot of women would have envied: she had an interesting well-paid job, she had her own apartment and the choice of half a dozen or so uncommitted lovers. She also had discretion, which was something that Joanna appreciated. 'I opened Mr Brame's private safe here in the office. There was no key to the combination here, I presume he must've taken it with him. I went up to your apartment at lunchtime and yes, there was the combination in the notebook where you suggested. I've opened the safe. Besides other papers, there are hand-written notes that he never dictated to me. Maybe he intended to when he – when he got back here.' There was a moment's hiatus on the line. Joanna knew that Connie had had real affection for Orville, though it had never amounted to more than that. 'It's as you thought – things were happening that Mr Brame didn't like at all . . .'

'What do the notes say?'

'Some of them say very little. Mr Brame never doodled like some people when they're on the phone. He'd write a word or a phrase. There's one here –'

The conversation lasted fifteen minutes, with Joanna taking notes of her own on the hotel's notepaper. She rang off with the admonition, 'This is just between you and me, Connie. Put everything back in Mr Brame's safe and set the combination again. Don't mention what you've told me to anyone else in the office, not to Mr De Vries or anyone. And keep the safe locked, don't tell anyone you know the combination.' She was not accustomed to such intrigue; later she would marvel at her behaviour. 'Come and see me as soon as I get back to New York – I'll call you.'

'Mrs Brame – I hope you don't mind me saying this – you're not going to play detective, are you?'

There was a note of real concern in Connie's voice; Joanna smiled. 'Someone else asked me something like that. No, Connie, I'm not going to play detective. There are enough of them already on the case.'

'How are you?' The concern was still there: Joanna hoped Orville had provided for Connie Letoni in his will.

'I'm bearing up, Connie, thank you. I probably will feel worse later on.' Then she hung up, feeling worse immediately.

At nine o'clock, after a glance at the newspapers that told her the world was still tearing itself apart, she rang Milly Channing. 'Milly, would you care to come in here to the hotel? I have something I think we should discuss.'

'Oh, I don't think I can. Rod is coming here at eleven, before he goes to golf – he always comes to see me on a Saturday. Filial duty, I think he calls it – I love these legal terms when it comes to motherhood. In my day we called it going to see your mum. Would you mind coming out here?'

Joanna looked at her watch. She did not want Rod

Channing walking in on them before she had time to finish telling Milly what she had learned. 'May I come now or is that inconvenient?' She *never* invited herself to other people's places; her mother's ashes would be turning into embers if she knew.

'Of course.' Milly gave her the address. 'It sounds urgent –'

'It is,' said Joanna and hung up.

She went out to Rose Bay by taxi. Back home she never travelled by taxi. On Manhattan there were the Carey limousines, in Connecticut there was the Rolls-Royce driven by the gardener doubling as chauffeur, a word she had inherited from her mother. The taxi driver was a health fanatic: he gave her a rundown on his illnesses and the merits and demerits of the national health scheme.

'They tell me health costs are off-the-planet in the States. That right?'

'Possibly.' Her banker always paid her bills.

'What's it cost to die?'

'Only pain,' she said, and he shut up, catching the coldness in her tone.

Milly Channing lived in a two-bedroom flat in a block of six in a quiet street off the main road. In pockets around her lived the purse-thin rich surviving on the scraps of their lost affluence; their names still appeared in the gossip columns, they still drove luxury cars leased from month to month, they shuffled mortages like professional gamblers, which they were. But none of them impinged on Milly; she had troubles of her own.

The flat was nicely furnished; Joanna guessed that *nicely* would be the word used. The rooms were small, the living and dining rooms being one. The furniture was comfortable, the wall-to-wall carpet looked new. There were a dozen or more paperbacks in a small bookcase, a piece of furniture that Joanna saw at once was too good for the books it held.

'Murder mysteries,' said Milly. 'I read them all the time. I never dreamed . . .'

On a sideboard were framed photographs of her grand-children. She picked up three photographs, faded and bent at the edges, that were lying on the sideboard.

'I dug these out, I thought you might like them. That's Orville when he was, I think, twelve or thirteen. That one was taken his first year at university, he was in the rugby team. And that one was taken at his graduation.'

Joanna looked at the three strangers, the man she had married and loved. Even in those days, however, even in the photograph of him as a boy, there was the hint of the reserve that would distinguish him in later life. He was smiling in only one of the photographs, the one of him as a rugby player, but it was a reluctant smile, the sort ordered by whoever was on the other side of the camera.

'I may keep them?'

'Of course. Now what would you like to tell me? Tea or coffee? Let's go into the kitchen.'

Joanna went into her kitchen every day to speak to her cook; but she had never sat at a breakfast bar to drink instant coffee and eat fresh scones. She was uncomfortable on the breakfast stool; it was all right, she thought, for crooners and stand-up comedians but not for matrons like herself. But Milly looked right at home on the stool and Joanna did her best to appear the same.

'Milly, I think Rod is in over his head –'

Rod's mother nodded. 'I'm not surprised. Go on.'

Joanna told her about her call to New York. 'In Orville's private safe there were notes that sound as if he made them on a phone conversation he had with Rod. There were also some notes on a meeting he had with Exxon two days before he left New York to come here –'

'Who are Exxon?' Then Milly blinked, a habit she had, like a gentle slap, when admonishing herself. 'Oh, *Exxon*. The oil company that spilled all that oil in Alaska or somewhere?'

Joanna was neither a moralist nor an eco-conservationist: 'Among other things,' she said dismissively. 'It is one of the *biggest* oil companies in the world, it's worth –' She looked at the notes she had taken from her handbag. 'It's worth eighty billion dollars.'

Milly appeared unimpressed; or perhaps the figure was beyond her comprehension. 'Go on.'

Joanna was beginning to lose some of her patience: 'Milly, someone was buying up Exxon stock – shares, as I think you call them here. Millions of shares. There were several companies doing the buying, but Orville represented only one of them – they were companies registered in the United States. The point is, Rod had recommended the company –' She looked at her notes again: 'It's called Bodensee Trust. Over five months ago it bought a billion dollars' worth of stock in Exxon.'

'One-eightieth,' said Milly, concentrating now.

'Yes, one-eightieth. But there were other companies buying Exxon stock at the same time, buying big. From Orville's notes, it seems that Exxon were worried enough to be going to Washington –'

'But how does Rod fit into this? Other than recommending – what was it? Bodensee Trust? – to Orville? Is this the deal where he's expecting to make millions? He's never had that sort of money to invest –'

'Milly, I don't know what's going on, but it's obvious Orville was worried by it. He was trying to warn Rod, but evidently not getting anywhere with him. Connie –'

'Connie?'

'Sorry. Orville's secretary. She said there was one slip of paper in the safe with just the one word written on it. *Dangerous*, underlined three or four times. Dangerous to whom?'

'Orville, I'd say. He was the one who was murdered.' Milly got off her stool, leaned with stiff arms on the breakfast bar as if for support.

'Yes, I thought of that. But if he had been in any danger, real danger, he would have told me. We were *close*, Milly. Not about what went on in the firm, but on a personal level. He would have told me. No, I think he was warning Rod.'

Then the security buzzer made them both jump; Joanna fell off the stool, but managed to keep her feet. Milly looked at her watch. 'It can't be Rod. He's too early.'

But it was Rod, dressed for golf and, on seeing Joanna, looking as if he had just put his ball into the water hazard. 'Joanna, what are you doing here?'

She put her notes back into her handbag, moved away from the breakfast bar, glad to be off the stool. She wanted a firm floor beneath her if she was to face Rod; she had not expected to see him before she had had time to sort out her approach. Milly had been no help, though now she wondered why she had hoped there might be any help from that quarter. Suddenly she felt *alone* and, irrationally, wished for Orville's support.

'I've been talking to New York, Rod. I think I know half the story of what's been happening.'

He went behind the breakfast bar, switched on the electric kettle and prepared to make himself some instant coffee, spooning out the granules as if for a medical dosage. He even put butter and jam on a scone, though he did not bite into it. Joanna recognized that he was playing for time, that he was as unprepared as she for what had to be said.

'Joanna, I don't think you should be playing detective. And I don't like you bringing my mother into it.' He was stiffly formal, as if reading from a brief.

'Speak for yourself, not for me,' said Milly, gathering up her and Joanna's cups; housework can tidy up oneself as much as the house itself. Though it was not a method Joanna had ever used. 'I'm not sure I understand everything Joanna has been telling me, but I'm sure you're being stupid. You're putting yourself in danger – and maybe Ruth and the children. For what? More money?'

He ignored his mother, looked at Joanna. 'What did New York tell you?'

'What were you and Orville engaged in? Why did he tell you that what you were doing was dangerous?'

'He told you that? He talked to you before he left New York? Come on, Joanna, you've been saying all along that you hadn't a clue what was going on. Who have you been talking to in New York?'

'Orville.'

He had been about to sip his coffee, but stopped with the cup halfway to his mouth. Somewhere outside a lawn-mower started up, a Saturday-morning sound. '*Orville?*'

'He left notes of a phone conversation, maybe two or three, he had with you. About Exxon and two companies here in Australia, BHP and – Ampolex? Something like that. Exxon, I gather, had been in touch with Washington. What's going on, Rod? Orville was murdered because of it and you won't tell me, Orville's wife, and your mother, *his* mother, why it happened.'

He put down his cup with a crash on its saucer. 'Jesus Christ, if you know so much, don't you see I'm trying to protect the two of you? And myself, for Chrissake! I never dreamed it would come to this –'

Milly turned from the sink, drying her hands on a tea-towel, unagitated, at home in that most sensible of rooms, her kitchen. 'Are you going to tell us what's going on?'

He hesitated, then shook his head. 'No, it's better you both stay right out of it. Will Lazarus and I are trying to sort it all out –'

'What, for God's sake?' Milly suddenly lost her calm; she threw the tea-towel across the small room. 'Jesus, you make me so wild! You and your bloody secrets – all your life –' She was a different woman: Joanna was shocked at the change in her. 'For once in your life, be honest with me –'

It was ugly to see: too ugly for Joanna, who turned and walked out of the kitchen. Sophisticated though she was, she had always avoided other people's scenes; she had no armour against them. She stood at a loss in the middle of the small living room, trying to shut her ears against the bitter argument out in the kitchen; Milly and Rod had at least lowered their voices. She picked up her topcoat, pulled on her gloves, was heading for the door when abruptly she stopped. I'm fleeing, she thought, I'm running out. I came here to ask Milly for help and now I'm abandoning her. She turned back as Milly, furious-faced, came through from the kitchen.

'He makes me so *mad*! Was Orville like that? No, no, he couldn't have been! Not *two* of them! I –' Then abruptly she shut up for a moment, wiped her face with the back of her hand, though Joanna noted there were no tears on her cheeks. 'Ah, why'm I dragging you into this? I never knew how to handle men – my husband, my sons –'

Joanna went to her, took her hand in her own gloved one. 'I'm going to the police. Do you want to come with me?'

Milly wiped her face again with her free hand. 'I'll get my coat. Rod –' She turned as he came through from the kitchen. 'We're going to the police.'

He shook his head almost frantically. 'No. No, don't! What are you going to tell them?' He took out a handkerchief, blew his nose. It was almost as if he had been crying, but it was no more than that his cold had not improved.

Milly looked at Joanna, who said, 'What we know. It's only half the story, maybe less, but if it helps find who killed Orville, then it'll be enough.'

'Yes,' said Milly and went on into her bedroom.

Rod stared at Joanna. He was dressed in a bright green shirt, a yellow alpaca cardigan and brown-and-white checked trousers, a clown's outfit topped by a clown's red-nosed mournful face. The clown image was Joanna's: she

237

did not like men in brightly coloured clothes, in what she called Florida plumage. Mournfully Rod said, 'You don't know what harm you're going to cause.'

'All the harm I'm interested in has been caused. That happened when Orville was murdered.'

4

Malone went out to meet the two women. 'We'll go along to our interview room.' He nodded to Phil Truach and John Kagal to follow them.

'Detectives Truach and Kagal have been working on the murders.'

'I've met Mr Kagal. I was so sorry to hear what happened to that nice young woman with you that day. Are you going to turn that on?' Milly Channing nodded at the video recorder on the table as she took the chair Malone pushed towards her.

'You've been interviewed by police before, Mrs Channing?'

'Heavens, no! I've just seen it on TV –' Then she looked embarrassed. 'I suppose that's what most of us think, I mean that's how real life works.'

'Only worse,' said Malone, remembering some of the horror stories that had been recorded by this machine.

He had not met Milly Channing before this and he was studying her while he tried to put her and Joanna Brame at ease. She had produced one son who from all accounts was a brilliant lawyer and another who had, by Malone's estimate, failed brilliance by a long mark but wouldn't admit it. He was no more adept than most men at summing up a woman, but experience had taught him there were signs that could be recognized. He would look for them as the interview went on.

Settled in his chair, with Truach seated beside him and

Kagal leaning against a wall (just like on TV, he thought: real life couldn't help imitating it), he looked across the table at the two women. 'What've you come to tell us?'

Joanna did not open her handbag and produce her notes; she had marshalled her thoughts and would depend on them. She had no doubts about coming to the police; Orville, and her father, had taught her that in law there was an order of battle just as there was in war. Professionals, her father had told her, had not been invented out of whim; they were a necessity and as such should be used. Both her father and Orville, she was sure, would have recommended Inspector Malone as a professional.

'I had someone in our New York office open my husband's private safe –' She went on to tell the three detectives what she had learned. 'My husband was obviously disturbed by the buying up of Exxon stock –'

'Did he mention who was doing the buying?'

'Just the one, called Bodensee Trust.' Her memory for company names would have got her a job on the floor of the New York Stock Exchange. 'But there were others, Exxon told him. There were also notes mentioning BHP and – Ampolex? – here in Australia.'

'We know about the local buying. Did Mr Brame mention anything in his notes about Arabs?'

'Arabs?' She frowned; then understood. 'Oh, you mean they're all oil companies, the Arabs might be buying into them? No, there was nothing in his notes about them. You could call Exxon –'

Malone smiled. 'They wouldn't talk to us, Mrs Brame. Big corporations are as shy of the police as – well . . .' He was going to say the Mafia, but managed to hold his tongue. 'No, we'll have to go through our Securities Commission, who'll talk to your Securities and Exchange people, who'll talk to the Justice Department . . .' He looked at Kagal. 'John, do you have a contact in Securities here?'

Kagal nodded: *of course*. The bugger probably had a contact in Buckingham Palace and the Vatican, too. 'I'll get on to him now, he's one of their investigators.'

He went out of the room and Milly Channing said, 'I knew we did the right thing in coming here. Mrs Brame and I would've been running around in circles.'

'We have our network.' His own network was amongst the criminals, but that wasn't enough these days; the network was frayed, too small. Junkies and punks, outside the professional criminal ring, were difficult to trace. And with the burgeoning of white-collar crime a different network was needed, one that was still being woven; the successful cop of the future would have a connection with *everyone*. The prospect exhausted him, but that could be because he was on the point of exhaustion anyway. 'How are you involved in this with Mrs Brame?'

'Because of Rod, my son. My other son,' she added, as if she thought she might have offended Joanna. 'I think he could be in some sort of danger.'

'Does he know you were coming to see us?'

'Yes.'

'How did he feel about that?' *Why do I bother to ask?*

Milly traced a loose pattern on the dust of the table; the cleaners did not come in Saturdays. 'Very upset. He came to see me this morning – Mrs Brame was there –'

'Where is he now?'

'At his office, I think. He was going to play golf, but changed his mind – he said he would have to see his partner Will Lazarus –'

'I think we'd better see him, too,' said Malone.

Then Jim Creek, one of the duty men, knocked and opened the door of the interview room. 'Inspector, you're wanted on the phone. Urgent.'

Malone's first reaction was that something had happened to Lisa or the children; his thoughts were too close to home. He stood up hastily, knocking his chair back against the wall, excused himself and hurried out after Creek. 'Who is it? My wife?'

Creek looked at him curiously. He was another of the young officers who had come into Homicide at the same time as Peta Smith, one who had started on the beat, gone into Physical Evidence and now was proving one of the better recruits to Malone's domain. He was medium height and slim, with thick very blond hair, a surfer's tan that apparently lasted through the winter and a quiet air of confidence that didn't grate on the older man.

'Your wife? No, it's one of the guys on the phone tap at Arncliffe, on that wog's phone.' He was one of the new men, but he had old prejudices. 'They got something, they said.'

Malone went into his office, picked up the phone. A voice at the other end of the line said, 'Inspector Malone? This is Constable De Groot. We been tapping the Dourane phone, nothing up till now. But we've intercepted two calls in the last five minutes. The first was from a Mr Channing, asking if he could get in touch with a Mr Federal.'

'Did Dourane give him a phone number or an address?' He could feel the adrenalin beginning to stir, like a spring pushing its way up through dried mud.

'Mrs Dourane answered the phone, Dourane didn't come on to it. She must of put her hand over the phone, we didn't hear anything for a minute or so, then she come back on. Said she couldn't give him a number, but they'd try and get in touch with Mr Federal and they'd call him back.'

'What about the second call?'

'That was to Mr Federal. It was too short for us to trace where the guy is at. All we got was that he'd meet the Douranes at the gallery.'

'Which gallery?'

'I dunno, Inspector. I presume he meant some sorta art gallery. It could be the New South Wales Gallery in the

Domain or any of a hundred around Sydney, we dunno. All we can do, I guess, is tail the Douranes when they leave the house.'

'Where are you tapped in?'

'Up the street and around the corner. There's a coupla Telecom guys tapped into a box there, they're supposed to be tracing faults, anyone asks. They been there two days now and they're complaining it's not good for Telecom's reputation, they take two days to correct a fault.'

'Tell 'em we'll take all the police business to Optus. That should shut 'em up.' Since the government telephone service had been opened up to private competition, consumers had been wooed like compliant virgins just waiting to be asked.

'Righto, tail the Douranes as soon as they leave the house. If they split up, one stays behind, you two also split up, take one each. You got a car phone or a mobile? Keep me informed. Soon's we find out what gallery they're meeting in, we'll be there.'

When De Groot got off the line Malone rang Clements. 'Sorry to spoil your day off, but you'd better get in here quick. Things are beginning to break.' The adrenalin had also broken through.

'The missus isn't gunna like it. She was taking me to a symphony concert this afternoon.' Clements must feel well and truly married: Romy had become *the missus*.

'You don't want to come in?'

'Of course I'm bloody coming!'

Malone hung up, looked at Creek. 'Stick by this phone, Jim. Soon's it rings, grab it and come and fetch me. Don't let anyone but De Groot or his sidekick hold up the line, tell 'em to get off and we'll call 'em back.'

Homicide had no central manned board to which detectives could call in on their radiophones or their mobiles. Police funds rarely seemed to stretch to the essentials; the government preached law and order but at bargain rates. But then, Malone had once suggested, they were lucky to have mobile phones: messages could still be arriving in a cleft stick if some Treasury officials had their way.

He went back down the hall to the interview room. Truach noticed the difference in him, but made no comment other than a raised enquiring eyebrow. It was Joanna Brame who said, 'Good news, Inspector? You look as if it is.'

She was as sharp-eyed as Lisa; or he was more easily read than he imagined. 'It could be,' he said cautiously. 'I'm afraid, Mrs Channing, we're going to have to bring Rod up here and hold him. For his own safety.'

Her face clouded, but she didn't protest. 'That might be the best thing. But he's stubborn –'

Then Kagal came back into the room. 'I got on to my mate at Securities. He's on his way in now, he lives just up the road in Paddington. He'll be here in ten minutes.'

'May we stay?' said Joanna.

'By all means,' said Malone. 'But we'll have to talk to him alone at first. Whatever he can tell us may still be classified. Phil –'

Truach stood up. 'Take one of the fellers with you, go down and bring Mr Channing back with you. And Mr Lazarus if he's with him. Threaten 'em with anything you can dream up, if they get obstreperous.' He grinned at the two women; he was feeling much better. 'We bend the rules a little when we have to.'

'Who doesn't?' said Joanna, who had never bent a rule in her life.

Milly Channing smiled indulgently. 'You've got to sometimes, haven't you?'

Truach went out of the room, a packet of cigarettes already out of his pocket and in his hand, half a breath short of dying for a smoke.

'We sit and wait now,' said Malone and sat down.

'For Channing and Lazarus?' said Kagal. 'Or my mate from Securities?'

'No, for Mr Federal, our killer,' said Malone and almost laughed at the look on Kagal's face. He hadn't felt so good all week.

Chapter Ten

1

Will Lazarus arrived at the offices in Martin Place ten minutes after Channing. Separated from his wife and young daughter, he lived in a flat overlooking Elizabeth Bay, a few minutes' drive from the heart of the city. He drove a Porsche, black of course, and lived a life that Channing secretly envied.

This morning he was dressed in dark grey slacks, a black turtleneck sweater, a black roll-collar cardigan and a black corduroy cap. Beside him Channing all at once felt like a peacock, one with its tail drooping between its legs.

'I hope this isn't going to take long,' Lazarus said. 'I have to pick up a bird, then we're going out to Coogee to see Randwick play Easts.'

Bird: it was the slang they had used when they had been at university together. So long ago, mused Channing: he thought of the birds he had missed, the opportunities lost. There had been singers and bands then like Alvin Stardust and Paper Lace, gone even from memory, or anyway his memory till this odd moment. He had met and fallen in love with Ruth back then. Now, over the past two years, he had fallen out of love with her, though he couldn't see himself ever asking her for a divorce. Unlike Lazarus he would always stay married for the sake of the children. He would never put them through what he had suffered from his own parents.

'I rang Dick De Vries, he'll be here soon.'

Lazarus took off his cap, ran a hand through his thick

black hair, adjusting the elastic band that held his eye-patch in place. 'It's as bad as that, we need him? Fill me in before he gets here.'

But before Channing could do so, De Vries arrived. He was dressed for the weekend, less colourfully than Channing, less sombrely than Lazarus. 'The convention ended last night. We go our own way from today. Most people are heading home. I wish I were.' He sounded and looked worried. 'What's happened?'

Channing told them: 'I don't think my mother had anything to do with getting in touch with New York, but she's backing Mrs Brame all the way. They've gone to the police.'

'Fucking women!' De Vries couldn't contain his anger. 'Why do they have to interfere?' Then he belatedly realized whom he was talking about. 'Sorry, I didn't mean to criticize your mother, Rod. It's that fucking Joanna – she still thinks she has a proprietary interest in our firm –'

'She does, doesn't she?' said Lazarus quietly. His own temper could be volatile, but the eye-patch never made him one-eyed. 'She's protecting Orville's interest.'

'I thought he was bullshitting me when he came to see me last Sunday.' Channing was pulling nervously at his moustache. 'About Exxon going to Washington and the Securities and Exchange Commission. I've tried to get in touch with Federal,' he told De Vries, 'but their manager here, Dourane, wouldn't give me his number. I spoke to his wife and she said they'd call Federal and then get back to us. What gets me,' he said plaintively, 'is what have we done wrong?'

'That's what I tried to argue with Orville,' said De Vries. 'Christ, if you look into the money that's invested in American companies, *legitimate* investment, you'll find billions coming from the Mafia, the Japanese *yakuza*, Chinese Triads, Colombian drug cartels . . . A lot of people know where the money comes from, but nothing can be proved. So nothing is done. This money is cleaner than any of that . . .' He had not sat down since he had entered Channing's office, but now he dropped on to the green leather couch. He had been wearing a floppy tweed hat and he was crumpling it between his nervous hands as if looking for a loose thread to pull it apart. 'Or I thought the money was clean till – till the murders. Then . . .'

'We had nothing to do with the murders,' said Lazarus.

'Who did then – this guy Federal? Is that really his name? I've never met him, you know. He never came to the States, they had a different director who talked with Orville. And me,' he added, as if not wanting to sound like the junior partner. 'Smooth as silk, a guy named Walter Bosch, said he was Swiss-German. Polite, smooth like I said, but a real Nazi, I'd say.'

'I met him in Zurich last week,' said Lazarus. 'Smooth as silk, as you say. But Federal is pretty smooth, too. He just happens to be a killer, that's all.'

'Jesus,' said Channing, 'how can you be so matter-of-fact!'

'Because that's the only way to be.' Lazarus sat down in Channing's own chair; the latter was still on his feet, pacing up and down by the window. From the wall the spurious Channing looked down; a trick of light gave the painting a wry smile. 'We don't know that he won't murder one of us. Or all of us.'

'Why, for Chrissakes?' De Vries dropped his hat on the couch beside him as if giving up any idea of tearing it to pieces.

'Because who else knows as much as we do? Orville was the one who found out the truth and look at what happened to him. And he told you two and you told me.' He put a hand on the desk and looked at it, at the faint tremble in the fingers. 'I'm matter-of-fact, but I'm scared shitless, too.'

Bob Anders, Kagal's mate from the Securities Commission, was a tall languid man in his mid-forties, with close-cropped thin dark hair, a full moustache, an ear-ring and, as Kagal said, lived in Paddington. Malone was just glad that Russ Clements was off-duty and for the first time he could recall he looked at Kagal with suspicion.

They were in Malone's office, just the three of them. 'It's only been in our lap, Inspector, just over a week. Three days before Orville Brame was murdered, to be exact.' His voice was not languid at all, at least not while talking business; it was crisp and deep. 'The SEC in Washington got in touch with us, although we'd been looking at the BHP and Ampolex buying for a couple of weeks before that.'

'You hadn't made any move?'

Anders spread a well-manicured hand, displaying a bracelet. But he was not limp-wristed: this man was as fitness-conscious as Dicey Kilmer. 'The buying was perfectly legitimate and above board. Then two days ago ASIO heard about our enquiries and came to us –'

Malone tried to contain his anger. 'You had word from the Yanks ten days ago and our spy spooks came to you two days ago and you still didn't bother to get in touch with us? Didn't you connect Brame's murder with all this?'

'Washington never mentioned Brame to us, they didn't tell us his firm were the legal advisers for the American end –'

Malone came off the boil, shook his head at the labyrinthine ways of bureaucracy. 'Would the FBI know anything of this?'

'Probably, by now.'

'A pity they didn't know four or five days ago, when we asked them to check on Rockman, the guard who was murdered. And before one of our officers was also murdered.' He couldn't keep the bitterness from his voice. 'Why did ASIO come in on this? Has it got something to do with national security?'

'Evidently. The Yanks think so, too.'

Malone looked at Kagal. 'That means we can expect the bloody Feds to be on our doorstep, next.'

Kagal nodded sympathetically. 'We'll keep 'em out as long as we can. Too many cooks spoil the broth,' he told Anders.

Malone stood up. 'Well, national security's got nothing to do with Homicide. I'm now going out to put Mrs Brame in the picture. I think she's entitled to know why her husband was murdered.'

'Do you think we could have prevented any of these murders, Inspector?'

Malone sighed, surrendered. 'No, probably not. But you don't expect me not to be upset, do you?'

'No,' said Anders. 'I'm sorry we didn't move faster. But . . .' He spread his hands again, the bracelet glinting on his wrist. 'Despite the so-called information highway, Inspector, a lot of things still move at their own pace. Computers will never beat human nature.'

Malone liked the man; he smiled: 'You're philosophers in Securities?'

'We have to be.'

'Join the club.'

They walked back down the hall to the interview room where Joanna Brame and Milly Channing, drinking coffee from the office mugs and munching on Iced Vo-vos, the office biscuit, sat waiting with impatience neither of them tried to hide. Joanna was not accustomed to being kept waiting and Milly, no matter what chair she sat on, would forever be tilting towards the edge of it.

'This is Mr Anders, ladies. He will explain the background to why Mr Brame was murdered.'

The two women looked at the tall man who, finding no

chair vacant, had to stand against the wall in the small room. Malone remarked Joanna Brame's glance at the ear-ring and the faint twitch of the patrician nose, but Milly Channing seemed to notice neither it nor the bracelet.

'Inspector Malone tells me you know about the buying up of shares in those companies in oil search. The money, which has come out of Switzerland, we are now almost certain is Russian money.'

'Russian?' said Joanna. 'Communist money?'

It had the same sound as if she had said *blood money*. She had been only a child when John Foster Dulles had tried to run the world like a Presbyterian parish, when Joe McCarthy had been allowed to run amok, but her father had believed in both men and not even Orville, a fair man, had ever been able to convince her that not all Communists were evil.

Anders nodded. 'Communist *Party* money. We know –' He did not look at Malone and Kagal when he said *we*. It had not been the Securities Commission but the security organization ASIO that had divulged the information on the Russians; but bureaucracies, like politicians, generals and boxing promoters, never give credit where credit is due. It goes against the grain, is human nature as the philosophers would say. 'We know that for years, right from the start of the so-called Cold War –'

'It was a war,' said Joanna. 'Cold or otherwise.'

'Of course,' said Anders, recognizing a warning sign. 'Well, way back then the Party invested in companies outside the USSR. Perhaps it was just looking to the future, to the possible collapse of Communism – some shrewdies are always prepared for the worst. It happened in Germany in Hitler's time – IG Farben, the big chemical company, bought into American companies. It took years after the war before that one was straightened out by the US Justice Department –'

Skip the history lesson, Malone silently told him; and

Joanna said, 'Please get on with it, Mr Anders.'

Anders recognized another warning sign. 'Well, in some cases, the Russians actually controlled the companies they invested in. Just as the Germans did,' he said, getting in his last lick.

'Then that's what Orville meant when he said, *Look to the past*.' Joanna looked at Malone and he nodded.

'The money came out of Russia,' said Milly, 'and nobody *knew*? I mean, all you experts?'

Anders fingered the ear-ring for a moment, looked uncomfortable. 'I think you'd have to ask the experts about that, Mrs Channing. I wasn't with them back then.' He smiled and Milly returned it, but Joanna remained stiff-faced. 'The money didn't actually come out of Russia, not directly, that is. It had been deposited in Swiss banks, in holding companies there, and in France –'

'France?' said Malone.

'Don't ask me why, except that for years the French Communist Party was the biggest in Europe, it or the Italians. The Russians were rumoured to have seven thousand bank accounts in France alone, most of them in small banks in ports. Marseille, Le Havre, places like that.'

'How much money?' said Joanna, who was not astonished by large sums.

'All the figures are only guesses,' said Anders, 'but the biggest estimate was that the Party had one hundred billion dollars in assets overseas.'

Joanna *was* astonished; Milly was breathless: 'How much?'

'One hundred billion?' said Joanna, recovering. 'So what they have been investing in Exxon and the others is almost small change?'

The three men managed to keep straight faces as the loose change in their pockets froze. Anders said, 'Not exactly, Mrs Brame. They've invested enough, not to get a corner on the oil market but to give them a big stake in oil profits.'

'But why?' said Malone. 'The Communist Party in Russia is *kaput*. Finished.'

'It can always make a comeback under another name. It's just happened in Hungary, they don't give up that easily. There were fourteen million members in the USSR Party in its heyday. Let's say three-quarters of them were members in name only, trying to keep a job. That still leaves enough true believers to form a fair-sized rump Party. How many are in the Liberal Party here? Or in the Republican Party in America?' he asked Joanna.

'Enough,' she said, but her tone told him he should not have asked the question. 'So you are saying my husband found out all about this?'

'It would seem so, from what Inspector Malone thinks. I don't know, Mrs Channing, if your son Rod knew any of it, that the money was Russian money —'

'But why?' said Milly. 'Why kill Orville?'

Anders looked at Malone, leaving it to him, the expert in murder. But that didn't make him an expert in motives, only in methods. 'I don't think we'll know that till we catch whoever killed him. Maybe the Russians are fighting amongst themselves, each trying to get a share of the loot they've stashed abroad. Maybe they think Communism is going to be revived in Russia and they are prepared to eliminate anyone who upsets the apple-cart. They were secretive about what they were doing and they wanted it to remain secret. What we may never know, Mrs Brame, is how your husband found out.'

'I won't be satisfied with that,' said Joanna.

Malone recognized the symptoms: the bereaved partner who had to sieve every grain of every sod that covered the dead one. He had seen it countless times and none had ever got the complete answer.

Then Russ Clements knocked on the door and opened it. He was in a grey open-necked shirt and a pink pullover. 'I've just got in. There's a call on your phone, Inspector.'

Malone jumped out of his chair, followed Clements down the hall. 'I like the sweater. You look sweet.'

'You think it'd look better with an ear-ring?' Clements had missed nothing in his five-second glance around the interview room.

'Lay off. He knows his job . . . Who is it?'

'The guys on the Douranes' tail.'

Jim Creek was holding the phone and Malone took it. 'Constable De Groot, where are you?'

'We're heading towards town, sir.' Malone could hear the peripheral sound on the car phone. 'Mr and Mrs Dourane are up ahead of us. I'm with Detective-Constable Powell, from Rockdale. We're coming down Rocky Point Road, they're moving pretty fast. She's driving, she's a real Speedy Gonzales.'

De Groot must be elderly: Speedy Gonzales had been dead for years. 'Stay with them. I can't get another car out there now to take over from you, so make sure they don't spot you. We'll keep this line clear, report in every five minutes or as soon as you get an idea where they're heading.'

He handed the phone back to Creek, went out into the main room with Clements. 'This is the picture now –' he said and went on to fill it in for the big man.

Clements nodded. 'It fits. What do we do – ask for back-up?'

Malone was suddenly worried; the adrenalin had wiped out the local aspect of the picture. 'I dunno. We don't know where they're going to meet. If it's in some crowded place, we don't want armed cops running around. Federal, or Ballinger, whatever he calls himself, he's already killed Peta in a public place, even knowing she was a cop. *Because* she was a cop. He's not going to stop at killing another of us. And if we start shooting back . . .'

Clements nodded. 'Someone's bound to get hurt. There's always some idiot who'll pop his head up to see what's going on and get it blown off . . . Okay, no back-up. Who've we got?'

'You and me. John Kagal and the two fellers doing the tail, De Groot and the other one. That's enough. Any more and we're going to look like a convention.'

The next call from De Groot said, 'We're in King Street, Newtown. The Dourane car is three cars ahead of us – it's a blue Saab, incidentally. We're being held up by the traffic, this must be the worst bottleneck in the whole of the State.'

'What's the licence?' Malone remembered the car, but there was more than one blue Saab in Sydney.

'I got that earlier. Would you believe Hot Tip. Yeah, H-O-T T-I-P.'

'That'd be the wife's choice. Righto, don't lose them. Even if you have to go through traffic lights. You've got my okay to do that if it's necessary.'

He told Clements to stay with Creek and he went back to the interview room. 'We may have to leave before my men come back with Rod and Mr Lazarus. You can stay or you can leave, it's up to you, ladies.'

'What's happening?' said Joanna.

He hesitated; but he knew better than to offer false hope. 'I can't tell you that at the moment, Mrs Brame. But if I'm called away, you're welcome to stay till I get back. Unless you don't want to face Rod and Mr Lazarus?'

'Why should I not want to face them?'

'Yes, why not?' said Milly.

These women, he decided, had found strength in each other. Or, at worst, Milly Channing had found her own strength in Joanna Brame. 'I'm short on staff, we may have to leave you alone –'

'I'll stay with the ladies, if they don't mind,' said Anders. 'I have an interest in what happens, Inspector –'

The Securities man and the two women now appeared to be at ease with each other. Anders, indeed, seemed to be gently considerate of them, as if only now had he come close to the personal tragedy of what he had been investigating. Malone left the three of them and went back to Clements and Creek.

'They're down in George Street now,' said Clements, ear to the phone. He put his hand over the mouthpiece. 'De Groot says they're going down into the car park under the Queen Victoria Building.'

'Of course!' Malone snapped his fingers, picturing in his mind the huge old building that had been converted into a swish shopping complex. 'The QVB has galleries, three or four of 'em. Not *art* galleries, walk galleries. Crumbs, they'll be packed on a Saturday –'

Clements held up a hand for quiet. 'I'm getting static . . . Come on, De Groot, for Chrissake!' He gestured in frustration. 'We've lost him!'

'Keep it open . . . Jim, rustle up three mobiles for Russ, John and me. When we move out, you stay here on the line in case I have to call for back-up. Though I hope to Christ that won't be on . . . What's happening?'

Clements had held up his hand again. 'He's back on the air . . . Mr and Mrs Dourane are up on the main level of the QVB. They're looking in shops, window-shopping, he says.'

'They're checking they're not being followed,' said Malone. 'These people must be professionals. I hope De Groot and his mate are not standing out in the middle of the floor with the bloody phone stuck to his ear. Are they heading for one of the galleries?' He was trying to remember the elegant galleries that tiered the big building, most of them fronted by boutiques that catered for every want so long as it wasn't serious. He felt the frustration that must grip a blind man in an emergency; De Groot was his seeing-eye dog.

Clements held up a hand again: 'Shit! . . . They're separating. Mrs Dourane's leaving the QVB.'

'What's Dourane doing?'

Clements repeated the question into the phone, got an answer. 'He's sitting on a bench on the main floor. He's looking around, but it doesn't appear he's looking for anyone in particular.'

Malone made a snap decision: 'Tell De Groot to follow Mrs Dourane. Tell what's-his-name, Powell, to stay with Dourane . . . John, get down there now, keep Powell company –'

'What does he look like? Powell?'

Frustration did blind Malone for a moment. 'Jesus, I dunno what either of them look like! Ask De Groot –'

'He's gone,' said Clements, putting down the phone.

'You know Dourane,' said Malone to Kagal, 'you saw him when we brought him in here on Thursday. Big feller, dark hair, looks like Wasim Akram –'

'Who?' said Kagal, who wouldn't have known Don Bradman from Joe DiMaggio; he followed basketball.

'The Pakistani fast – forget it. Get down there, take your mobile. Keep in touch either here or with me on –' He looked at the number on the cellular phone Creek had just brought him, gave it to Kagal. 'If Mr Federal turns up at the QVB –'

'What does *he* look like?'

'John, are you trying to be –' Then he shook his head. 'No, we're all dense on this one. We don't know what he looks like, except that he's anonymous-looking and wears thick-rimmed specs. But if he sits down next to Dourane or Dourane gets up and follows him and speaks to him, that'll be him. Don't be heroic, be careful. If he turns up, Russ and I'll be there in five minutes. If *Mrs* Dourane has gone to meet him, then we'll be on her tail – if De Groot gets back to us. Righto, go!'

Kagal left on the run and Malone, Clements and Creek stood looking at the silent phone. Then it rang and Malone grabbed it. It was Greg Random: 'Just checking, Scobie –'

'Get off the line, Greg! I'll explain later –' He hung up in the ear of the Chief Superintendent, looked at Clements. 'Just as well it wasn't the Commissioner.'

The phone rang again; this time it was De Groot. 'I'm in a cab following Mrs Dourane. She caught a cab outside the QVB and I had to knock an old lady down to get one right behind her. We're going down George Street, turning now into Hunter – you getting me, Inspector?'

'A bit staticky –'

'We're at the top of Hunter, turning right into Macquarie –' There was faint static on the line, then: 'We're going round into the Domain – she's heading for the Art Gallery! That's it – all along it was an art gallery!'

'We'll be there in five minutes! I'll – wait a minute. What do you look like, De Groot? I've never seen you –'

'Eh? Oh, what do I look like? I'm a hundred-ninety tall, weigh eighty kilos –' Malone cursed the metric system. 'I'm wearing a navy-blue blouson, jeans, Reeboks, a Yankee baseball cap –'

Malone suddenly longed for the cop in the suit and the pork-pie hat, such as he and Clements had once been. Were he and Russ the last of the fashion plates? 'What's Mrs Dourane wearing?'

'A yellow topcoat is all I can see –'

'Righto, don't lose her. We're on our way.'

They raced out of the office, Malone pulling on the Burberry, Clements dragging on a golf jacket over his pink sweater. They used the siren till they were in College Street and about to turn into the road that led to the Domain, the city's main park, and the Art Gallery of New South Wales. Clements drove down with the tree-bordered park on their left and pulled into a No Parking zone in front of the gallery. They got out of the car and looked around for someone who might resemble De Groot's description of himself, but saw no one remotely like him. A few people stood under the portico at the top of the broad steps, apparently waiting for friends; a bus had just drawn up and was unloading a group of Japanese tourists; another bus was disgorging a group who sounded as if they might be a party of the American lawyers. Immediately in front of Malone and Clements sat a wino with a full bottle of plonk in one hand and a mobile phone in the other: the economy had indeed turned the corner, if seeing was believing. Then a parking patrol officer appeared out of nowhere, as they invariably do.

'Move it!' She was talking to the illegally parked motorists, not the wino. 'You can see that sign.'

Malone produced his badge. 'Book us and I'll have you for obstructing the course of justice, law and order and the well-being of the public, not to mention half a dozen other things.'

She smiled, authority falling from her like a snake's skin. 'You wouldn't, would you? You here to pick him up?' She nodded at the derelict, who, without having dialled, was holding the mobile phone to his ear as if expecting messages on the ether.

'No, he's not ours. You see two taxis draw up here in the last five minutes? A woman in a yellow topcoat got out of one of them?'

'Sure. She went into the gallery. A young guy followed her, he was in the second taxi. Looked like he was her boyfriend chasing her.'

'That's them. Keep an eye on our car, will you?'

'You're kidding.' She smiled again, showing a blatantly honest set of false teeth. 'I'm behind on today's quota.'

Malone and Clements left her, ran up into the column-fronted sandstone pile that looked as if it had been designed to protect the State's bullion hoard rather than its art treasures. Once inside they separated, Malone going right off the main lobby, Clements turning left.

Malone came here to the gallery only occasionally and always at the urging of Lisa. He was not an art enthusiast, but he had an eye that was better than he gave it credit. He had come here to the French Impressionists exhibition and admired everything he saw; he had come to last year's Bienniale and made no attempt to understand the artists' pretensions. The gallery was between exhibitions and, thank God, it was too early for the Saturday afternoon crowd. Nonetheless there was a sprinkling of people everywhere, their voices magnified in the high reaches of the various halls. He walked slowly down the nineteenth-century Australian gallery. Above him was the high curved glass ceiling letting in natural light; on either side of him were the teal-blue walls, split by off-white columns. The wooden floors click-clacked under the high heels of some of the women visitors. He walked slowly, keeping an eye out for De Groot or the yellow topcoated figure of Mrs Dourane; he passed the standard Australian landscapes, dusty leaves and peeling bark suggesting the forests were about to die in yet another drought or fire. Which they never did: he had seen the evidence only this morning.

He paused in front of a painting, trying to look as if he were interested in what was before him. It was a Gruner, of several cows silhouetted against the misty morning light of another age. Still no sign of De Groot or the yellow topcoat. He turned into a side gallery: this was the nineteenth-century European hall. Cherry-red walls, gold-leaf frames, Leighton, Watts, Burne-Jones, Wilson Steer with his portraits of women in yards (not metres) of silk and satin. A tall young man stood in front of Waterhouse's *Job*: he – the young man, not Job – was wearing the blue blouson, jeans and trainers, baseball cap in hand. Malone approached him. 'De Groot?'

The young man looked at him blankly. 'De what?'

Oh Jesus, thought Malone: he thinks I'm trying to pick him up. Then he was tapped on the shoulder. 'Mr Malone?'

A second young man in blue blouson etc. stood behind him. 'De Groot?'

'Yes, sir. Mrs Dourane is in that side gallery there.'

'Anyone with her?'

The first young man had moved on after a curious glance at the two of them, leaving them standing in front of Job, who looked at the end of his mythical patience. Behind them on the other side of the gallery, a group of American women were being lectured on the run by a bearded young man who looked as impatient as Job. A few couples, with the natives' penchant for free-loading, were attaching themselves to the paying group.

'No, sir, nobody there yet. She's sitting on one of the benches, obviously waiting for someone. She's not interested in any of the paintings.'

'What makes you think that?'

'She walked straight through this gallery and into that side one without even a glance at anything on the walls.'

'Are you interested in art?' He was making conversation, pretending interest in the painting in front of them, in case they were being observed by someone further down the long hall.

'I did two years at East Sydney before I found out I had no real talent.' He was broad-cheeked and heavy-jawed, with intelligent blue eyes: intelligent enough to size up his own talent or lack of it.

'What's your first name?'

'Hans. My parents are Dutch.'

'So's my –'

Then a man in a covert topcoat, carrying a hat in his hand, went by them and into the side gallery. Malone caught only a glimpse of him, not enough to identify him. But then how was he going to identify Federal anyway? Only by seeing him meet Mrs Dourane.

'Stay here. Don't let anyone come into that side gallery. If any shooting starts, get everyone out of the way.' He took his gun out of its holster, put it in his raincoat pocket. 'I hope to Christ Mr Federal is going to be sensible.'

The adrenalin was pumping away like a burst artery; he paused before leaving De Groot to steady himself. He was apprehensive; he was not reckless. Reckless cops got themselves killed; or got other people killed. Hand on the gun in his pocket, he walked slowly into the side gallery. This room was almost a retreat: one or two busts on pedestals, some small paintings on the beige-yellow walls, a place to pause and think. There were only three people in it: Mrs Dourane in her yellow topcoat and a black beret, the man in the covert topcoat and an elderly man in a red knitted beanie and a dufflecoat standing in a corner in front of a small painting and studying it through a large magnifying glass. Mrs Dourane and Federal, if it was he, were seated side by side on the backless bench in the middle of the room.

Malone walked up to them from the rear, not hurrying, and stood above them. Mrs Dourane looked up and her eyes widened, the pouted lips opened. The man turned his head quickly when he saw the expression on Mrs Dourane's face, but Malone had taken his gun from his pocket.

'Don't do anything stupid, Mr Federal. Or is it Mr Ballinger? No, sit still, Mrs Dourane! The game's over, I'm afraid. I'm arresting you sir, for the murder of Detective-Constable Peta Smith. Anything et cetera, et cetera . . .'

'You can't hold me —' Mrs Dourane made as if to stand up, then changed her mind when Malone turned the gun on her. She bit her lips, smearing her teeth so that they looked as if they had drawn blood. 'I had nothing to do with —'

'Be quiet, Mrs Dourane.' Federal had not moved, but sat, turned awkwardly to look up at Malone. There was no expression on his thin bony face, nothing in the dark eyes behind the horn-rimmed glasses. Malone, staring hard at him, thought, Christ, he *is* anonymous. A face easily forgotten.

The old man in the corner had turned round and was looking at them in puzzlement; then he raised the magnifying glass and studied them as he had studied the painting. Malone put two fingers in his mouth and whistled; both the old man and Mrs Dourane jumped, but Federal just twisted his lips in what could have been a smile. De Groot appeared instantly in the wide doorway.

'Search him, Hans. Sit still, Mrs Dourane!' He spoke over his shoulder to the old man. 'Would you mind leaving, sir? This is police business.'

The doorway now was crowded with spectators more interested in drama than in art. There were gasps as De Groot took a gun from the pocket of the covert topcoat, then produced handcuffs and snapped them on Federal. The old man had not moved, was either bemused or had not heard Malone tell him this was police business. He just stood shaking his head in wonder at what one found these days in art galleries.

'Is this what they call performance art?' He had a thin reedy voice.

'If you like, sir,' said Malone. 'Shall we go, Mr Federal? Mrs Dourane?'

Halfway down the main gallery, flanked on either side by a growing crowd of spectators, they met Clements. 'I heard that whistle –' He looked at Federal. 'Is this the bastard?'

'It's him,' said Malone.

3

'If you are going to believe in capitalism, you have to be a success in it. The same when we believed in Communism. How many idealists survived under our old system? Do you think Stalin and Brezhnev were idealists?'

Federal lounged in his chair in the second interview room, separate from where Joanna Brame and Milly Channing were. Homicide was crowded with visitors. The two women in one room; Federal here with Malone, Clements and Anders; Channing, Lazarus and De Vries in Malone's office with Kagal and Truach and Creek. The two Douranes were in the big main room with De Groot, Powell and a young uniformed policewoman Malone had asked to be sent across from Police Centre.

Federal did not appear disturbed that he was here on a murder charge. 'We have done nothing wrong, just invested our money in perfectly respectable companies.'

'*Oil* companies,' said Anders.

'Okay, oil companies.' His English was excellent, there was virtually no trace of accent that Malone could pick up. It was an anonymous voice, he decided, one that could be used effectively wherever Federal happened to be. Malone, like most of the natives a poor linguist, felt a grudging admiration.

'Whose money?' Malone asked. 'You said *our* money.'

For the first time Federal shifted uncomfortably in his chair. 'I thought you knew?'

'We do,' lied Malone, 'but we want you to confirm it for this.' He tapped the video recorder.

Federal looked around the small bare room, then he looked back at the two detectives and the Securities investigator. He smiled, the smile of a co-conspirator, one who knew all the tricks. 'Force of habit. No bugs?'

'Why force of habit with the bugs?' Malone tapped the video recorder again.

'You know I'm Russian?'

'Yes,' said Malone, though it had only been an educated guess.

'I worked for fifteen years for the Committee for State Security. The KGB.'

'Not now?' said Clements, who had been silent up till now. He was showing more open resentment of the Russian than Malone or Anders.

The Russian smiled again, shrugged. 'It's finished. Spineless. What sort of deal will you give me for what I tell you?'

'No deal at all,' said Malone. 'We can't offer you anything. If the government intervenes . . .'

Federal smiled again; he seemed to be all smiles. Malone knew little of Russian history or the Russian character, but he had read of Russian fatalism, bred of centuries of oppression under both Tsarist and Communist rule. Federal seemed to be true to type, though more good-humoured than dour.

'Governments! They're always willing to make deals, don't you think? You buy this from us, we'll buy that from you, you give us this spy, we'll give you that one . . .'

'Are you still a spy?' said Clements.

'What future would there be in it? No.'

'But does someone still control you?' said Anders.

It seemed that Federal had not yet made up his mind about Anders; he kept looking at him curiously before he answered any of the Securities man's questions. 'Our holding company in Zurich is controlled by the Party – or what remains of it. The Old Guard, as the newspapers call them.'

'People like this Zhirinovsky?' said Anders.

The smile widened, he shook his head. 'A nut case. A ratbag, as you Australians say. No, not him. Men you've possibly never heard of.'

Malone was studying the Russian. He was affable, relaxed, seemed totally unconcerned that he was in the company of men whose woman colleague he had killed in cold blood. *What makes the bastard tick?* But it was a question Malone had asked on other occasions about other killers and, despite what criminal psychologists might tell him, he had never found a true answer.

'When Kruchina committed suicide three years ago –'

'Who?'

'Nikolai Kruchina, controller of the Party's monies – when he committed suicide some of us knew that was the end and something had to be done about all the money we had invested overseas.'

'How much?' said Anders.

Federal shrugged again. 'Your guess is as good as mine. An awful lot. Our holding company has access to twenty-eight billion dollars.' If he was expecting a reaction from the three men he was disappointed; partly because that sum was beyond their comprehension, or at least that of Malone and Clements. 'The source of our money has nothing to do with the West, it's honest money – or so we think. The Mafia, the Colombian drug cartels –'

'We've heard that argument.' Malone for the first time sounded testy; the Russian's composure, quietly arrogant, was getting to him. 'What's the purpose? To control the oil market if the Party makes a comeback? If Russia starts another Cold War?'

'Do you really think it will, Inspector?' He shook his head. 'I don't think so, nor do my fellow directors. Mr Brame and the Americans obviously thought so, but certain Americans are lost without Russia as an enemy. We should have to have another revolution and it's too soon for that, our people don't have the energy, not now. Maybe in the future . . .' He took off the horn-rimmed glasses, wiped them with a handkerchief; without the glasses he looked even more anonymous. 'No, we were investing for profit, not control. A perfectly respectable capitalist ploy, wouldn't you say?'

'Why didn't you turn the money around?' said Anders. 'Invest it in the new Russia? It's crying out for money.'

'You must be joking. Can't you see all the new republics crying out for their share? Would you pour champagne down a drain?'

'Did Channing and Lazarus know what you were up to?' asked Clements.

'Not at first, no. They never asked questions, I think they were blinded by the prospect of the fees they would earn. They are what I think you Australians call greedy buggers. The world is full of greedy buggers. I'm one.' Once more the smile.

'Who told them who you really were?'

'The American, Mr Brame.'

'Did you ever meet him?'

'Just the once. I had a drink with him last Sunday night at his hotel, in the coffee lounge. He wouldn't listen to my argument. He was very strait-laced, for a lawyer. It was like talking to the Pope.'

Malone was about to ask, *Was that why you killed him?* But Anders was pursuing his own line, the money line: 'How did you come to choose Channing and Lazarus, and then Mr Brame's firm? Or was it vice versa? Did you know Channing and Brame were brothers?'

'Of course.' Federal seemed to have accepted that, if nothing else, Anders knew his job. 'But I'm not going to tell you the sequence of whom we chose first and why. What I've already told you we'd guessed would come out eventually. But if I tell you too many secrets, my life wouldn't be worth a current rouble.'

'About two cents,' Anders told the two detectives.

'If you expected yourselves to be exposed, why did you kill Brame?' said Malone.

'It was too soon, we hadn't completed our plan. Personally, I think the killing of Mr Brame was a mistake.'

'If it was a mistake, why did you do it?'

'Why did *I* do it?' He was still holding his glasses in his hand; his eyes were exposed but they told Malone nothing. 'I didn't kill him. Or Murray Rockman.'

'Who was Rockman?'

Federal shrugged. 'It doesn't matter now if you know.

The KGB planted him here twelve years ago. He was here as an industrial spy. What better cover, what better opportunities, than as a security guard? His mother was a Chechen, you would have to know them to appreciate how dreadful they are. They still think they are at war with us Russians, after over a hundred years.'

'Who killed him, then?'

'I don't know.' He put the glasses back on.

He's lying now, thought Malone. 'Do you know why he was killed?'

'I suspect because he was taking something that didn't belong to him. I told you, he was half-Chechen, they will steal anything. There were seventy thousand BHP share certificates missing.'

'There were only ten thousand in his safe deposit box.'

'He must have had another box in another name.' Then he seemed to lose interest in Rockman. 'He really was a nuisance at times.'

Then Clements leaned forward. 'You did kill Detective Peta Smith?'

Federal remained steady in his chair; he didn't lean back away from Clements. 'Yes, I admit that. By then things had started to get out of hand with the other two killings. It was beginning to look like the Mafia –'

Malone could see that Clements was ready to explode; he intervened: 'When you killed her, why didn't you leave the country? We expected you to.'

'I knew that. I guessed you would have Immigration waiting for me.'

'Where did you go? We traced you to your hotel.'

'To a motel, a cheap one. It was like being back in the KGB. They always wanted us to do things on the cheap, if you were low down on the totem pole. We used to envy the CIA, they liked to do everything first class. Especially when Reagan was President.'

'You're a cold-blooded sonofabitch, you know that?'

said Clements. 'That girl was just doing her duty, bringing you in here for questioning –'

'You think I don't know what duty is? I apologize for shooting her –'

'You fucking *apologize*! Christ, I'll –'

Clements made a lunge towards the Russian, but Malone pushed him back into his chair. 'Mr Federal – is that your real name? Or is it Ballinger?'

The Russian pushed his chair back, as if afraid that Clements might make another lunge at him. 'It's Viktor Belinkov, ex-Major Belinkov.'

'Righto, Mr Belinkov, if you didn't kill Orville Brame and Murray Rockman, who did?'

'I don't think I have to answer any more questions,' said Belinkov and leaned back in his chair, one eye on Clements.

4

Though it disappointed him, for every cop loves nothing more than a case with all the ribbons tied, Malone had believed the Russian when the latter had said he had not murdered Brame and Rockman. Belinkov had had the air of a man who had the confidence of truth, a truth that could be proved, though it still had to be proven.

'You have an alibi?' Malone had said.

'Of course. I spent Sunday night at the Touch of Class. You can check with the madam or the girl I spent the night with, Dawn.'

Malone knew Tilly Mosman, the madam who ran the city's classiest brothel. She was a typical brothel-keeper, with a heart of gold which she kept in a bank vault, but she always told the truth to the police, within reason.

'I was there from midnight till seven in the morning. A charming house, better than most I've known. But Mrs

Mosman has a quaint house rule that everyone must be off the premises by seven a.m. In Moscow they used to serve breakfasts.'

'There were brothels in Moscow?' said Anders. 'In the old days?'

Belinkov had smiled at such naïveté. 'I'm sure there are brothels in Vatican City, Mr Anders. Why do the Swiss Guards always look so satisfied?'

Clements had looked at Malone, the Catholic, but the latter was not going to get into a defence of the Vatican, another bureaucracy.

Malone checked by phone with Tilly Mosman: a Mr Hammer, answering to Belinkov's description, had indeed spent the night with Dawn. 'You remember her, Inspector? You questioned her once before, when we had that nun dumped on her doorstep?'

He had a clear memory of the case, but only a vague memory of the girl. 'Is she there? Put her on.'

Dawn came on the line. 'Hello, Inspector.'

'You're on the day shift?'

'Around the clock. All these American lawyers in town, most of 'em haven't got their wives. They've heard of us. One guy was from Oshkosh, Indiana, he said they'd heard of us there.'

'I'm pleased to hear it, Dawn. The Tourist Board must be proud of you. Was Mr Hammer with you all night Sunday?'

'Yes, Inspector. Quite nice, really, very Continental, if you know what I mean.'

'I don't, actually. Describe him.'

'Well, he was – I dunno, you know, anonymous-looking. You see a hundred guys like him. Thin-faced, horn-rimmed glasses – oh, he had a nasty scar on his belly, just above his dick. All shrivelled up. The scar, not his dick.'

'I'm sure *that* wasn't, Dawn, not with you.' He remembered her now, a beautiful girl of half a dozen mixed

269

bloods, who had had her ambition. 'You any closer to getting your own establishment?'

He could almost imagine her wry smile. 'No, Inspector. I'll send you an invite when I do.'

He had hung up and told Belinkov to take down his trousers. The Russian did so without embarrassment, as if this had been part of the KGB training. There was an ugly wrinkled scar on his lower belly. 'I got that in Mexico in 1987.'

'A brothel?'

'No, the Mexican police. They thought I was a double agent.'

'Who for?'

'The CIA. Who else?'

He's not telling the truth this time, Malone thought. He's decided to joke. Malone had seen it before, the surrender to the inevitable, the laugh that was a nervous reflex. He had to be joking when he said, 'May I have my lawyers in here? Mr Channing and Mr Lazarus.'

'Not yet, Mr Belinkov. They are suspects too, you know.'

There was no reaction other than a nod. 'Of course. In the KGB we always had an advantage. There were never any suspects, just people who had to prove they were not guilty. It's a better system, saves an awful lot of time. We learned it from the Spanish Inquisition. They were always inventive, the Catholics.'

He's baiting me. Malone had had enough of the man's cynicism. He wanted to lean across the table, grab him and belt him one, just as Clements had wanted to do. But all he did was to say, 'You'll be held over at Police Centre, Mr Belinkov. Arrange it, will you, Russ?'

He left the room while his temper was still in check and went out to the main office. Weariness was starting to cloud his mind like a drug. The Douranes sat there in the room, the husband dejected, the wife nonchalant, legs crossed provocatively. The pouted lips had been repaired, the eyelashes touched up: she would go down, if she went down at all, in full battle kit. The two young Rockdale detectives and the young policewoman stood up as Malone came in. He motioned for them to resume their seats and pulled up a chair for himself.

'You're in trouble, Mr and Mrs Dourane. Accessories to murder –' It was a bluff, but bluffing was not a crime.

Mrs Dourane looked at her husband, but he had decided to remain silent. He was obviously afraid of what might happen to them, but there was a dignity to his silence; he would not beg to be understood, he was no camel driver. Mrs Dourane was more pragmatic: 'Bullshit. We know nothing about the murders. They were stupid, we dunno what got into Mr Federal –'

'His name's Belinkov, for the record. And he says he committed only one of the murders, that of my colleague, Detective Smith.' At once he was aware of the stiffening in the three young police officers; nothing physical happened, but it was almost as if one could hear their minds set. 'He denies knowing anything about the other two murders. You knew Rockman, the security guard, didn't you?'

'Never heard of him.'

Malone looked at her husband. 'You'd heard of him, hadn't you, Mr Dourane? We suspect he may have murdered the owners of two firms, one out at Carlingford, the other at Homebush, two firms that you bought up for Bern Investments and Alps Securities. Two of the firms that have been buying shares in BHP and Ampolex, the dealing that started these three latest murders. You knew him, didn't you?' He was leaning forward, his face only inches from Dourane's.

'Bullshit,' said Mrs Dourane again.

'Or camelshit or whatever you like,' said Malone. 'It doesn't alter the question I've put to your husband. Mr Dourane?'

Dourane ran his hand through his thick hair, nodded dejectedly. 'Yes, I knew him. He was the one who first came to me, I had no idea he was just a security guard, he looked like a businessman. He offered me the job as manager of the holding company for those two firms and some others.'

'When did you find out he was just a security guard?'

'He came to the office one day in uniform, just after we'd opened –'

'And you had no doubts about him? A security guard and he'd offered you a job like that?'

'Don't you know who he really was?'

'Yes, we do. A KGB agent. Did you know?'

Dourane hesitated, looked at his wife, who turned her back on him. Then he looked back at Malone. 'He told me who he was, the second time he came to see me, told me why I'd been chosen for the job. The word had come from Moscow, I had friends there.'

'You had friends in Moscow? You weren't in the KGB too, for Chrissakes?' He was tired of holding all the strings.

'No, no –'

'Be quiet,' said his wife, back still turned.

'What's the use?' he asked her, but, getting no answer, he looked back at Malone. 'I was a member of the government in Kabul, back in the days when Moscow ran it. I was the Under-Secretary for Finance, I'm a graduate of the LSE – the London School of Economics. When the Russians withdrew, I knew it was the end, it was too dangerous to stay on, the *mujaheddin* had me on their list . . .'

Malone remembered the days when the local crims had had only locals to fear, when crime had been a parish affair. Now there were fugitives from the *mujaheddin*, the *yakuza*, the Triads, Mafia . . . God bless multiculturalism.

'I had to leave. So I – I emigrated.'

'Are you a Marxist, too, Mrs Dourane?' He kept a straight face.

The pouted lips sneered. 'I'm not anything, I wouldn't give my vote to Jesus Christ. I had nothing to do with all this –'

'Then why were you the one who went to meet Belinkov?'

'That was purely accidental. I'm an art lover –'

Malone sighed, stood up, grinned at her. 'Camelshit, Mrs Dourane. Excuse me –' he said to the young policewoman, who smiled her forgiveness. 'Detectives De Groot and Powell have had your phone tapped for two days –'

She turned her head sharply towards the two officers. 'You bastards! That's against the law –'

'Not when you have a warrant,' said Malone, laughing; she really was a trier, this one, a battler for any fortune that offered itself. One could almost see her hand out, clutching for money going down the drain. 'You and Mr Dourane have a little think about what you want to tell us. The truth, that is. When you've made up your minds, Detectives De Groot and Powell will take down your statements. Will you come with me, Constable?'

The young policewoman got up and followed him out into the hallway. She was small and neat, with long blond hair drawn back in a chignon (just like my wife's, he wanted to tell her, but refrained).

'What's your name?'

'Kate Arletti, sir.'

'Italian? You don't look it.'

'My parents were from northern Italy, the Val d'Aosta.'

'How'd you get that scar?' There was a scar, partly hidden by make-up, running down her left jawline.

'A junkie tried to carve me with a razor.'

So she had been around. 'What happened to him?'

'I broke his nose with my gun. He's doing three years now.'

'Good for you. Righto, go back and get onside with Mrs Dourane. Don't interrogate her, just get her to loosen up.

Her husband's not the dangerous one, she is. She was in all this just for what she could get out of it. I don't know whether she would have killed to get what she wanted, but she might have.'

'How many suspects do you have, sir?'

He pondered a moment before answering: 'Three, including her.'

And so the afternoon wore on. The questioning continued. That was the basis of detection: questions, questions, questions. Nothing ever fell out of the sky, although occasionally a psycho wandered in with all the questions answered before they had been asked. Except perhaps the main one: what had driven him?

In his own office Malone was questioning Channing and Lazarus. 'When did Zurich Private Holdings come to you to represent them?'

The two men exchanged glances. They and De Vries all gave the impression that they resented being held here, especially the American. But they all knew enough about the law to recognize that a certain amount of co-operation was required. It was Channing who answered, 'About two years ago.'

'Who recommended you to them?'

'No one, as far as I know.'

'You mean they just stuck a pin in the phonebook? Come on, Rod.'

'I tell you, Mr Dourane just presented himself, asked us if we'd represent them.'

'Did you know Belinkov – Mr Federal to you – and Murray Rockman, the security guard, were ex-KGB? And Mr Dourane once had friends in Moscow? Were you two Marxists when you were at uni? It wouldn't have been unfashionable in your time.'

The two partners were shocked; so, too, was De Vries. Channing almost spat with indignation: 'I was president of the Young Libs! Jesus – a *Marxist*? Will and I –' He shook his head, aghast at the thought of being a *Marxist.* 'You're trying to say the KGB – the *KGB*?' Again the shake of the head. 'They had some sort of tick against us? No way, no way in the world.'

Malone changed tack: 'Mr De Vries, when did ZPH come to your firm?'

'I don't rightly know. They'd been with us some time before Orville Brame mentioned them to me. Look, Inspector, I'm not wanted here –'

'In a moment, Mr De Vries. You were going to say something, Mr Channing?'

Channing seemed to have recovered a little from what he had been told about the KGB. 'Let's cut this short, Inspector. I – well, it was us, Will and I, who recommended them to Orville. They wanted an American firm, a New York one, and I thought my brother's firm would be the answer.'

'Your brother and you had become reconciled?'

'Well, no. When I wrote him, it was the first time in – well, years.'

'Why choose his firm then?'

Channing sat back in his chair, refusing to say any more. Malone didn't press him, made his guess. The younger brother had wanted to impress the elder, introducing a client who wanted to spend millions. *Look, you're not the only success in the family* . . . It was only a guess, but Malone was sure he wasn't wide of the mark.

He turned to Lazarus. 'I take it you weren't in Sydney last Sunday night or Monday morning?'

The one-eyed man, it seemed, had retreated behind his eye-patch. He had sat saying nothing, the visible eye sliding back and forth like an abacus bead. 'I was on a flight between Zurich and Bangkok. You can check –' He gave the Thai Airlines flight number and his first-class seat number; his pedantry was arrogant. 'If you are thinking I had anything to do with the murder of Mr Brame, you're dead wrong.'

'We often are, Mr Lazarus. But occasionally we're dead right. We only get to be right by asking the obvious and some of the not-so obvious questions. You can go, Mr Lazarus, but we'll keep in touch. If you're going to make any more sudden overseas flights – like to Zurich – let us know.'

'You'll have a check on me at the airport?'

Malone didn't answer, just smiled. Lazarus hesitated, then got to his feet. Channing also stood up, but Malone waved a hand at him. 'Sit down, Mr Channing.'

'Look –'

'Siddown!' The two of them stared at each other, then Channing sank back on to his chair.

Lazarus looked as surprised as Channing, then he said, 'I'll be at the office, Rod,' and left. Malone looked at De Vries. 'You're eliminated, too, as a suspect, Mr De Vries.'

'Thank you.' His voice rasped. 'As I said before, you have a talent for insults.'

Malone shrugged. 'That sounds good coming from a lawyer.'

'Another insult. I'll wait outside for Mrs Brame.'

That left Malone and Channing together. The lawyer had seemingly lost all his bearings. He looked around Malone's office as if seeing it for the first time, though he had been here almost an hour. 'Comparing it with your own office?' said Malone.

'What?' Channing was puzzled.

'Nothing.' *I should pack up and go home. I'm not looking at any of these people objectively.* 'Rod, I don't know why we haven't asked you this question before. Where were *you* Sunday night?'

'Sunday night?' Channing frowned; then the point of the question seemed to stick into him like a poniard: 'Oh, come off it, for Chrissake! Are you asking did I kill my brother? Jesus, that's the end! Why would I kill him?'

'He was trying to stuff up a deal that was going

to make you and your partner a fortune in fees.'

Channing moved his head around as if trying to get out of an armlock. 'No, no!'

'You're the logical suspect. Where were you Sunday night?'

'I was home, in bed! Ask my wife –'

Malone looked at him with mock pity. 'Rod, you're a lawyer. You know as well as I do that a wife's testimony isn't worth a pinch of the proverbial. If she's a loving, loyal wife, she'll lie for her husband. If she hates his guts, she'll just as likely also lie to convict him.' Lisa would tear strips off him if she could hear this. 'You'll need better corroboration than that.'

'My kids?'

'Did any of them get up during the night and see you asleep in your bed?'

'How would I know, if I was asleep? Come on, Malone – I didn't kill my brother! Okay, I was pissed off with him for wanting to – to expose the share dealing. But Jesus – *kill him*?' He shook his head again at the thought.

Malone stood up and went out into the hallway room as Clements came in. The big man, in his pink sweater, was the only bright note in the place; or perhaps Malone's gloom made everything seem duller than it was. 'You get Belinkov locked up?'

'He didn't put up any sorta protest. He must be a fatalist or something.'

'Maybe it's the Russian in him. You and I should practise it. I've got Channing in my office. He's got to be one of those who could've killed Brame, but I don't know that I can hold him just on suspicion. Put a tail on him. Ask Chatswood if they can spare anyone, he lives in their area.'

'You said he's gotta be one who might of. Who're the others?'

'Mrs Dourane.'

Clements nodded. 'And?'

'Channing's mother.'

Clements sat down on the edge of a table. In a far corner of the room Dourane sat sullenly with De Groot and Powell, the two detectives drinking coffee, the Afghan staring out the window at the slanting rain. Clements bit his lip, his old habit. 'You're stretching it, mate. Why would she kill her own son, one she hadn't seen in thirty years?'

'That could be the reason. He comes home after thirty years to bugger up a scheme that was going to make her other son rich, the son who'd stuck by her.'

Clements considered this, then nodded. 'Okay, that's a reason. But she wouldn't have done in Murray Rockman, too.'

'One at a time.'

'All the killings are still connected.'

'Sure. But as I said, let's do 'em one at a time. I'm going to talk to Milly Channing, after I've got rid of Mrs Brame.'

He went along the hallway to the interrogation room where the two women still sat with Anders. The three of them were chatting, Anders telling the two women how he had been an organizer of the Gay and Lesbian Mardi Gras this year; Milly was nodding her head, full of interest, and Joanna sat listening with a quiet fascination, like a latecomer to the facts of life. Anders stood up as Malone came in. 'The ladies were wondering, Inspector, how long they were going to be kept –'

Malone explained the delay. 'We've charged a Mr Belinkov, a Russian, with the murder of Detective Smith.'

'And my husband's murder?'

Malone looked at Joanna. 'I'm afraid he's not our man, Mrs Brame, not for that murder. Mr De Vries is waiting outside for you, he'll take you back to your hotel.'

There was just the slightest twitch of her nose. 'But I'll leave tomorrow and still not know who killed Orville?'

Out of the corner of his eye Malone was watching Milly Channing, who was the only one who had remained seated. It struck him that she had the prim look of someone who was completely organized; she held her handbag as if it contained the elements of her life, her hands grasping it were steady, no white knuckles showing. Another image formed in his mind, subliminally: his mother sitting just like that, handbag held just like that, secrets in it that he could only guess at. Such as what had really happened in Ballyreagh long ago.

'Anything could happen between now and tomorrow, Mrs Brame. We're not going to stop trying just because we've cleared up one murder.'

His tone had been gentle, but she recognized it for a rebuke. 'I'm sorry, Mr Malone. I –' For once she was at a loss for words; it had been a long long day. 'Will you mind if I call you tomorrow before I leave?'

'I'll come to the airport,' he said on the spur of the moment, his tongue this time on his side.

She gave him her hand, taking off her glove to do so. 'You have been very kind, Mr Malone. Thank you.'

She said goodbye to Milly Channing, who also rose to leave but stopped when Malone waved her down. Anders took Joanna out of the room and Malone closed the door.

'You and I have to talk, Mrs Channing –'

'About Rod? Or about Orville?'

'About you.' He sat down opposite her.

She stared at him, then nodded at the video recorder. 'Are you going to turn that on?'

'Not yet. It depends on what you tell me. I've asked everyone else this question, Mrs Channing – where were you Sunday night?'

She frowned, not as if trying to remember where she had been Sunday night but at the question itself. 'Am I some sort of suspect or something?'

He nodded. 'Among others. The way we work, Mrs Channing, is we start with a crowd and work our way inwards.'

'And now you've got to me?' She was still holding the handbag, but not clutching it, the knuckles still not white. She wore a brown wool topcoat and a paisley scarf which had covered her head but was now draped round her neck. She pulled the ends of the scarf together, but that was the only sign that she might be feeling nervous. 'You think I might have killed Orville?'

'He came to see you?'

'Yes, last Sunday morning, before he saw Rod. It was awkward, I have to admit that. After thirty years, what was I supposed to be? The loving mother, all forgiveness? It doesn't work like that, Mr Malone, not immediately. Given time . . .'

Malone could not argue against that. It occurred to him that the only serious forgiveness he had ever had to offer had been to criminals; and there had been no reconciliation with any of them. 'Where were you Sunday night? Monday morning early?'

'I was home, alone. Like a lot of women my age,' she said tartly. She was sitting on the edge of her chair now, leaning forward against the table. 'Why would I kill my son?'

Facing her, he hesitated; then he told her what he had told Clements.

She looked at him almost with pity. 'Do you think I'm a madwoman or something?'

He stood up, exhaustion crippling him again. 'You can go, Mrs Channing.'

She tied the scarf under her chin; her hair hidden, she suddenly looked pinched and aged. 'I'm disappointed in you, Mr Malone.'

He nodded. 'That's a policeman's lot, Mrs Channing. I'll have someone take you home.'

'Never mind,' she snapped and stalked out on legs surprisingly steady for a woman of her years.

Malone, suddenly feeling his own years, sat on the edge

of the table. He looked at the video recorder and, for some reason he was too weary to examine, was glad that he had not turned it on. Then Clements came to the door. 'So?'

'So I could be wrong. But you nominate someone else.' Clements shook his head and Malone went on, 'Put a tail on her, too. One of ours.'

'We're running out of bodies –' Then he shook his head; he, too, looked tired. 'No, we've got enough bloody bodies. I mean personnel. I'll find someone.'

'See if we can borrow that girl outside, Kate Arletti. Put her in plainclothes.'

'You really think Milly Channing might of murdered Orville and she'll try to do a bunk?'

'I don't know what I think –' He ran a hand over his brow, wiping away sweat that wasn't there. 'She wouldn't have shot Murray Rockman, Christ knows who did that. We may never know and frankly, between you and me, I don't care very much. But yes, she could have done Brame . . .'

'Okay, I'll have her tailed. You going home now?'

'Russ, my eyes are crossed, I'm bitched, buggered and bewildered. What are we going to do with Dourane?'

'I don't think he's gunna go anywhere. He's besotted with that wife of his, he's not gunna piss off and leave her. She's still in with Kate Arletti.'

'Righto, take her across to Police Centre, charge her with being an accessory, helping Belinkov evade arrest, you know the drill. If she can get bail, okay, so long as she reports to Rockdale once or twice a day. I'm going home.'

Clements looked at him solicitously. 'Drum up a smile before you go in the house. You've got no right to take a face like that home to Lisa.'

Chapter Eleven

1

Saturday night Malone and Lisa spent alone. As if they had pre-arranged it all, the children went out: Claire with her boyfriend-of-the-week, Maureen to a girlfriend's, Tom to a school chum's. The exodus was without fuss or comment and Malone remarked upon it. 'Three Sensitive New Age Kids. SNAKS.'

'I had to spell it out for them,' said Lisa. 'They were all going to stay home and keep us company. A family night, they said.'

'So what are we having instead?'

'A lovers' night. Have you forgotten how?'

'Are you up to it? I mean –'

'Darling –' They were sitting side by side in front of the television set. Angela Lansbury was solving another murder with an ease that left Malone mystified. Lisa stretched out, put her head in his lap and looked up at him. 'Does the thought of the tumor put you off?'

'It doesn't exactly turn me on. I'm thinking of you, not me. That thing sticking in the back of your neck isn't my Smith and Wesson.' He bent his head and kissed her. 'Don't let's get worked up, darl. There'll be plenty of it when this is all over.'

She reached for the remote control, swamped Angela Lansbury in blackness. 'To be honest, I don't have the itch. I just thought you'd –'

'Don't you know me better than that?'

But of course she did. She drew his head down again and

kissed him hungrily, then let him go. 'Get that thing out of the back of my neck.'

'Sit up. We'll watch Columbo, he's coming up next. Maybe I'll learn something from him.'

He learned nothing. But he and Lisa went to bed still loving each other.

2

Sunday morning Malone went to Mass with Lisa and the children. Normally he said a perfunctory prayer, then let his mind wander while the priest went through the rituals. This morning he prayed earnestly, calling on God to do the decent thing and spare Lisa. He went to communion with her and the children, kept the Host on his tongue as if it were a last hope, till it melted and he was left with the dry taste of fear.

After he had taken them home he drove into the Hat Factory. He checked the running sheet in the computer. Belinkov was being held without bail; Mrs Dourane had been released on an assurance by her husband; she, Rod and Milly Channing were under twenty-four-hour surveillance. He took another look at the flow chart, the map of three murders. He knew that when it came time to erase the chart he would have to leave it to someone else to wipe out Peta Smith's handiwork. It would be too much like erasing Peta herself.

Then he drove out to Kingsford Smith airport, found a space in the crowded car park, then went across to the departure terminal. He enquired after Joanna Brame and was told she was upstairs in the executive lounge. He went up the escalator, knocked on the door of the lounge and was admitted, with raised eyebrows from the hostess, when he showed his police badge.

'You're not going to arrest anyone?' Her tone suggested

that was no more permissible than coming in without a proper pass.

He reassured her, went in and found Joanna Brame with De Vries, Rod and Milly Channing. And at once wished he had not come.

Only Joanna Brame greeted him with any warmth. 'You did indeed come, Mr Malone. Thank you.' She looked wan and older this morning; Malone wondered if she had been supervising the loading of her husband's coffin into the plane's hold. 'Do you have any more news?'

He shook his head. 'We have nothing we can bring against the Russian I told you about, Belinkov, not regarding your husband's murder.'

'So you're no closer to solving that?' De Vries could not have made the question sound any more critical.

To Malone it seemed that both the Channings leaned forward for his answer. He decided perversely to increase their unease. 'Yes, we are.'

'And you'll make an arrest soon?' De Vries persisted.

Malone smiled, though he felt no humour. 'We cops always say that, Mr De Vries, I'm sure even in New York. It makes the crim, when he hears it or reads it, just that little bit uneasy.'

The Channings, it seemed, leaned back satisfied.

The lounge was clamorous and crowded; the American lawyers were going home. As with other nationalities, those in the majority had taken over the place: the rooms could have been in a terminal in Los Angeles or Seattle or New York. Karl Zoehrer appeared out of the crush, looking and sounding less bombastic. Perhaps the week had worn him out or perhaps his mind, too, was on what would be going home with them in the hold of the aircraft.

'Mrs Brame told me about the arrest of the Russian. But for a different murder?'

Joanna Brame evidently hadn't explained fully *which* murder; but Malone was in no mood to lay it on him now. 'Yes, a different one. But not Mr Brame.'

'Well, these things take time.'

Why didn't you say that the other day in the Commissioner's office?

'There are some of us who still want to know who *really* shot President Kennedy.'

I'm not going to get into that one. 'I'll let you know, Mr Zoehrer,' he said and for a moment Zoehrer looked puzzled by the ambiguous answer. 'Have a good trip home.'

Then he turned away to say goodbye to Joanna Brame. 'I'll let you know, Mrs Brame, if and when –'

'I've been thinking, Mr Malone, even while standing here. Perhaps when I'm home and my husband has been cremated, perhaps I shan't want to know.'

He wanted to tell her: *yes, you will*. But he said, 'Then I shan't write unless you do. But of course you'll read about it in your newspapers. They carry the occasional story from us, I understand.'

De Vries, standing beside them, said, 'The lawyer in me wants all the loose ends tied up.'

Joanna Brame just looked at him, then without a word, shook Malone's hand, turned and made her way through the crowd, disappearing into it as into thick scrub, going home to all the familiar things that she would now suffer or enjoy alone.

Malone didn't put out his hand to the Channings. He just said, 'I'll be seeing you,' and left. As he was going out the door of the lounge he met Adam Tallis coming in. He put out his hand to him, someone who had tried, no matter how ineffectively, to help.

Tallis put down his heavy briefcase and his laptop, shook Malone's hand vigorously. 'I'll be coming back, bringing my girlfriend. I've seen enough to want to come again . . . Mrs Brame told me you'd got a killer, some Russian.'

'Not Mr Brame's killer, though. We're still trying there.'

'Orville gave us the clue all along, didn't he? *Look to the past*. He went to Russia, you know, two years ago with a law delegation, to show 'em how our systems worked. He wasn't impressed. Maybe that was when they marked him down for future use.'

No, it wasn't like that; but there was no time for explanations and they didn't matter anyway, not to Tallis. 'Will Schuyler, De Vries and Barrymore lose money now all this looks like collapsing?'

Tallis grinned. 'Law firms never lose money, Mr Malone, not competent ones who prepare for every contingency. It's one of the irrefutable laws of nature.'

'You're too frank to be a lawyer.'

'Not frank, just naïve.' He grinned again. 'But I'm learning. Goodbye, Inspector, and good luck.'

Outside in the car park Malone waited beside his Commodore. A morning wind had stretched the air till it seemed that it thrummed; the cloudless sky was a tight blue drum. A plane took off into the shining air, its faint exhaust smoke a desecration of the purity. Three Taragos drew in across from Malone's car and a crowd of Greeks, men, women and children, got out, roped together by shrill excitement. They raced towards the arrivals terminal, bearing a huge welcome for whoever was arriving from Athens or Ithaca or wherever, Greeks bearing gifts.

The Channings, mother and son, came into the car park, followed by two young men at a distance who Malone guessed were the surveillance cops. Channing and his mother paused by a blue BMW some fifty yards from Malone and continued what looked like an argument they had brought with them from the terminal. Then Channing looked towards Malone and saw him, said something to his mother and she turned and shaded her eyes against the glare of the sun reflected from the line of cars. He walked unhurriedly towards them, looking beyond them to see the two young plainclothesmen break off and head towards their respective cars.

'Were you waiting for us?' said Channing challengingly. 'Why, for Chrissake, can't you leave us alone?'

'I'll do that. I'm taking a week's leave. Sergeant Clements will be taking over from me. You'll find he has less patience than I have.'

'Is that usual?' said Milly Channing. 'You walk away from a job while in the middle of it? No wonder the country's getting nowhere.'

Don't make me dislike you, he thought. He still strongly suspected her, not maybe that she had done the actual murder of her other son but that she had been somehow involved. Yet there was a basic niceness about her that appealed. Or had been: now she was turning nasty. He had seen it before: the line between acceptance and resentment of the police was very thin.

'The job will be done just as effectively by Sergeant Clements. Stay tuned.'

He went back to the Commodore, got in and drove away without looking back at them. By the time he came back to duty tomorrow week he hoped the remaining two murder cases would have been solved. As he turned on to the perimeter road round the airport he was surprised to find he didn't care whether the murders were solved or not. He was praying that a life, Lisa's, would be saved and the dead, after all, were dead.

3

That afternoon he and the children took Lisa into St Sebastian's. Then he took the children to a Pizza Hut for supper.

'Mum's going to be okay, okay? None of us forgets that. She'll hold a gun at our heads if we think otherwise.'

'She's always such an optimist,' said Claire.

'A pragmatic one,' he said. 'On Cloud Nine with a parachute.'

'Listen to him,' said Maureen, the cynic who could weep.

'My trouble is, what prayers do I say?' said Tom from behind a dripping pizza. 'Do I talk to God like I do to you?'

'Just like that, with a little more respect,' said Malone. 'I think He likes a heart-to-heart occasionally. He must get sick of the Our Fathers.'

He looked at them, the warm lining of his life; had his mother ever looked at him in the same light? Dear Jesus, that should be the first commandment: Tell your children you love them. But in a Pizza Hut?

He took them home, then drove back to the hospital. Lisa was in bed in her room, her hair loose, light make-up on, looking beautiful and inviting.

'You want a bit?' she said, making a pretence of moving over in the bed.

He kissed her, sat down, held her hand. 'It's hard to believe you have that damned thing inside you.'

'It'll be gone tomorrow. Then there'll be some chemotherapy –' She made a face. 'I hope I don't go completely bald.'

'You think I won't love you bald?' He ran a hand over the thick blond hair, pressed and felt the skull beneath. 'A woman's crowning glory . . . There are other parts just as good.'

'You make a girl feel so wanted.' She smiled, lifted his hand and kissed it. 'Look after the kids, keep them happy.'

Once again he felt the fear in her; she was, he realized with his own terrible fear, contemplating the chance that she would not recover. He held her to him, saying nothing because his throat was too thick. When he let her go neither could clearly see the other for the tears in their eyes.

She dried her tears. 'As soon as I'm well again, you take us all to dinner at the most expensive place I can think of.'

'I almost told the kids tonight how much I love them.'

'Why didn't you?'

'Not in a Pizza Hut. Not with cheese and anchovies dripping from their jaws. They looked like slobbering dobermans.'

When he left her he paused for a moment in the doorway and looked back at her. She smiled, raised a hand and gave him a small wave; it was a tiny gesture, her regal wave as Claire called it. He waved back, just a flick of the wrist, then went quickly down the corridor to the lift.

As he got out of the lift he was aware of someone coming at him from an angle. 'Why, Inspector Malone!'

He stopped, turned: it was Mrs Johns.

'I've been visiting an aunt. You have someone in here?'

'My wife.'

'Nothing serious, I hope?'

He didn't feel disposed to discuss his wife's insides with another woman, one he didn't like at all. 'No.'

They walked out of the lobby, past the statue of St Sebastian, arrows sticking out of him and an expression on his face that suggested he was having second thoughts that maybe life would have been gayer if he had accepted the Emperor Diocletian's offer of a homosexual relationship. They went out into the chill night air. Mrs Johns shivered and drew the fur collar of her coat up round her neck. 'I have to find a cab.'

This evening she sounded unexpectedly affable; as if she wanted to talk. Maybe, just maybe, she had something to tell him about Channing and Lazarus. On the spur of the moment he said, 'Where do you live? Maybe I can give you a lift?'

'Why, that would be nice! Kensington.'

It would be five minutes out of his way, no more. He led her across to the Commodore, opened the passenger's door for her, waited till she was in the seat, then closed it. He did not want to appear over-solicitous, but if he, too, were affable, maybe she would talk.

He got in, took the car out of the space reserved for doctors where he had parked it, and turned south. They caught the lights at Oxford Street and crossed into South Dowling. He said, 'I hope there's nothing serious wrong with your aunt?'

'There is no aunt,' she said and took a gun from her handbag. 'Turn left at Flinders Street, then left again when we get to Moore Park Road.'

How could he have been such a bloody fool? He drove automatically, for the moment more angry than afraid. He looked sideways at the gun in her hand; it was one he didn't immediately recognize. 'What's that? The gun?'

She didn't take her eyes off him. 'A Tokarev. Murray Rockman had two of them.'

'You knew him?'

'Shut up, Mr Malone.' They had turned left into Flinders Street, were heading towards the next cross street. There was a lot of traffic, all of it moving too fast for him to call for help. 'Left here.'

'This isn't the way to Kensington –' He was stumbling for words, trying to stumble out of this situation that his stupidity had plunged him into.

'We're not going to Kensington. Turn right up ahead, at the road that leads past the Football Stadium.'

He turned right into Driver Avenue, for one mad moment thinking of jerking to a stop as he cut across the oncoming traffic. If they were hit, she would be on the smashed side. But self-preservation was too strong; he shot across the front of the traffic to a herald of horns and flashing headlights. Then they were passing the Football Stadium on their left, dark now but with cars still parked in the members' car park and lights on in the club rooms. His foot eased on the pedal as he realized he was going to be shot somewhere along this lonely road. The Stadium, then the Cricket Ground, loomed on their left; on their right was the black desert of Moore Park. Two cars were following him, but before he could make up his mind how to enlist them, both of them had swooped by him and were gone. This road was notorious as a speedway.

He said, doing his best to keep his voice steady, 'Did you kill Orville Brame?'

'No. Pull up.'

He kept the car moving, almost sedately. 'Who did?'

'Murray Rockman. Pull up!'

'Not just yet.' He was going to stretch his luck; he had nothing to lose. 'If you shoot me, I'll put my foot down hard on the accelerator and chances are you'll die with me. Why did Murray kill him?'

'Because he was the one who was spoiling it for all of us.'

'Us?'

She put the gun against the side of his head. 'Pull up!'

'I told you, you shoot me and the car's not going to pull up till it hits something. You forgot to put your seat-belt on.' He was far from calm; but he sounded calm. 'You said *us*. Who?'

'Us. Murray and Major Belinkov and me.'

'You were KGB, too?' His foot went down involuntarily, the car speeded up. The crims in this case were a club.

'That was another life –' She didn't sound as if she missed it. She took the gun away from his head. 'You are being stupid, Mr Malone –'

'I was stupid offering you a lift. Who killed Rockman? You or Belinkov?'

'What's it matter now? I did!' She was growing angry; or afraid. 'He didn't need to kill Brame. He was a killer, that was his trouble, he was getting out of hand –'

'That was what Belinkov said.'

They had reached the end of Driver Avenue, come past

the darkened Showgrounds, had come to the T-junction with Lang Road. He was out of the danger zone for the moment, unless she shot him as he now slowed down as streams of traffic, going both ways, passed up and down in front of them. He could not afford to come to a full stop; if he did, he was dead. Suddenly he saw a narrow gap, no more than two cars long; he stamped on the accelerator, shot across one stream of traffic and into the other, swinging hard right with a shriek of tyres. He went up on the inside of the traffic, sometimes scraping the kerb; he came to the lights at Anzac Parade, the main artery south out of the city. He swung left into the speeding traffic; he didn't hear the horn-blowing or the screech of tyres as cars braked sharply. He went south, weaving through the traffic, shot through the red lights at Robertson Road, veered left at Alison and headed up towards the ridge of Randwick. And all the time he was praying for a police car to appear; what were all the bloody yuppies with their car phones doing, not ringing in to report a madman loose? He went through another set of red lights, narrowly missing a car coming in from the right. *That's how accidents happen . . .* He heard the echo of his own words a few nights ago. What he was doing was stupid and theatrical and criminal; he might kill someone else besides himself and Mrs Johns. The alternative was that he would surely die and, with the natural instinct for survival, he took the roulette chances.

He had gone through two more sets of lights before he saw the police car do a U-turn and come after them, siren wailing, lights flashing. He slowed down, but kept the car moving. 'Are you still going to kill me?'

'Keep going!' But she was wavering.

The police car was right on their tail now, siren still going. There had been a spate of tragic accidents during police chases earlier in the year and there had been talk that police would no longer take part in chases; he thanked

God that that suggestion had not prevailed. A traffic light loomed up ahead at the busy intersection of Alison and Belmore Roads and he began to slow.

'Go through it!'

He did so, shutting his eyes at the car coming in from the right. It clipped the back of the Commodore and he felt the rear end slide away; he fought the wheel, managed to steer away from the cars coming towards them. Then he had had enough. He took his foot off the pedal, let the Commodore coast to a stop by the kerb. The police car skidded round them, jerked to a halt and two uniformed men jumped out, one of them drawing his gun.

Malone looked at Mrs Johns. 'You can shoot me, but killing a cop will get you longer than killing Murray Rockman. Or you can kill yourself.' He said it without any compunction; he was past mercy. 'Take your pick.'

Then the car door was snatched open and the officer with the gun said, 'Out! Don't try anything!'

Malone slid out of the car, to find that his legs were shaking. He leaned both hands on the roof of the car while the officer frisked him. Then he heard the soft whistle as his police badge was flipped open.

'Turn around!' Malone did so. 'Inspector Malone? Christ, who's the woman then?'

'She's wanted for murder. She has a gun, but I don't think she's going to use it.'

Leaning on the car's roof he watched while Mrs Johns was taken out of the passenger's seat, cuffed and led back to the police car. She stopped, glared back at him, then was bundled in by the two policemen.

Malone looked at his hands on the cold roof of the Commodore. They were trembling, like an old man with palsy. Then he looked across the road and remarked for the first time where he had come to a halt. He was half a mile from home, opposite Marcellin College, Tom's school and his own old school. Where he had been a star sportsman and a so-so scholar, where he had sung in the school choir, belted out with fervour his favourite hymn, *Be Not Afraid*. Balls, he thought. Always have a little fear, it made you value the safe moments such as this.

4

'She's told us the lot,' said Clements. 'It was Rockman's idea to kill Brame. Seems he was a bit of a psycho, just like we thought. I think Dicey Kilmer was lucky he didn't do *her* in. Incidentally, I called her in Cawndilla, told her it was all over. She's coming back to Sydney, said they don't appreciate women body-builders in the bush.'

'How did Rockman get Brame?'

'He stalked Brame when the latter went out for a walk Sunday night, shot him, then took him up and put him in the monorail. He knew how to work it, he'd ridden on it enough times. But why the hell would Brame go for a walk on a freezing Sunday night?'

'I went for a walk on a freezing Monday morning, this morning. If it's a habit, you do it. His wife said he liked to walk at the end of the day, did it all the time in New York. He probably figured if no one mugged him in New York, nobody was going to do it in Sydney. He was thirty years out of date.'

It was late Monday afternoon and Clements had come up from Homicide to join Malone at St Sebastian's. The two big men sat in the small waiting room; across from them sat Brigid Malone and Elisabeth Pretorius. Above their heads the usual insipid painting of Christ looked benignly down on them, His Sacred Heart exposed in what looked like an advanced case of fibrillation. Malone wondered why so many religious paintings looked like the work of novice artists, unsure of their paints and even of their piety.

'He shot Brame without telling Belinkov or Mrs Johns what he was gunna do. She reckons she and Belinkov were both ropeable. She and Rockman were both still under the control of Belinkov. The KGB may be dead, the old one anyway, but the system still works. She shot Rockman with one of his own guns, she didn't say why he'd given her the gun. Maybe she just acted like the office manager and he did what he was told. Anyhow, there were three murders and three different murderers. And you might of been the fourth.'

'Don't remind me.' He had slept fitfully last night, red traffic lights rushing at him like shell-bursts. 'What about Channing and Lazarus?'

Clements shrugged. 'We've got nothing on 'em. Maybe the Securities Commission will give 'em a slap on the wrist. They've made money outa this, but they're not gunna make the millions they expected. You gunna tell Lisa what happened last night?'

'No,' he said emphatically. 'Not now, anyway. I've told the nurses she's not to see a newspaper or look at TV. She's still in intensive care, so she's cut off for at least twelve hours.'

'The doctor's optimistic?'

'He said it looked like a clean-cut job. There's no sign that it's spread. We just have to hope that it stays that way.'

'It will,' said Clements with the confidence of someone who didn't have to bear the worry. He stood up, said goodbye to Brigid and Elisabeth, squeezed Malone's shoulder and left, taking his air of confidence with him.

Malone looked across at the two old women. They were so dissimilar, yet the concern in their faces made them sisters. Elisabeth, her white hair styled by a Double Bay hairdresser, wore a twin-set and well-cut skirt on a figure only slightly plumper than Lisa's; her slim feet were fitted into Ferragamo shoes. Brigid, her iron-grey hair still with curl in it and still worn in the almost schoolgirl cut that had been her style for as long as Malone could remember, wore a plain wool dress and her thick ankles, fluid-affected, bulged over her comfortable Footrest shoes. He was surprised and touched to see they were holding hands.

Elisabeth stood up and, going out of the room, said, 'I'll go and see what's the news.'

Malone crossed and sat down by his mother. 'Thanks for coming, Mum.'

'Could I not come? And Elisabeth, too. Don't worry yourself sick, Scobie. Lisa will be all right. I've been round and around my beads.' She held up her rosary, her safety net against everything. 'You really love her, don't you?'

'Yep.'

She pressed his hand and the unexpected intimacy let slip his tongue. 'Mum, which feller back in Ballyreagh did you love? The one who was killed or the other one?'

Instantly he regretted asking her; he saw the sudden pain in her eyes. But the unexpectedness of the question had caught her off-guard: 'The one who was hanged.'

Oh Jesus! He put his arms round her shoulders, something he hadn't done in so many years; she did not push him away. 'Mum, I'm sorry I – Does Dad know?'

'Yes. But we never talk about it. And don't you *ever* mention it again.' She eased herself out of the loop of his arm.

Then Elisabeth came back: he was glad of the interruption. 'Scobie, they said you can go in and sit with her. We can go in later, when she wakes up.'

He went gingerly into the intensive care ward, sat down by Lisa. She looked much better than he had expected her to look; she certainly did not look *dead*. He sat there for another hour, reliving memories, and then finally she opened her eyes. He pressed her hand and she turned her head and smiled wanly at him.

'I knew you'd be here,' she murmured. 'How'd it go?'

'The doc says you're as clean as a whistle. Nothing has spread.'

She squeezed his hand. 'What have you been doing?'

'Nothing. Just waiting.'

Kirribilli
December 1993–June 1994